The Crystal Ship

The Glassmaker Series

Book One
The Glass Dagger

Book Two
The Crystal Ship

Book Three
Blood-Red Goblet
To be published at a later date

To Angela

The Crystal Ship

Second Adventure Of The Glassmaker Series

Have a happy

By

birthday

Peter Cooke

7/07/2010

Petan Publishing

First Edition
Published in Great Britain in 2008

by

Petan Publishing
20 Dorchester Crescent,
Baildon, Shipley,
West Yorkshire, BD17 7LE.
peter.cooke@petanpublishing.co.uk
www.petanpublishing.co.uk

Paperback ISBN 978-0-9553418-1-6

This book is printed on FSC compliant paper stocks
using digital printing technology to minimise wastage

London & Venice

1570 – 1572

Historical Characters

Elizabeth I - (September 1533 – 24 March 1603) Queen of England and Ireland from 17 November 1558 until her death, sometimes referred to as The Virgin Queen, Gloriana, or Good Queen Bess, Elizabeth was the fifth and last monarch of the Tudor dynasty, succeeding her half-sister, Mary Tudor.

William Cecil - 1st. Baron Burghley, (13 September 1520 – 4 August 1598), Principal Secretary of State (1558–1572) and Lord High Treasurer from 1572.

Sir Francis Walsingham - (1532 – 1590), French Ambassador, Principal Secretary (1572 – 1590)

Admiral Sir John Hawkins - (1532 – 1595) English shipbuilder, naval administrator and commander, merchant, navigator, privateer, slave trader, politician, treasurer, (1577) and controller, (1589) of the Navy,

Roberto Ridolfi - (1531-1612) Count, of Ridolfi di Piazza family, Florentine banker.

Sir Francis Drake - Vice Admiral, (c. 1540 – January 27, 1596) second cousin of Admiral Hawkins, English privateer, navigator, slave trader, politician and civil engineer, first Antarctic explorer, first circumnavigation of the world.

George Fitzwilliam - relative of Duchess of Feria, former shipmate of Admiral Hawkins

Gilbert Gifford - (1561-1590), English Catholic

Sir Henry Babington - of Dethick Hall, Dethick, Derbyshire

Anthony Babington - (1561–86) son of Sir Henry,

Mary Stuart - (December 8, 1542 – February 8, 1587) was Queen of Scots (the monarch of the Kingdom of Scotland) from December 14, 1542, to July 24, 1567, daughter of Mary of Guise. Mother of James (19 June 1566 – 27 March 1625) who was King of Scots as James VI, and King of England and King of Ireland as James I succeeding Elizabeth I.

Marie de Guise - (November 22, 1515 – June 11, 1560) Queen Consort of James V of Scotland and the mother of Mary, Queen of Scots. She was Regent, or Governor, of Scotland 1554–1560.

Thomas Howard - 4th. Duke of Norfolk, (1535 -1572.)

Robert Dudley - 1st Earl of Leicester, Master of Horse To Elizabeth I(1533 – 1588)

George Talbot - 6th Earl of Shrewsbury & Waterford, Earl Sheffield (1528 – 1590)

Bess of Hardwick - Elizabeth, Countess of Shrewsbury (1527 – 1608)

Robert Devereux - 2nd. Earl of Essex, (1566 - 1601)

Guerau de Spes - Spanish Ambassador to the English Court.

John Lesley - (1527 – 1596) Bishop of Ross, Scottish Roman Catholic supporter of Mary Stuart.

Charles Baillie - messenger in the employ of Count Ridolfi.

William Herle - spy in the pay of Lord Burghley

Higford - secretary to Thomas Howard

Bannister - steward to Thomas Howard in Shrewsbury

Thomas Browne - a Welsh draper and haulier

Sir Thomas Smith - Servant to the Queen's Council

Doctor Thomas Wilson - Servant to the Queen's Council

Sir Henry Neville - Servant to the Queen's Council

Henri de Lorraine - 3rd. Duke of Guise

Doctor Bayly - Royal Physician to Queen Elizabeth I

Reverend Rad Bentley - Rector of St. Olaves Church, Harte Street, London,

All other characters depicted in this book are fictional. The Ridolfi plot occurred substantially as described except for the events involving Jacob Bell and the other fictional characters.

See Historical Notes.

Chapter One
Tottenham, England, June, 1570

Jacob Bell, the Queen's Glassmaker, rode out of the front gate of his house in Tottenham just as the sun broke through the rain-filled clouds. The lush, buttercup-strewn meadows smelled clean and fresh after the early rain and Jacob sniffed appreciatively. Carefully skirting the newly tasselled corn, his horse breasted the rise about a hundred yards from the gate and he looked back at the attractive stone house with its distinctive Dutch gables. The house, a gift from Queen Elizabeth, for his services to the Crown, had formerly belonged to the traitor, Sir Richard Urie. A wonderful retreat from the hustle and bustle of London, he was sad to leave, but needs must if he was to answer the urgent call from Quiff, the leader of the Ring, his information gatherers. He searched for a glimpse of Roberto, his partner and friend. Sure enough, there he was by the front entrance with Elizabeth his wife and their young son of two months, waving their goodbyes. With a cheerful wave in return, Jacob spurred his horse beneath the sturdy oaks that stood guard by the London road and it soon settled into a smooth canter. It was an hour's ride, but fortunately the threatening rain failed to materialise, so Jacob made the most of the countryside. All too soon, however, the houses became more frequent and keeping alongside the wall's outer ditch, he rode along Houndsditch until the gate into the city appeared.

The gate was already thronged with lumbering carts bringing farm produce for the city's markets, waiting to pay their entry dues. Passing them with difficulty under the narrow, vaulted arch of the city gate, Jacob turned his horse into Poor Jewry. Leaving his horse at the nearby Aldgate livery stable Jacob strolled along keeping a wary eye open for cut purses, his hand ready on the hilt of his sword. The crowds thronging the narrow streets jostling on their unheeding way, made life easy for these rogues to make a living. Despite the early hour, the teeming streets were alive with the sound of street sellers and apprentices trying to attract customers.

'Buy a fine toast fork. Give your husband a treat.'

'Fine oysters! Who will buy my fine Wainfleet oysters?'

A little further on there were more cries.

'Buy rue: buy sage: buy my fine rosemary and bay?'

'Buy your barnacles here and you'll never miss a word again!'

'White radishes: white young lettuce. Who will buy?'

Jacob ignored all of their blandishments and hurrying along Crouched Friars Street, passed the Crouched Friars Glass-works, his place of business. Resisting the temptation to call in, he carried on to his house in Harte Street. Mistris Simpkin, his housekeeper, welcomed him at the door with her usual cheery greetings and informed him that Quiff had already arrived. Accepting the offer of some fresh lemonade, he went upstairs to the reception room. It always felt so welcoming and Jacob looked forward to evenings spent there after a hard day's work. He just wished that his beloved Maria could be here in London to share it, instead of wrestling with the Venetian courts to obtain his pardon.

A figure rose from the comfortable chair by the fireplace and greeted him warmly. 'You look as though the rest has done you good, Master Jacob,' said Quiff, with a cheery smile. 'I hope Elizabeth and young John Jacob are in good health now.'

Jacob shook the outstretched hand warmly. 'They have fully recovered from the nasty fever and are very well indeed. They send their regards.'

'I suppose the boy is shooting up,' said Quiff sagely, for one who had yet to have his first child, 'they seem to grow up so quickly.'

'That's true,' Jacob agreed, 'he is already a sturdy fellow and of a very pleasant nature. He sleeps well and hardly ever cries.'

He regarded Quiff with interest. The distinctive white shock of hair from which he took his name had not changed, but the drawn, sunken cheeks and hangdog expression produced by years of beatings and starvation had gone. Quiff, the leader of the 'Ring', a band of London apprentices and servants who kept a steady stream of information flowing to Jacob, was now a confident, married man and father-to-be, next spring.

Motioning him to sit down Jacob looked at him enquiringly. 'What have you found out then Quiff? I hope it's important enough to warrant dragging me away from Tottenham!'

Quiff took no offence, his eyes crinkling at the corners with humour. 'You know me better, Master Jacob,' he said with a wicked grin. 'I wouldn't have asked you to come unless it was important. Especially as I know how much you were looking forward to spending some time at Tottenham.' His grin became even wider as Jacob shook his head in mock disbelief. 'One of the servants has turned up an interesting story that you ought to know about. It's about another Count I'm afraid.'

Jacob made a grimace of distaste at his memories of the late, unlamented Count Maldini.

'This Italian gentleman is called Count Ridolfi,' said Quiff. 'He's been visiting the Duke of Norfolk in the Tower for months. Several times recently, one of the Duke's servants has collected large sums of money from Ridolfi, after he has been to Flanders. It's supposed to be for the Duke, but my informant has seen a letter to the Bishop of Ross explaining the money is for the imprisoned Queen of Scots and the Catholics who support her cause.'

Jacob was intrigued. 'Has he now! I don't suppose he managed to obtain this letter?'

When Quiff shook his head, Jacob sighed. 'I thought that would be too much to hope. I must say I'm surprised at the Duke of Norfolk being involved. It was only last November that he was thrown in the Tower for promising to marry Mary Stuart. The Northern rebellion raised by his supporters was crushed in only six weeks and several of the leaders executed. You'd have thought it would have put him off getting involved again.'

Quiff assumed an innocent expression. Jacob, not taken in for a second, questioned him further. 'Who is this Count Ridolfi anyway? I assume from the expression that you have some more information about him?'

Quiff gave a sly grin. 'I have, and it's even more interesting,' he said, unable to keep the glee from his voice. 'His full name is Roberto Ridolfi, an Italian, belonging to the Florentine family of Ridolfi di Piazza. He's a banker and has lived in London, on and off, ever since Queen Mary's reign.' The smug expression told Jacob that the next piece of information was going to be out of the ordinary. With a resigned look, he said. 'Come on Quiff let me know the worst. What has he been up to?'

'It's not what he's been doing, Master Jacob,' he replied, 'but more who he's been doing it for. Among others in high places, he has been employed by Sir William Cecil, to advise him on financial matters.'

Jacob gaped at him in astonishment. 'Sir William Cecil! Are you sure?'

Quiff smiled enigmatically. 'I'm sure, Master Jacob and I believe he's had dealings with Sir Francis Walsingham too.' With this final piece of news, he settled back in his chair with a self-satisfied smile.

Jacob regarded Quiff incredulously. 'Let me get this straight, Quiff. You're implying that this Count Ridolfi is a Spanish plotter and that he advises both Sir William Cecil and Sir Francis Walsingham on financial matters?' He looked at him with disbelief as Quiff gave several solemn nods then broke into a beaming smile.

'Not only that, Master Jacob, but I'm sure that he's not being used by either of them as a counter-plotter if my information is correct. I'm pretty certain it is too!'

'How can you be so sure, Quiff?' said Jacob, wanting to be in no doubt on this point before he considered the implications.

Quiff became serious. 'You should know me well enough by now, Master Jacob,' he said, in a slightly aggrieved tone. 'I don't rely on just one source of information. When I first heard about this, I put the word out round the Ring that I wanted to know everything about this Count. Since then several reports have come in, which confirm he's been giving financial advice to various important persons including Sir William Cecil. Although I've no proof of his spying activities as yet, I'm sure it's only a matter of time.'

Sitting back in his chair, Jacob pondered his next move. From experience, he was sure that barring something very well concealed, the information in Quiff's report was correct. In all probability, both Sir William Cecil and Sir Francis Walsingham were employing a man for financial guidance who at the very least was a spy for the Spanish and possibly a plotter against the Queen.

He would need to be very careful how he made use of this

information. The last thing he wanted was to get on the wrong side of Sir William Cecil, or Sir Francis for that matter. They were frequently on opposite sides of the political fence and often disagreed on the right way to advise the Queen. Undoubtedly, they both had her best interests at heart, but unfortunately, there was no great empathy between them.

However, on some matters, like plots against the Queen, they worked closely together. To inform one and not the other would lead to trouble. Not to mention the political implications for both of them. It could undermine their credibility as protectors of the Queen at the very least.

While Jacob digested the information, Quiff sat quietly in his chair waiting for his next move. Since Jacob's glass was empty, he poured him some lemonade. Acknowledging it with a nod, Jacob took a deep draught then put the glass down purposefully. 'I want you to put the word round the Ring. This Count Ridolfi is the most important target we have.'

When Quiff looked questioningly at him, he answered the unspoken query. 'I'm not prepared to risk telling either Sir William, or Sir Francis, without something more solid in the way of proof. The word of apprentices or liverymen will simply not do in this case. No, we must have something much more definite. See if they can get hold of letters, or instructions. Particularly any he sends to the Duke of Norfolk, or the Bishop of Ross.'

He thought for a moment and then went on. 'Should he send a letter to the Spanish Ambassador, or to France, or Spain, I want to know about it at once. In fact, I would like to get my hands on it. We might be able to intercept it, copy it, and send it on its way without them being any the wiser. It won't be easy, but see what you can do.'

He got up and paced around. He liked to walk when he was thinking over a problem. It was undoubtedly a tricky situation. With the Duke of Norfolk involved, it was likely that other Catholic Lords would be too. They would defend themselves from exposure by any means at their disposal.

Coming to a decision, he sat down and let Quiff into his thoughts. 'I want you to make sure that everyone in the Ring knows that they're not to take any unnecessary risks. Some very powerful men are involved in this affair. The Duke of Norfolk is the premier Earl and it will take a lot more than rumour to unseat him,' he cautioned. I'll get in touch with Sir Francis's man Phelippes who deals with opening letters, ciphers and making copies. If we're lucky enough to intercept a letter or instructions, he would be the man to copy it. A suitably incriminating letter would make sure we are believed about the Count. I can't see it taking less than that, unless I'm very much mistaken.'

Quiff nodded solemnly. 'I think you're right, Master Jacob. I wouldn't in their place. I'll start putting the word out straight away, if that's what you want.'

'It is indeed Quiff,' said Jacob. 'The sooner we get the word out, the sooner our chances of success. In fact, you can tell them that the one who brings me the proof I need will get five gold royals. That should help to concentrate people's attention. But don't forget the advice on caution.'

'I won't,' Quiff promised, 'and it certainly will concentrate minds. I'll be keeping an eye out too,' he said, rubbing his hands. 'I could certainly use the money.'

Having dealt with the matter of the Count, Jacob enquired how things were getting on at the Crouched Friars. He was relieved when Quiff told him that Peter Tyzack was doing a good job. Quiff was of the opinion though, that Jacob needed to spend a little more time at the Works, since the English workers were not progressing as well as previously. 'It's not Peter's fault,' he hurried to explain. 'He just doesn't have the time to be training them as well as running the Works and everything else.'

Jacob could see the sense in this, but it was going to be difficult to achieve, if this Count Ridolfi turned out to be the plotter that Quiff thought he was. He knew that once the information he had obtained reached Cecil and Walsingham, they would drag him into the affair. It was likely he would have less time, not more! With this in mind, Jacob decided to go and have words with Peter Tyzack.

It soon became apparent that as Quiff had suggested, the English workers were not the problem. Peter explained that they had too many orders and not enough workers. The Works had only its original complement of six Venetian glass-blowers. With

Peter running the works on a regular basis, he had only five glass-blowers and whatever time he could spare in the 'chair', the glass-blower's workplace.

Jacob realised at once that things were even worse. He had not made a glass for weeks and neither had Roberto. 'Peter, my friend, I must apologise for the fact that I have put such a lot on your shoulders.' He looked him squarely in the eyes. 'I will see you are not the loser for coping like this. However, that will not solve the problem. Do you, or any of the other glass-blowers, know of any suitable men who would join us?'

Peter gave a smile of relief. 'I was hoping you would see it like that. How many did you have in mind?'

'Three glass-blowers and the usual workers needed for three more chairs,' said Jacob decisively. 'In fact, bearing in mind the orders we have coming in we could even take four. The Glass-Sellers are already receiving more orders than usual and the troubles in Antwerp will result in even more.'

'I know of one glass-blower who has just come to London,' said Peter, 'he is Murano trained and so is his brother, in Antwerp. He is also hoping to find work in London. Do you want me to arrange for them to come in?'

Jacob thought for a moment. 'Do you think they'll be up to our standards, Peter?'

When Peter nodded, he told him to set him on straight away and to send for his brother. 'If he knows any others looking to get out of Antwerp, get them in. Have a word with Captain Roberts. He can arrange passage on the Bona venture.' The Bonaventure was a merchantman of 300 tons previously owned by Sir Richard Urie and on permanent hire to the Glass-Sellers. Jacob had been surprised to find he was the owner. Thomas Pepper, his lawyer, had discovered this when examining the full extent of the Urie estate: Jacob's reward for his help with the Maldini Plot.

'I'll leave it to you to organise it and set them on.' He shook his finger at Peter, 'But no more than four chairs, mind you.'

With that friendly warning, Jacob went to his office, but he found it difficult to concentrate. His mind kept harping back to Quiff's report and its implications.

Thinking back to the Maldini Plot, there had been some perilous moments, but he had to admit that he had never felt more alive than when he was battling against the evil plotters. Life since then had become rather mundane. He enjoyed the danger and whatever this new Count was up to, he couldn't wait to pit his wits against him.

Chapter Two
Murano, Venice, June, 1570

The golden-haired young woman at the window stared out across the Grand Canal of Murano towards the Ponte Vivarino. Her dress was of heavy cream silk damask, elaborately decorated with a peony motif and having a slanted lace ruff that emphasised her high cheekbones. Around her neck was a long knotted necklace of matching pearls that hung low between the swollen breasts.

As she watched, a sudden deluge of rain from the looming black clouds sent the people on the bridge scurrying for shelter. Pulling her woollen cloak more securely around the prominent swell of her stomach, she shivered and turned towards her father.

'It's so cold and wet for this time of year, it's worse than when I left London. I do hope it improves before the baby is born.'

'In some ways it might be better if it is cool,' said Ricardo Morisini seriously. 'You know how hot and humid it can be in June.'

He regarded her fondly. 'I want to tell you about my research into the legal position regarding the surname of your baby.'

'What have you found out, father,' asked Maria eagerly. 'Can I use whatever surname I like?'

Ricardo frowned and shook his head. 'I'm afraid not. The child must bear the name Ragazoni.'

'That is so unfair,' said Maria. 'Surely the fact that I'm now a widow entitles me to name the baby as I wish.'

When Ricardo solemnly shook his head, Maria ran into his arms and he wrapped them around her protectively.

'When I returned to Venice,' she said bitterly, fighting back the tears, 'all I could think about was having my revenge on Adrian Ragazoni for all the heartache and strife he caused and for the terrible way he beat and raped me. I thought that if I said the baby was his, the Ragazoni estates would come under my control.'

Ricardo held her at arms' length. 'Are you saying you don't want that now?'

She was thoughtful for a short while and then she nodded, slowly at first and then more vigorously. 'I want Giam to be recognised as the father. He will come back to Venice as soon as we have cleared his name. He promised me before I left London.'

She gazed steadily at her father. 'I truly believe that Giam is the father and that the baby was conceived in love after Adrian died. It would be hateful if he came back to find out that Adrian Ragazoni has been named as the father.'

Ricardo sighed heavily. 'It will not alter the fact that as far as the courts are concerned, you were married to Ragazoni and the baby was conceived before he died. Therefore Ragazoni is the father. Anything else is unthinkable.'

He gave her a fond look. 'What you believe about Giam may be true, but there is no way of telling. Should you name Giam as the father you will almost certainly be charged and found guilty of adultery. Under Venetian law, the court could send you to a convent for the rest of your life and award custody of the baby to Pietro Ragazoni, Adrian's father.'

Maria gasped in horror and clung to her father, who comforted her, stroking her hair. 'It may not come to that,' he said reassuringly, 'they could fine you, or stop you from inheriting any of the Ragazoni estates and confiscate your dowry. However, I must counsel you against naming Giam. Whatever the outcome, of the court case that would surely follow, you would certainly be shunned by society. The Old Families would try and force both of us out of Venice.'

Maria began to cry bitterly and her father comforted her. They talked for a long time and eventually Maria accepted she had no real option other than to name Ragazoni as the father of the baby.

'After all,' her father consoled her, 'when you marry Giam you'll be able to change the baby's name to Bellini quite legally.'

'If he still wants to marry me,' thought Maria sadly.

In the weeks that followed, Maria kept putting off the task of writing to Giam. She was desperately worried about his reaction to the news concerning the baby. As the weeks went by it became increasingly difficult, until sick with worry, she put off sending the letter until after the baby was born.

'I can't imagine how he will feel when he learns about the baby,' she thought wearily. 'I only hope he loves me enough to understand why the baby is named after Ragazoni.'

Ricardo Morisini, Senator and Avogador of Venice, shielded his eyes against the blazing noonday sun and, accepting the steadying hand of the gondolier, stepped on to the quayside outside the Casa Da Mula. He was surprised when his daughter's companion, Anna, came hurrying across to greet him. Alarmed at her expression, Ricardo enquired what ailed her.

'It's Lady Maria and the baby, Senator,' she said, making a hurried curtsy. 'They're both burning up with fever and the baby has come out in a red rash. I fear the baby has the measles and that Lady Maria has caught it from him. Can you remember if she had it as a child?'

'I don't think so,' said Ricardo, his brow wrinkled with thought. 'No, I'm almost certain she missed it.'

Anna looked troubled. 'That's very bad, especially as she's been so weak after the birth of the baby.'

The birth had not gone well. The boy was in the breech position and had been born feet first. He was a large baby and the midwife had been forced to make a substantial cut to ensure the head came out correctly. The stitches had become infected and Maria had a high fever for many days. Once the child bed fever had broken, thanks to the herb potions of the midwife, Maria had recovered her strength a little, thanks to careful and devoted care by Anna.

And now this!

Ricardo knew that measles was far worse for an adult than it was for a child, but he was worried for both of them. Since his silence was disturbing Anna, he told her not to worry, he would arrange for a doctor. Telling her to return to her mistress immediately, he threw a heavy purse to the gondolier. 'Take Mistris Anna back to Lady Maria's house and then go with all haste to the Casa Bella Nova, the residence of Doctor Nguyên. It's on the Fondamenta Nova.'

The gondolier nodded and said he knew it.

'Tell him I have urgent need of his services,' Ricardo said with authority, 'and say that he will be well rewarded if he attends me immediately. If he argues, tell him to remember what I did for him in Bursa and say that my daughter's life is at stake.'

Turning to Anna, he gave her an encouraging smile. 'Inform

Maria I will be with her shortly and that I have every confidence that the good Doctor Nguyên will know what to do.'

The doctor was a fugitive from the wars that had ravaged Vietnam for years. Nguyên Kim Hung was a member of the Nguyên clan and studied with an old Chinese doctor in Than Hóa province. When civil war broke out between the Mac King and the Trinh Nguyên Alliance, the King's army overran Than Hóa province. They burnt down the town where he lived, massacring soldiers and civilians alike. The Chinese doctor was killed and Doctor Nguyên was forced to flee for his life leaving behind everything except his medicine bag. After much hardship, he eventually reached Istanbul, travelling along the Silk Route.

It was at Bursa, the main centre for contact between Venice and the Ottoman silk traders, that Ricardo first met the good doctor. Ricardo had been injured in a clash with pirates on the way to Istanbul. The wound in his side was not life threatening, but by the time the galley reached port, it was infected and he was very ill. The doctor had cured him with his Chinese medicines and was well rewarded. He begged Ricardo to take him to Venice, which he had heard was a very liberal regime. The grateful Ricardo had readily agreed and the doctor had now been in Venice for almost ten years practising medicine. He was very highly regarded by the Old Families.

As the gondolier steered his craft away Ricardo hurried into the Casa Da Mula, calling for the Sigisbei to attend him immediately. When Sigisbei Vercelline arrived, he explained the situation to him.

'My daughter's companion fears the Lady Maria and the baby may be suffering from measles. Since my daughter did not have it as a child, I understand it is more dangerous for her, particularly as she has only just recovered from the child bed fever. I have sent for Doctor Nguyên and I want you to make sure that when he arrives, I am notified immediately.'

Since the Sigisbei was looking concerned and about to speak, he silenced him with a gesture. 'Make sure the gondolier waits for me. I will take the good doctor to see Maria, and God willing he will restore her to health as he once did for me in Bursa.' He regarded the Sigisbei with a kindly expression. 'Do not fear that I will catch the measles. I had it twice as a child and though I have been exposed to it since, I have not succumbed.'

It was two hours before Ricardo and the doctor attended Maria. The doctor questioned Anna carefully and found out everything she could tell him about the onset and progress of the illness. When she had told him all she knew, he left Ricardo waiting anxiously in the antechamber while he examined Maria and the baby.

A short while later, his worst fears confirmed, the doctor discussed his findings with Ricardo. 'The baby I am pleased to say has a most favourable prognosis,' he said, nodding in satisfaction. 'The fever is not too high and the rash has reached the hands and feet, turning dull red. I will make up a mixture that will ensure that the healthy qi expels the yang evil from the spleen and induces cooling. I expect the spots to die away in three to five days as the yang evil is eliminated.'

Ricardo was relieved at the news, but still anxious about Maria. 'What about my daughter, Doctor Nguyên?'

The Doctor shook his head sadly. 'Am afraid prognosis not so good. Your daughter showing advanced lung-wei disorder and healthy qi failed to expel yang evil.' He sighed. 'Am afraid she very ill, with high fever. Evil is blocking lungs leading to failure of descending of lung-qi. Has already attacked the throat causing hoarseness and a cough. Should it spread to heart and liver, could lead to coma, convulsions and delirium; even death.'

Seeing the alarm on Ricardo's face, he hurried to reassure him. 'Do not fear, Senator. Have treated many cases such as these and believe daughter will survive.' He took him by the arm and led him to a chair. 'Must warn though,' he said kindly, 'recovery not quick. The qi of Lady Maria already low due to child bed fever. Must first treat heat and bring eruptions to climax, using acrid-cool drugs. Once eruption of rash happen, sweet-cool drugs used to nourish yin and clear away remaining heat. It imperative doses of drugs exactly I recommend. Overuse most inadvisable.'

He stood up and collected his ornate bamboo case. 'Please to show me where I make up mixtures,' he said, indicating the case. 'Have brought all ingredients needed, but time short. Must begin treatment.'

Although Doctor Nguyên was sure that the baby would recover, Ricardo decided he should be christened and called the local priest. The baby was duly christened the next morning and named Ricardo Giacomo, as Maria had intended. Maria was present, but she was so ill, that later she could remember nothing of the brief ceremony

A week later, Doctor Nguyên emerged from Maria's bedroom with a worried expression in his dark brown eyes that alarmed the waiting Ricardo. 'Is Maria worse, Doctor Nguyên?'

The doctor frowned. 'Not worse, but not responding as well as expected. Fever showing no signs of improvement and no signs of rash erupting.'

'What are you planning to do now?'

Doctor Nguyên gave it some thought before he answered. 'Will increase dose of potion, but need to get fever down. There is herb known in China as Hi-la-pa. You call Fenugreek. Try infusion using both the leaves and the seeds. There is merchant, in square by fish market. He have stock. Send someone to buy for me? Please see if has herb Aiye. It is known as Mother of Herbs. Not sure what it called here in Venice. Merchant will know.' He handed Ricardo a piece of paper. 'Send list to merchant and he supply.'

Fortunately the merchant had supplies of both herbs and an hour later Anna helped the doctor to prepare the medicinal teas. First, Fenugreek tea was made, by infusing the leaves of the herb with boiling water. Then, adding a small palm full of seeds to a cup of boiling water for about five minutes, he made a decoction. The resulting mixture of rich saffron coloured tea was sweetened with honey to remove the bitter after-taste.

The Aiye herb, known as Mugwort, was prepared by infusing a handful of leaves and flower tops in half a litre of boiling water. Doctor Nguyên gave Anna very strict instructions. Maria was to drink one small cup of Fenugreek tea morning, noon, and night; a half-cup of Aiye tea was to be given mid-morning and mid-afternoon.

'Must give Lady Maria only these doses. Teas must be made exactly as shown you. Not do this, you poison mistress.'

For two days Anna made sure that Maria drank the tea,

although it was difficult to persuade her at times as she tossed and turned in delirium. The baby had recovered well and the doctor advised that he should be kept in a separate room to avoid further disturbance. When Julia Labie, the wet-nurse, came to take him, Maria was so delirious, she thought the Ragazonis were stealing her baby and started screaming. It was some time before Anna managed to soothe her and she sank into an exhausted sleep.

Later that night the fever worsened. Maria was drenched in perspiration and she went into a series of body-racking convulsions. When Ricardo and the doctor were aroused, the latter took one long careful look at Maria then took Ricardo on one side.

'No time for discussion, Senator. Your daughter in critical state. We not break the fever, she die.' He regarded him solemnly. 'Please to trust my judgement. What I propose not something your doctors find acceptable, but know from own experience has been successful in few such cases.'

Ricardo, who had blanched at the news of Maria's state, made his decision. 'I have every personal reason to trust your judgement, Doctor Nguyên,' he said, his voice choked with emotion. 'Tell me what you wish to do and it will be done.'

'I believe you have a specially lined ice house kept partially under water in the basement of the Casa.'

'Yes I do,' said the puzzled Ricardo. 'Do you want some ice? I believe there is still a little left.'

The doctor gave a bleak smile. 'All you have, my friend. Want put into bath and place Lady Maria in.' He held his hand up as Ricardo started to protest. 'You said you would trust me,' he said solemnly. 'Shock to system great, but if fever broken have chance to get better. We continue present treatment, or do nothing, she die.'

So it was that a little while later, Maria, clad only in a cotton shift, was lowered into a bath of icy water. Immediately her body convulsed as the shock hit her. Her back arched, her eyes opened wide and she screamed. It seemed to Ricardo it went on for an age, but in reality, it was only a few minutes. As suddenly as it began, the screaming stopped and closing her eyes, Maria slid down into the icy water, her body racked by intense shivering.

Doctor Nguyên supported her head and carefully checked her forehead. Her limbs began to turn blue with cold and the watching Ricardo found it difficult not to beg them to take her out. The shivering became more intense and the doctor felt her forehead and pulse. 'Enough,' he shouted, 'take out of bath quickly.'

They lifted her out and rubbed her with warm towels to get some circulation going. Wrapping her up in blankets, they laid her on the temporary bed that had been made up in front of a roaring fire. The shivering intensified for several minutes and then slowly subsided and with a long sigh, Maria sank into unconsciousness, breathing shallowly.

The doctor stood up. 'It is done,' he said. 'Fever broken, but only time tell if she pull through.' He ran his fingers over his black hair with a weary gesture, screwing up his eyes. 'Will not deceive you. Shock to system immense and in weakened state, could be too much for heart. She alive by morning, has a very good chance.' He turned to Ricardo and taking him by the arm led him into the other room. 'Must get some rest. Anna and I sit with her. We call if change. All can do now is wait. Have done our part, now her life is in hands of her God.

Chapter Three
London, July, 1570

Jacob left the Glass-works and emerged from the gate into Harte Street feeling much happier than he had for some time. He almost bumped into an apprentice wearing the livery of the Mercer's Guild who was just about to turn into the Works. On seeing Jacob, he doffed his cap politely.

'Do I have the honour of addressing Master Glassmaker Bell?' he enquired.

Jacob acknowledged he was and the apprentice handed him a letter from John Isham, his friend and financial backer. In it, he requested Jacob to attend him at the Mercers' Hall as soon as possible that day. Deciding there was no time like the present, Jacob told the apprentice to lead the way and they set off for the Mercers' Hall in Cheapside.

It was a long walk and the jostling crowds made progress difficult at times. Turning into a quieter side street, Jacob had a near miss from some rubbish unceremoniously thrown into the street from an overhang: a common hazard in the narrow streets. When they arrived at the Mercer's Hall, he was shown into one of the private rooms, where refreshments had been provided

John greeted him warmly when he entered the room. 'Thank you for coming so promptly, I trust you have not been inconvenienced.'

When Jacob replied he hadn't, John gestured to the table and bade Jacob help himself from the fruit and pies. 'I've asked you here because I have a business proposition to put to you. Ordinarily, I would not make it in such haste, but the decision will not wait for another day. From what you have told me, you are making good profit from the Glass-works. I'm seeking some extra funding for a speculative venture.' He gave an encouraging smile. 'It could return you a tidy sum for your investment and I urge you to give it some serious thought.'

Jacob regarded him warily. Not all of John's investments were sound, but to be fair, he made money from most of them.

'Is this one of your trading voyages, or had you something else on your mind?'

'It is a voyage of sorts, but definitely not one for trading,' said John, a little mysteriously. 'Have you heard of Captain Francis Drake from Plymouth?'

Jacob thought the name was familiar and then it came to him.

'I believe I've heard him mentioned at St. Paul's. He sails with Admiral John Hawkins on his raids against the Spaniards; a cousin, or so I've heard.'

'The very one,' said John. 'You must surely have heard about their last venture. They were treacherously attacked by the Spaniards, at San Juan de Ulua, on the Spanish Main, you know,' he said, shaking his head in disgust. 'It was an act of base treachery. Hawkins had captured the fort at the mouth of the harbour and the Spanish ships were outside with a bad storm blowing up. He let them in on condition that they wouldn't attack him. The Spaniards broke their word given in a signed treaty and he was lucky to get away with his life. Many of his men didn't and mark my words, Jacob, both Hawkins and Drake will make Viceroy Don Martin Enriquez pay for it.'

Jacob remembered it now, it was when he'd first heard of Drake. 'Wasn't it rumoured that Drake deserted Hawkins?'

'There were some stories to that effect,' said John. 'I don't know the details, but Hawkins has never had anything other than praise for his cousin's bravery and leadership qualities. In fact, it was the Admiral who suggested that I might like to become a backer for Drake's next voyage, which is the venture I am recommending.' He regarded Jacob shrewdly. 'I must tell you, however, that the one he made last year made little profit, but Hawkins believes Drake has learnt enough to make a good profit this time.'

Jacob looked thoughtful. 'Is Hawkins putting any of his own money into this expedition?'

'He is indeed,' said John, nodding vigorously. 'It is not to be a large force, there will only be one ship, which the Hawkins family is providing and payment for the men and their provisions.'

Jacob came to a decision, but had one more question. 'How much do you intend to put in? I assume you've already decided to invest.'

'Most certainly; I suggest we invest two hundred pounds each and Roberto one hundred pounds.'

'Have you spoken to Roberto already?'

'Yes I have and he will put up the money, but only if you agree it is a good investment. What do you think, Jacob?'

Jacob had heard many tales over the past couple of years about the vast profits made from some of these privateering voyages. He found the tales exciting. He'd even thought of fitting out the ship he owned through the Glass-Sellers to make a voyage of his own. However, he knew from the example of Admiral Hawkins' trip that some of them were disasters. In the end, one factor alone decided him. Because of the Queen's generosity following the Maldini affair and the revenue flowing in from his glass monopoly, he had a considerable sum of money at his disposal. 'I'll do it on one condition. I want to talk to Francis Drake first. I'll decide what to do, after I've spoken to him.'

The frown, which had been threatening for some time, faded away and John smiled in delight. 'I anticipated you might want to meet him,' he said, with his schoolboy grin. 'He's in London trying to get backers and he's coming to my house this evening for a meal. Why don't you join us?'

Jacob agreed and later that evening he arrived at the Isham house to find John already entertaining Drake in his study.

'Come in, come in, Jacob,' said John cheerfully, ushering him into the study. 'Allow me to introduce Captain Francis Drake of Devon.' Turning to Drake, he introduced Jacob. 'This is my friend Jacob Bell, of the Crouched Friars Glass-works and Glassmaker to Her majesty the Queen.'

Having made their courtesies, the two men regarded each other with interest as John Isham went on with his fanciful story about a strange beast that lurked in the forests around Antwerp.

Drake was a man of medium height and his stocky body gave an impression of restless power. He wore a fashionable doublet and hose in yellows and browns and had a fine sword at his side. His eyes were piercing and his ruddy, weather-beaten face sported a short pointed red beard, with a moustache that curled up at the ends. These combined to give him a somewhat satanic look.

When John had finished his story, he led them into the dining room. The table laid with gold plate had two fine candlesticks in silver at each end and there were chargers laden with all manner of fruits. The drinking glasses were fine examples of façon de Venice style and drew admiring comments from Drake. 'Are these imported from Venice?' he asked, studying his glass with interest as the servant poured fine malmsey into it.

'Not at all Captain Drake, they are the product of the Crouched Friars Glass-works and made by my friend Jacob's talented hands,' said John.

Drake looked impressed and complimented Jacob on his skill. 'I've seen no better from Murano; I assume you trained in that part of the world, Master Bell?'

Jacob acknowledged the compliment gracefully and agreed he had grown up in Murano where he had learned his skill. Not wishing to go into further details, he changed the subject and asked Drake about his recent voyage.

Drake needed no further urging and launched into a detailed and succinct description of his last expedition and his intents. 'We set off in November of last year, with two ships, the Dragon and the Swan. The intent was to explore the coast of Panama to find a suitable base for our incursions and of course to trade, and stop Spanish ships and appropriate whatever of value they carried.'

He paused a moment and a frown came to his face. 'In financial terms, this voyage was not a huge success. We managed to capture some small coastal craft, but they were not carrying a lot of jewels, or bullion. We did however, pick up a lot of information about the movements of gold and silver around Panama and found a likely place for a base, before we set off for home.' Taking a large drink from his glass, he regarded them intently as though trying to read their minds.

'We managed to do some trading on the way,' he said, a slightly bleak smile crossing his face, 'so that in the end, John Hawkins and I didn't lose too much on it.' Taking another long draught of malmsey, he wiped his moustache. 'In terms of information, it was a valuable voyage indeed.' Jacob could see that he was pleased with this thought. 'I intend to go back later this year in the Swan, provided I can get the backing. She is a vessel of only twenty-five tons, so in all honesty it will not be a large expedition.'

Jacob was amazed at this piece of information. 'Isn't that rather small to be taking on the Spanish galleons?'

Drake gave a barking laugh. 'I certainly won't be looking to take on any galleons. Not on the high seas at any rate. It's the coastal ships I'll be after, which for the most part have very little in the way of armaments. The Spanish are very complacent,' he said, giving a shrug of disdain.

'However, I dare say my last voyage may have stirred them up a little,' he said with a chuckle. 'In any case, I intend to try out the use of pinnaces, which I will take and assemble in the West Indies. The French used them very successfully to ferry armed men into enemy harbours. I believe they will prove to be very effective against the Spanish ports. Then I might tackle a galleon, especially if it's well laden with gold' He gave a barking laugh. 'I can't guarantee we will return with huge profits. Although if God is with us, who knows,' he said, his smile widening at John Isham's grimace at this news.

'As you can see, I do not attempt to make too much of this expedition,' he said, regarding them both with a shrewd expression. 'What I will promise you however: I will do my best to see that you show a profit on your money. I also promise that if you'll back me on this occasion, I will ensure you have the chance to back the main expedition I'm planning.'

Ah, thought Jacob seeing the gleam in Drake's eye, now we're getting to the real point. With heightened interest, he listened as Drake outlined his scheme.

'The next expedition will be a real force to be reckoned with,' he said. His passion keeping his audience spellbound as he went on. 'It will help us to bring home many more like these,' he explained, pulling a handful of gold coins and gems from his purse and scattering them carelessly on to the table. 'Many more of them,' he said, sitting back with a mysterious smile as he awaited their reaction.

The two men examined the coins, beautiful rubies and fine emeralds scattered before them with expressions of appreciation. Jacob was the first to speak as he regarded Drake quizzically. 'I assume you have some long-term goal that these fact-finding voyages are to further, Captain Drake?'

Drake regarded Jacob shrewdly. 'You are indeed correct, Master Bell, but before I tell you what it is, I must first have your decision on this year's voyage. Will you back me based on what you have seen and heard?' he challenged.

Without hesitation, Jacob nodded. 'I can't speak for John, but I'm prepared to back you. You've convinced me with your sincerity and your obvious knowledge of the Spanish Main. What say you John?'

'Here's my hand on it, Captain Drake,' said John, walking round the table. When Drake took it in a firm grasp, he said. 'Hand and heart, Captain Drake, hand and heart, you have my word on it and Jacob will tell you I do not renege on a promise so given.'

Jacob joined the two of them and shook hands with Drake. 'I can vouch for the truth of that, Captain Drake. I benefited from John's honesty when I needed his help to set up the Glass-works.' Drake gave a small bow in obvious acceptance of this assurance and Jacob went on. 'I may be able to persuade one of my partners to come in as well,' he said, much to Drake's delight. 'I will leave it to John to explain.'

John nodded his thanks to Jacob and turned to Drake. 'Jacob and I have agreed that we will put up two hundred pounds each and I am sure that Jacob's young partner, my son-in-law, will put up a hundred to make a grand total of five hundred pounds. Will it be sufficient for your purpose, Captain?'

'It will do famously,' said Drake with relish, toasting the pair of them with his glass. 'With the contributions of John Hawkins and Sir Richard Hatton, it is all I need to set up the expedition.'

They finished off the meal and then retired to John's study with yet another glass of malmsey. When they were settled in their chairs, Drake regarded them thoughtfully. 'What I am about to tell you must be kept a total secret. Unless I have your solemn word on it, I shall say no more.' When they had both promised to keep the secret, Drake told them his grand plan. 'I intend to capture the gold and silver of the annual Spanish treasure fleet from New Spain to the Old. What think you of that?' he said, sitting back to watch their reactions with a self-satisfied smile.

'The annual treasure fleet!' exclaimed John. 'Surely, some of the most powerful ships in the Spanish fleet will guard it?'

'They will indeed,' smiled Drake, 'and I have a workable plan to seize it all, despite them. And to return safely to England with it, God willing.'

For the next few minutes John and Jacob bombarded Drake with questions. However, try as they might to persuade him, all he would say on the subject of the treasure was that he had every expectation of achieving its capture. 'You must understand that if the Spanish get wind of my intentions, they will be on their guard. That will effectively ensure that the plan will fail. It must remain a total secret, or the Spanish will strengthen their defences and cost us many lives.' Having received their promise that the finance would be available by the end of the month, he took his leave of them.

When he had left, John and Jacob sat down and discussed Drake's project. Jacob was excited and enthusiastic, but for once, John tried to be more practical. 'I have been making investments for a long time, Jacob,' he said evenly, 'and I have to say, that there will always be a large element of risk. Remember what happened to Hawkins. The perfidious Spanish Viceroy almost succeeded in wiping him out at San Juan de Ulua. Had it not been for Hawkins, it was doubtful if any of them would have lived to tell the tale. The only way any of them could survive was to leave a hundred volunteers to the mercy of the jungle and the Spaniards. Hawkins has vowed that nothing would stand in the way of his efforts to get them released.'

Before Jacob left for home, John Isham suggested that they should get together with Roberto at John's home in Tottenham on the coming Saturday. 'My wife will be delighted to entertain Elizabeth and her grandson while we talk business. She's been so worried about them both. Thank the Lord it was nothing more serious than a summer fever. I assume now they are better it will not be long before Roberto is back at the glass-works?'

Jacob smiled. 'Much as he loves Elizabeth and the baby, now they are recovered he is getting restless at his inaction. He was all for coming back to London with me, so he could call at the Crouched Friars, but I managed to persuade him against it. However, I fully expect to see him there on Monday.'

Chapter Four
London, July, 1570

Sure enough, Jacob's prediction came true. Early on the Monday he'd gone to the glass-works to see Peter Tyzack. Just as they were finishing checking the order book, Roberto walked in with a big smile on his face.

'A very good morning to you both,' he said cheerfully. 'There's nothing like an early morning ride to set you right for the day.'

Jacob turned to Will with a grin. 'This is from the man who had never seen a horse before he came to London.'

Will laughed. 'Aye and I'm willing to bet he fell off more than a few times too, before he got the hang of it.'

Roberto joined in the laughter with a good grace enjoying the camaraderie that he'd been missing during his illness. For the next hour or so, they discussed how to keep the glass-works running smoothly. Jacob was relieved to find that the arrangements he had made to secure a new supply of timber were going smoothly. He was also more than satisfied with the way that Peter Tyzack was coping with running the glass-works.

Feeling the need to make some glass to keep his hand in, Jacob asked Roberto if he would like to be his feeder. Roberto was delighted as he too had been missing the good feeling he received when helping Jacob to produce a new piece of glass. For the rest of the day they immersed themselves in the needs of the glass-works. When the time came to leave for the evening meal, they were both weary but satisfied with their day's work.

Roberto stretched his aching back. 'I don't know about you Master Jacob, but I'll be glad to have a meal and a good rest. I'd almost forgotten what hard work glassmaking is and that summer fever does take its toll of your stamina.'

With a grimace, Jacob stood up and stretched his shoulders back to straighten his back. 'I know what you mean Roberto it's always the same when you go back to work after a break.' Gingerly he bent down and picked up his things from the floor. 'How are Elizabeth and the baby by the way? I trust they're in good spirits?'

'They are indeed, Master Jacob, I took them over to stay with her mother before I left. No doubt she is spoiling the two of them.'

'John Isham has invited all of us to go to his house on Saturday. We want to put you in the picture about this business with Captain Drake. We intend to put money into his next voyage, but I'd rather John was there to help with the details.'

The following weekend saw them all together at Tottenham, where John Isham's wife had prepared enough food for the whole of the Queen's court: or so John said. They brought Roberto up to date with the voyage plans of Francis Drake and without a moment's hesitation he agreed to put up the suggested amount. Having settled the matter, the talk then moved on to other things.

John had been much more subdued than usual and Jacob enquired if anything was bothering him. John gave a short barking laugh. 'Only my own mortality I suppose. I am sixty next month, and my wife has been urging me to retire from the city and move to Northampton.'

'Northampton?' Jacob enquired. 'What is there at Northampton for you?'

'I bought Framington Hall in Northampton last year. It is a rather splendid manor house, not so many miles from Cambridge. To be honest, I've spent rather a lot of money on renovating it in the past year and then last week I was asked by the locals to become the magistrate.'

'At least you'll be on the right side of the law if you do,' joked Jacob. 'Your ventures into court are the stuff of legend. This time it will be you dispensing justice not some poxy magistrate,' he said, with a wink at Roberto.

John joined in the general laughter at this quip. He had used that description on more than one occasion when a case had gone against him. 'Have a care, Jacob Bell,' he threatened, with a broad smile, 'or you might find yourself in contempt of court and I would be forced to send you to the cells for an unspecified time.'

The banter went on for a little while and then John called a halt. 'There was a serious point I wanted to make,' he said, when they were all listening. 'I wanted to tell you that I have decided to take up their offer and I will be moving to Framington Hall later this summer.'

Jacob broke the silence that greeted this announcement. 'I will be very sad to see you go, my friend, but at least Northampton is not the end of the world; even if some at court might not agree.'

Roberto had sat quietly throughout this exchange and John sensing this, went across to him. 'You're very quiet Roberto, have you nothing to say on the matter?'

'I was wondering if you've told Elizabeth,' Roberto said hesitantly. 'I'm not sure how she'll feel about this.'

'Why young Roberto, she has you and John Jacob as family now.' said John with a smile. 'It's time for her make her own life. Surely, you know you'll always be welcome to visit.' He clapped him on the back. 'Have no fear for Elizabeth my friend, her mother is breaking it to her. Elizabeth is very like her mother, she'll take it all in her stride.'

Roberto seemed a little unsure to Jacob, even though he said nothing further on the subject. Jacob resolved that Roberto would have every opportunity to visit his father-in-law in the future.

John, never a man to let a conversation be dull or serious for long, asked them if they had heard his latest story about a sea serpent that Francis Drake had encountered on his last voyage. Jacob was about to make some excuse, but was saved the trouble when Elizabeth announced that the midday meal was ready. John led them into the hall. In a small alcove they washed their hands in basins and dried them on towels, then, having completed their ablutions, he led them into the dining chamber.

When they had sat down, he said Grace and then offered some slices of radish dipped in salt. 'Please help yourselves of the radishes which my dear wife has grown in the cottage garden. They will procure you an appetite for the meat.' His wife smiled cheerfully at his compliment and motioned the servants to serve the meal.

Jacob nibbled gently at a slice, but it was not to his taste. He noticed as usual, contrary to the Venetian custom, there were no forks, just a plate and spoon. He had found this difficult to get used to at first, but needs must. Pulling out his knife, Jacob checked it was clean, wiping it on the damask napkin set out for him and placed it next to the plate.

The servants brought in four large dishes containing a stewed broth, chicken and bacon, a golden brown goose, roast conies and various others platters containing pies and vegetables. John bade them help themselves of the food and the fine malmsey wine, which together with some of Jacob's fine glasses stood beside the wooden tub of water on the buffet at the side. It was the custom to wash the glasses between pledges, or toasts, the glasses being less likely to break against the wood than in a porcelain basin.

Sitting opposite to Jacob was Rebecca, Elizabeth's older sister, a widow of two years. Jacob had met her for the first time at Roberto's wedding, although it had not made any real impression on him at the time. The presence of Maria had ensured that he'd no eyes for anyone else. Now he noted she was tall, with light brown hair and brown eyes, an attractive oval face and lissom figure.

As the meal progressed, she paid a lot of attention to Jacob, asking questions about Venice and conversing with wit and knowledge on current affairs. Later on, she began to rub her foot against the calf of his leg, whilst looking expectantly at him with raised eyebrows. Jacob was flattered, but feeling very restrained by the presence of John Isham on his right, made no response.

By the time the final course of fruit tarts, cheese, pies and fresh fruit had been consumed, Jacob was feeling replete. In company with everyone else, he had also downed several glasses of wine. Contrary to many houses, John liked the meal times to be full of joy and laughter, entertaining them all with his fanciful stories, while a local minstrel played pleasant music on the lute.

When the meal was over, John suggested they should try some bowling, but Jacob decided a gentle walk in the fruit orchard at the side of the house was more to his liking. It was a balmy afternoon and he strolled gently along through the avenue of trees groaning under their load of ripening, red fruit. The pleasant voice of a woman singing a lovely ballad drifted gently through the trees. He missed the early part of the ballad, but now with the singer nearby, he stopped to listen.

Thou couldst desire no earthly thing
But still thou hadst it readily

Thy music still to play and sing
And yet thou wouldst not love me

Greensleeves was all my joy
Greensleeves was my delight
Greensleeves was my heart of gold
And who but my Lady Greensleeves

As the last line of the refrain died away, not wishing to disturb her, Jacob made to move away, but unfortunately trod on a twig, which made a loud cracking noise. There was a startled exclamation from behind the tree in front of him and a surprised voice called out, 'Who's there?'

Making no further attempt at stealth, Jacob walked forward. The singer was Rebecca. 'Oh it's you, Master Bell, you startled me,' she said, making a curtsy. 'I thought you'd gone to play bowls.'

'I'm sorry, Mistris Rebecca,' he said with an answering bow. 'I didn't want to interrupt your lovely ballad.'

'It is lovely, is it not? It is said that King Henry himself wrote it, but I know not if that's the truth of it.'

'Any ballad would sound beautiful with a voice like yours, Mistris Rebecca,' said Jacob gallantly.

'I'm glad your ears are more sensitive than your other parts,' she replied with an arch smile. 'I think perhaps you prefer a more circuitous approach.'

Jacob gave a surprised look. 'It was not unpleasant, but more than a little unusual in my limited experience. However, the proximity of your father made it somewhat difficult.'

'Father isn't here now,' she said eagerly, moving closer.

Before Jacob could reply, they heard Elizabeth calling Rebecca's name. With a muttered comment under her breath and a reluctant sigh, Rebecca replied and then with a meaningful glance at Jacob, hurried off to join her sister.

Jacob watched her disappear with mixed feelings. She was an attractive woman and very direct! It might be interesting to see if she was just flirting. He gave a shrug and sighed. It really was much too nice a day to worry about what might be, so continuing his stroll through the orchard, he found an inviting grassy bank and lay down in the long grass. Hands behind his head, he chewed on a sweet stalk, enjoying the warm sunshine.

Some time later, someone calling his name woke him. Sitting up, he saw Elizabeth walking through the orchard towards him. When he answered her call, she made her way across to him.

'Father was starting to worry about you; you've been gone such a long time.'

'I'm sorry Elizabeth, I must have dozed off,' he confessed. 'It was a large meal, the sun was warm and the grassy bank was inviting. Didn't Rebecca tell you she'd seen me in the orchard?'

'No she didn't. In fact, she's been in a bit of an odd mood since she came back into the house,' said Elizabeth. Her voice sounded puzzled. 'Did you notice anything when you saw her?'

Jacob shrugged. 'Not really, I heard her singing and went closer to listen, but it seemed to startle her. I complimented her about her singing and we talked for a short time, then she rushed off muttering, when she heard you calling.'

Elizabeth gave a knowing look. 'Oh,' she said, 'so you're the reason she didn't say anything. I knew there was something.'

Jacob was puzzled. 'What do you mean?'

Elizabeth gave him an exasperated look and simply ignored the question, suggesting they should return to the house. Jacob would have liked an answer, but Elizabeth had already set off, so there was nothing else to do but follow.

Later, on several occasions he came across Rebecca and Elizabeth with their heads close together, whispering conspiratorially,. Each time as he approached, they giggled and hurried away without a word, looking over their shoulders as they went. Jacob could tell he was the subject of their conversation, but what it was all about, he had no idea.

Chapter Five
Tottenham, July, 1570

Jacob went to bed early that night and had just fallen into that languid state that precedes sleep, when a noise disturbed him. Before he had time to investigate, there was a rustling of clothing and a warm naked body slid into bed and nestled up to him.

'It's Rebecca,' she said, snuggling up to him, 'I thought we could have a little comfort for a change.'

'Rebecca! What are you doing? If your father finds out about this he will go berserk,' he said, trying ineffectively to pull away. Jacob was astonished by her actions, but in truth, he rather liked the feel of her lithe body against his. Despite his protest, he was already feeling his desire rising.

Rebecca simply snuggled closer and wrapped her legs round him. 'Are you saying it's all right if he doesn't know about it then?' She began to stroke his back and kiss him on the side of his neck. 'You needn't worry that I am trying to trap you Jacob, I just want to feel like a woman again; it's been two years since my husband died.'

By now, Jacob was fully aroused and turning her over on to her back, he slid on top of her. She opened her legs and guided him to her, clasping her legs over his back and matching his thrusts, whimpering with desire. They made love with a passion that all too soon came to a shuddering climax. Afterwards, lying close together in drowsy lassitude, Rebecca sighed in contentment. 'That was wonderful, Jacob; it was every bit as good as I thought it would be.' She sighed again. 'I suppose you think I'm a wanton. But I don't go around doing this all of the time. You're the first man I've looked at since my husband died.'

'I feel very honoured then,' said Jacob, meaning every word.

He stroked her face and she turned to face him leaning on her elbow. 'Have you been with anyone since she went back?'

'No. I haven't.'

'You must miss her.'

'Very much, but I don't know if we'll ever be together again. I thought I would have heard from her months ago, but there's been no word from her at all.'

Rebecca hugged him. 'I'm sure you'll hear soon. Anna, Roberto's mother, told us at the wedding what Lady Maria had gone through after your reported death and how she had been forced to marry that swine Ragazoni. She said that she took all sorts of risks to find the evidence to clear you.'

Jacob said nothing, for in truth he was beginning to have doubts about Maria. Why hadn't she been in touch with him since her return to Venice? He'd asked himself that question so many times. At first he'd put his fears to one side, but as the months slipped by, he could find less and less reasons for her silence.

Several weeks ago, he had received a short letter from his father that further fuelled his doubts. There was virtually nothing about Maria except that they were working to bring his case before the full Giunta and that Pietro Ragazoni was doing his best to delay, or stop the appeal. He finished by promising to write as soon as he had something more positive to tell. This and the lack of even a brief letter from Maria made him fear the worst.

Maria was a very wealthy woman in her own right, but as the widow of Ragazoni, she would also inherit all of his estate. This made her a prime goal for every fortune hunter in Venice and beyond. Perhaps she had decided to enjoy her position and had found a new lover. He should have gone back to Venice with her and hang the risk.

Before he could continue with this line of thought, Rebecca turned to face him. 'You seem so sad Jacob, are you worried about Maria?'

'Of course I am. I think she's forgotten me and found someone else.'

Putting a finger to his lips Rebecca remonstrated with him. 'You mustn't think like that Jacob. Elizabeth is a good judge of people and she has often said that Lady Maria is devoted to you. Why else would she have put herself through the misery of living with Envoy Ragazoni except to find evidence to clear you?'

Even now, he couldn't think of any reason other than her love for him; nevertheless, why hadn't he heard from her. He couldn't understand it. He lapsed into a withdrawn silence.

Rebecca, thinking that it meant that he was falling asleep, gave him another hug and then slid out of bed. 'I must go,' she said, picking up her chemise and pulling it over her head. 'I would not cause my father any upset. I wish I could stay longer, but we might fall asleep and be discovered and that would never do.'

Jacob, who'd been admiring Rebecca's lovely figure, was surprised at his disappointment and at his lack of guilt. He slid out of bed and taking her in his arms kissed her soundly. Rebecca responded eagerly then slipped out of his embrace with a husky laugh. 'Stop that Jacob; you know where it will lead.' Jacob nuzzled at her neck and gently pulled her towards the bed again. Disengaging herself with a writhe wriggle she kissed him and stepping back pulled down the chemise, which had somehow nearly come off again. 'I must go now, but I'll try to come again tomorrow night.' Stepping quickly to the door, she opened it carefully, listened for a moment and then with a wave she was gone. Jacob went back to bed, lay down with a satisfied sigh and was asleep almost at once.

The next morning, after the best night's sleep for a long time, he went down to look for Rebecca. Elizabeth was in the kitchen and gave a very knowing grin when Jacob, trying to sound as casual as possible, enquired about Rebecca. She simply told him she'd gone to a neighbouring farm with her mother, to buy some meat. Jacob was sure she was aware of Rebecca's visit to him, but wisely said nothing.

Just then, John Isham and Roberto came in with a messenger who, from his dusty clothes, had ridden post-haste. He bowed to Jacob and handed him a letter. 'Sir William Cecil sends his greetings and I am to wait for an answer.'

Taking the letter from him, Jacob went and sat in the window seat and examined the seal carefully. It was still intact and bore Sir William Cecil's seal. Intrigued, he eased open the seal with his knife and read the letter quickly. The contents were even more fascinating. Sir William Cecil requested Jacob to meet him that afternoon at two-o'clock at Jacob's house in Harte Street. He stated that the matter was of the utmost importance, two other persons would attend and the meeting must be private.

Jacob was astonished on two counts. Firstly, it was the urgency of the meeting and secondly the fact that Sir William had requested instead of instructing him to attend. This alone decided Jacob and he instructed the messenger to tell Sir William that he agreed to his request.

When his two friends asked him about the note, he fobbed them off, by saying that it was simply a meeting with Sir William. 'You know what he's like,' said Jacob, by way of explanation. 'Everything is urgent and must be done immediately, if not sooner.'

John looked so disappointed at his departure that he promised he would not stay in London, but would return that evening in time for the family meal if it were at all possible. 'I don't suppose the meeting will go on for more than a couple of hours, so I should have time to get back.' He was relieved to see that John now appeared happier, so with a further brief word with him, he asked Roberto to help him pack, while John went off to tell his wife that Jacob would not be in for the midday meal.

On the way upstairs to get his things together, Roberto asked him what was really behind the letter. 'There's more to it than you said downstairs. Let me come with you.'

Jacob smiled. 'Not this time, Roberto, I can only tell you that it's important and very secret. I don't know any more than that, so it's no use pestering me.' He thought for a moment and then asked Roberto if he would ask Elizabeth to come and have a word with him in private. Roberto looked surprised at the request, but Jacob was relieved that he simply agreed and went off to find her.

By the time she arrived, he had already collected his things and was in his travelling clothes. Jacob went straight to the point. 'I have to return to London on urgent business and I would like you to give Rebecca a message, but it must be done in private.'

Elizabeth smiled. 'I take it you want me to apologise for your sudden departure, but not to let my parents know what is going on.'

'Indeed,' said Jacob. 'I assumed you are aware of the situation.'

'We are sisters and we tell each other everything,' she paused and pursed her mouth. 'Well …er, nearly everything! What shall I tell her?'

'That I will return at the earliest possible moment so we can…' he hesitated trying to put it more subtly.

'Take up where you left off,' completed Elizabeth with a

knowing smile.

'Exactly,' said Jacob sheepishly. 'I suppose you have already told Roberto.'

'Aren't married couples supposed to be honest with each other?' she replied, with an innocent expression that didn't fool Jacob for a second.

'I see,' he said. 'And will you tell him now? He's sure to wonder what this is all about.'

'I will tell him if I can't avoid it, but I don't want my sister to be embarrassed in any way. You're very honoured, you know, this is the first time she's looked at a man since her husband died. She nursed him all through his illness with the smallpox and nearly died from it herself. She's not short of suitors either, but she hasn't shown the slightest interest in anyone until now. I do hope you'll not cause her any hurt, Jacob.'

'You have my promise I'll not do that. But Rebecca is the one making all the running. But I admit to being a willing partner. Rebecca knows all about the situation with Maria. We comforted each other, that's all.'

Elizabeth gave Jacob a hug and a peck on the cheek. 'I'll keep this a secret from everyone and I'll pass on your message to Rebecca. Roberto will worry until you return, so God speed you back and keep you safe.'

Chapter Six
Murano, Venice, July, 1570

Anna awoke with a start and looked hastily across at Lady Maria. There was no sign that she had stirred, just her gentle breathing. Looking around, Anna realised from the shaft of bright light coming through the gap in the curtains that morning had come at last. Moving the curtain a little more, Anna peered out across the canal towards the Ponte Vivarini, the main bridge of Murano. It was busy with workers hurrying towards the Canal de Vetrai where the main glass-works were situated. Judging by the number of workers in the street, it must have been the Campanile bell that woke me, she thought. They only had twenty minutes to reach their place of work after it had sounded.

Just then, the sound of a loud yawn startled her and looking hurriedly around, she saw Lady Maria stretching her arms as she yawned again. With a scream of delight, Anna rushed over, embraced her and then rushed wildly out into the corridor shouting for the doctor and the Senator. Maria looked after her in amazement wondering what on earth was going on and then, realising that her arms were covered in itchy spots, she began to scratch distractedly.

Her puzzlement was short lived. First her father and then Doctor Nguyên, came hurrying in with smiles wreathing their faces. The doctor helped her to sit up and then gently restraining her scratching hands, studied her carefully, taking her pulse, examining the spots and feeling her forehead. A smile lit up his face. 'The fever has subsided thanks to the herbal teas and the eruption of spots is the sign that the qi is much healthier and has expelled the yang evil. Now we must use the sweet-cool drugs to nourish yin and clear away the remaining heat.'

When Maria looked back on that period, she could make little sense of what had happened. She was vaguely aware of being forced to drink foul-tasting medicines and having wild feverish dreams. When her head cleared enough for her to understand she had been very ill, she was appalled to find that almost a month had passed.

When her father next visited her, she asked him to write to Giam to inform him about the baby. She bitterly regretted not doing it herself before he was born, but so much time had elapsed! She was not sure what he would think now.

'I would do it myself, father,' she explained, although it was a huge effort to talk, 'but I just haven't the strength. I don't know how long it will be and I don't want to put off telling him any longer.' When her father promised to do it immediately, she sank back on to the pillows exhausted and almost immediately fell asleep.

By the time she was well enough to sit outside on the garden room veranda, the weather was cooler and Anna insisted she wrapped up warmly. 'You don't want to get another fever, Lady Maria.'

'Please don't fuss, Anna. It's so lovely to get outside at last.' She looked round at the house, but not seeing what she was seeking she turned back to Anna. 'Has the wet-nurse fed Rico yet?'

'I imagine so by now. Perhaps she's changing him. I told her to bring him out so you could spend a little time with him.'

Maria smiled in appreciation. 'I have a lot of bonding to catch up on. It was lucky you were able to find Julia Labie, she's been wonderful.'

'It has been good for her as well,' said Anna. 'She was heartbroken when she lost her own baby and she readily agreed to look after yours while you were ill, and she was able to breast feed him.'

Just then, Julia arrived with the baby. She placed him carefully in Maria's arms and looked down in satisfaction. 'He is asleep now, my lady. He has fed very well and is a very happy child.'

Maria moved the shawl away from his face, kissing his forehead and smiling as Rico snuggled closer to her. 'I can't tell you how it feels to be able to hold him at last. There were times when I thought it would never happen.' She regarded them with gratitude. 'I can never repay you. Without your care and love we would not have survived.'

'Forgive me, Lady Maria, but that's not true. The baby was not as seriously ill as you and would have been safe. It was the good

Doctor Nguyên's medicines that made you well.'

Maria gave a weak smile. 'I don't have the strength to argue now, but when I have rested I will make sure you both understand how grateful I am.' Anna busied herself fluffing up the cushions as Maria settled back in the chair. Then, as Maria closed her eyes and gave a contented sigh, Anna crept quietly away.

At the Casa Da Mula, the Sigisbei had just shown Doctor Nguyên into the Senator's study. 'Come in, come in, my dear doctor, it was good of you to come so promptly. Please sit down, I have a matter of importance to discuss with you.'

The doctor frowned. 'I trust the Lady Maria is not ill again,' he asked in a worried tone.

Ricardo laughed. 'Not at all, she continues to improve with each passing day, thanks to your great skill.'

The doctor inclined his head in gracious acknowledgement of the compliment. 'For which I have been well rewarded,' he said, making a little bow. 'I am pleased that your daughter's health is progressing. I planned to call on her later this week to reassure myself that all is well with both of them.'

Ricardo nodded. 'By all means and since you have mentioned the topic I wish to discuss, I will tell you what is on my mind.'

The doctor looked puzzled, but simply waited for Ricardo to continue.

'It is the matter of the service you have rendered to my daughter,' said Ricardo. He held a hand up as the doctor tried to say he had been paid. 'I know I have paid you the fee you asked for at the outset, but the manner in which you saved my daughter's life went way beyond the call of normal duty. I know of no physician in these islands, or beyond, who could have saved her,' he said, his voice husky with emotion. 'Maria is my only child and without your knowledge and devotion to duty she would almost certainly have died. I owe you a debt that goes much further than simple payment. I want you to know this, all of my resources and influence are at your command.'

He smiled at the stunned expression on the doctor's face. 'It's the first time I have seen you lost for words, my dear doctor,' he chuckled, 'but I mean what I say. If I can be of any service at all, no matter what, if it is within my power to grant it, consider it done.'

He sat down and studied the doctor who was obviously having trouble coming to terms with Ricardo's offer. It was some time before he could speak, but eventually he stood up and walked towards Ricardo, who rose to meet him. The doctor bowed and then held out his hand. Ricardo took it in both of his and shook it solemnly.

Looking deep into Ricardo's eyes the doctor said. 'Your offer is gratefully accepted. There is one thing I desire above all else, but I'm unable to achieve it on my own. With your help, it might be possible.'

'Name it,' said Ricardo without hesitation.

They both sat down while the doctor explained. 'Senator, you are one of the few people aware of my background before I came to Venice. The Chinese doctor I studied under in Than Hóa province in Vietnam had a daughter and the father was wholeheartedly in favour of us marrying. When I fled from the army of the Mac king, I left thinking she had been killed with her father. Fortunately, she was visiting an uncle at the time and like me, they escaped. About a year ago, they came to Venice. At twenty-four, she is a lot older than most unmarried Chinese women. I have enquired about the bride price, but they refuse to discuss it. Perhaps they are not in favour of her marrying a former student of her father.'

'What do you wish me to do?' said Ricardo. 'Is it a matter of money, or is the uncle involved in a business where I could use my influence?'

'Nothing as simple as that,' said the doctor. 'In China it is very important when approaching the parents or guardians to follow a basic principle of three letters and six etiquettes that are essential to a marriage.'

'What are these three letters?'

'They consist of a betrothal letter, gift letter and a wedding letter. The important point is that a matchmaker, who presents them, must ensure strict adherence to six etiquettes. Preferably, he should be a man of influence and someone the family can trust. If I teach you the etiquettes, will you be my matchmaker?'

Now it was Ricardo's turn to be speechless. It was not at all what he had expected. The more he thought about it, the more he could see the sense from the doctor's point of view. To have one of the most influential Senators in Venice as his matchmaker could alter their thinking about the suitability of the doctor as a suitor.

This indeed proved to be the case. The wedding took place three weeks later, on the auspicious date selected by the astrologist. Ricardo was best man and his present was an elaborate wedding banquet held at the Casa Da Mula. Maria insisted on attending and as the happy couple set off to begin their married life, Ricardo and Maria waved goodbye from the quayside.

Chapter Seven
London, July, 1570

When Jacob arrived at Harte Street, Mistris Simpkin was surprised. 'I'm sorry Master Jacob, I was not expecting you until Monday and I've given the servants the day off.'

'That's quite all right Mistris Simpkin, I intend to return to Tottenham tonight, but in the meantime, I am expecting some important visitors and wish to have a private meeting with them.' He smiled conspiratorially. 'A very private meeting! I will use the glass showroom office and I want you to make sure that after I signal you, no one disturbs us, not even Roberto and Quiff. Do you understand me?'

Mistris Simpkin nodded. 'Of course Master Jacob, will you require any refreshments?'

'You can put a bottle of malmsey and some of that excellent lemonade of yours in the office and then return to your quarters. I will answer and bar the door and then ring the hand bell in the hall to signal the meeting. When the meeting is finished I'll ring the bell again. If anyone should enquire, you know nothing about any visitors, I'm away visiting friends and the house is empty'

If Mistris Simpkin was in any way surprised by this secrecy, there was nothing in her expression to indicate it. She simply curtsied and went off to follow his instructions.

Promptly at two o'clock, Sir William Cecil and Colonel Young arrived, followed shortly afterwards by a man dressed in crimson velvet breeches, knitted stockings and a scarlet leather jacket trimmed with silver braid. Over all, he wore a silk cloak and a long gold chain. He was vaguely familiar and Jacob was sure he'd seen him at court. When they were together in the office with the door bolted, Sir William introduced him. 'Master Bell, allow me to present Sir John Hawkins of Devon, you may have heard of him? Colonel Young is of course well known to you after that little affair with Count Maldini.'

Jacob nodded and smiled at the Colonel and bowed to Hawkins. 'Your recent battle at San Juan de Ulua is on everyone's lips, Admiral. Everyone condemns the perfidious behaviour of the Spanish. Welcome to my home and showroom.'

John Hawkins returned his bow. 'My thanks to you Master Bell,' he said and then gestured at the shelves of gleaming glass in the showroom. 'I have never seen so much Murano glass in one place before.'

With a grin, Jacob invited him to sit down. 'Façon de Venice it may be, but it was all made here in London at the Crouched Friars Glass-works.'

Hawkins was astonished. 'Then you must be from Murano yourself, since I know of none in this city who could make glass of that quality. I thought you must have imported it from Murano, or possibly Antwerp. I would love to buy some from you.'

Sir William interrupted them. 'Perhaps we can get down to the matter at hand,' he said dryly. 'You can buy as much glass as you like when our business is concluded, Admiral.' Turning to Jacob, he gave a quizzical smile. 'You are aware of the affair at San Juan de Ulua, but are you aware of the plight of over a hundred of the expedition's men?'

'Only that some men were left behind, but I don't know the circumstances,' said Jacob. 'What has this to do with me?'

'That is what we are about to discuss,' said Sir William testily, 'can we get on?'

They settled down in the chairs and then Sir William turned to Jacob. 'What you are about to hear is not for repeating. Do I have your word on this?'

'Of course Sir William,' said Jacob, his annoyance showing, 'as you should well know, I am not in the habit of telling tales.'

Sir William bowed to him. 'My apologies Jacob Bell, no insult was intended, it was simply my desire to keep these discussions strictly private.'

Jacob nodded. 'Apology accepted. Now, how can I be of assistance in this matter?'

'First, there is the matter of Admiral Hawkins. I want you to support him in his quest to release his men from the Spanish authorities.' Brushing aside Jacob's attempts to say something, he continued. 'You may not be able to do much at present, but there may well be an opportunity to play a more active role later. For now, I want you to act as a liaison between us so that the Admiral can keep in touch with me without arousing suspicion.' He gave his grim smile. 'Given his interest in your glass, you have a ready-made excuse.'

Sir William gave a meaning glance at John Hawkins who gave a nod in return. 'Since January of last year, Admiral Hawkins has been trying to arrange the release of his men, or what is left of them, from Spanish hands. He has been to see Guerau de Spes, the Spanish Ambassador, but to no avail.' He paused and then with a gesture to Hawkins said, 'I will let John Hawkins tell you the story for himself.'

Hawkins stood up and began to pace about. 'Forgive me if I move about, it doesn't do to stand still on a ship when in a fight, so it's become rather a habit.' His weather-beaten face became serious. 'It was one of the worst days of my career as a Captain when I had to leave a hundred men behind in Mexico. I vowed then that I would do everything in my power to get them released.' He grimaced. 'Or what is left of them after the cursed Inquisition is finished with them.'

Jacob didn't need to ask further questions, he knew very well the extremes of the Inquisition; it was one of the reasons that he was not a practising Catholic. Venice with its tolerant attitudes had so stifled the Inquisition as to render it almost ineffective. Even the Jews and Greeks were safe in the Islands, as the Inquisition was not allowed by the Council of Ten to have any jurisdiction over members of other religions. 'What are you planning to do?' he asked.

Hawkins smiled. 'It seems that the Spanish Ambassador may have got the impression that I am a supporter of the Catholic cause. I can't imagine why, the remarks I made were only slightly seditious.' His smile became wider when he saw Cecil's grimace. 'I can see it was fortunate I had your permission to mislead the Ambassador, Sir William.' Even Cecil had to laugh at the droll expression that accompanied the remark.

Hawkins, his mood becoming serious again, turned to Jacob. 'Unfortunately, Master Bell, I'm not sure that his master, Philip of Spain, will find it so convincing without some sort of confirmation.'

'Confirmation?' asked Jacob. 'What can I do?'

'Hawkins is going to need some help in convincing the Spanish and we want you to give him a hand,' said Cecil.

Jacob looked surprised. 'I'm not sure…'

He got no further before Cecil interrupted. 'Of course you aren't sure Bell, but if you listen instead of asking questions, I will explain,' he said waspishly.

Recognising that any future argument was pointless, Jacob gave a shrug and waved for him to continue.

'I believe you met the Countess of Feria when you were at court?'

Not for the first time, Jacob was amazed at the things Cecil knew. 'As a matter of fact I did, although she has returned to Spain with her husband, who is a courtier of the King of Spain.'

'Excellent, that will make things a lot easier.' Because Jacob was looking bewildered by this comment, he explained. 'A number of Hawkins men have been transferred from Mexico to Spain to await trial by the Inquisition.'

'God help them,' muttered Jacob.

'Amen to that,' said Hawkins.

Cecil just ignored the comments and went on to explain that one of the men called Fitzwilliam, a relative of the Countess of Feria, had contrived to smuggle out a letter to Hawkins.

'The Countess knows about her kinsman from Hawkins and is travelling to England to plead Fitzwilliam's case with Mary Stuart. With Mary Stuart's support Fitzwilliam will go free.'

He could see Jacob was confused and tried to clarify matters. 'Because the Countess is married to a Spanish court official, it would need the permission of the Queen's Council for her to meet Mary Stuart. This would involve a personal plea to the council. To bring it into the open like that, might lead to the exposure of Admiral Hawkins's plan. I cannot risk this, so I have advised the Countess that she must send a letter to Mary Stuart asking for her help. I have promised that this will be delivered. I asked her if there was anyone who is not directly involved in court circles and your name came up. The Countess remembers your kindness when she was sent from court. In view of this, I want you to act as a go-between for Hawkins and myself, with the Countess of Feria. She will visit you here, ostensibly to buy some glass. You can then exchange messages without anyone being the wiser that we are involved.'

Jacob thought that it was taking caution a little too far, but since it didn't create any real problems as far as he could see, he readily agreed.

Cecil then went on to explain that he wanted Jacob's help in discovering if certain important people were involved in a plot against the Queen. Although there were grounds to suspect that they were plotting something, proving it was another matter entirely. The Duke of Norfolk for one. had been under suspicion for some time. Even before the failed rebellion of the Northern Earls and his imprisonment.

'I wish to use the services of your Ring to discover if the Duke of Norfolk is plotting with Mary Stuart and her advisers. The Ring was helpful in the Maldini affair and I think they might prove effective again. There is some background, which you all need to know, so please be patient while I explain.'

He then went on to give details of events of the past two years and the information that he had obtained recently from Walsingham's spies in France, Holland, and Spain. 'I first became aware from various sources that throughout the summer of fifteen sixty-eight, Mary Stuart was plotting to marry the Duke of Norfolk. The Northern Catholic Earls raised an army to support her cause and Norfolk and his supporters made such a strong political case that Mary and the Spanish Ambassador were both convinced that they had won. On my advice, Queen Elizabeth, banned the marriage with a fine show of royal wrath.'

Norfolk's courage failed he explained and he fled from the court to consult with his friends. The Queen at once commanded him on his allegiance to return. Faced with the alternative of obedience or open rebellion, his nerve deserted him and he set off for court, only to be arrested and flung into the Tower.

'I had Walsingham investigate the ramifications of the conspiracy. His attention was drawn to a Florentine banker called Ridolfi and he examined him, but concluded he was simply what he purported to be, even though he had moved some amounts of money from the continent to supporters of Mary Stuart.'

Jacob listened with mounting excitement and his face must have betrayed his thoughts. Cecil asked him if he knew Ridolfi.

I can't say I do,' said Jacob casually, 'but his name came up recently in a conversation with a business acquaintance about some financial affairs.'

'Ah I see. He has advised a number of prominent people.'

Jacob thought this remark was more than a little ironic if his information was correct, but wisely refrained from any comment as Cecil continued his tale.

In the past couple of months, Walsingham's spies had reported to Cecil that there had been an increase in the number of messages passing between the Spanish Ambassador, Bishop Ross and the Spanish Court. There was sufficient evidence to set alarm bells ringing and Cecil explained that he was increasing the guards around Mary Stuart and redoubling his efforts to intercept her mail.

'I am hoping you can find some information relating to these people,' he said, looking at Jacob expectantly. 'I will of course reimburse you for any expenses.'

Jacob thought carefully for a moment and then gave his agreement. He had no intention of bringing up the matter of Ridolfi unless he had something more specific to go on.

Having concluded their business, they walked out into the hall, while Jacob went to find Mistris Simpkin. He sent her to Quiff to ask him to collect his horse from the livery, then returned the hall. Cecil advised Jacob he would send him full instructions shortly and then took his leave with Colonel Young.

Hawkins stayed a little while longer and gave Jacob a healthy order for stem ware before he left with his grateful thanks to Jacob for agreeing to help. He also offered his help and advice, if Jacob ever required any assistance regarding ships, or shipping.

After saying goodbye to Hawkins, Jacob saw Quiff approaching along Harte Street with his horse. Mistris Simpkin came to the entrance with Jacob's things and with thanks to them both for their help, he set off for Tottenham, but not before reiterating to Quiff the need for obtaining information on Ridolfi and the necessity for vigilance. These plotters were dangerous!

Chapter Eight
Greenwich, July, 1570

The horse picking its way carefully through the dense thickets of the woods close by Greenwich reared in alarm as a startling outburst of high-pitched screeches possessed the woodland and whirled around them. The horseman patted the neck of the nervous steed, talking in a soothing voice until it settled again. He shook his fist in the direction of the reddish-fawn bird with its conspicuous white rump and erect white and black crest and it flew deeper into the forest at his gesture, leaving its strident alarm call trailing behind.

Urging the still uneasy horse forward the rider looked around cautiously, cursing the jay for alerting any forester within half a mile as they resumed their way through the thickets. Reaching the edge of a glade, his destination, he stopped where he could see the whole of the area and listened intently. The only sounds were those of birds and insects of the forest going about their business, so the rider dismounted and tying the reins carefully to a nearby sapling, he eased his way forward towards the shattered oak on the far side.

Riven by a lightning strike a few years earlier, the oak had torn asunder about a third of the way up the main trunk: not the only one to suffer in that violent storm. Its proud crest now lay in ruin across a corner of the glade Searching for the former squirrel hole that served as a hiding place for messages, the horseman was about to place his letter when a man stepped out of the shadows nearby.

'I heard you coming a mile away, father, you're getting careless.'

Count Ridolfi looked at his son in relief and studied him carefully. His wiry frame had slimmed down since the last time they had met, but his distinctive red hair, pockmarked face and narrow features had not changed. He was Ridolfi's son by Agnes Sutton, a distant relative of Robert Dudley, the Earl of Leicester. The Earl had changed his name from Sutton when he acquired the Dudley lands.

Ridolfi gave a grimace. 'That damn jay made sure of that. It so frighted the horse, it nearly unseated me.'

'You're too soft with horses, father, you must show them you're the master.'

Ridolfi did not comment. His son was an excellent equestrian with immensely strong wrists, but he was cruel to horses, believing they needed taming. He has the same attitude to people as well, thought Ridolfi. Whilst not admiring the trait, he found it useful at times. Finding a suitable place, he sat down and indicated the letter.

'I'll not need to give you this now that we're well met. I have received a message from your mother.'

When Ridolfi first met her, Agnes was a chambermaid in the service of Queen Mary, Queen Elizabeth's sister. Ridolfi, a tall, lean and handsome man with dark swarthy looks, was a frequent visitor to the court as financial advisor to the Queen and his affair with Agnes had been discreet. The birth of his illegitimate son had occurred whilst Agnes was away from court, ostensibly looking after her dying mother. Jedediah had been farmed out to an aunt until he was old enough to work, sweetened by payments from Ridolfi. Agnes returned to court without anyone knowing she had borne Ridolfi's child.

When Elizabeth came to the throne, Leicester became her favourite and Master of Horse, Agnes through her family connections was appointed a chambermaid to the Queen and a prolific source of information for Ridolfi. She had managed to get Jed, as she called him, employment as a groom in the Royal stables.

'What gossip has she picked up this time?' asked Jed.

'The Queen intends to ride alone with Leicester on the morrow. They will give their escort the slip to spend time alone, no doubt to get some whoring done,' he commented waspishly. 'Thankfully her base desires will give us the opportunity we need.'

'Do you want me to shoot her in the woods, or make it seem like an accident?'

Ridolfi grimaced. 'We need to be subtle about it, Jed. Besides, you couldn't guarantee where they'll ride and the escort would likely discover you, either before or after the shooting. No, an accident it must be.' He regarded Jed fondly. 'I don't want you to take any undue risks. Have you anything in mind?'

'I've been waiting for the right opportunity to rid us of this bastard Queen. I'll make sure that the saddle girths of the horse she rides are so weak that when she attempts to race with Leicester, which she usually does, the girth will part. I hope she falls under the hooves of Leicester's horse,' he said nastily. 'Few women could survive a fall at full gallop.'

'Excellent, but I suggest you leave as soon as they set off.' He thought for a moment then his face lit up. 'I have it. I will arrange for your mother to go home later today saying she's ill. You'll receive a note early in the morning saying that she's very sick and asking for you. This will explain your sudden departure and rouse no suspicion. Come straight to my house in London. You're going to be the new steward of my household. As for Leicester, he will not implicate you in an attempt on the Queen's life for fear of being arraigned himself as an accomplice.'

Jed smiled evilly. 'I could tell Leicester about the letter and get his permission to leave. He will surely not deny me visiting my sick mother. I'll make sure there are witnesses, so he can't claim otherwise at a later date.'

Ridolfi gave a satisfied nod, then with a boost from Jed, mounted his horse and with a wave of farewell, rode away without a backward glance.

Next morning, Jed was hard at work soaping some of the harnesses when Leicester bustled in. He was dressed in his best riding clothes and Jed noted he was wearing his favourite sword, a present from the Queen.

'Prepare my horse, Jed, and be quick about it,' he shouted, aiming a playful kick at him. He was obviously in very high spirits at the news that the Queen was riding with him. 'Get the Irish gelding I've been gentling for the Queen and put on that new side-saddle we had made to Catherine de Medici's design: the one with the high second pommel. She has a mind for a gallop today, so you'd best not keep her waiting.'

Jed hurried off and fetched the saddle and, turning over the girth strap to inspect the stitches at the rear of the buckle, smiled in satisfaction. He had frayed several of the stitches and broken some of the others, but with the girth fastened, they were underneath and not visible. They would hold for normal riding, but at full gallop, or a jump, the full weight of the rider thrusting down would cause them to part. Jed felt his chest tightening in delicious anticipation. Putting the side-saddle firmly in place on the gelding, he slapped the horses belly and tightened the girth quickly. He didn't want Leicester re tightening it in case he used too much force and broke it prematurely. That would be disastrous. So long as Leicester found it tight when he checked, which he always did, he wouldn't touch it.

Leading the two horses out into the yard, Jed was just in time to see the Queen arrive with her escort. Leicester signalled Jed to bring forward the horses and made a deep bow to the Queen. Taking the reins of the gelding from Jed he paraded it around the Queen, finally bringing it to a halt beside the mounting block. 'Your majesty,' he cried in a ringing voice, making another courtly bow, 'allow me to introduce you to your new mount Diarmaid, so named for the mark on his face that makes all women fall in love with him.'

The Queen's eyes lit up as Leicester paraded the horse in front of her. Its coat, the product of hours of patient grooming, shone in the morning sunlight. She clapped her hands in delight. 'He is most aptly named, my lord. If he rides half as well as he looks, it will be a joy. I will probably fall in love with him.'

As if knowing he was the subject of discussion Diarmaid threw up his head and pranced in front of her. Leicester, ever wary for such a move, held the reins in a firm grip. 'I have gentled him myself, your majesty. He will give you a fine run today.'

Favouring him with a flashing smile, the Queen climbed up the steps of the mounting block. With Leicester holding the horse steady, she climbed on to the saddle, hooking her knee over the high pommel as Leicester had shown her, and gathered the reins. At Leicester's signal, Jed brought up his black stallion and grasping the pommel firmly, with an athletic swing, Leicester sprang into the saddle. Immediately, the Queen dug her heels into the gelding and it raced away across the yard, with Leicester in close pursuit. The escort was left straggling behind and with a curse, the Colonel urged his men to catch up.

Jed gave a smile of relief as the girth strap held. He had

experimented for months to produce the right amount of wear on the buckle strap. He watched in keen anticipation as they rode across the heath and out of sight into the forest ride. Leicester said she liked to gallop up the ride and on a number of occasions they had shaken off the escort. The strap would likely part during such a gallop.

Hurrying to the stables, he collected his things and hurried out of the yard. He did not intend to be around if his plan came to fruition. The letter from his mother had achieved its goal and he had permission from Leicester to leave as soon as the Queen had left. Mounting his horse, he rode out of the stables heading for London. In his mind's eye, he saw the Queen falling under the pounding hooves of Leicester's stallion and made a silent prayer. 'Do not save her Lord. Remove this foul abomination from this world so the true faith may once more flourish in this land.'

Chapter Nine
Greenwich, July, 1570

About a mile away from the Greenwich stables, the gelding and the stallion turned into the wide forest ride. The Queen's eyes lit up with a mischievous smile as she challenged Leicester. 'Let's see what this horse can really do, Robin. I'll race you to the fallen oak.' Even as she spoke, she spurred the gelding and given his head, he sprang away, ears pricked forward.

Leicester smiled indulgently as the Queen opened up a gap of about ten yards. Patting the stallion on the neck, he leaned forward and whispered in his ears. 'Let's go and catch her boy.' The stallion, its ears pricked forward responded immediately and leaped into a pounding gallop that once more left the Colonel cursing as his troops were left trailing fifty yards behind.

Just as the Queen was approaching the fallen oak, Leicester came alongside her. She gave an exultant laugh and urged her horse forward again, driving her foot hard against the stirrup as the horse landed after soaring over the trunk, with Leicester a fraction behind. Her whoop of delight turned to one of horror as with a loud snap, the buckle parted and the saddled lurched to one side.

Seeing what had occurred, Leicester spurred the stallion cruelly and it bounded alongside the gelding. Leaning over, at great peril to himself, he plucked the Queen from her horse just as the saddle slipped away entirely, to be brutally mangled under the hammering hooves.

By the time the escort caught up, they were sitting on the fallen log with the Queen ashen faced and shuddering as she realised how close to disaster she had been. The Colonel threw himself from his horse and seeing that the Queen was unhurt, turned on Leicester. 'This is your doing, my lord,' he roared. 'Your gross negligence could have killed the Queen.'

The noble lord said nothing, his face taut with strain, waiting anxiously for the Queen to speak. To his intense relief the Colonel's bluster roused her from her stupor. 'Do not blame my Lord Leicester for this; blame my own impetuous nature,' she said in a chastened voice. 'It is only thanks to his superb horsemanship and quick wits that I wasn't badly injured, or worse.' She favoured Leicester with a warm smile, and then her mercurial temper flared as she turned on the Colonel and angrily ordered him to catch the horses and get them back to the stables.

Later when Leicester examined the battered saddle, one glance told him the whole story. The stitches holding the buckle had broken. He was sure that when it had come from the saddle makers there was no poor stitching anywhere. A few Ladies of the Court had tried out the saddle and the Queen had used it once. It was difficult to comprehend how the stitches could have become so weak after so little use.

As the implications became obvious, he blanched and the hairs on the nape of his neck rose, sending a shudder through his shoulders. This was no accident. Jed looked after the tack and kept it maintained, although the head groom had the responsibility. Assuming Jed had weakened the strap, his hurried departure had to be part of the plan.

His neck was at stake: as Master of Horse, he was responsible. It would do him no good to denounce Jed. Although only a distant relative, Jed was appointed on his recommendation. My enemies will seize on this he thought. They will accuse me of plotting against the Queen and arraign me for treason. Head in hands, he racked his brains for a way out.

Later that afternoon, Leicester's worst fears were confirmed when he was summoned to appear before a hastily convened Council to explain what had happened. The letter, signed by Cecil, although stopping short of an indictment, told him all. Calling for the head groom, he talked quietly to him for some time then, when the groom nodded in agreement, passed him a well-laden purse.

At the appointed hour, Leicester strode into the council chamber and his heart sank when he saw the Queen's chair was unoccupied. No sooner had he sat down than Cecil got to his feet and asked Leicester to explain the accident to the Queen. Before Leicester could say a word, the Earl of Essex rose to his feet. He rounded on Leicester and accused him of engineering the whole incident, and in doing so, putting the Queen at grave risk of her life.

Jumping angrily to his feet, Leicester was about to reply when the Queen, who had entered the chamber quietly, laughed loud and long, causing everyone to turn round.

'My Lord Essex,' she said scornfully, 'your words show how little you understand about horsemanship. Had anyone sabotaged the saddle, they would have had no inkling of when the saddle would slip. To expect someone to be on hand for such an eventuality is utter nonsense,' she gave a wry smile in Leicester's direction, 'especially when it is one such as myself, who thrives on the challenge of riding fast and furiously.'

Turning to Cecil, she gave him a warning look that he did not miss. 'Methinks the Council should offer a vote of thanks to my Lord Leicester for saving you the job of appointing a new Queen: probably the Stuart woman you all so hate!' With this telling remark hanging in the air, she stalked to the back of her chair and regally inclined her head to the Council.

'And now my lords, I take my leave of you. I wish to have words in private with my lord Leicester. You, I suggest, would be better employed finding some suitable way of rewarding the noble lord for saving my life.'

She swept out of the room followed closely by the relieved Leicester. The Queen's intervention had stifled any debate on the matter and he could breathe easily; unless of course, she had something different to say in private. He need not have worried. When she asked him what had happened to the saddle, he threw himself at her feet. 'Beloved Queen, forgive me for not taking better care of you. The stitches on the buckle holding the saddle have parted. There was no evidence of any attempt to sabotage them, so they must have been of inferior quality. I blame myself for not checking them more carefully.'

Elizabeth stepped closer and ruffled his hair. 'Oh Robin, you cannot check every little detail yourself, you have to rely on others to do their jobs.'

He looked up at her. 'That is why I have dismissed both the head groom and a distant relation of mine, the man who saddled your gelding. They were supposed to check for any signs of wear or weakness.'

The Queen held out her hand and raised him to his feet.

Linking her arm in his, she walked him along the gallery. 'You have nothing to reproach yourself for, Robin. You are the only horseman in the land who could have done what you did and I owe you my life. You will not find me ungrateful.'

Leicester stopped and looked into her eyes. 'The only reward I need is that you are safe, dearest Bess. Thank God I was in time! If you had fallen…'

His voice broke off in distress and Elizabeth hugged him tightly and kissed him on the cheek. 'Come Robin, this is not like you. We must put this behind us, for there is much to do. Leave me now and we will talk again soon.'

Later, sitting at his desk with a large glass of sack, Leicester reflected on the whole incident. He was still not sure if it was an accident, or a deliberate attempt on the Queen's life. He took a long draught. Luckily, he'd come out of the affair with an even better standing with the Queen. There was nothing she admired more than a brilliant horseman. He was glad he'd got rid of Jed. He had to trust the people around him and Jed was best placed to fray the stitches if that is what had occurred.

The head groom was a different matter. He'd been paid well to take the blame. He may be just a scapegoat, but Leicester had vowed to make sure he was not the loser. That's why he was now on his way to Warwick to oversee the stables with a substantial purse and a cottage for his family. Jed Sutton was the one he'd never trust again. And if their paths crossed again, he'd bear it firmly in mind that Jed was probably a traitor and act accordingly.

Chapter Ten
London, August, 1570

At the Crouched Friars, Jacob sat in his office, looking back over the events of a week ago. The reunion with Rebecca had not gone to plan at all. Certainly, Rebecca had come to his bed and they had enjoyed a leisurely coupling that satisfied them both. Afterwards as they lay comfortably together, Rebecca had thanked him for making her feel like a woman again. She then informed him that this would be the last time, as she planned to accept an offer of marriage made by a neighbouring farmer. Apparently, it was the third time he had begged her to marry him and she had decided to accept him.

Astonished by this sudden announcement, Jacob asked her to explain. Rebecca said she had thought about nothing else since the farmer's latest marriage proposal. She had made it clear to Jacob that when she came to his bed it was nothing more than a dalliance. Unfortunately, it had not remained like that and she found herself attracted to him. However, when Jacob started to talk about Maria, it became clear to her that while there was the slightest chance that Maria still loved him, he could not offer her marriage. Whatever he might say to the contrary, he still loved Maria.

For Rebecca, this changed everything. She longed for children and thanks to Jacob awakening her dormant feelings, she could now contemplate marriage once more. The farmer was very fond of her and he would be a good husband and father. He was steady, reliable and a landowner. He might not give her the excitement that Jacob represented, but it would help her to fulfil her desire for children and give her a secure and good life in the country.

On mature reflection, Jacob had to admit Rebecca was right about Maria. Rebecca was a lovely woman and a lively lover. He had no qualms about their affair; Rebecca had been a pleasant interlude, but nothing more. Maria was the love of his life and he would never settle for anyone else, unless she no longer loved him. He was worried at the lack of news from her. He had to find out the reason. The time they had spent together at Harte

Street and the house at Tottenham had been the most satisfying time of his life. They had loved and laughed with no worry for the future and Jacob wanted that feeling again.

Before he left for London, he spoke to Rebecca again and she invited him to her wedding. Jacob promised that nothing would keep him away and that if she needed a friend, she only had to call and he would be there to help.

He'd sent a letter to Maria that morning, asking why she hadn't contacted him and promising to go to Venice if she needed him, no matter what the consequences to himself. Now all he could do was wait for a reply. In the meantime, he decided it was no use sitting around moping; it would take months to get a reply. He began to plan the reorganisation necessary to leave him free to focus on Cecil's instructions.

His first worry was Roberto. Now that Jacob was again involved with Cecil, Roberto would be faced by a dilemma. He would be torn between Jacob and Elizabeth. The last thing Jacob wanted was to drive a wedge between them.

When he broached the subject to Roberto, he learned that Elizabeth had told him that he must stay in London during the week and only return to Tottenham at the weekend if it could be arranged. 'It's not that she doesn't want me, it's the way she's been brought up,' Roberto explained, when Jacob expressed his surprise at Elizabeth's suggestion. 'The man must be allowed to get on with his business and the wife must do everything to support him,' Elizabeth had told him. Roberto gave Jacob a knowing look. 'She knows you are more than just a glassmaker and that you enjoy the confidence of people in very high places. She expects that I'll be away from home for extended periods.'

'What about the house in London? Why can't she come here?'

'Because she's a country girl at heart, her mother was the same. She brought up Elizabeth and Rebecca with those same values.'

Realising that there was no more to be said, Jacob moved on to the situation at the Crouched Friars and the Glass-Sellers. After some discussion, they agreed that when Jacob was away, Roberto would handle the Bourse and the Glass-Sellers and Peter Tyzack would run the glass-works. Quiff would of course continue as normal, helping Roberto and controlling the Ring. In the case of a problem arising that couldn't wait until Jacob returned, they must agree a solution between them. When Roberto made no objection, Jacob had a feeling that the agreement had come all too easily. Whether Roberto would be happy to let him go on a dangerous mission on his own, time alone would tell!

Two weeks later, Jacob was in the showroom in Harte Street dealing with a customer, when Mistris Simpkin announced the arrival of the Countess of Feria. Once the other customer had left, Jacob led the Countess into the showroom. She was a tall, stately lady wearing a green day dress that owed much to Spanish fashion and which showed off her figure to perfection. The years had handled her kindly, the high cheekbones and unmarked complexion giving her the looks of a much younger woman.

Jacob remembered her from her last day in court, when Elizabeth had behaved petulantly towards her for marrying a Spanish courtier and becoming pregnant. Even though the Countess had been a trusted lady-in-waiting, she was kept waiting for hours in oppressive heat before receiving only the most disparaging dismissal. She had shown wonderful forbearance and impressed all present at court. Afterwards, Elizabeth had confessed shame at the way she had treated her.

After a cursory look around, the Countess could contain her impatience no longer. 'Have you a letter from Sir William Cecil for me?'

Jacob did not reply, but immediately handed her the letter. Opening it quickly, she scanned the contents then broke into a delighted smile. 'Sir William informs me that Queen Mary has sent a letter of support for my petition to King Philip of Spain, via the Spanish Ambassador. Hopefully my kinsman will be released soon. Will you pass on my thanks to Sir William for his help.'

Jacob promised he would and then going over to the rear shelves, he brought out a small parcel. He handed it to the Countess who looked puzzled. 'Sir William suggested that to avoid any suspicion, we should pretend that the purpose of your visit was to buy some glass,' said Jacob. 'I have taken the liberty of giving you two goblets from my Serissima range. These are the ones here,' he said, indicating the display at the end of the aisle.

'Please accept them with my compliments.'

She thanked him gracefully, a slight colour coming to her cheeks as she studied both Jacob and the glasses with new interest. 'Your glasses are superb, Master Bell, I will show them to my husband and perhaps he will order some more.' She regarded him shrewdly. 'Your English is very good, but from your skill with glass I suspect that Venice is nearer to home.'

Jacob recited the now familiar story of living with a Murano family as an apprentice glass-blower. He almost believed it himself, the details being so familiar.

'So you are not married to a nice Venetian lady then?' When he said he was not, she did not attempt to hide her pleasure. 'I was wondering,' she said with a bold glance, 'would you do me another service, Master Bell?'

Jacob murmured something polite and she explained. 'I have been invited to a reception at the house of the Spanish Ambassador, tomorrow night. It would be difficult for me to go alone, but the Ambassador has kindly extended the invitation to one of my friends. Would you care to accompany me? It is an imposition and short notice I know, but I would be most grateful.'

Jacob was wary of the emphasis in her words, but intrigued at the thought of meeting the Spanish Ambassador, a chance he would not have passed up for the world. 'I'd be delighted, Countess, so long as it will not cause any embarrassment. Your husband is a diplomat and the attendance of an unmarried escort might be considered incorrect.'

The Countess put her hand lightly on his arm. 'That is so sweet, but you need have no qualms. I will introduce you as an old friend of my husband's from court, anxious to ensure I am able to enjoy the social scene. I will look forward to the reception with much anticipation.'

The words were formal, but the look she gave him promised much. Jacob sensing the undercurrent of excitement, groaned mentally - what have I let myself in for this time!

Chapter Eleven
London, August, 1570

There was a stream of people entering the imposing entrance to the Spanish Ambassador's house as Jacob escorted the Countess into the entrance vestibule. Jedediah Sutton dressed in his Ridolfi livery cut an imposing figure at the entrance to the main reception room. He scowled as he scrutinised the invitation and noting that Jacob's name was not on the card he said rather condescendingly, 'And how shall I introduce the other guest?'

The Countess regarded him levelly. 'As Jacob Bell, Glassmaker to the Court of Queen Elizabeth, of course.' Taking Jacob's arm, she led him forward without a backward glance and stopped at the reception door. When they were announced, she guided him to the Ambassador, who gave her a welcoming smile and an answering bow to acknowledge Jacob's. 'My dear Countess,' he said, bowing over her hand, 'and Master Glassmaker Bell. I have heard so many good things about your glass. I am told it rivals that from Murano.'

Jacob acknowledged the compliment gracefully and then once more gave his fictitious account of his early life. He thought it would be better if the Ambassador heard it from him. Since other people were coming in, they passed on into the reception and for the next half hour, Jacob was introduced to a number of prominent citizens, many of whom were familiar to him as customers of the Crouched Friars.

They had just started to talk to the Bishop of Ross, when a tall, wiry man joined them. Bowing to Jacob and the Countess, he apologised for interrupting and then informed the Bishop that the Ambassador wished to have a word with him. When the Bishop had made his apologies and left them the man turned to the Countess. 'My dear Countess, you are looking more radiant then the last time we met. Could it be your handsome escort that has brought the bloom to your cheek?'

The Countess laughed politely. 'I declare Count, you get more outrageous each time we meet.'

Turning to Jacob, she placed a hand lightly on his arm. 'May I introduce Count Ridolfi de Piazza. He is a banker of many years repute in very high circles in England. Count, this is Master Jacob Bell, the Queen's Glassmaker.'

Jacob bowed a little deeper than usual to hide his reaction to the name, as the Count studied him with interest and Jacob returned the compliment. 'I am most impressed with your glassmaking, Master Bell,' he said in a friendly voice. 'I was surprised to find that an Englishman could make glass to such a standard. The ones I have seen are the equal of any from Murano.'

Acknowledging the accolade gracefully, Jacob was about to explain, when the Countess did it for him. 'Master Bell studied in Murano from an early age. He has worked with some of the best glassmakers there and has brought his skills to London.'

'I see,' said the Count, 'and how are you finding life in London, Master Bell?'

'I was most fortunate in obtaining Letters Patent from the Queen and my business is doing well. London is a very different city to Venice however and I miss the liberal attitudes.'

'I imagine you were brought up as a Catholic in Venice. How do you find the religious situation here in London?'

Jacob smiled. 'I follow the advice given by Saint Ambrose "When in Rome, do as the Romans do". Since I understand you have been in England for some years, I assume you do the same.'

The Count was about to take up this remark when there was an announcement to take their places at the table. As the Countess held on to his arm she whispered, 'You were very naughty to tease the count: he has no sense of humour where religion is concerned.'

When Jacob laughingly remarked that he wasn't teasing, the Countess shook her head in mock despair and said no more on the topic as they took their seats. The meal was excellent and by the time it was finished Jacob could not have eaten another morsel. Although he had given the impression of drinking a great deal, he had contrived to keep his consumption low. He wanted to ensure he had a clear head in case Ridolfi renewed his conversation.

After the meal, the Countess led him towards the group containing the Ambassador. He greeted her warmly. 'I am glad you could make the reception tonight, I have some good news for you about your relative in Spain. Queen Mary has listened to your plea and has petitioned King Philip on your behalf. I have every reason to suppose that he will grant a pardon to Fitzwilliam.'

The Countess gave a very good imitation of surprise and delight. When she had finished her effusive thanks, the Ambassador asked if she could do a favour for him in return. She readily agreed and he asked if she had any personal knowledge of Admiral John Hawkins.

The Countess shook her head sadly. 'I'm sorry, but I only know him slightly from my days in the English court. Perhaps Master Bell could give you the information you seek.'

Surprised that the Ambassador had made this query in front of him, Jacob was at once on his guard. 'All I can tell you is that the Admiral is a customer of mine. In fact, he came to see me only a few days ago to buy some glass. He was most polite and seemed to be a very open man. He bought some of my Serissima range and paid cash. Those are my favourite sort of customer,' he added with a broad smile. 'Other than that, I have no personal knowledge of the man.'

'I see,' said the Ambassador, 'I was hoping you might be able to tell me if he was trustworthy.'

'He pays promptly, so I suppose that makes him so,' said Jacob lightly. 'At St. Paul's, I have heard he is well thought of in Navy circles, but that is the extent of my knowledge.'

The Ambassador inclined his head. 'Thank you for your contribution, Master Bell, it is useful to know he pays his dues promptly, I know many who do not. What say you Count?' Count Ridolfi, together with the servant from the entrance hall had just joined them.

'I could not agree more, Ambassador. I always advise paying bills promptly or they have a habit of getting out of hand.' He indicated Jed. 'My steward informs me that there is a problem that requires your attention.' He bowed to the Countess and Jacob. 'Please excuse us if we take the Ambassador away for a little while.'

With that, they hurried off with Ridolfi whispering urgently to the Ambassador, who, from his expression, seemed to be alarmed by what he was hearing. They went through a door at the rear of the salon, with Jed looking carefully around before going through and closing the door behind him. As soon as he disappeared, Jacob seeing the Countess was engrossed in conversation with the Ambassador's wife, slipped quietly away. Opening the door at the rear of the salon, he saw a flight of stairs leading downwards. Listening carefully, he set off down with great caution. At the bottom was a short corridor with doors in either direction. As he hesitated, he heard a cry of pain and the muffled sound of a man shouting from a door to the left. With all senses alert, Jacob crept up to the door. It was slightly ajar and through the hinge Jacob could see a man sitting in a chair, his hands tied behind the back and his face showing signs of a vicious beating. To the right stood Ridolfi and the Ambassador and with his back to Jacob was the man from reception. He suddenly stepped forward and slapped the man in the chair hard across the face, jerking his head round with the force. The man groaned and the steward came round to the side of him. His expression was vicious and he snarled at the moaning man, 'Why not save yourself more pain and tell me why you were looking through the Ambassador's papers.'

The man said nothing.

'Again, Jed,' said Ridolfi.

The steward immediately hit him again and the man slumped forward without a sound. Lifting his head up he examined him then letting it drop he turned to Ridolfi. 'He is unconscious and I don't think he will talk without some proper torture. What do you want me to do, Count?'

Ridolfi turned to the Ambassador. 'The man is obviously a spy, probably one of Walsingham's. A thief wouldn't waste time reading letters. We must dispose of him.'

The Ambassador nodded and with a gesture from Ridolfi, Jed, as Jacob now thought of him, produced a knife, gave a leer of pleasure, stepped behind the man in the chair and slit his throat. Cutting the bonds on his wrists, he cut the man's purse away, then putting his hands under his arms, dragged him to a chute in the wall and slid the body in.

Jed turned to Ridolfi as the body slid out of sight. 'If they find his body, after the fishes have done with it, Count,' he said, with an evil smirk, 'they will assume it was the work of cut purses London can be a dangerous place.'

Jacob was appalled. The man is a sadist: he enjoys giving pain to people,' he thought. He obviously holds a very close position both to the Count and the Ambassador. I will need to watch out for him.

Ridolfi gave an answering smile. 'It can indeed: especially for spies.' Turning to the Ambassador he took his arm. 'We must return to the reception before people miss us. Should the Countess or anyone enquire where you were, there was an urgent message from Spain that needed your attention.'

They turned to leave and Jacob beat a hasty retreat up the stairs as quietly as he could. Slipping unnoticed through the door, he obtained two glasses of wine from a passing servant and made his way back to the Countess. Passing her a glass, he slurred his voice a little as he sang the praises of the wine. The Countess looked a little surprised, but fortunately said nothing.

When the Ambassador rejoined them again, Jacob was regaling the group with a sea serpent story that John Isham had recounted to him. He deliberately gave the impression he was a little worse for drink. They all laughed when he had completed the tale and the Ambassador put a friendly arm on his shoulder. Jacob resisted the desire to shake it off and steeled himself to smile. When the Ambassador said he would like to visit his showroom with a view to buying some glass, Jacob was able to make his tone light and friendly as he invited them all to Harte Street.

Later as they were leaving, Count Ridolfi came across with Jed close behind. The steward whispered something to him and the Count laughed. Turning to Jacob he offered to take them home in his carriage. 'Please allow me to put my carriage at the disposal of the Countess and yourself. You appear to be perhaps a little less able than usual to look after her.'

His tone was patronising and the words insulting. Jacob declined, saying he needed to get some fresh air. Jed took hold of his arm and urged him towards the carriage. Jacob resisted and with a quick twist, broke the steward's grip and stood hand on sword ready for any further move on Jed's part.

The Count immediately realised that Jacob was ready for a confrontation. 'Jed, what are you doing, if Master Bell wishes to walk, that is his business.'

'I'm sorry, Count,' he said, backing away from Jacob, 'I thought Master Bell would be better off with us, London can be a very dangerous place after dark, especially if you have had rather a lot to drink. He might fall in the river.' Although the words were placatory, the eyes certainly were not. He gave Jacob a look of pure hatred, for a moment only and then his eyes became guarded. He bowed to Jacob. 'My apologies, Master Bell, I meant no disrespect.'

Like Hades you didn't, thought Jacob. Removing his hand from his sword, he inclined his head in acknowledgement and said, 'No harm done.' Turning to the Countess, he suggested she took up the Count's kind offer. She was obviously put out by this, but when he insisted, she agreed very reluctantly. With a bow in acknowledgement he turned on his heel and walked away without a backward glance.

A short way along the street, the coach passed him with Jed riding pillion. He gave Jacob a hard look as they passed and Jacob waved airily. The Duchess turned her face away in high dudgeon.

I don't think I will hear from the Duchess again, thought Jacob, but I'm afraid I've not heard the last of Ridolfi's steward, Jed. He's not a man you turn your back on with impunity.

Chapter Twelve
London, September, 1570

There was no opportunity to speak to Cecil since he was away for two weeks, so Jacob settled into the work routine again. He was intrigued, when about a week later, he received a note from the Countess of Shrewsbury asking if it would be convenient for her to call at the Harte Street showroom on the following day.

As the time for the visit approached, Jacob found himself looking forward with some anticipation to her visit. The Countess, or Bess of Hardwick as she was universally known, was a charismatic woman whose exploits, looks and manner rivalled that of the Queen. She was a constant source of gossip at court, not the least for her marriages. From the age of twelve, she had four husbands, each one richer than the last. Her house Chatsworth, in Darbieshire, was often mentioned in glowing terms.

When the Countess was shown in, with two brawny servants in attendance, Jacob had a surprise. She was dressed all in black with the usual ruff, but it was her hair and pearls that surprised him. He hair was a deep carrot colour and the multi-stranded necklace of matching pearls reached her waist. It was worth a King's ransom. No wonder she was attended by the servants. Motioning them to remain in the entrance hall, she took Jacob's arm in a firm grip and together they went into the showroom.

The result of the visit was an order for three dozen glasses in three sizes to be made to the Serissima pattern with the initials ES engraved in a cartouche. There was also an invitation to stay at Chatsworth when he brought the glasses. The forceful Bess would brook no argument on that score!

A week later, Jacob was shown into Cecil's study at Greenwich. 'Come in Master Bell, I'm sorry for the delay in bringing you here, but there were a number of things to arrange. I had intended to invite you anyway, so your note saved me the trouble. Is it to do with the Countess of Feria?'

'Not really, Sir William, it's more to do with events at the Spanish Ambassador's reception.' When Jacob recounted the evil deeds that had occurred in the cellars of the residence, Cecil cursed. 'Damn them to Hades,' he roared, 'he was one of my best men. I'll see they pay for this.' He began to pace around. 'It is a pity I can't haul them in and put them to the torture, but until we can establish what's going on, I need to keep them safe.' Then a thought struck him. 'You say that Count Ridolfi and his steward were heavily involved in this matter?'

'Indeed so, Sir William,' said Jacob, 'I believe that you are well acquainted with the Count in his role as a banker and you mentioned that Walsingham had interviewed him.'

'That is undeniably true. Many at court have used him to advise them on financial matters. It would appear that the Count is more involved than we thought. Have you heard any more about him?'

'Only rumours at present and nothing I can prove. I have set the Ring on it after the business at the Ambassador's residence and made sure they are aware that he's a very dangerous man.' Jacob had no compunction in this slight distortion of the truth. He didn't intend to tell Cecil everything he knew until he received some confirmation.

'Let me know as soon as you have anything certain to go on. It's important not only for this matter, but also for Admiral Hawkins. He's waiting nearby and I will call him in.'

When the admiral came in, Cecil explained. 'We want you to give a hand in convincing Mary Stuart, Queen of the Scots, that Hawkins is a good Catholic and a trustworthy fellow.'

Jacob reacted with astonishment. 'Mary Stuart? I don't know anything about her, so how am I supposed to achieve that miracle,' he concluded sarcastically.

Cecil smiled knowingly. 'Ah, but you will get to know the lady, when you take the glasses to Chatsworth for the Countess of Shrewsbury. Mary Stuart is very fond of personable fellows, especially if they are Catholic by religion.'

'How on earth did you know about the glasses for the Countess? I've only known about them myself for a week.'

Cecil put on an innocent expression. 'I might have suggested to the Countess that no self-respecting household was complete without some façon de Venice glasses and it's possible that your name might have cropped up in the same conversation,' said Cecil, with a smug expression. 'I believe the redoubtable Bess has invited you to Chatsworth for a stay when they are complete.'

Jacob shook his head in mock sorrow. He might have known Cecil was up to something. It had not registered at the time, but the Countess did mention having a conversation with Cecil. The whole thing had been arranged, just to get him to meet Mary Stuart. He gave a sigh. 'I suppose the Queen of Scots is currently imprisoned at Chatsworth, Sir William.'

Cecil nodded. 'For the moment. She was sent to Chatsworth from Tutbury in May, as the plague was rife in the castle. I intend to visit her myself later in the year, but whether she will still be at Chatsworth, or at Sheffield Castle, I know not. In view of the likelihood of more plots, it seems best not to leave her too long in one place; otherwise, it will make it easier for the plotters to arrange to release her. Besides, Sheffield Castle is a much more formidable prison. Chatsworth is a very suitable house, having no town or resort where any ambushes might lie, but it is not as easy to defend in the event of a large scale attack.'

Hawkins had been listening to this conversation with mounting impatience. 'This matter might proceed more speedily Sir William, if you refrained from this baiting of Master Bell. Just tell him what we're about and let's be done with it.'

Cecil took no insult, but simply nodded in agreement and explained. A few weeks earlier, he had received information that ten of Hawkins' men were being held in prison in Spain. One of them, George Fitzwilliam, managed to send a letter to him. In it he informed Cecil that four of the men had died at the hands of the Inquisition and the other six were dying of starvation. Unless they received help soon, it would be too late.

Cecil had arranged for Hawkins to make a definite offer to put his private fleet of fighting ships at the service of the King of Spain, in return for the release of all of his men. Hawkins told De Spes that he was a good Catholic. Apparently, De Spes had accepted this, but on conveying his offer to Philip of Spain, he was told to seek assurance from Mary Stuart, that Hawkins was above suspicion.

'What happened about Fitzwilliam?'

'I am pleased to say that thanks to the intervention of Mary

Stuart, Fitzwilliam has been released.'

'Indeed he has,' said a delighted Hawkins, 'he arrived in Plymouth two days ago and has agreed to act as an intermediary with the King of Spain. Because of the bait of my ships, the Spanish have eased the conditions of my men and also arranged for all other survivors to be brought to Spain.'

'That's very good news,' Jacob said with a smile, 'you must be worried though in case they don't take the bait.'

'Fitzwilliam is going to see Mary Stuart next week to thank her for her help and to plead for Hawkins,' said Cecil, 'with my permission, of course. We want you to go with him. Can you have the glasses ready by then?'

Jacob thought a moment. 'Assuming I agree to go, yes, they will be ready by the end of this week.' He gave Cecil a puzzled look. 'I still don't understand my part in all this.'

Cecil and Hawkins exchanged glances. 'From what we have already explained, you will understand that I'm convinced there is another plot against the Queen involving the Spanish Ambassador. You were very helpful in crushing the Maldini plot, have a natural talent for intrigue and your sources of information are exceedingly useful. I would like you to help Hawkins get his men out of Spain and to discover who is behind this plot, if plot there be.'

Jacob's mind was working overtime, but he refrained from any reaction until he'd considered all of the implications.

Cecil, becoming worried by Jacob's lack of response, made a further plea. 'You have proved to be a resourceful, brave and accomplished fighter against the evil men who would kill the Queen and I would welcome your help in this matter. I do not expect you to fund this out of your own pocket, Master Bell. The Crown will pay all reasonable expenses. As for the men in prison, I believe that there is a good chance of releasing them and keeping the Queen from any harm at the same time. What say you?'

Jacob did not need to consider his response since he had decided already. 'I will agree to help on two conditions; neither of which should cause you any problems. Firstly, I want to be free to make my own decisions how I go about finding out about this plot. I will of course do nothing to hinder John Hawkins in his own quest.' He looked expectantly at Cecil who, after a moments thought, nodded in agreement.

'Secondly, I need both of you to agree that I may keep my two able assistants, Roberto and Quiff, fully informed.'

Cecil and Hawkins went out of the room for a few minutes to discuss Jacob's request. When they returned, Hawkins said, 'Are we agreed Sir William?'

Cecil nodded and turned to Jacob. 'We agree to both your conditions and trust your judgement. It is a measure of the esteem in which you are held that we agree to this. The lives of Admiral Hawkins' men will depend on it.'

Chapter Thirteen
Darbieshire, September, 1570

The business with Hawkins had to come first, but Fitzwilliam was ill, so the trip to Chatsworth was delayed. Jacob decided to use the time to make an armorial goblet as a present for Mary Stuart. It was a bucket-bowled goblet, about eight inches high with a folded foot. The Stuart coat of arms was enamelled on one side of the bowl in white. He was pleased with the result and hoped it would help him break the ice with the Queen of the Scots.

He was also experimenting with making filigree glass models. It was an idea of Quiff's. One of the men had been given a wooden model of a ship, which Quiff liked. During a conversation with Jacob, he had mentioned this and asked Jacob if he had ever seen a model ship made from glass. When Jacob had admitted he hadn't, it set him thinking why not? He decided to try it out and it proved to be very difficult. Once the glass for Mary Stuart was ready he spent his spare time trying out different methods with mixed success.

By late September, with the weather seemingly set fair and Fitzwilliam recovered, they set off from Tottenham for Darbieshire: a part of England that Jacob knew nothing about. He had been warned that the journey would take four, or five days of hard riding.

Cecil had arranged for them to ride with the post, on commission. This meant that they had to pay only a penny ha'penny per mile for each horse on the stages. Stages varied in length, being normally twelve to twenty miles. Thomas Randolph, Master of Post, employed the guides, but the traveller usually had to pay them a groat, or fourpence a stage.

As Fitzwilliam advised, they took the Chester road as far as Lichfield and then took the road to Darbye. The main post routes did not go into Darbieshire. The nearest village to Chatsworth was Edensor and fortunately a system of bridleways and packhorse trails led to it. Every time they met travellers, or every third of a mile, the guide had to blow a blast on a horn, which amused Jacob no end.

They made good progress to Lichfield, which they reached late on the second day. Cecil's commission ensured that the proprietor of the Fleece Inn gave them superior rooms and after an excellent supper, they retired to bed.

Jacob slept well and when he wakened next morning, Fitzwilliam was already dressed. After a hearty meal, they paid their dues to the landlord and he advised them to travel with some other merchants heading in the same direction. 'There have been some robberies on the Darbye road, so you best keep a sharp lookout. A strong party is less likely to be attacked.' Bearing this in mind, they set off for Darbye in the company of some merchants who were able to act as guides. They welcomed this addition to their party as they too were wary of footpads.

The track was simply a packhorse trail, being much narrower than the well-used West Road. Progress was often slow and it was well after midday before they had reached the village of Repton. They stopped at the Bull's Head for a short rest and refreshments. Afterwards, the merchants agreed to pay while Jacob went to check on the horses. A little while later, he was joined by Fitzwilliam. He looked worried.

'There's a shifty looking individual talking to one of the merchants,' he explained. 'He was telling him that there had been footpads sighted on the main Darbye track and was advising him to take the ford at Willington to avoid them. He says the ford is often deep, but at the moment it's quite low and passable.'

'Why are you concerned?'

'I'm sorry Jacob, but I don't like the looks of him. There's something in his manner that doesn't ring true to me.'

'What was the merchant saying?'

'He seemed to think it was all right.'

Just then, a man came into the entrance to the stables and shouted to the ostler for his horse. 'That's him,' hissed Fitzwilliam, pulling Jacob back out of sight. They watched as the man mounted his horse and rode hurriedly away. As they led the horses out, Jacob threw a coin to the ostler and said jovially, 'He seems to be in a hurry to get where he's going.'

The ostler deftly caught the large value coin and then tapped his nose with a forefinger. 'Aye, and up to no good I'll be bound.' He pulled a face. 'You'd do well to steer clear of that one.'

Sure enough, when the merchants joined them, they said they had decided to take the Willington ford, which was the shortest way. Not wishing to alarm them, Jacob and Fitzwilliam decided to say nothing for the moment, but to take very great care on the way.

Leaving the village, they passed the ruins of the former monastery and headed along a ridge with good views of the valley below. Jacob and Fitzwilliam rode on ahead when they sighted the ford. Where the road led down through a small wood towards it, they dismounted and Fitzwilliam pulled out a small expanding brass telescope.

'That's handy,' remarked Jacob.

Fitzwilliam laughed. 'The admiral gave it to me, he said it might come in useful.' He scanned the ford and its surrounds carefully, and then passing the telescope to Jacob, bade him look at the line of bushes just to the nearside of the ford.

After a moment, Jacob spotted a movement. Studying carefully he was able to identify three men in the bushes. A moment later one of them waved and there was an answering wave from the trees on the other side.

'There are five of them I believe,' he said, 'three on this side and two more on the other. They must plan to catch us between them as we cross the ford.'

'What do you think, Jacob?'

'There's good cover on this side, right up to those bushes just behind them. We could creep up and give them a real shock.'

After a short discussion, the three merchants gave Jacob and Fitzwilliam time to get into position and then with pistols at the ready, but hidden from sight, rode down to the ford. As the merchants started to cross, the three men stood up from cover. At the same time two men emerged from the trees on the other side.

Without any qualms Jacob discharged his pistol while Fitzwilliam did the same rushing directly at the men. Two of the robbers were killed immediately and Jacob dispatched the other with his sword.

At the first shot, the merchants revealed their pistols and discharged them at the two men on the far side of the ford.

Seeing their companions fall, they turned to run for their lives, one staggering as he was hit. Shortly afterwards, two horsemen raced away along the valley bottom, one of them swaying in the saddle. They were very glad to let them go. The three men engaged by Fitzwilliam and Jacob were all dead. One of them was the shifty looking individual who had advised the merchants to use the ford, when they stopped at the Bull's Head.

By the time they had searched the men and removed any belongings they had been substantially delayed. It was well into the afternoon before they reached the Dolphin Inn at Darbye and told their tale to the landlord. He promised to inform the authorities and pass on the belongings. He also said they had been luckier than several other merchants in the past few weeks. 'The constable will be well pleased to hear that this gang has been routed. No doubt he will put the word round to look out for a wounded man. Where are you heading for?'

When Jacob explained their final destination the landlord advised them that it would be impossible to reach Chatsworth that day. He might however, be able to arrange a guide who would show them a shorter way to reach the Earl of Shrewsbury's house than by the Ashborne to Bakewell route. The guide turned out to be the chief steward of Sir Henry Babington of Dethick. He was escorting a visitor to Dethick, which lay only a few miles south of Chatsworth. For a consideration, the landlord was sure he could persuade him to act as a guide.

The landlord was as good as his word and the next day together with Richard Lees, the steward and his charge, introduced as Gilbert Gifford, they set off along the heavily wooded banks of the River Derwent. The guide was very friendly, pointing out places of interest, but Gifford, aside from acknowledging them with a bow when they first met, rode along in silence.

They crossed the river at a ford named for the mill, which stood beside it, then passed through a small town called Belper. It was apparently one of the premier sites in England for making nails, especially horseshoe nails and the industry went back hundreds of years. It turned out that the steward was a distant relative of the Lees family, one of the oldest in the town. He had few good words for the nailers, describing them for the most part as uncouth, brawling drunkards.

Progress was slow due to the terrain and the river was wide and deep, being swollen by the heavy rain of the night before. In places it had burst its banks and they had to make detours around flooding. It was fortunate that they had crossed the ford by the mill, before the effect of the downpour had reached it.

The ground was sodden and the track, often deep in mud, made the steep climbs they were forced to make, even more treacherous. It was late in the afternoon when, after another long hard climb up heavily forested slopes, they arrived at a fine honey-coloured stone house, in a small settlement, which Lees explained was Dethick Hall, the home of his master Sir Henry Babington.

Excusing himself for a moment, he hurried the visitor into the house and shortly afterwards emerged with an elderly man and a young boy of about ten year's of age. The man introduced himself as Henry Babington and the boy as his third son Anthony. He invited them into the house for refreshments and led them to a very agreeable sitting room with a large wood fire burning in the grate. There was no sign of their fellow traveller.

After they had introduced themselves and gratefully partaken of the excellent blackberry cordial they were offered, Sir Anthony enquired about their visit to Chatsworth.

Jacob explained his occupation and that he was delivering some of his glasses to the Earl of Shrewsbury's wife. He was also bringing a gift of a goblet for Mary Stuart. Babington immediately begged Jacob to show him the glasses. 'I have heard much of your glass on my visits to court, Master Bell,' he said excitedly, 'but have never possessed any.'

When Jacob reluctantly agreed to unpack one of them, Babington showed his appreciation. 'I do believe that your glass is every bit as good as the Murano glass I have seen in London.' He gave a rueful smile. 'We are not so fashionable out here in the wilds of Darbieshire that we use glass for everyday drinking, it is mainly pewter. In fact, to be truthful, apart from the Earl of Shrewsbury, I know of no other families locally that possess any drinking glasses.'

'In that case,' retorted Jacob, 'I shall make it the business of the Glass-Sellers and myself to see that glass is more widely disseminated.'

He brought out the goblet he had made for Mary Stuart. When Babington saw the Stuart coat of arms embossed on the side of the bowl, Jacob was intrigued by the almost reverent way he handled the goblet.

'Pardon my asking Master Bell,' said Babington, 'but from your accent and your skill with glass, I would imagine you must have trained in Murano, for some years.'

Jacob agreed that he had indeed learnt his skill on Murano, while living with a Venetian family, but purposely left out any further details. Babington became excited. 'Do I take it, that you were brought up in the true religion?'

Jacob agreed he was a Roman Catholic and that his companion Fitzwilliam, who had been a silent onlooker to these exchanges, had recently returned from Spain. He explained that he was visiting Mary Stuart with a message from the Countess of Feria. At once, Babington insisted that they remain at Dethick Hall overnight, promising that his steward would guide them to Chatsworth the next day.

Weary after the hard ride, Jacob readily agreed. In truth, Babington intrigued Jacob. He was obviously a Catholic, but Jacob was sure there was more to his invitation than merely a kind gesture. Babington rang for his servant and instructed him to prepare rooms for his guests and to inform the cook that there would be two more for the evening meal.

Jacob did not have long to wait before his suspicion was confirmed. When the servant had hurried away, Babington became very friendly and begged Jacob to do him a favour when he met Mary Stuart. 'I know it is a lot to ask of someone at such little acquaintance, but I have a need to send a letter to her majesty.' He hastened to assure Jacob that there would be nothing treasonous in it. 'I simply want to assure her majesty of my undying loyalty and that she still has friends in the area. Also, I would like my son Anthony to serve the Queen, perhaps as a page when he is a little older.'

Meanwhile, the subject of their discussion had been examining the goblet with interest. He asked Jacob if he might handle it, promising to be very careful. Jacob nodded and the boy studied the coat of arms with animated eyes and then looked enquiringly at Jacob. 'Are these the arms of her majesty, the Queen of the Scots?' he asked excitedly.

'They are indeed,' said Jacob. 'You have done well to recognise them.'

The boy's face took on a dreamy expression. 'When I am older, I will serve her majesty well. I hope to become a page soon and find favour with her. Did my father tell you?'

'He did, but I feel you might have to wait a little while. You are young to be a page, especially in the Queen's situation.'

He drew himself up to his full height. 'When I am older, I will do all I can to see that her majesty takes her rightful place on the throne of England.'

Henry Babington was alarmed by his son's lack of discretion and reprimanded him. He apologised to Jacob and asked him not to take a young boy's dreaming too seriously. Jacob assured him with a laugh that he was not in any way concerned about the remark. 'Her majesty has been ill-used. Although her stay in England is said to be as a guest, it is little more than an imprisonment. However, your son would be well advised not to express those sentiments in some circles.'

Fitzwilliam suddenly joined the conversation. 'The way the Queen has been treated is openly condemned at the Spanish court,' he enjoined. 'There is much talk of an invasion to bring the rightful heir to the throne of England and to restore the true religion.' He hesitated as he gauged the reaction to this, then seeing Sir Henry was nodding in approval, continued. 'I have even heard it rumoured that his Holiness the Pope will soon excommunicate the Boleyn bastard, Elizabeth and urge all Catholics to rise up against her.'

Jacob was rather startled by this extremely treasonous statement, but Sir Henry simply said, 'Amen to that day.' While young Anthony clapped his hands in delight. It was obvious to Jacob, that despite the outer trappings of a Protestant family, the Babington's were staunch Catholics. This was further re-enforced a while later, at the table for the evening meal, when Sir Henry introduced Gilbert Gifford to them as the cousin of Dr William

Gifford, one of the leaders of the Secular Party of Catholics. While Gifford had not been present during the earlier conversations, it soon became apparent that he'd been eavesdropping. He excused himself by saying that a man in his position had to be careful until he was sure of their sympathies and that he welcomed them warmly. He then explained that he was travelling around to various supporters to keep them informed of events and to see they were in good heart.

'Have you met Queen Mary as yet?' he enquired. When Jacob remarked that he had not the pleasure of her acquaintance, Gifford smiled. 'You are in for a rare treat, Master Bell. Her majesty is charmante and la plus parfaite. I will not say more, but leave you to judge for yourself.'

The conversation then turned to other topics and after a fine meal, Jacob and Fitzwilliam made their excuses and retired to bed. Jacob was about to discuss events with Fitzwilliam, but he put a finger to his lips and shook his head. He obviously feared that they might be overheard again. Jacob realised he was right and saying how tired he was, said goodnight and turned in.

Chapter Fourteen
Dethick, Darbieshire, September, 1570

The following morning, after breakfast, they were readying their horses and checking the saddlebags when Sir Henry appeared and handed a letter to Jacob, who stored it carefully in his doublet. 'I will see it is handed to her majesty in private,' he promised. Then in company with Lees, the steward, they set off with the Babingtons and Gifford waving until they were out of sight.

The weather was now very warm and the path was much drier than the previous day. They made good progress and shortly before ten they headed up a long hill. Breasting the crest, they were greeted with a magnificent view across the river, where a splendid house was tucked against the base of a steep slope on the other side of the valley. Cecil had described the house as "a jewel set in the wilderness" and Jacob could see what he meant. The countryside was wild all about, with little more than tracks to reach it, but the house was magnificent.

Approaching from the west, the house was spread before them. It was the largest house Jacob had seen outside of London, rising to five turreted storeys, in the same honey-coloured stone that Jacob had found so attractive at Dethick Hall. Descending to the river, which Lees said was the same Derwent they had been following, but only a few miles from its source now, they came to a stately stone bridge with a tower on it. On crossing this bridge, the raging torrents swelled by the recent rain, poured over many cataracts and smote their ears with a noise like thunder.

They were halted at the tower by armed retainers. Stating their business, they were conducted through the imposing portal of the west gate into the inner courtyard, where the steward of the house met them. He was well known to Richard Lees and on learning their identities, he soon had the servants scurrying to attend to them. While the grooms of the stables dealt with the horses, the grooms of the chamber took away their baggage except the panniers with the glass, which Jacob insisted were carried carefully where he could see them. 'My mistress is waiting for you in the parlour, Master Bell,' said the steward respectfully, 'and is, I believe, most anxious to see her glasses.'

'Then we must keep her waiting no longer,' said Jacob gallantly and followed the steward as he led them along the long gallery at the side of the courtyard to the parlour in the south-east corner. At the door, the steward announced them to his mistress who was taking her leisure on a chaise langue. The Countess was dressed in a marvellous pearl-encrusted gown of russet silk, with a high lace ruff in the manner of the Queen. She had a large matching pearl necklace and the ring-encrusted fingers of the hand she offered was yet further evidence of her wealth.

'Master Bell, you are most welcome,' she said, as Jacob bowed over her proffered hand. 'I have been anticipating your arrival with impatience, but no doubt the rains have delayed you. The tracks are treacherous at this time of year after heavy rain.'

Jacob agreed that this was very true, as she indicated for him to sit down. Before he did so, Jacob introduced Fitzwilliam.

'Countess, allow me to introduce George Fitzwilliam, cousin to the Countess of Feria - Fitzwilliam, the Countess Shrewsbury.'

He explained that Fitzwilliam was here to see the Scots Queen with the approval of Sir William Cecil. Fitzwilliam paid his respects. 'I regret, Countess that I have not been well since my arrival from Spain and the journey has been most fatiguing. I beg your permission to retire.'

The Countess acknowledged this request with a gracious nod of approval and then turned to Jacob indicating the panniers that a groom had placed by Jacob's side. 'I hope those are the glasses you promised me, Master Bell.' When Jacob said they were, she clapped her hands in delight. 'I am impatient to see them,' she said. 'May I see them now?'

Jacob agreed and unwrapped the glasses with great care. He was relieved to find, that despite the hard journey, the packing had protected them well. Placing them on the side table, he watched as the Countess picked them up and handled them with cries of delight. 'Master Bell,' she said finally, 'you have exceeded my greatest expectations. Your glasses are superb and worth every penny of the exorbitant amount you charged me.' Her smiling face took any insult from the words.

'Your delight is my reward, Countess,' he replied. 'Any craftsman is pleased when his work is appreciated.'

'You must call me Bess, when we are in private like this,' said the Countess, 'I believe that your given name is Jacob. May I use it too?'

'I would be honoured Bess. What do you intend to do with the glasses.'

'Use them of course and the sooner the better.' Calling to her steward who had been hovering within earshot, she instructed him to take the glasses away and prepare them for the evening meal. The grooms gathered up the glass and made to take the panniers as well, but Jacob stopped them. He did not want the glass for Mary Stuart to be out of his sight.

Bess who had been watching the activity saw that there was another glass in the pannier and asked Jacob what it was. He explained it was a gift for the Scots Queen as he had learned that she was fond of façon de Venice style glass. He was reluctant to show it in case Bess thought hers were second best, but he needn't have worried. When he showed it her she was entranced and congratulated Jacob warmly when he explained what he had attempted with the goblet.

'I am sure that Mary will be delighted. It is absolutely wonderful.' She examined it pensively for a moment then her face lit up. 'Would you make me a goblet with my own coat of arms on it,' she asked breathlessly, 'I will pay you anything you ask for such a glass for my personal use.'

The yearning in her voice surprised Jacob. By reputation, Bess was a very abrasive, strong woman, rather in the same mould as Queen Elizabeth, but this was another side of her personality. 'Of course I will. We will discuss the details before I leave.'

Bess was delighted and she jumped out of her chair and embraced him. It was easy to imagine why she had been able to attract four husbands, each richer than the last. Bess linked her arm in his and led him out into the vestibule in the corner of the courtyard that led to the stairs to the upper storey, stopping by the door to the lower hall. 'Would you like to refresh yourself before the evening meal? My husband will not be joining us this evening, as he is away to Sheffield to inspect the arrangements for Queen Mary's stay there. She is to be moved later this year and he has gone to oversee the refitting, to make sure that the apartments are suitable for the Queen.'

'Does he receive an allowance that will pay for these luxuries?' said Jacob in surprise.

Bess laughed mirthlessly. 'I see you have had little experience of trying to extract money from Cecil, or the Queen. My lord's allowance for keeping Queen Mary is but fifty-two pounds a week and is months behind already; to keep her in the style she insists, costs more like thirty pounds a day.' She stopped and pointed to the men guarding the gate. 'Although we have asked for an increase in the allowance to cover the extra guards ordered after the Maldini plot, nothing has been forthcoming. The Earl is always complaining that the cost will ruin him.' She shrugged. 'Still he likes the attention it brings to Chatsworth well enough. Many prominent people in the county come to visit Queen Mary.'

Jacob could tell from her voice that it was very much to the Countess' liking too. Before he could think more on the subject, he was treated to a demonstration of the other side of Bess's character. As she turned to mount the stairs, she noticed by the far door of the hall, one of the grooms deep in conversation with a kitchen maid with his arm familiarly around her waist. She was simpering and giggling.

Calling them both to her, she gave the groom a buffet round the ear and told him to report to the steward for extra duties. The girl was threatened with dismissal if she was caught flirting again during work time. Bess then went on to warn the frightened girl about the groom. 'Keep away from that one,' she said curtly. 'Didn't you know he was sent here from Sheffield for siring two bastards among the maids? You'll just be another on his list of conquests, you silly girl.' The girl gave the Countess a sharp look then with downcast eyes and a quick curtsy, she scuttled off back into the kitchen.

Bess, guessing that Jacob was feeling sorry for them explained that she had a simple rule for her servants. Work was work and what they did in their spare time was their business, unless it was against her interest. She was a hard taskmaster, but rewarded and appreciated good service. Jacob could see that she was indeed a formidable woman, but based on this incident she was also fair and looked out for her servants.

When they had mounted the stairs to the first floor, Bess led him along a gallery decorated almost entirely in blue. A little way along they reached Jacob's chamber. Bess informed him that Fitzwilliam was in the chamber next door. She left Jacob with a warning not to go up to the next floor without permission. 'The Queen of Scots chambers are directly above us. The guards had orders to arrest anyone without the correct authorisation.'

When she'd left, Jacob lay down on his bed felling very weary. Some time later, he awoke to the sound of voices echoing down the gallery. Dashing some cold water on his face and hurriedly drying it, he put on his doublet and rushed towards the stairs at the end of the gallery. Just as he reached them, the steward appeared and asked politely if he would wait for a moment. He explained that the servants were carrying the Queen of Scots midday meal up the stairs and there was little room for passing.

As Jacob watched in mounting surprise, dish after dish was carried up to the floor above. He counted thirty-two in all and later, when he mentioned this to Bess, he was informed that this happened twice a day. The meal they were served was no less gargantuan and Jacob was feeling replete by the end. After the meal, Bess showed Jacob and Fitzwilliam the beautiful formal gardens and the lake. Wonderful examples of the gardener's art presented themselves at every twist and turn. There were sculptures and arbours, each with views of the house, which soothed the senses and Jacob thought it must be wonderful to live in such a captivating place. When he said as much to the Countess, he was most surprised therefore, when she told him how much she envied him for living in London and being able to attend court.

'You do surprise me, Countess,' he said. 'For myself, I believe this is the most tranquil place I have visited in all my life.'

'Tranquil soon becomes boring when there is little else,' said Bess tartly. 'The gentlefolk of Darbieshire are mainly farmers and know little of the finer points of society. They talk of nothing else except the weather and the price of cattle.'

'I'm sure you exaggerate,' he said with a smile. 'Although I have only met one of the local families, Sir Henry Babington, he is anything other than a rustic.'

Bess smiled. 'Perhaps you are right. A few families make entertaining rewarding, although it is probably Mary Stuart who is the attraction.'

Jacob seized on the chance to further their quest. 'When will we be allowed to present ourselves to the Queen?'

'I am afraid it will not be until my husband returns tomorrow. Only he can grant you permission.'

Bess left them a short while later, saying she normally spent this time of day with Mary Stuart working on embroidery. The two men continued the walk, using the privacy to discuss how they should make contact with Mary Stuart. At first they decided that Fitzwilliam should see the Queen first and then try to distract anyone else who might be present while Jacob passed on the letter from Babington. Eventually, they agreed that this was too likely to be detected and Jacob settled for hiding the letter in the packing for the goblet.

The following afternoon when the Earl of Shrewsbury presented them to the Queen of Scots, it was a very different occasion from that expected. Although in reality, she was a prisoner, she enjoyed most of the trappings of a Queen in exile. Her staff numbered in excess of forty and her two main rooms were set up as a privy chamber and a reception room.

When they entered the reception room, Jacob was surprised at the luxurious tapestries on the walls and the exotic Turkish carpets strewn around. At the far end of the room was a raised dais on which a chair upholstered in crimson velvet and cloth of gold stood surrounded with a number of low stools. Above the chair hung a cloth of state with the Stuart cipher, Mary's personal symbol the lodestone and the motto "En ma fin est môn commencement," which Jacob translated as "In my end my beginning". It was a puzzle. The coat of arms he had used on the glass was not the same. He had used the impresa of a marigold turning to face the sun with the motto, "Its virtue draws me". Cecil had assured him that Mary had chosen this in France and if memory served him right, this cloth of state bore the arms of the Queen Mary's mother, Mary of Guise. It's like a royal court thought Jacob. She may be a prisoner, but she's behaving like a Queen!

Just at that moment, a courtier announced the arrival of the Queen. Emerging from her privy chamber with her attendants, she took her place on the dais with her attendants around her on the stools. Acknowledging their bows with a gracious gesture, she bade them welcome in a most courteous manner. During the speech, Jacob studied her carefully.

She wore a cloth of gold and silver dress in the French style with a small gold crown on her headdress. The face above her fine lace collar was attractive with high cheekbones and almond-shaped hazel eyes that were bright and penetrating. Her lustrous dark hair was set in tight curls that were visible at the side of her headdress. Her nose, although slightly aquiline for Jacob's taste, was set in a perfect marble-like complexion.

When she had finished, the visitors were announced separately. Fitzwilliam bowed low and presented the gift from the Countess of Feria then presented his petition on behalf of John Hawkins. Mary asked a number of shrewd questions and seemed satisfied with the answers. Promising to give him an answer soon, she turned her attention to Jacob, giving him a most welcoming smile.

'Master Glassmaker Bell, you are most welcome at my court,' she said in her delightful Scottish accent. 'I have heard much of your skill with glass and having seen the goblets you have brought for the Countess of Shrewsbury, I am most anxious to see the present she tells me you have brought.'

Jacob bowed low and signalled to the servant who was carrying the boxed glass and he placed it on a table at the side of the dais. Jacob removed the goblet from the packing, taking great care not to disturb the note from Babington, hidden under it. Mary craned forward eager for a glimpse and when Jacob held it aloft there were cries of delight from the Queen and her ladies. The Queen was enchanted with it and turned it round to see the coat of arms.

Jacob immediately begged her forgiveness for using the wrong arms, but the Queen dismissed his apology with an alluring smile turning the full force of her charm on him. 'Master Bell, you have nothing to reproach yourself for. These are indeed my arms, but I recently adopted those of my mother as better representing my position here in England as a guest of my sister Elizabeth.'

It was impossible to miss the irony in her words and the

humour that was reflected in her eyes and smile. Jacob found himself warming to this extremely attractive woman who was in no way cowed by the reality of her captivity. Passing the glass to one of her ladies, she thanked Jacob most sincerely. 'I can see that my informants have not exaggerated your skill, Master Bell. I will treasure your gift and promise to use it carefully.'

'I am delighted it meets with your approval,' said Jacob with a bow, 'but can I suggest you repack it carefully before you put it away.' The Queen regarded him shrewdly and then with an almost imperceptible nod, continued as if nothing had passed between them.

For the next ten minutes, she chatted gaily with Jacob on a number of subjects and he was impressed with her intelligence and wit. It was as if they were alone together, such was the force of her personality. Eventually, she gave a loud sigh and said that reluctantly they must end their visit. Holding her hand for Jacob to bow over, she promised to grant him a further audience. She turned to acknowledge the other visitors and then with a flash of eyes at Jacob, she swept out of the presence chamber.

Chapter Fifteen
Chatsworth House, September, 1570

Lying in the dark room, Jacob carefully slid his hand under the pillow and grasped the hidden stiletto. Whatever it was that had awoken him was silent now and all he could hear was the beating of his own heart. There was a metallic click and Jacob, his eyes now adjusted to the dim light, could see the door moving quietly open. Tensing himself for rapid action, he waited silently as the light from a candle shone into the room.

'Monsieur Bell, are you awake?' came the whispered query. Jacob said nothing. 'Monsieur Bell, are you awake?' The woman's voice was louder now as the door opened wider and in the light from the candle, Jacob could make out the figure of one of Queen Mary's attendants in her distinctive French dress.

'What do you want?' he said, sitting up in bed. The woman curtsied. 'Your pardon for disturbing you sir, but my mistress bids you to attend her. But it must be done secretly,' she went on hurriedly, 'for the guards will arrest you if we are discovered.' She came into the room and closed the door. 'The guards are sleeping helped by some lightly drugged wine, but they are changed in about an hour and we must waken them before the new guards arrive.'

'Very well,' said Jacob, motioning for the young woman to turn round. He dressed hurriedly and when he was ready, the woman led him up the stairs and into the Queen's withdrawing chamber through a partly-open door. The woman motioned him to a deep chair at one side of the fireplace then disappeared into the Queen's chamber.

He did not have long to wait before the Queen,in a long dressing gown, entered and waving him to remain seated, settled into the matching chair at the opposite side of the fire. Jacob said nothing waiting for the Queen to begin, while she studied him shrewdly. Her hair, which had been up in an elaborate style, was now tumbling over her shoulders in well-brushed waves. In the soft light from the fire, her attractive face looked much younger than earlier and Jacob thought she looked beautiful.

She favoured him with a dazzling smile. 'Thank you for

meeting me like this, Master Bell. I know it is most irregular and it is putting you in some danger, but I needed to speak to you in private.'

'It is no matter your majesty, please go on.'

'I have received the note that you so cleverly passed to me. Do you know of its contents?'

'Only that Sir Henry Babington was offering his son as a page and sending his expressions of loyalty.'

'I see,' said Mary, 'well it also contained a paragraph on you, Master Bell.'

Jacob showed his surprise and Mary smiled. 'You have nothing to fear, for Sir Henry speaks very well of you. Have you known him long?'

Jacob had the feeling that there was more to the query than just a simple question. 'No your majesty, I can claim little acquaintance with Sir Henry. I was simply a guest of his at Dethick Hall on the way to Chatsworth He was kind enough to put us up for the night and we had a most pleasant meal in the company of his family and Master Gilbert Gifford.'

Mary nodded in recognition of the name. 'I do not know the gentleman, but I am acquainted with his cousin Doctor William Gifford.' She took a sip of wine and then gave Jacob a friendly smile. 'Forgive my questions, Master Bell, but what about Master Fitzwilliam, how well do you know him? I have to consider his petition on behalf of Admiral Hawkins and I would value your opinion.'

'I'm not sure I can be too much help there either,' said Jacob cautiously. 'I have only known Fitzwilliam for only a few days. Just the time we travelled from London together. I believe he has recently returned from Spain. Other than that, I can only tell you that he has been an agreeable companion and showed he was a handy fellow to have around in a crisis.'

When Mary asked him to explain, he told her about the ambush on the way to Darbye and built up Fitzwilliam's part. 'He is more of a man of action than myself and has served with Admiral Hawkins for some years, or so I understand. He certainly seems to be an admirer of yours, since he spoke out well in your favour at the meal with Sir Henry.' Seeing Mary was nodding in obvious agreement, he took a further chance. 'I am more acquainted with the Admiral. He has been a customer of mine for some time and I see him at court in London. Since the Queen made me her Glassmaker, I get regular invitations.'

Mary leaned forward eagerly. 'And what is your opinion of Admiral Hawkins?'

'Well your majesty, he has always been a man of his word in his dealings with me. From what I have heard from others, he seems devoted to his men and I am told he is a supporter of the true faith.'

'As are you I believe Master Bell, I understand you were brought up in Venice.'

'Indeed your majesty, I lived with a staunch Catholic family from an early age, while I studied glassmaking in Murano. They are the best glassmakers in the world.'

Before he could say more, a lady in waiting interrupted them. 'Madame, your pardon, but it will not be long before the guards are changed. Master Bell must return to his room so I can wake the guards before the changeover. It would not be good for them to be found asleep.'

Mary nodded. 'You must go, Master Bell. I will ride tomorrow morning. Will you accompany me?'

Jacob bowed. 'It will be my pleasure, your majesty, if I am allowed.'

'I will insist on it,' she said, offering her hand and Jacob, seeing the ring of state, instinctively kissed it. Mary gave a delighted smile and as Jacob bowed, she wished him au revoir.

There was quite an entourage next day for the ride. As well as Mary and two of her grooms, there was an escort of six well-armed troopers. Together with the grooms, they stayed a respectful distance behind. Both the Earl and Countess had excused themselves, the Earl on the grounds he was returning to Sheffield and the Countess because of some prior engagement.

Jacob was instructed how far they were allowed to ride and that he must obey a command to return to the house immediately. Other than that, he was allowed to ride with Mary out of earshot. They rode along in silence for some time with Mary obviously enjoying the freedom from the walls of Chatsworth. As they breasted a rise, they turned and looked back at the house, which was bathed in warm sunshine.

Jacob commented how fair the house looked. 'True enough,' Mary replied, 'but it is still a prison.' Then with a shrug of her shoulders, she moved her horse alongside Jacob's. 'The Countess told me this morning that you intend to return to London tomorrow is this true?'

'I'm afraid that I must, your majesty. Regretfully, I can spare no more time away from the Crouched Friars Glass-works. We are very busy at present and we have recruited some new Venetian glass-blowers from Antwerp and I must see to their training.'

'I will be sorry to see you go. I was hoping that we might have time to sit together and talk. The Countess does her best and we do quite a lot of embroidery together, but her conversation is limited.' She sighed theatrically. 'Oh, how I miss the intellectual conversation of the French court: the Scots were for the most part savages and cared nothing for the finer points of discussion. Here I seldom get the chance to have a lively discussion.' She sighed dramatically again and then changed the subject. 'What think you of my cousin Elizabeth? Is she as pretty and intelligent as they say?'

This is dangerous ground thought Jacob. I must be very careful what I say. 'They say she was most attractive when she was your age, your majesty, but I have only met her recently. As for her intelligence, I believe she speaks several languages fluently, but I can only speak for her Italian, which is most fluent.'

This seemed to satisfy Mary and she was silent for a while, then leaning a little towards him, she said quietly, 'Do you think I should grant Admiral Hawkins' petition, Master Bell?'

Jacob instinct was to be wary of showing too much support. He knew that eventually she was going to feel betrayed and he did not want to compromise his own position for the future. 'I'm afraid I can add little more to what I have said already. I do not know him well. As to the decision, it must be your own.'

Seeing she was still looking far from convinced, he took a further chance. 'There may well be some risks in trusting him. However, the Spanish Ambassador seems satisfied, or he would not have sent Fitzwilliam to you. Perchance, the opportunity to bring Admiral Hawkins and his ships to your cause would far outweigh any risks. Regrettably, with my limited knowledge of the Admiral, I cannot advise you more.' Mary was nodding her agreement with his reasoning and he hoped it would be sufficient to persuade her without going further.

Glancing back at the troopers, he saw that they were signalling them to return to the house. He informed Mary as the troopers moved closer and quickly before they came within earshot, Mary asked Jacob to do her a favour and take a reply back to Sir Henry Babington, without anyone knowing. Jacob readily agreed and she instructed him to look under his pillow when he returned to his room after the midday meal.

He found the heavily sealed letter addressed to Sir Henry Babington as she'd indicated. He wished that Phelippes, Cecil's cipher and copying expert, was available, but as he was not, it left him little choice other than to deliver it intact and hope it was not too significant.

A short while later, Fitzwilliam came in and triumphantly informed him that Queen Mary had granted Hawkins' petition. She had given him a letter of support begging King Philip to release the prisoners and a present of a gold-bound service book for the Countess of Feria. He felt in his doublet and produced a small parcel, which he passed to Jacob. 'She also asked me to give you this as a token of her thanks and regard.'

The parcel contained a ring with a phoenix engraved on a shield. Fitzwilliam gave a wide grin and clapped Jacob on the arm. 'You know what this means, Jacob, she trusts you and with this ring, so will any other Catholic. They are bound to recognise its significance.'

'I'm not sure how long that will last after Hawkins gets his men back,' Jacob said sourly. Nevertheless, when he rode back towards London next day, he wore the ring on his right hand.

Chapter Sixteen
Plymouth, October, 1570

As he hastily packed the last of his things into the saddlebags, Jacob thought how little he had expected to be travelling again so soon. Fitzwilliam had departed for Spain and Jacob hoped he had managed to cross the Channel safely before the storms set in. The gales raging in the Channel had an unexpected consequence for Jacob. He'd been at Harte Street barely a week when he received a message about his armed merchant ship. The Bonaventure had been badly damaged in the storms and had barely managed to reach the safety of Plymouth. That's where he was heading to assess the situation.

At Cecil's request, Jacob had sent a full report of his discussions with Mary to the court at Reading, where Cecil was to be with the Queen. It had to be forwarded to Buxton since Cecil was taking the waters for his health. He was a martyr to gout! From their earlier conversations, Jacob was sure Cecil would probably use the opportunity to visit Mary Stuart. Whether the illness was a cover for his visit to Chatsworth, Jacob could only guess.

His journey to Plymouth was long and tiring and Jacob went straight to his lodgings at the Navy Inn. He'd decided to get some sleep and check the ship out in the morning. As he entered the hostelry, a cheery voice hailed him. 'Master Bell, what ill-wind brings you to Plymouth?'

Turning round, Jacob saw John Hawkins, dressed like a peacock as usual, grinning at him from the recesses of a nearby porter's chair. 'Ill-wind indeed, Admiral, we are well met. I intended to seek you out tomorrow.'

'Then you would not have found me,' said Hawkins, striding over to shake his hand. 'I depart for London in the morning.'

Jacob showed his disappointment at this news and Hawkins enquired if the matter was important. 'My ship the Bonaventure has been badly damaged in the recent storms, or so I am informed. You offered to assist me if I had any such problems and I was hoping to seek your advice.'

'Do you know the full extent of the damage yet?'

'Not yet, I have only just arrived from London. I was planning to get some sleep and visit the Captain in the morning.'

Hawkins stroked his beard and looked thoughtful. 'I did promise to help and my trip to London is not so important it can't wait for a day I suppose. Very well, Jacob, I will meet you at the dock tomorrow at eight o'clock, and meanwhile I will make some enquiries.'

Jacob retired to his bed in a more optimistic frame of mind. The next morning he arrived at the dock early to find Hawkins already on board the Bonaventure talking to Captain Roberts. When Jacob went aboard, he was appalled at the damage. Teams of men were manning the pumps continuously and the vessel had a decided list. It was a miracle that the ship had made it to port and he congratulated the Captain on his seamanship.

Hawkins added his own compliments and told Jacob he was very fortunate in having Captain Roberts. 'We are old friends,' he informed Jacob,' having served together on many a skirmish with the Spanish.'

'That's right,' confirmed Captain Robert's in his soft West Country brogue, with more than a little hint of a Welsh accent. 'I would have been with the Admiral at San Juan de Ulua, except for accepting this post.'

'You were well out of that fiasco,' said Hawkins bitterly. 'Many of the men I left behind are dead. The others are rotting in a Spanish goal. Not to mention those who died on the journey home.'

Jacob clapped him on the back and tried to cheer him up. 'God willing, the end of that might be in sight now, although there is still some work to do on the matter.' He was reluctant to say more in front of Captain Roberts and changed the subject. 'Have you made any progress with this?' he said, indicating the ruin all round.

Both men nodded grimly. Captain Roberts was the first to speak. 'I'm afraid to report that the Bonaventure is very badly damaged and in the need of a major rebuild.' He indicated the stump of the main mast and the ruined spars. 'This is the tip of the iceberg, the major problems lie below the surface. The timbers are badly sprung and the cargo suffered extensive damage.' he grimaced. 'It was only thanks to the new shipping crates sent by Master Rosso that any of the glass survived.'

Jacob turned to Hawkins with a grim smile. 'I suppose that you would concur with that Admiral?'

Hawkins did not reply at once, but seemed deep in thought. He gave a nod and then looked at Jacob with a curious expression on his face. 'There is no doubt that the Bonaventure will need to be rebuilt and most of the masts, spars and rigging replaced. This will not be a cheap exercise. However, I have a suggestion to make to you, which you might like to consider.' He nodded to Captain Roberts and asked Jacob to join him in the office of the Hawkins Company, which was nearby.

When they were sitting comfortably in the well-appointed office, Hawkins explained. 'My father-in-law, Benjamin Gonson, is Treasurer of the Navy and we have been working on a design for a new kind of ship. One that I believe will give the English fleet a huge advantage over other countries.'

Jacob was puzzled. 'I don't see how this is going to help me. My ship is a merchantman.'

Hawkins smiled. 'That is true, but it hasn't always been so. It was originally a French galleon, which was seized as a prize and converted when the Glass-Sellers needed a ship quickly.' He smile became wider. 'I can vouch for this, since it was converted here in Plymouth in the family yard.'

When Jacob still look puzzled, he explained what he had in mind. 'My thought is to new-build the Bonaventure and produce an armed merchantman that will carry the same cargo as at present, but one that will be a match for any vessel currently afloat of at least twice its tonnage. It will also be much faster and more manoeuvrable.' He grinned at Jacob's expression of doubt. 'I see that you are thinking, how much is this going to cost me?'

Jacob had to laugh. 'You took the words out of my mouth.'

Hawkins asked him to give him a short while and began to do some calculations. Ten minutes later he looked up. 'Are you ready for this?' When Jacob nodded he gave him the figures. 'To repair the Bonaventure to a good standard exactly as it is, a merchantman of two hundred tons capacity, with only five small cannons for protection, will cost you four hundred pounds.'

Jacob nodded. 'That certainly seems fair in view of the current value of the Bonaventure.'

'Now I would like you to listen to my alternative,' said Hawkins. 'I will new-build the Bonaventure to produce an entirely new type of ship, of two hundred tons capacity, with a twin deck armament of sixteen cannons, eleven larger ones being on the lower deck.' He paused to see how this was being received and smiled as Jacob looked impressed.

'It will be at least five knots faster, more manoeuvrable, have a sheathed hull and other improvements, like a capstan for weighing anchor, a chain pump and anti-boarding netting. All of these improvements well tried in my own vessels: except the hull design that is.'

Jacob was very impressed by the figures, but noted that so far Hawkins had not told him how much it would cost. Before he could ask, Hawkins beat him to it. 'You're thinking this will cost a lot more and I must confess that this is true. I estimate it will cost, almost one thousand pounds.' As Jacob opened his mouth to reply, he hurriedly continued. 'However, I want this to be a viable offer, so I am prepared to offset this figure by providing materials at cost, using the family yard and forgoing any profit. That means you will get a vessel that is faster, more seaworthy, able to hold its own against even the most powerful attacker for the sum of six hundred pounds.'

When Jacob's expression betrayed his interest, he added a further incentive. 'There is also the possibility that I may be able to offset as much as a further one hundred pounds if I can persuade my father-in-law that the Naval Yard should provide timbers. I believe he will sanction that if he can use the vessel for Naval purposes from time to time, when it is available.'

Jacob had been listening to Hawkins figures with rising excitement. The prospect to have such a powerful ship at his disposal had set him thinking about the idea of a privateering venture. The stories told by Drake and others had fired his imagination. Assuming the ship performed as Hawkins predicted, it could even be used for obtaining supplies of glass from Murano. With this in mind, he asked Hawkins how he thought the new ship would perform in the Mediterranean and its vulnerability to galleys.

Hawkins was unequivocal. 'This ship will carry far too much fire-power for any galley. Even if becalmed, its all-round gunnery will easily keep them at bay.' His confidence was absolutely assured and he went on to explain that because of its better sailing characteristics, it was far less likely to be becalmed.

Jacob was persuaded. He told Hawkins to come back to him with a proper estimate and he saw no reason why it could not go ahead. Hawkins promised to have the figures for him next day and true to his word, he arrived at the hostelry late in the afternoon with a firm proposal. The price they eventually agreed was to new-build the Bonaventure for five hundred and forty-two pounds. One of Hawkins ships was to be available for cargo work at a nominal rental while the Bonaventure was in dock.

Jacob was more than pleased with this figure, but wondered if it was too good. He was obtaining a lot of extra ship for only one hundred and forty-two pounds. When he made this point to Hawkins, he had the grace to look a little shamefaced. 'You are correct. I'll be subsidising the rebuild with some of my own money.' He smiled sheepishly. 'And before you ask, it is not altruism on my part. You are giving me the opportunity to test out my ideas without the necessity of new-building a ship, which would cost at least a thousand pounds. This way we both gain.'

He assured Jacob that he was confident that the re-built Bonaventure would be a fine ship. 'There is one other condition that I would like your acceptance on. When the ship is complete, I want to invite the Queen to see it: probably at the Palace of Placentia at Greenwich. It's her favourite palace: she was born there, you know. I assume you will be having the ship sailed to London anyway when it is complete?'

'That's true,' said Jacob. 'I don't see any real problem in taking the ship to Greenwich.' He was a little puzzled at the request though and enquired, 'Why do you want the Queen to see it?'

Hawkins was silent for a moment obviously weighing up his options. 'Since you enjoy the confidence of Sir William, and mine, I might add, I will explain. The Queen and the council have made it clear they want me to stay in England and forgo any further ventures to the Spanish Main.' He gave a sigh. 'I can't say it sits well with me, but I serve the Queen first. Cecil has charged me with the long-term renewal of the Navy. It may be some little time before that comes to pass, but in the meantime, I am looking to make the English ships the finest in the world and that is what this design is about.'

Jacob interrupted. 'From the way you explained the changes to the Bonaventure, it seems that you are proposing a change in strategy.'

'You are correct, Jacob. The ships of today are little more than floating castles. They exist to bring the large contingent of soldiers alongside the enemy, so they can fight a battle. From a sailor's point of view, there are several objections to this. Existing ships are top-heavy and can't mount heavy guns, or they would turn turtle. The high forecastle and stern castle catch the wind and make the ship difficult to sail except with the wind directly astern.'

'So what will the changes mean?'

'The sleek hull design and lower forecastle and stern castle will all improve the sailing characteristics. It will also make it possible to mount a weighty broadside: thirty pounders replacing the more common five pounders. The new ship will have no need to get alongside to fight. It will be a floating gun platform that will out-sail, stand off and pound another ship until it is crippled and forced to surrender.'

Jacob listened carefully to Hawkins' explanation. He could see how these changes could alter the balance of power in Europe. After all, Venice had become the major power of the Mediterranean because of its superb fleet of galleys. If Hawkins was right, Jacob would possess one of the most powerful ships afloat. He hesitated no longer. 'I will be happy to accept your conditions and offer. Here's my hand on it.'

They shook hands on the deal and then sat down to a celebration meal in a private room at the rear of the hostelry. They toasted their joint venture and then Hawkins raised the matter of Fitzwilliam.

'I want to thank you for your part in persuading Mary Stuart to back my cause.' He indicated the ring that Jacob was wearing on his right hand. 'I see that you are wearing the Scots Queen's ring.

It should hold you in good stead with the Catholics.'

'I hope so,' said Jacob, 'but I'm not so sure they will think so well of me after you have your men safely home. I know Cecil is hoping that if Fitzwilliam is successful in Spain, you will get to know the whole of the current plot. Once that is exposed, they will be unlikely to trust me again.'

Hawkins gave it some thought before he replied. 'It depends how it's done. From what Fitzwilliam tells me, you managed to persuade Mary Stuart, but cleverly, distanced yourself from recommending it, other than as a worthwhile risk.'

Jacob nodded. 'That's true. I tried to put the emphasis on that aspect, as I could see she wanted it to be true that she had another powerful supporter.' He pulled a face. 'I felt very bad deceiving her. She's a remarkably attractive and vulnerable woman.'

'Aye and a dangerous one to boot: especially for Queen Elizabeth,' growled Hawkins. 'Make no mistake about that. Now that the Pope has excommunicated Queen Elizabeth, she's a target for every radical Catholic. They've been told that it would not be a sin to kill her, damn them all.' He had the grace to apologise when Jacob pointed out that he was brought up a Catholic. 'I didn't mean you, nor those people in England who are Catholic, but would do nothing to harm the Queen.'

Jacob thought they were getting side-tracked and brought the conversation back to a possible plot. 'Will you promise me you will inform Cecil and myself whatever you discover about a plot and not do anything to make the Spanish suspicious?'

'Of course,' promised Hawkins. 'In any case, they will have to inform me what's happening before they release the prisoners. I will insist on having them safe and sound before I commit myself to their cause,' he said, with a huge smile and a look that said quite the opposite. 'Perhaps you could give them a warning, but too late to stop Cecil's men from capturing them.'

Jacob thought this was an extremely good idea and after they had parted cordially, he retired to his room to consider it. It occurred to him that if Count Ridolfi was a plotter, both Cecil and Walsingham would be spared embarrassment if he were to escape. Taking the thought further, he might retain goodwill if he was the means of Count Ridolfi's deliverance!

It was an interesting possibility. It would certainly help to offset any accusations from the Catholics that he was plotting against them. With a sigh, Jacob decided there was nothing more to be gained at present by any further speculation. He would keep the idea in mind, but he knew he was playing a dangerous game against ruthless opponents, who would kill him without a qualm if they knew he'd betrayed them.

Chapter Seventeen
London, October, 1570

Having made his arrangements with Admiral Hawkins and disposed of the surviving glass to a local merchant, Jacob returned to London. It was going to take two to three months to rebuild the Bonaventure, by which time it was hoped that Fitzwilliam would have returned from Spain with the answer to Queen Mary's letter. It was a time-consuming exercise trying to see a King!

Whatever happened, the fact that he was involved with Cecil once more meant a lot of time spent away from the Crouched Friars. Not to mention getting involved with some vicious and treacherous people, if Jed Sutton was anything to go by. Perhaps it was time he began to practise fencing again. He was very rusty now and it wouldn't do to be caught out. Accordingly, he made enquiries about a good fencing master and shortly afterwards began attending the school of Giacomo di Grassi when he had any spare time.

It also occurred to him that it would be a good idea if he could identify apprentices who could be trusted with a message. Jacob had been mulling over an idea for some time. Being part of the Ring meant it was likely they could be trusted, especially when they were well-paid for information. There would have to be an arrangement to pay a standard fee for delivering a message. But identifying a Ring member was fraught with danger. He could hardly ask an apprentice if they knew Quiff, or belonged to the Ring! It would have to be something simple. He thought about how he had acquired his own name. Perhaps a ring might be a suitable symbol? The more he thought about it, the more he liked the idea. He decided that it was time to have a word with Quiff.

The following evening after the meal, he mentioned his idea to Quiff.

'We could have some copper rings made,' Quiff said excitedly. 'They wouldn't cost much, even if we had them engraved. Perhaps we could put a number on them.'

Jacob liked the idea, but then he thought of something else. 'Why don't we have the ring engraved with a bell and a number?

We could use a simple password as well.'

After some discussion, it was finally agreed that Jacob would have a gold ring with one bell on it, Quiff's would have two, and Roberto's three. Quiff was to keep a list of apprentices and assign them a number. They would receive a ring with a bell on it and their number engraved in the bell.

They would wear the ring at all times. When someone wearing a bell ring enquired about it they were to say, 'mine has twelve bells on it' if their number was twelve. Jacob's reply would be 'mine has only one bell.' Using this simple exchange, apprentices would know whom to trust, as would Jacob and the others. Each apprentice who joined would be vetted by Quiff and paid a gold royal as a retainer. Every time they carried a message, they would receive two shillings.

Within a few days, Quiff was able to report that he had issued seven rings already and word was spreading round the Ring like wildfire. Feeling more confident now that he had a lifeline, Jacob thought it was time to see Cecil.

He was unable to do this, as Cecil was supposedly still in Buxton taking the waters. Since there were no further results from the Ring on the affairs of Count Ridolfi, Jacob decided to carry on with his research to make a glass model of a ship. He borrowed the wooden carved ship that had caught Quiff's imagination. Using the model, he made an impression of the hull in sand and then used clay to produce a mould. He poured molten glass into the mould and when it had cooled and the mould was removed, he had a good representation of the hull.

The sails proved to be relatively easy. After blowing a bowl to the curved shape he wanted, he allowed the glass to cool slightly, then using a pair of shears, he quickly cut the bowl into two: one he held with the pucellas, the other was held by Roberto who was assisting.

He reheated the glass in the glory hole and quickly cut it to the correct size and shape with the shears. Handing it to Roberto to hold while it cooled, he repeated the operation on the other half. By the time they had finished for the afternoon, they had managed to produce all of the sails.

As they cleared away Roberto looked at the results and

laughed. 'I do believe that we've beaten the record for the least production with the most waste this afternoon.'

Jacob nodded. 'You are quite correct my friend, but we had never done it before.' He picked up one of the sails and examined it. 'It is quite tricky to get the glass to the right temperature, so that you can cut it with the shears, but it doesn't lose its shape when it cools.'

One trick they learned was to make the larger sails first. The ones that were incorrect they reheated and cut down for the smaller ones. Nothing was lost except time. The faulty glass was used as cullet.

When they had cleaned up Jacob tried out a thought on Roberto. 'What do you think of the idea of making a model of the New Bonaventure to present to the Queen, when she comes to Greenwich to see the ship?'

Roberto was very enthusiastic. 'You'll need to have a model of the ship from Admiral Hawkins.'

'That shouldn't be too difficult,' said Jacob. 'He intends to produce detailed drawings of the design. He's sure to know someone who can make a faithful model.' And so it proved.

Over the next few weeks, Jacob continued his efforts to produce the model ship. The rigging proved to be the most difficult. It was not that it was an insurmountable technical problem; trailing decoration had been part of Jacob's repertoire for years. It was the complexity of the rigging attached to the sails, masts and yards. It took many hours to produce, but eventually, it was done. They had purposely not told Quiff how they were getting on. In fact, they had completely misled him into believing that the task was proving too difficult and not worth the effort.

That evening at the evening meal Jacob arranged for the model to be concealed under the lid of Mistris Simpkin's largest covered dish. While the first course was being cleared away, Quiff was asked to bring the dish to the table and take the cover off. His face was a picture and his hands flew to his mouth as he gasped in surprise. He almost burst into tears when Jacob told him that the model was for him.

When eventually he could speak, he went to Jacob and shook

his hand solemnly. 'This is the most wonderful thing that anyone has ever done for me.' He paused for a moment as he reconsidered. 'Well, except for Master Jacob buying out my apprenticeship, but this runs it very close.'

When everyone had admired the model again and sat down to resume their interrupted meal, Quiff told Jacob there was one problem. 'I don't think that the model and a young child go together. Would it be possible to keep it here?'

'Of course it will,' said Jacob immediately. 'In fact, I would like to put it on display in the showroom: with a suitable label of course. Display kindly donated by Quiff,' he said, in a very important tone.

When the laughter had subsided, he told Quiff that he didn't intend to put it on display just yet. 'I don't want anyone to know about it until after we have produced the model of the New Bonaventure for the Queen.'

'I understand,' said Quiff nodding seriously. 'It wouldn't do for the Queen to know she was only the second person to have such a beautiful glass model.'

Chapter Eighteen
Venice, January, 1570

Maria Morisini-Ragazoni looked around the Chamber of the Justices and wondered how Giam must have felt when he came here for his trial. The circular apartment on the second floor of the Palazzo Ducale was almost empty at present; the Giunta was in recess while they considered their verdict and the teller counted the votes.

The chamber had large windows looking out on to the canal at the rear of the Palazzo, looking across to the Piombi, the main prison in Venice. The walls of the whole apartment were lavishly decorated with friezes. Four of the most prominent artists in Venice had contributed these, Aliense, Bassano, Marco Vecellio, and Veronese. The paintings were beautiful, but Maria had no eyes for them. It had been an exhausting week, especially coming so soon after the serious illnesses she had suffered following the birth of her child. It was only hope that sustained her now as she waited for the verdict of the Giunta.

It was impossible to tell how the hearing had gone. At least it had not been held in front of the Three, the Inquisitori, but a full Giunta: the Council of Ten and six co-opted Councillors from each of the executive bodies. This constituted a final court of appeal.

The hearing, unlike Giam's trial, had been scrupulously fair. The testimony of Ragazoni's servant had been crucial. His evidence had provided the proof that was lacking in the Chief Avogador's dossier.

Maria was extremely grateful to Sir William Cecil. He had given her Adrian's confession to plotting to murder Queen Elizabeth and she had in turn passed it to the Chief Avogador. The evidence given by Ragazoni's servant, the assassin, sent back under threat of death unless he told the truth about Ragazoni, proved to be the turning point of the appeal.

The papers supplied by Cecil had helped to show how far Adrian was prepared to go in pursuit of power. The testimony given by his servant, whilst failing to mention his own main occupation, had confirmed the suspicions of the Avogadors by filling in missing information: particularly Adrian Ragazoni's preparation of the letter of denunciation signed by Marco Baffo and his subsequent murder.

Faced with this evidence, Adrian's father, Senator Pietro Ragazoni, had broken down under sustained questioning from the Chief Avogador and confirmed the truth of the statements. During the original trial, he insisted that he had believed that Giacomo Bellini was a traitor. He had used all of his considerable influence to stop, or delay the appeal, but at last, not even his own deteriorating health had prevented it.

Now, at last, he admitted that at the Senate meeting to review the Three's verdict his son, Adrian, had confessed to his lies: even boasted about them! He had threatened to bring his father down with him if he was exposed, so to protect his position as Rossi and avoid a scandal, Pietro had kept quiet. Full of remorse, his health broken by the death of his son and the full exposure of his machinations, he apologised for his weakness and asked for forgiveness.

The case was made, but Maria knew that politics could not be ignored. Was the Giunta prepared to admit that the court of the Three had been corrupt? That was another matter entirely. Her father and father-in-law had cautioned her about this. She knew very well that originally, politics, not the rule of law, was responsible for Jacob being sent to the galleys.

At that moment a court usher announced that the Giunta was reconvening and that the complainants must resume their seats. Hardly had they sat down when in filed the members of the Giunta. The Council of Ten came first in their violet robes, then the Councillors in crimson and the Decemvirs in black. The secretary of the Ten, who was acting as the teller, stood up, bowed to the members and began to speak. Maria held her breath and then letting it out with a sudden gasp, she threw her arms round her father's neck. The verdict of the Giunta was unanimous: the late Senator Adrian Ragazoni was guilty of perverting the course of justice by manufacturing evidence. He had falsely accused Giacomo Bellini of treason by virtue of passing information of glassmaking to a foreigner. The verdict of three years in the galleys against Giacomo Bellini was set aside and the Ragazoni estate must pay him the sum of ten thousand ducats in reparation.

Senator Pietro Ragazoni, a Capi of the Ten and Rossi at the time of the original trial, was found guilty of conspiring with his son to pervert the course of justice, after the original trial and barred from office for life. Further, he must pay five thousand ducats in reparation to Giacomo Bellini. Only his state of health saved him from more serious punishment.

The president then stood up and made a statement. The Giunta had decided that a small committee was to be appointed to study the implications of the appeal. The scale of the failure of the system in the face of the actions of one unscrupulous nobleman had made the judiciary determined to ensure it could never happen again. The committee would consist of the Advocate General, the Chief Avogador and Senators Dalle Fornaci, Morisini and Bellini, with full powers to call witnesses, hand out punishment for non-cooperation and recommend changes to the law.

The Chief Avogador was delighted with the verdict and the setting up of the investigating committee. He had lobbied long and hard for this, so that the injustice done to Giacomo Bellini could never be repeated.

Walking across the lobby, he thanked Maria for her courage and congratulated Senators Morisini and Bellini on the important role they had been given on the Committee in recognition of their courage in fighting the case. Maria felt drained and could only murmur her thanks for his help, whilst the two Senators insisted they were simply protecting their families.

When the Chief Avogador had left, Maria collected her papers together and trudged wearily down the stairs of the Palazzo. She just wanted to get out into the fresh air now it was all over. When she emerged from the Palazzo Ducale into the Piazzetto San Marco, the weather was wet and grey, but she didn't notice. Her tiredness left her and her heart was suddenly full of elation as the reality hit her. They'd done it at last! Giam was vindicated and had a free pardon. Hugging herself in delight, she twirled round to look for her father. He was walking towards her across the piazza with the familiar figure of Eduardo Bellini, Giam's father.

'A wonderful day Maria,' Eduardo burst out excitedly, taking her hands in his. 'I can't thank you and Ricardo enough for pursuing and overturning this terrible injustice, especially after your long illness. It has been such a shock: Giam alive and well in London, Adrian Ragazoni dead, now this wonderful news. It's almost too much to take in. You must be very proud of Maria,' he said, turning to Ricardo.

'I am indeed,' he replied. 'It has cost her a lot. However, when you think about it, we are all victims of Adrian Ragazoni, even his own father. Everyone became embroiled in his evil schemes.' He gave a long sigh. 'I don't like to confess it, but I'm glad he's dead. Perhaps we can get on with our lives now.'

Maria knew it wasn't going to be so simple, especially for Giam. There was their son to think about: she still considered that Giam was his father. Once again, Maria regretted her decision to pretend Ragazoni sired the baby. But it was too late to correct it now. The damage had been done. She knew the news should have come from her. She had agonised about sending a message to explain, or even taking ship for England. The first was too late and the second impractical with a young baby. One thing was for sure, the whole affair would come to a head and soon. The Giunta verdict concluded with the condition that Giam must give up making glass in London and return to Venice as soon as possible after the decision reached him.

Chapter Nineteen
London, January/February, 1571

Many times in the past three months, Jacob had felt like taking ship to Venice and hang the consequences: none more so than when he received his father's letter telling him of Maria's illnesses. Now that he had taken the time to think about it, it wasn't that the letter was late that bothered him, it was Maria naming the boy a Ragazoni and the reasons given for it. Maria hated Ragazoni for what he had done to Jacob, just as much as for forcing her to marry him and then raping her, he understood that. That was motive enough for revenge, but then to name the boy a Ragazoni, he couldn't stomach it. Unable to talk it through with her, he began to imagine all sorts of reasons, but primarily, that Ragazoni really was the father.

Shaking his head in distress, he looked at the model ship standing on the desk and brought his mind back to problems nearer home. Admiral Hawkins had presented the model to him on his last visit to Plymouth. He was astonished at the changes that had been made to the Bonaventure. The sleek ship with its double deck of cannons was everything that the Admiral had promised. Now all he had to do was to make a model in glass for the Queen!

As soon as he had seen it, he knew that it was a far more difficult task than the small schooner he had made for Quiff. It was not that it would need a different approach; it was the complexity of the spars and rigging. On the schooner, it had taken far more effort to get the rigging correct than the rest of the ship.

However, the die was cast and the sooner he got on with it the better. The Bonaventure would be ready in two weeks' time and this left him about a month before the ship had finished its trials and sailed to Greenwich. Calling over one of the apprentices, Jacob sent him to fetch Roberto.

Three weeks later, he was ready to tear his hair out as the model was far from finished. The earlier model had made the task of producing the basic hull, masts, and main spars relatively simple. Making the sails was a matter of perseverance rather than problematical, but the rigging! Not for the first time that day, Jacob surveyed the latest mess.

'I just don't seem to be able to get it right,' he complained to Roberto. 'There must be a better way of doing it than this.'

Before Roberto could answer, a thought struck Jacob. 'Have we got any olive oil here at the Works?'

'I'm not sure, Master Jacob. Mistris Simpkin is sure to have some though. I'll go and check.'

About half an hour later, he came back with a bottle of oil. 'What do you want me to do with it?'

Jacob, who had been measuring the rigging on the foremast of the model, looked up. 'Lightly oil the top of the marver, please Roberto. I'm going to try something.' Using the measure and some chalk, he made a pattern in the oil, corresponding to the rigging of the foremast. Heating up a glass rod, he elongated the end to produce a trailing and laid it over the first part of the design. Working quickly, he rapidly filled in the remainder of the rigging. Once it had cooled, he carefully picked it up with the pucellas and heating both ends of the rigging, he applied it to the foremast and held it until it cooled.

'What do you think, Roberto,' he asked, stepping back to look at it critically.

Roberto examined the models carefully. 'It's very nearly exact,' he said, his voice showing pleasure. 'This will certainly speed up the main rigging. The other yards, whilst more tricky to apply, don't need to be so exact.'

Three days later, the model was complete and was moved into the office with great care and trepidation. Roberto came in carrying a large parcel covered with cloth. Setting it down carefully, he whipped off the cover. To Jacob's immense surprise, it was a glass-sided box with a secure cradle for mounting the model ship. The base surrounding the cradle had been sculpted from coloured clay to look like waves.

The box lid had an engraved label with the legend: "This Crystal Ship was made and presented to Her majesty, Queen Elizabeth, by the Royal Glassmaker, Master Jacob Bell of the Crouched Friars Glass-works, in February of this year of our Lord, fifteen hundred and seventy-one."

When the ship had been mounted in the box and the lid securely closed, Jacob was relieved. 'This case is a splendid idea. It complements the model and keeps it safe. The carrying handles will also make it so much easier to carry.'

'I can't claim all of the credit,' said Roberto, happy that he'd been able to contribute. 'The joiner who makes our new shipping crates did some of the work. He has also made a crate for transporting the box. It works rather like the shipping crates we made for the last shipment of glass from Antwerp.'

'It should survive the trip to Greenwich quite well then,' said Jacob. 'We had fewer breakages that trip than ever before.'

It did indeed survive the trip and two weeks later it was placed ready on the table in the owner's cabin and covered with a blue velvet cloth. Jacob had not let anyone see the model, or even hinted at its existence. Admiral Hawkins, resplendent as usual, had enquired about it, curious to get a glimpse, but even he had been denied and made to wait like everyone else.

As they waited for the Queen to arrive, Jacob looked across at Roberto and Elizabeth, dressed in their finest clothes. Turning to John Isham who had just joined Jacob and the Admiral he indicated the young couple. 'A handsome pair they make, don't you think, John?'

'They do indeed,' he replied proudly. 'I could not wish for a better son-in-law than Roberto. Elizabeth has really blossomed since their marriage.'

'She's become a most attractive woman and a feisty one too,' Jacob said, with a laugh.

John joined in the laughter. 'Most certainly she has. Just like her mother when I first met her. She's not above giving her father a few home truths, if she thinks I need them.'

'I'll warrant that is fairly frequent then,' said Jacob, with a twinkle in his eye and a wink for the Admiral.

Before John could reply, a fanfare of trumpets heralded the arrival of the Queen, together with a number of her ladies-in-waiting and several members of the council, including Sir William Cecil, the Earl of Leicester and Sir Richard Hatton.

Together with Jacob, Admiral Hawkins strode down the gangplank and made a gracious leg to the Queen, as did Jacob.

The Queen bade them rise and after a brief word with Jacob, turned to the Admiral. 'I confess, Admiral,' she said, in a disappointed voice, eyeing the five cannons visible on the deck of the ship. 'I had expected something rather special from your description, but this new ship of yours looks very much a lightly armed merchantman to me.'

'Indeed, your majesty,' he said with a smile, 'but that is a deliberate ploy on our part as Master Bell will demonstrate when we go aboard.'

Offering his arm, the Admiral escorted her on board followed by Jacob and the members of the council. Leading her along the line of the people present, he introduced them. When it was Roberto's turn, the Queen stopped to talk. 'So this is the redoubtable Roberto Rosso that Master Bell is always telling me stories about. You have rendered us some valuable services Master Rosso. We are most grateful for your help in confounding our enemies.'

Roberto was totally overwhelmed by the Queen's remarks and stammered his thanks. He introduced Elizabeth and the Queen gave her an approving nod. 'You have done well for yourself Master Rosso. Your wife is most pretty.' The Queen passed on, and Roberto gave Elizabeth a hug of delight. Reaching the end of the line, the Queen could contain her impatience no longer. 'Now Admiral, are you going to satisfy my curiosity about this ship of yours, or are we going to have yet more distractions.'

Without further ado, the Admiral led the Queen on a tour of the ship, pointing out all the new features, but leaving the main gun deck until last. When the Queen saw the broadside, she was most impressed.

Taking his cue from the Admiral's signal, Jacob waved a kerchief above his head. In answer to his signal, there was a flurry of activity, the gun ports on the side facing away from the quay were flung open and the guns run out.

The Queen clapped her hands in delight. 'Most exciting, Admiral: this ship will undoubtedly give a good account of itself.'

'Indeed, your majesty, as we hope to demonstrate to you shortly.'

The Queen gave him a questioning look, but the Admiral did

not elaborate, but escorted her up to the quarterdeck. As he stood with the Queen beside the wheel, he drew her attention to a large pinnace that was moored at the far side of the river. With a nod to Captain Roberts, he asked the Queen to prepare for two of the guns to fire. There was a loud command and then the two guns fired almost together. The pinnace, cut in two by the thirty-two pound balls, sank immediately with only some shattered timbers to mark its position.

There was a stunned silence for a moment and then the Queen gave a loud huzza. 'Magnificent demonstration, Admiral, the Spanish will be well advised to steer clear of such a ship.'

Seizing his moment the Admiral dropped on to his knee. 'It is my greatest wish to ensure that your majesty's ships are of a similar or better standard. With a fleet of these ships, your Navy will be the strongest in the world.'

Waving him to his feet, she turned to Cecil and Leicester. 'We will discuss this ship at the next meeting of the council, but meanwhile, prepare estimates of what such a programme of rebuilding would cost.'

Cecil bowed in acknowledgement and Jacob stepped forward. 'Your majesty, as your Royal Glassmaker, I thought it appropriate to mark this special occasion by making a new type of gift for you. Please accompany me to the owner's cabin where it is waiting and after the presentation, refreshments will be served.'

When Jacob unveiled the model in its case, the Queen was silent. She walked all round the table and carefully studied the model and the inscription on the plaque. Walking across to Jacob, she regarded him with a stern expression that had Jacob quaking and the onlookers holding their breath. 'Master Bell, why have you not produced anything like this before?' She said sternly. Then seeing Jacob crestfallen look her eyes sparkled and she threw her head back and laughed heartily. The tension in the room which had built up during the Queen's silence was suddenly released in spontaneous applause. 'I do declare you thought I did not like it,' said the Queen. 'It is truly the most magnificent model I have ever seen. Your ship too is remarkable, thanks to the Admiral's design. However, I venture to suggest that the name New Bonaventure does not do justice to it and it is my wish that she shall be named 'The Crystal' as foreshadowed on the inscription on this beautiful model.'

Jacob could only say one thing and a few hours later, Captain Roberts and his newly-named ship, The Crystal, set sail for Antwerp.

Chapter Twenty
London, February, 1571

Count Ridolfi looked up from the papers on his desk as Jed Sutton came into the room. 'Ah, there you are Jed. I need this letter delivering to the Duke of Norfolk,' he said, waving the heavily-sealed letter in his hand. 'It must be delivered to the Duke's hands personally. It would not do for anyone else to see it. I don't suppose they would be able to crack the cipher, but it's best not to take chances. Send one of the servants you can trust and make sure he understands that only the Duke must receive it.'

'In that case, I'd better take it myself,' said Jed, with a frown. 'The servants know better than to cross me, but they're all numbskull's and might do something silly, like give it to one of the Duke's servants.'

'Unfortunately, I can't spare you the time. I must visit the Bishop of Ross and I need you to come with me. He's been less than enthusiastic about the plot of late. He's easily discouraged and I might need you to give him some encouragement. We can't afford for him to get cold feet now, he might go running to Cecil. I think a little pressure might do the trick.'

He could see that Jed was looking forward to that. Indicating the letter again he continued. 'Choose the most reliable man and make sure he knows the consequences of making a slip up.'

Jed nodded and taking the letter went out into the hall. The senior footman was talking to one of the grooms and Jed called him over. Motioning him to follow, he led him into the small anteroom off the hall and closed the door.

'I have a very important letter for the Duke of Norfolk,' he said, glaring aggressively at him and brandishing it in front of the footman's nose. The footman backed away and, placing the letter on the desk, Jed followed him. When he reached the wall Jed, moving quickly forward, seized him by the throat. Pushing his face back and almost lifting him off his feet he smiled evilly at the terrified, man, 'Have I got you're your full attention, Jenkins?'

The man, his face starting to turn purple, managed a nod and Jed released him suddenly, watching as he rubbed his throat, looking fearfully at Jed. Jed picked up the letter and moved towards the cringing footman. 'As I was saying, Jenkins, this is a most important letter and ordinarily I would deliver it in person. However, the Count desires me to accompany him, so I must entrust the letter to someone I can trust.' He fixed the man with a fierce expression. 'Can I trust you to do exactly as you are told, Jenkins?'

Jenkins made no answer, simply nodding his agreement. Jed was not happy with this and threatened to seize his throat again. When the man croaked hurriedly, 'Yes, Mr Sutton, of course,' Jed turned away with a satisfied smile, missing the flash of hatred that flared briefly in the man's eyes, which was quickly suppressed.

'Very good, Jenkins, now listen carefully. You will take this letter to the Duke of Norfolk at Arundel Castle and you will deliver it personally into his hands. Personally mind you, you hear me, not by a servant, by you personally!' He thrust his face forward aggressively again. 'No excuses, if I find out that you've disobeyed me, you had better not come back, or I'll beat you to a pulp.' The terrified Jenkins was left in no doubt from Jed's expression that this would indeed be his fate. 'Here is some money for the livery and the Post,' Jed said, handing him a small pouch of coins. 'Now take this letter and make sure you do exactly as you've been told.'

Taking the letter and the pouch, Jenkins scurried off while Jed congratulated himself on how well he had enforced his will. Then with a quick look in the mirror and reassured by what he saw, he set off to make ready for the trip with the Count.

A short while later they set off in the Count's coach and neither of them noticed Jenkins the footman, hiding at the corner of the road as they drove past. Once they were out of sight Jenkins twirled the copper ring on his finger and then with a determined expression on his face, set off for The Swan to meet Quiff.

Although it was well before his usual time to go to The Swan, the message from the landlord said the matter was urgent and Quiff wasted no time in getting there. When he entered by the back way, the landlord indicated the private booth he kept for Quiff and his visitors. 'He's waiting for you in there,' he said, 'and he's in a right state too. If you need any help, just give me a shout, but meantime this might help.' He passed Quiff a glass with generous measure in it, which Quiff regarded quizzically. 'Don't worry it's good brandy. I've just got a new supply from the coast.' He tapped the side of his nose with a forefinger and gave Quiff a knowing wink. 'I've put it on your slate. Give it to the lad, he looks as though he needs it.'

Quiff grinned, he was well aware that the landlord got his brandy from smugglers. Taking the proffered glass he went into the booth where the nervous Jenkins was waiting, handed him the glass and he told him to drink it down. This he did, coughing as the fiery liquor burned its way down. Once the coughing had stopped, his cheeks began to look less pale. Quiff told him to take his time and explain what was so urgent that it couldn't wait until the usual time.

Jenkins was hesitant at first, but as the brandy loosened his tongue, he told Quiff about the letter and the violent threats from Jed Sutton. He produced the letter from his doublet and passed it to Quiff who examined the address and seals with rising excitement. 'How long will the Count be away, do you know?'

'I heard Jed tell the groom that they would be back in about a week, but I must deliver the letter to the Duke as soon as possible. If Jed finds out what I'm doing, he'll kill me.'

Quiff reassured him, his mind working overtime. The seals on the letter made it a tricky task to open and it needed someone skilled to do it. Walsingham employed a man to open and copy letters. What was his name? Quiff racked his brains. Phelippes that was it! Perhaps Jacob could get him to do it quickly if he was at home. Turning to Jenkins who had being sitting nervously waiting for a reply, he told him to go to the livery at Aldgate and to wait there.

When Jacob heard the story, one look at the letter convinced him of its importance and he set off at once to see Phelippes. Fortunately he was in and it took him only a short time to lift the seals and open the letter.

When Jacob saw what was written he was disappointed, but Phelippes just laughed. 'Surely you didn't think it would be written in plain English, it is obviously in cipher.'

'Can you decipher it?'

'I can decode anything,' Phelippes boasted, 'but how long it takes is another matter. It can take weeks.'

'But we don't have weeks,' said Jacob in dismay. 'We don't even have hours. Unless this letter is delivered to Arundel as quickly as possible, the life of my informant will be at risk and the Count will know we have intercepted it and change his plans.'

Phelippes smiled. 'We don't have to do it here and now. I can make a fair copy and reseal it in half an hour and then it can be on its way. I will decipher the letter as soon as possible and let you know what it says.'

'Excellent,' said Jacob, taking out a purse and passing it to him. 'I would prefer that Sir William doesn't know about this letter, for the moment, but I assure you I will inform him of its contents, as soon as necessary.'

Phelippes hefted the purse. 'It will be between us for now, but if it is important, don't take too long in informing Sir William. He takes a dim view of those who keep things from him.'

Once back at Harte Street with the expertly resealed letter, he gave it to Quiff. 'Give him these two gold royals and tell him to ride like the wind to Arundel. The delay should not be noticed in a journey of that length. It must be all of fifty to sixty miles. When he gives the letter to the Duke of Norfolk, he must pretend to be exhausted. It probably won't bee far from the truth. He must tell him that the horse was blown and he had to lead it for the last few miles. That should explain any delay.' He put his hand on his shoulder and led him to the door. 'Thank him for the risk he took in bringing this to me and tell him to be careful of Jed Sutton, he is very dangerous. My advice is for him to get out of there as soon as possible.' He thought for a moment. 'Should he decide to leave, he should contact you and I will use my influence to get him another job.'

When Quiff returned and told him that Jenkins had set off for Arundel, Jacob went to the living room and sat by the fire. He hoped that the letter might give him sufficient cause to tell Sir William what had been going on. It was a dangerous game he was playing withholding information from him, as Phelippes had observed.

Four days later, he had his answer. Phelippes had broken the cipher and produced a copy of what it contained. 'It wasn't a very difficult cipher to break,' he bragged. 'They'd have to be a lot more intelligent to fool me.'

Jacob read the letter with mounting excitement. It informed Norfolk that Charles Baillie, a Scotsman in the employ of the Bishop of Ross, would come to England in April bringing books and a packet of letters. There would be money from Count Ridolfi, to further the cause of Mary Stuart. The Count would soon be leaving to raise the money from various sources including the Guises in France and he was hoping to see the Duke of Alva to convince him that the time was right for an invasion.

Baillie was charged with delivering the portmanteau of books and letters to the Bishop of Ross. The money was to be given to Norfolk. He was to arrange to send half of it to Scotland where Mary Stuart could have access to it. The remainder was to pay the expenses of "arrangements made by the Bishop of Ross concerning the Queen of Scots person and divers other expenses sanctioned by him". Nothing further was mentioned as to what these might be. Unfortunately, the letter was couched in cautious terms and although it was not difficult to make a shrewd guess, it did not constitute certain proof.

When he had finished reading, Phelippes looked at him questioningly. 'Is it your intention to inform Sir William now?' he asked pointedly.

'I think now would be the right time,' Jacob said, with a wry smile. 'I doubt it would go well for me if I wait longer.'

'Very wise,' said Phelippes, 'for I would have felt obliged to tell him myself. I have little liking for being in Sir William's bad books.'

Despite the imminent ceremony to raise Cecil to the peerage, Jacob was admitted to his presence with little delay. When he explained what he had found out, Cecil was pleased, but a little subdued.

'I knew that Ring of yours was going to be very useful. I hope your informant has not put himself in peril. From what you told me in your earlier report, this Jed Sutton is a most violent man.'

'He is indeed Sir William, although I am the only witness to that and it would be difficult to prove.'

Cecil pulled a disappointed face. 'I believe you are correct, but for now we have bigger fish to catch. Fortunately, in this case time is on our side. Baillie will not be coming to England until April.' The wry smile came back. 'I am sure we can ensure a warm welcome for him.'

He shuffled through some papers on his desk until he found the one he wanted. 'As for the scheming Count, he has already obtained a passport to travel to France on banking business,' he said, indicating the paper. 'He is departing for France later this week. I will get a message to Walsingham in Paris and ask him to keep an eye on him. It will be useful to see if he visits the Guises.'

He began to pace up and down. 'I am saddened that Norfolk is implicated in this affair, although not completely surprised. Too often he is driven by blind ambition to recognise the dangers to himself.' He regarded Jacob shrewdly. 'He has been my friend and supporter for many years and I had hoped that his period in the Tower would bring him to his senses where marriage to the Scots Queen is concerned. Friend or not, should it be proved that he is involved in treason, my friendship will not save him.'

Sitting back, he shook his head sadly then, his face brightening, he regarded Jacob with a warm expression. 'And what about you Jacob Bell? Once more you have been of service to the Crown. It has crossed my mind that some more tangible reward of our gratitude would be in order.'

Jacob tried to say it was not necessary, but Cecil waved aside his protests. 'I was not suggesting monetary considerations, but in view of your peculiar status with Venice...' He smiled when Jacob laughed at this coy description. 'You may laugh, Master Bell, but I am serious. What I had in mind was to offer you the chance to become a naturalised English subject and therefore not subject to the laws of Venice.'

Jacob was astonished and thanked him for the offer. Cecil continued. 'I assure you that her majesty is in full agreement. In fact, she commented that you had done more to protect her than many who were English by accident of birth. She asked me to tell you that she would be delighted to have you as one of her people.'

'I'm overwhelmed by the Queen's confidence in me,' said Jacob at last, 'but there are so many things to consider. Do you need an answer right away?'

'Not at all, Master Bell; you may think about it as long as you wish. It might prove helpful in negotiations relating to your present difficulties with Venice. My Ambassador informs me that your father and the resourceful Lady Maria are trying to reopen your case. He believes that they have a reasonable chance of success, unless Venetian politics rears its ugly head. In the meantime, you might like to have this.'

Opening a drawer in his desk, he took out a rolled scroll and handed it to Jacob, who regarded it quizzically. 'It's an invitation to my investiture at Westminster Palace in two days time. My clerk will ensure you get a good view. In the meantime, please give my offer some thought.' He stood up and walked around the desk. 'And now if you will excuse me, I must attend the Queen. Until we meet again, Master Bell, I bid you farewell.'

Chapter Twenty-One
London, , 25th, February, 1571

When Jacob arrived at Westminster Palace, crowds were gathering in the street outside, eagerly waiting to catch a glimpse of the Queen. He had some difficulty getting through, but when he showed his invitation to the sergeant-at-arms, the sight of it allowed him immediate entry.

The presence chamber was already crowded as Jacob, wearing his raven's wing coloured cloak bearing the emblem of the Queen's Glassmaker, was shown in by the side entrance. The clerk explained that the main door at the rear of the chamber was closed, as the procession was being formed. Shortly after Jacob had settled into his place, the Queen arrived to a fanfare of trumpets. Acknowledging the obeisance of the assembly, she took her place on the dais then motioned for them to rise.

The Lord Chamberlain, standing to the right of the Queen, made a signal and the doors opened. Every eye turned to see the procession. Jacob, near the front, still managed to see clearly due to his height.

It was a magnificent and colourful sight. First came the heralds, two-by-two in their colourful tabards, followed by the Garter King-of-Arms. He carried the charter of creation in his hands. Behind him was Lord Hunsdon carrying the baron's cloak. Next came Cecil himself, escorted by the Earl of Leicester on his right and Lord Cobham on his left.

This colourful array moved towards the dais where they all made their obeisance. The Garter King-of-Arms stepped forward and presented the charter to the Lord Chamberlain, who handed it to the Queen. She untied the ribbon and after a careful look, passed it to her Latin Secretary, John Wooley to read it out. When John Wooley had finished, he bowed to the Queen who rose and taking the cloak from Hunsdon, hung it around Cecil's shoulders. Handing Cecil the charter, in a loud ringing voice she pronounced him Baron of Burghley.

When the prolonged applause had died down Cecil responded with words of thanks. A trumpet blew, the procession reformed and filed out of the chamber with the new Lord Burghley acknowledging the many congratulations. The Queen and her entourage then left the chamber to join the new baron at dinner.

To Jacob's surprise, Cecil's clerk appeared by his side and led him to the dining room, escorting him to an assigned place near the foot of the table. Cecil was seated at the right-hand of the Queen at the top of the long table, with Leicester to her left. The remainder of the guests were seated according to precedent.

During the course of the sumptuous feast, the heralds gathered and having first proclaimed Elizabeth's titles in Latin, French and English, moved a little further away, then repeated the title of the new baron.

"Du très noble Seigneur Guillaume Cecil, chevalier Baron de Burghley".

As the cry died away, the heralds made their obeisance to the Queen and, uttering their customary cry for largesse, withdrew to end the ceremony.

Christopher Hatton, Member of Parliament for Higham Ferrers, was seated on Jacob's right. He was a colourful character, a dandy, who was always dressed in the height of fashion. Some years earlier, being a fine dancer, he had attracted the attention of the Queen at court and she had favoured him by making him one of her Gentleman Pensioners. The rumours abounded, that he would replace the Earl of Leicester as her favourite, but after six years in her service, it had still not happened.

For this special occasion, he was wearing a doublet of white, trimmed with braiding of red and gold. Down the front were gold buttons, between rows of perpendicular pinking. His knee breeches, known as Venetians - although from Jacob's memory, very few Venetians actually wore them - were in red and gold braid, together with white fancy stockings and French pantoufles. His cloak and hip-roll were in black velvet, diapered with pearls set in three leaves of gold. It was capped off with an Italian bonnet in the same material, with a row of gold jewelled ornament round the hat band, a brooch and a tuft of feathers. Even in his finest garments of slashed raven's wing, Jacob felt positively drab.

When the heralds had withdrawn, Hatton turned to Jacob and remarked that the words describing Cecil's attributes were hardly extravagant. 'He is well deserving of the honour that the Queen has bestowed. In the twelve years of her majesty's reign, she has created only three peers before him.'

Jacob agreed wholeheartedly. 'I have always found Lord Burghley to be a most intelligent and far-sighted man. He was supportive of my application for Letters Patent. Both he and the Queen favour manufacturing over importation from Murano or elsewhere. Since I became the Queen's Glassmaker he has bought a considerable amount of glass. I am most fortunate to enjoy his patronage.'

Hatton regarded him shrewdly. 'I believe you are being modest, Master Bell. Your glass rivals Murano and is recognised as such by knowledgeable people. A superb glassmaker and swordsman too, if Walsingham's description of the attempted assassination is to be believed, a man of many talents. Do you have a fencing master in London?'

'Yes I do,' said Jacob. 'I have recently started attending the school of Giacomo di Grassi. He is very interested in the use of the dagger as a defensive weapon and using the sword to parry attacks.' Jacob smiled ruefully as he recalled trying to parry the thrown knife in the attack on Walsingham. 'I am working on this aspect of my skill.'

'I have heard he is very good and was thinking of trying him myself. Would you recommend him?'

'Indeed I would. I believe he is extremely forward thinking and analyses attack and defence most carefully. I understand he is shortly to publish a book on the art of defence.'

'In that case I certainly will take up your commendation. Perhaps you would care to cross swords in a friendly bout,' said Hatton enthusiastically. 'I would welcome the opportunity to fence with a swordsman of your calibre.'

Acknowledging the compliment, Jacob gracefully declined to take up the offer at present. 'I can only fit in the occasional visit, but if you should happen to be present with Fencing Master Grassi when I call, by all means.'

Just then, there was a signal to Hatton that the Queen was about to retire. Hatton stood up and bowed to Jacob. 'I regret I must leave our conversation for now: I must attend her majesty as she is leaving. I may visit your showroom in the near future. In Harte Street, behind the Tower I believe.'

Jacob agreed it was and that he would look forward to Hatton's custom. With that, Hatton went to join the other Gentleman Pensioners to escort the Queen to her rooms.

After the Queen had left, people wandered away from the table and began conversing in groups. Jacob thought he ought to add his congratulations to the many that the new baron was receiving but found it difficult to get near him. Turning to leave, he was hailed by Lord Burghley's clerk. 'Excuse me Master Bell, but Lord Burghley particularly asked that you attend him in the anteroom. He requires an urgent word and will join you shortly. Should you require a drink, or any food, please ask the servant who will be in attendance.'

Having had a large meal, Jacob didn't require anything further. He wondered what Burghley might want. He had not made up his mind on the naturalisation, so he hoped it was not about that. When Burghley arrived, he acknowledged Jacob's congratulations then got straight to business. 'I wanted to let you know two things. I have studied the letter from Ridolfi most carefully and after some discreet enquiries, I am convinced that he is one of the prime movers of this plot and that De Spes, the Spanish Ambassador, the Bishop of Ross, and Norfolk are involved. Would you agree?'

Jacob nodded. 'I believe you are right and Hawkins is convinced about De Spes,' he said. 'He was delighted when Hawkins made his offer to put his ships at their disposal. He couldn't wait to tell his master, Philip.'

'I have also heard from Walsingham that Ridolfi was only in Paris for one night and visited the home of the Guises. He has now left and is on his way to the Low Countries: presumably to see the Duke of Alva.

'My second piece of news concerns Jed Sutton. Apparently, he has not travelled with his master, but is on his way back to London. It might be a good idea to see if your informant in the household can keep us advised about his movements.'

Having listened carefully Jacob agreed to put the word out to the Ring, to follow Jed Sutton. Taking his leave, Jacob headed straight to the Crouched Friars to talk to Quiff. 'I want you to contact Jenkins before Sutton gets back tomorrow. Ask him to keep us informed what Sutton is doing. Whatever you do though, make sure you warn him not to take any chances. That man is a sadistic bully and if he has the slightest suspicion that Jenkins is informing on him, he will kill him without a qualm.'

Quiff promised to ensure that this was done and then went off to The Swan to have words with the landlord. Following Jacob's warning about Jed Sutton, it occurred to him that if he found out about Jenkins, he might find out about Quiff and The Swan. He had a long conversation with the landlord and made arrangements to avoid any trouble. Passing over two gold royals, Quiff was confident the landlord would be careful to keep such a good source of income safe. You can't be too careful he thought.

Chapter Twenty-Two
London, 28th, February,1571

By the time Jed Sutton finally reached London, he was in a fine rage. Since leaving the Count at Calais, there'd been nothing but delays on his journey. At Dover, officious customs officials searching for contraband delayed the disembarkation of passengers until it was too late to set off to London. This was on direct instructions from Lord Burghley. The room at the inn was poor and Jed woke with a terrible hangover from the excessive amount of ale he'd drunk on the previous evening. The journey to London was little short of torture. Every jolt of the coach as they went over a pothole sent jabs of pain through his skull. There were many potholes on the road to London!

Reaching the Count's house, when the doorman was less than prompt in answering, Jed lashed out and smashed him to the ground, kicking him in the ribs for good measure. Feeling slightly improved by that, he roared for the rest of the servants and they came scurrying to follow his instructions, meted out with cuffs, punches and kicks.

When he had eaten and had a long drink of ale, he began to feel more like his normal self. Calling for Jenkins, he asked the apprehensive footman if he had followed his instructions and delivered the letter directly into to the hand of to the Duke of Norfolk.

Although Jenkins hurriedly explained that he had given it straight to the Duke, Jed's suspicions were aroused by his obvious nervousness. At first he put it down to the manner of his own arrival, but as he began to question him further, Jenkins admitted that he had been delayed in giving the letter to the Duke because his livery horse had gone lame on the way to Arundel.

Seizing Jenkins' arm, he twisted it savagely behind his back and marched him down to the cellar. Bolting the door, he pushed the terrified man into the chair. He began to beat him systematically; questioning what he had done from the time he'd been given the letter.

Although Jenkins pleaded that there was nothing to tell, eventually he admitted that he hadn't gone directly to the livery, but had met a friend at The Swan. Jed walked behind the cowering man and seizing his neck, began to choke him, demanding the name of his friend. Suddenly the unfortunate Jenkins went limp and with a curse, Jed felt for his pulse. There was none.

Cursing his heavy-handedness and realising that the other servants may have seen him going down to the cellar, he took two bottle of wine from the wine cellar. Leaving the body where it was he went upstairs. Shouting abuse at the servants and waving the bottles, he sent them all to bed. It was not the first time he'd done this and the bottles would convince them he was having a drinking session.

When the house was quiet, he went down to the cellar and began to search Jenkins. Removing all his belongings, he stripped him and then noticed the ring on his finger. Ripping it off, he saw it was made from copper with an engraving on it. Scoffing in disdain, he threw it into the corner with the rest of the clothes. Having disposed of the naked body down the chute into the river, he made a bundle of the clothes and sent them down too. It escaped his notice that the copper ring rolled into the shadows.

The following morning he sent the above-stairs servants away on various errands, much to their relief. When they had all left, he went to search Jenkins' small bedroom. Going through his meagre belongings, he found two gold royals hidden in his clean clothes. Now where would a poor servant like Jenkins get two gold royals?

Jenkins had blurted out about meeting a friend at The Swan. Perhaps there was more to this meeting than friendship. His suspicions were aroused. He would go and check it out, but first he must explain the missing Jenkins. To this end, he went into every servant's room, scattering things about to make it look as though they'd been searched. When the servants returned, he called them all together in the hall.

Lining them up, he brandished the two gold royals. Telling them that the money had been stolen from the study, he said he had searched all of their rooms. He'd found the royals in Jenkins room. On his return he'd been questioned and admitted the theft. Dismissed without a reference, he'd been thrown out of the house immediately with his meagre belongings. He warned them all that on no account was Jenkins to be admitted to the house under any pretext.

Stalking up and down the line of servants, he warned them what they could expect if there was any more thieving. They could rest assured it would be more than a dismissal next time. By the time he'd finished, the staff were thoroughly cowed and he sent them about their business convinced that they believed the story.

That evening he strolled into The Swan and ordering a tankard of ale, sat down at one of the tables. When the man brought it to him, he asked if he was the landlord. 'I am indeed and what can I do for you, sir. We don't often get gents like you in here.'

Jed smiled. 'I believe one of my servants was here two days ago meeting a friend.'

The landlord was wary. 'We get a lot of servants in here what did he look like?'

Jed described him carefully, looking intently at the landlord for any signs he knew something. He need not have bothered. The landlord was too experienced to give anything away. Since this approach was getting nowhere, Jed offered the landlord a half-royal.

He pushed the money back across the table. 'I'm afraid I can't help you, sir. I can't say I recognise the description and I won't take your money under false pretences.'

'Can't, or won't?' said Jed aggressively, getting to his feet. 'Perhaps you need a bit of persuasion?'

'Now then, sir, there's no need for any unpleasantness,' said the landlord, nodding his head.

Jed was about to step forward and grab him when he felt the prick of a knife in his back. He had not noticed the two ruffians who had crept up silently to stand behind him. His arms were pinioned and the knife pushed harder into his back, piercing his doublet and drawing blood.

'I think you're in the wrong place, sir,' said the landlord evenly, with no vestige of a smile. 'We have a bit of a rough and ready crowd here, sir. They don't take kindly to strangers asking questions. I haven't seen your man and I suggest you go back to where you belong. You might find yourself in serious trouble if you come in here again asking questions and throwing your weight about.'

Jed could see from the gleam in the landlord's eye that he was used to violence and if he wasn't careful, he would find himself in the alley with more than just a prick from a knife to show for it. With as much dignity as he could muster, he pulled his arms free and walked out without a backward glance. The two men taking their lead from the landlord let him go.

Once outside, Jed let out the breath he'd been holding. He realised that he'd been lucky to get out without injury. It was obviously a rough neighbourhood and The Swan a haunt of all sorts of criminals. He should have kept his temper and not tried to bully the landlord. That was a mistake. To survive in such a tough area the landlord was probably a criminal himself.

Whether Jenkins had met a friend there or not, he was probably up to no good and passing information to robbers about the Count. That would explain the money. Having convinced himself that this was the most likely explanation, Jed set off back to the house. He would report it to the Count when he returned. For now, he would tell the servants to be on their guard, but he wouldn't lose any sleep over it.

Later that evening, when Quiff made his usual visit to The Swan, the landlord told him about Jed's visit. 'Recognised 'im straight away from your description, I did: nasty piece of work, that one.' He sniffed. 'A bully and used to getting his own way, I'd say. Asked me about that Jenkins lad: offered me money 'e did.' He sniffed derisively. ''Alf a' bleedin Royal. And then he threatens me when that got him no joy.' He gave a snorting laugh. 'Take more than 'im to put the scares on me. I don't do business with the likes of 'im. My two lads saw 'im off with 'is tail between his legs. I doubt 'e'll be back.'

Slipping the landlord a couple of gold royals for his troubles, Quiff told him to keep his eye open in case Jed or anyone else kept watch on the place.

'Don't you worry, we're used to people asking questions and trying to find people. You can rest easy, me and my lads will keep our eyes peeled.'

When Quiff informed Jacob about the incident he was very worried. 'See if any of the other apprentices can find out what has happened to Jenkins. But tell them to be very discreet and not to go to the house. They may be able to bump into to one of the servants and ask about him. Casually of course: we don't want Jed to know anyone is asking questions. Do you have anything else to tell me, Quiff?'

'No, Master Jacob, but I have a bad feeling about this. I can't get it out of my mind that something has happened to Jenkins. You can rest assured I'll tell all the others in the Ring to be extremely cautious and to keep well clear of this Jed Sutton.'

Jacob agreed wholeheartedly and made a vow that if his worst fears proved to be true, he would see Jed Sutton got his true deserts.

Chapter Twenty-Three
London, April, 1571

Jacob regarded the heavily-sealed letter lying on his desk with some trepidation. He knew at once from the seals of the Council of Ten and the office of the Avogadors, that it was an official letter from the Venetian judiciary, probably the result of his appeal. He'd hoped to hear from Maria or his father first, but official letters tended to be delivered a lot quicker.

With a sigh, he picked up the letter. Carefully breaking the seals, he unfolded it. As soon as he read the first few words, he let out the breath he'd been holding and gave a gasp of relief. The sentence had been quashed and the court awarded him ten thousand ducats from Adrian's estate and five thousand from Pietro Ragazoni in reparation. Elation flooded through him: it was complete exoneration.

Revelling in the moment, he nevertheless realised the debt of thanks he owed Maria, their fathers and all the other people who had supported his case and worked so hard to clear him. Reading the document again, and savouring every word, he came to the last paragraph. He'd missed this before. He gasped. What was this? The Council informed him, that although they understood his reasons for faking his death and living in London, they could not agree to him continuing to make glass at the Crouched Friars. Therefore, he must desist from glassmaking in London and return to Venice as soon as his affairs were in order, or be charged with treason.

To say this had never occurred to him was untrue, but Jacob had concentrated on the thought of being cleared. Now he must face the consequences. He wanted to return to Venice to see Maria. There was the matter of the baby and who was the father. He needed to find out why she'd not written to him and why he'd been named a Ragazoni. But he'd become settled in London. No more than settled, I feel I'm needed and I belong here.

Just then, Mistris Simpkin came in with a letter that had just been delivered. She was very flustered. When Jacob enquired if she was unwell, she hurriedly explained. 'Oh no, sir, I'm quite all right. It's just that I'm all of a flutter. I'm not used to taking messages from the Queen.'

The letter was indeed from the Queen. Thanking Mistris Simpkin, he went into his office and opened it. The Queen instructed him to attend her at Greenwich Palace at three o'clock, as she had a commission she wished to discuss with him. She indicated that he should ask for Lord Burghley who would bring him to meet her.

Glancing at the clock, he saw that it was already after two. Realising he would have to leave very soon if he was to be on time, he dashed to his room to change and then hurried down to the river and hired a boat to take him to Greenwich, promising an extra royal if they got him there by three o'clock. The boatmen certainly earned the royal and Jacob was shown in to see Lord Burghley with five minutes to spare.

'Sit down, Master Bell you look a little flustered. I'm sorry that we could not give you more warning, but the Queen will not be available for several days after this and she is keen to resolve this matter.'

His tone was friendly and Jacob sat down feeling quite relieved. It couldn't be so bad if Burghley was being friendly. Once he was settled, Burghley looked at him shrewdly. 'Do I get the impression you were feeling a little apprehensive about this meeting?'

Jacob nodded. 'A little, but mostly I'm curious. It's not every day you get a summons from a Queen.'

'It can be a rather overrated honour, when you're one of her ministers,' said Burghley, with feeling. 'Her majesty can be very forceful at times. However, in this instance, there is nothing for you to be worried about. Let me explain. I believe that your present problems with Venice and our own requirements have a lot of common ground and we may find it mutually beneficial to combine the two.'

He smiled at Jacob's puzzled expression. 'I apologise for my oblique approach. I have been too long in diplomatic circles where it is unknown for anyone to come straight to the point. In your case, I will try to make an exception.'

'I wish you would, my Lord, since I have absolutely no idea what you mean.'

Burghley nodded. 'I thought so. Correct me if I am wrong, but I believe you have received a letter from the courts in Venice.'

Jacob shook his head resignedly. 'Is there nothing that escapes your attention. Yes, I did, and I have received a full pardon.'

'You don't seem as pleased by that as I would have thought,' said Burghley, with a puzzled look.

'I'm pleased about the pardon and the award of damages, but they've warned me that unless I give up glassmaking in England and return to Venice, I will be guilty of treason.'

'Ah!' said Burghley. 'I rather feared that might happen. Have you had time to consider it yet?'

'Hardly, since I only received the letter less than two hours ago.'

'Bear with me a moment,' said Burghley. 'I have an idea that might be a solution for both of us.'

Jacob waited patiently as Burghley left the room. He'd been gone for about twenty minutes and Jacob was getting rather impatient to know what was happening, when Burghley came to the door and beckoned Jacob to follow him.

'We are going to see her majesty,' he informed him. I have put a suggestion to her and she wishes to discuss it with you.'

The meeting was not in a reception room as Jacob had expected, but in the Queen's sumptuous private sitting room. When Jacob bowed, the Queen held out her hand to him. 'Sit down Jacob Bell and I will explain what this is about.' She made herself comfortable, then continued. 'You know that Venice does not have an ambassador to England, merely an envoy at present. Are you au fait with the reasons for this?'

'I believe I am, your majesty. Venice has for many years remained neutral in the disputes between England and Spain. It might not go down too well with both the French and the Spanish if Venice resumed full diplomatic relations with England.'

'Exactly so,' agreed the Queen, 'but since England has supported their cause consistently since I became Queen, there have been discussions, but in private. We have today received a request from the Signory to reopen discussions. We have been trying to decide who to send. A short while ago, Lord Burghley made a suggestion which I found most intriguing. That is why I now formally offer you the post of Special Envoy to the Doge so you can explain our wishes in this matter.'

Lost for words, Jacob just stared in amazement. Eventually he stuttered, 'Why me?'

'Because, Jacob Bell, your efforts on my behalf have been well beyond the call of duty and you have proved to be a resourceful and trustworthy ally.' She smiled warmly. 'You have earned much goodwill from my Lord Burghley and Sir Francis Walsingham who have been strong supporters of your cause. Our good Admiral John Hawkins is no less an advocate on your behalf. In short, Jacob Bell, we believe you are the right man for this task and are uniquely qualified to carry it out.'

Burghley took up the point. 'This is a mission of great delicacy. Both countries are anxious to further diplomatic co-operation, but are constrained by our relative positions with France and Spain.'

He leaned forward and regarded Jacob with a warm expression. 'You would not be suspected of passing diplomatic messages to the Doge. You would be returning to Venice as ordered, to bargain for your independence and to discuss trade in glass with Venice. Nobody will suspect you are acting in an official capacity for England.'

He stood up and made a final plea. 'Take up the offer of naturalisation and go to Venice as Glassmaker to the Queen, with the full power to control the import of glass for twenty-one years, given in the Letters Patent. They can either make a deal with you, or lose all of their glass trade to England.

'As the Queen's Special Envoy, you will have diplomatic status and as a naturalised subject, you are no longer subject to the laws of Venice. In short, to achieve their goals with England and retain their trade in glass, the Signory of Venice must bargain with you and you will be holding most of the cards.'

'A solution worthy of my good ghost, don't you think, Master Bell?' The scheme obviously delighted her. A master at playing off opposing factions herself, she recognised talent in others.

Jacob had listened with mounting admiration for Burghley's acute mind and strategic knowledge. It was a brilliant plan. The Signory, consisting of the Doge and his Councillors, held the key to solving his problems. They were also pragmatic when the lifeblood of Venice was threatened. Their very survival depended on trade. They were not self-sufficient in food and needed to earn currency to buy it. Trade with England was important and they would not jeopardise it to punish an errant glassmaker. Particularly one who was in a position to increase their trade!

All he had to do was to give up being a Venetian! But he wasn't sure that was what he wanted. In any case, it was a decision he couldn't make on his own, there were a number of people who had to be consulted. And there was the problem of Maria and her baby.

Recognising Jacob's dilemma, Burghley addressed the Queen. 'Your majesty, I fear we have presented Master Bell with a proposal that will require some thought. I beg to suggest that we give him some time to consider. It cannot be an easy decision to turn your back on the country of your birth.'

'Indeed not, my Lord Burghley,' said the Queen, 'but I pledge that he will not be the loser for doing so. We will give him until Easter day to make up his mind. It cannot be longer for both our sakes. Venice will expect him to wind up his affairs quickly and from us, the prompt opening of discussions.'

Jacob was grateful for their consideration. There was much to put in the balance. One thing he knew from bitter experience, the Venetian authorities would not countenance a long-delayed return. Take too long and they would soon resort to ways of forcing him back - or something infinitely worse.

Chapter Twenty-Four
London and Venice, April/June, 1571

During the course of the following day, Jacob tried his best to clarify certain aspects of the law relating to naturalisation. Early in the morning he paid a visit to Thomas Pepper, his lawyer. Thomas quickly confirmed that as an English subject the Venetian court would have no power in law to compel Jacob to return to Venice. Whether they could exert other types of pressure was another matter!

In view of his official position as Glassmaker to the Queen, the Letters Patent conferred on him complete control of the glass trade in England. This was further enhanced with his role as a senior partner in the Glass-Sellers Association. In short, he was in a position to stop Venetian glassmakers from carrying out any trade with England as Burghley had suggested.

Having clarified the legal position, Jacob sought out Roberto. Jacob valued his ability to see a problem in simple terms. He had a talent for getting right to the heart of a matter. On this occasion however, he was less than decisive. He confided in Jacob, that since his marriage to Elizabeth Isham, he had been considering whether to stay permanently in England, or return to Venice. So far, he had not made up his mind.

As he remarked to Jacob, 'It is not an easy decision, but at present, I have a few more reasons for staying here than you. My wife and child are here and although they would go to Venice if I asked, it would not be what they wanted most. You must weigh up what is important to you. I cannot advise you, other than that I believe you will regret making a decision before you have clarified the situation with Maria.'

This was a conclusion that Jacob had also reached. Thomas Pepper had offered one piece of advice, which had given him some hope. The immunity of a Special Envoy would prevent the courts of Venice from detaining him. The holder of Special Envoy status meant that he was de facto an Englishman. He did not need to be naturalised. The Signory would not wish to exacerbate relations with England by detaining their envoy.

That helped a lot to clarify his thoughts. He would accept the commission from the Queen and go to Venice as her Special Envoy, but he would not take up the offer of naturalisation, for now. Roberto was absolutely right, he must see Maria first and talk it over with her. Until that was settled, he could not commit himself to staying in England for good.

He wasted no time in informing Burghley of his decision. Two days later, he had an audience with the Queen and she presented him with his credentials and the letters she wished to be passed to the Signory. 'When you see the Doge, it is my wish that you tell him that we have great respect for Venice. We will continue to give her our support whenever we can; whatever the Signory decide about resuming full relations with England. I also want you to pass on a warning.' She leaned forward almost conspiratorially. 'Our information is, that while the Spanish are sending assistance to the Mediterranean to fight the Ottoman fleet, they are pursuing their own agenda. They want to limit the expansion of the Ottoman Empire, but they will not be at all concerned if the power of the Venetians in the area is weakened. Assuming the Christian fleet are able to defeat the Ottoman fleet, which is far from certain, Spain will refuse to assist in liberating Cyprus.'

'Forgive me, your majesty,' said a puzzled Jacob, 'but if you have such a good regard for Venice, why aren't the English ships involved. They would make a huge difference.'

The Queen gave a rueful smile. 'I would like nothing better, but because of my excommunication and the involvement of the Papal ships, we cannot be involved.'

She stood up indicating that the interview was over, but before she left, she gave Jacob one final message. 'Please make sure the Doge understands that the Papal Bull is the only reason I have not despatched vessels to his aid. God speed, Jacob Bell, may you have fair winds and return to us at the earliest opportunity to report your discussions. As for the other matter, I am sure the Doge will be swayed by your arguments.'

Following this audience, Jacob went to see Lord Burghley. He thanked him again for the advice in handling his meeting with the Signory. 'I have not ruled out your offer of naturalisation, my lord,' he informed him. 'Before I can be sure it is the right decision, I must discuss it with Lady Maria. She has been extremely ill following the birth of her son. Once I know the position in Venice, I can make a better judgement.'

'At least you have not turned it down completely. I confess I would have been most disappointed if you had.' He handed Jacob a carefully bound package. 'He majesty asked me to arrange for this to be made for your ship. Don't open it now, but use it at the appropriate time. When you see it you will understand.' As he led Jacob to the door, he told him there was something on another matter he should know. 'The man Baillie has been arrested on his arrival at Dover. A large portmanteau of prohibited books has been seized along with a packet of letters for the Bishop of Ross. These are being sent to London to Lord Cobham, Warden of the Cinque Ports. I plan to examine Baillie in a few days time, after I have read the letters. In the meantime, I wish you God speed, good sailing and a successful conclusion to your meetings with the Signory in Venice.'

Jacob spent the next three days in frenzied activity making all the necessary arrangements for his departure. Roberto of course was all for going with him, but Jacob explained that he needed him at the Crouched Friars. 'I am giving you full powers of attorney to act on my behalf both at the Crouched Friars and the Glass-Sellers. When you attend the meeting at the Glass-Sellers, I have arranged for Thomas Pepper to accompany you. He will ensure that they carry out my wishes through your voting power.

Roberto was touched by Jacob's confidence in him, but very upset that he could not go with him to see his mother. In the end, he accepted Jacob's wishes.

'As you said to me recently, Roberto,' said Jacob, 'your family commitments keep you here in England. I on the other hand have no such commitments and the woman I love is in Venice.' He put an arm round Roberto's shoulder. 'You may have started out as my apprentice, but you have become my closest friend. I trust you with everything I have and it is a great comfort to know that the Crouched Friars is in good hands while I am away.'

The following morning Jacob set off for Plymouth. On his arrival, he went straight to the Hawkins shipyard to meet the Admiral. The Crystal had arrived two days before and the

Admiral informed him that Captain Roberts was re provisioning the ship for the long journey to Venice.

While they were waiting for the Captain who had been summoned to the office, Jacob and the Admiral talked about the possibility of meeting Ottoman or pirate galleys. 'Do not be afraid for the ship, there is no galley afloat that can best her, not even the mighty galleasses of Venice. The Crystal will out-sail them and out-gun them with no difficulty.'

He then went on to tell him that Captain Roberts had been drilling the gun crews all the way to Antwerp and back. 'I do believe that you will have as fine a gun deck as any ship in the Navy.'

Jacob was pleased to hear it for he had been longing to put the ship to the test. He had even contemplated a little piracy of his own, but reluctantly he put it on one side in view of the Queen's commission. There would be other opportunities.

Once on board, he opened the package presented to him by Burghley. To his amazement it was his own pennant. The note inside from Burghley explained. The pennant incorporated the crusader cross of the Crouched Friars and his own arms. The Queen had instructed the College of Heralds to produce them for him to signify his position as Glassmaker to the Queen. He would be able to use the arms on any livery he used in the future. He was to fly the pennant whenever he came into port, or made contact with the Queen's ships.

They left on the next tide and made good time to the Straits of Gibraltar. The winds in the Bay of Biscay were almost gale force, but fortunately in a favourable direction. The ship handled very well and Jacob congratulated Captain Roberts on his handling of her.

'We had a few difficulties at first,' said Captain Roberts proudly. 'She was a little bow heavy, but by adjusting the ballast, we quickly cured that and now she is an absolute delight. She performs better than any ship I've ever sailed.'

Passing through the Straits they headed directly for Messina, their first port of call. Everything had gone well up to now and as they tied up at the quayside in the port, Jacob felt mildly disappointed.

Captain Roberts did not agree when Jacob said as much to him. 'It's better not to wish for a more exciting life. Fate has a habit of taking you at your word. An old Chinese curse says "may you live in interesting times" and I'm sure they don't mean it to be good times.'

As soon as they had taken on water and other provisions, they set sail through the Straits of Messina and entered the Adriatic. The journey to Venice was uneventful although they did meet with an Ottoman galley. Much to Jacob's disgust, as soon as it got a good look at The Crystal, it kept well away. They had no stomach for a fight with the wind against them.

When they entered the Venetian lagoon, Jacob stood on the quarterdeck looking at the familiar scene as it unfolded in front of him. Despite the intense hurt of his betrayal and ignominious departure, he felt a thrill as the familiar skyline came in to view. A pilot met them as they moved slowly down the main channel towards the Isla San Giorgio Maggiore and directed them to a secure anchorage under the guns of the Arsenal.

Captain Roberts looked up at the imposing structure and remarked that they must think that The Crystal was about to launch an invasion. Jacob explained that only the main channels were deep water and the deep-water quays were in constant use. All ships had to wait until there was a place available. Sometimes this could take days, as ships containing foods had priority.

While they waited for the port authorities, Jacob hired a passing gondolier to take a message to his father. Less than an hour later, he returned with both his father and Senator Morisini.

The reunion in Jacob's cabin was very emotional with both men embracing him warmly. They swept aside Jacob's apologies for keeping them in the dark about his reported death. 'Don't worry about it Giam, Lunardo has explained everything,' said his father happily. 'It's just very good to see you looking so well. And with a very fine ship too.'

How strange it was to be called Giam once more thought Jacob. He had got used to being Jacob Bell. Once things had settled down a little Jacob explained his mission. He had no hesitation in explaining his role as Special Envoy to Queen Elizabeth. If he couldn't trust them after all they'd done for him during his original trial and at his appeal, whom could he trust?

Ricardo told him that Maria and the baby were now well and went on at length about the boy. Eduardo too was fulsome in his praise for Maria and the way she had handled the trial and her illness.

They then bombarded him with questions until Jacob was forced to call a halt. 'Forgive me for cutting you short, but there is a pressing matter for which I must ask Ricardo for his help. Please sit down while I explain.' Once they were settled, he continued. 'From the list that Lord Burghley provided me of the Signory, the name Ricardo Morisini was very familiar. It would seem I'm not the only one who moves in exalted circles.'

'I sometimes wonder what happened to the rebel,' said Ricardo, with a chuckle. 'I never thought in my wildest dreams that I would become a pillar of the establishment.'

'A very influential one too,' said Eduardo.

Ricardo looked at Jacob shrewdly. 'I assume that you were not just paying a compliment and that there was a serious point.'

'I'm afraid so,' said Jacob. 'I really need you to contact the Signory and advise them that I come as Special Envoy with messages from England. You will of course, be aware of the reasons for this. I hope to use my return as ordered by the courts as a cover for being here. To clarify my own legal position in Venice, I wish to meet the Signory to discuss trade with England in my role as Glassmaker to the Queen.'

'I understand,' said Ricardo, standing up. 'I will go at once to the Palazzo Ducale. I can see no reason why we cannot combine the two meetings. It will make it easier to keep the discussions with England a secret.'

Jacob also stood up. 'Before you go, there is another matter which needs your help. I will explain after I show you something down below.'

When they saw the gun deck, they were both amazed. Eduardo was the first to speak. 'I had no idea this was such a powerful vessel. The guns on the main deck were impressive. But this…'

'It is indeed a most powerful vessel,' agreed Ricardo, 'and I venture to suggest that few vessels would be its equal in an engagement.' He was silent for a moment. 'Am I right in thinking you wish to keep this armament secret and you want my help to keep it so?'

'You are correct, Ricardo. We have gone to some lengths to conceal the lower guns and I would much prefer that they remain a secret. I was hoping that you could have a word with the port authorities and advise them to wait for instructions from the Doge before they come aboard.'

Ricardo took a little time to answer as he weighed up the situation. On the one hand, as it belonged to the Special Envoy, the vessel would have diplomatic status. In that case, it would not be inspected. However, because of the need for secrecy about this mission, they had to keep up the pretence that Jacob was here at the request of the judiciary. 'I will have a word with the port authorities,' he said at last. 'My status as an Avogador may well be enough to persuade them to wait for instructions from the Signory.'

'Perhaps this might help,' said Jacob, offering a bottle of French brandy.'

Ricardo smiled. 'I'm sure it will. Now I will take my leave. As soon as I have spoken to the port officials, I will contact the Doge and inform him of your arrival. I am sure he will instruct that the vessel is not to be boarded.'

'Thank you, Ricardo; once more I am in your debt. I hope to visit you soon and I want to see Maria as soon as possible. Will you tell her that as soon as the matter with the Doge is settled I will visit.'

Ricardo promised he would do so and then took his leave. For the next hour or more, Jacob and his father talked about everything that had happened since he left Venice. Jacob was pleased that his father at least had no qualms about the way that Maria had behaved. In fact, Eduardo went to some lengths to defend her decision, when Jacob said how difficult he found it to have his son brought up as a Ragazoni.

'I don't think you realise what it would have meant if she had named the boy for you,' Eduardo said firmly. 'Both Ricardo and I discussed it with her. We were both agreed that it was the only thing to do. Not only would naming the boy for you have offended the moral code of Venice, but also she would have been open to a criminal charge. In short, she would have been a pariah in society, could have been sent to prison and lost the baby to Pietro Ragazoni.' His father put a reassuring hand on Jacob's arm. 'I know it's hard for you. Adrian Ragazoni hurt you both so badly. Even his own father was a victim. I doubt you've heard, but Pietro Ragazoni died over two months ago, shortly after the trial.'

Try as he might, Jacob couldn't feel sorry for him. Pietro's prejudices during the trial fed on Adrian's lies and he was happy to accept them as truth. Even when he knew they were lies, he said nothing. His only thought was to protect his son and himself from the consequences of those lies and prevent them from becoming public knowledge.

He shook his head sadly. 'I can't find it in me to forgive the Ragazonis, but it's not my place to judge them; that's for a higher authority.' Both he and Eduardo made the sign of the cross. 'I hope I can persuade the Signory to grant my request. It's time this whole sorry episode was laid to rest.'

'Amen to that,' said Ricardo and embraced him warmly. 'I know you can't do anything until you hear from the Signory. Come and see me as soon as you're free.'

Jacob promised he would and after his father had left, he stood by the rail looking towards the Palazzo Ducale, wondering what the next few days had in store.

Chapter Twenty-Five
Venice, June, 1571

The news from her father that Jacob was in Venice, came as a shock. Maria had dreamed about this day for months: while she'd been lying ill and every time she looked at their son. Now he was here all her terrible fears were resurrected. Perhaps he no longer loved her? Maybe there was someone else? What if he really hated her for naming the baby a Ragazoni?

She bitterly regretted the decision she'd made on her return to Venice. Both her father and Eduardo had told her that it was the only thing to do, but looking back, she was not so sure. Her motives had been revenge on the Ragazonis, but in truth the idea of being a pariah in Venice, or worse, was not attractive either.

Why hadn't she written to Jacob straight away to explain? Racked with indecision, she had tried time after time to reach a decision until finally her illness intervened. By the time she'd recovered it was too late. Every night she prayed for his forgiveness, but what if he couldn't? Before she could go any further down this maudlin path, Anna, her companion, came into the room. 'Maria, Julia would like you to come to the nursery if you can spare a moment, she has something to show you.'

When she entered the nursery, Julia was playing with Rico, who was crawling on the floor as usual. As Maria watched, Rico reached up and pulled himself to his feet, holding on to the chair. Keeping a firm grip, he walked round to Julia, chortling in delight.

Maria clapped her hands with joy; this was his first attempt at walking. 'How long has he been doing this?' she asked Julia excitedly.

'Just since this morning, Lady Maria,' she said, her face wreathed in smiles. 'It'll not be long before he's walking, he's a very sturdy child.'

Maria laughed, her troubles forgotten in the joy of her son. 'There'll be no stopping him then. He moves like the wind when he's crawling and there's no telling what he'll be up to when he walks properly!'

Before she could say more, a footman came in and informed her that her father had called to see her with a guest. Intrigued,

Maria hurried down to the salon and as she entered, her father came over and greeted her warmly. Holding her at arm's length, he studied her face. 'You look a little flushed, Maria. I hope you are not overdoing it?'

'Not at all, father. Please don't fuss.'

Just then, she noticed the man waiting quietly to one side. Turning to her father, she looked quizzically at him. 'I see you have brought a guest, aren't you going to introduce us?'

'I didn't think he would require any introduction, surely you recognise him?'

Maria looked carefully at the immaculate, tall, dark-haired man. He looked vaguely familiar, but Maria couldn't think who he was.

He moved towards her and bowed, while Maria curtsied in reply. With a broad smile, he regarded her kindly. 'I know we haven't met since the night you got engaged to Giacomo Bellini,' he said playfully, 'but I'd hoped you might have remembered your last dancing partner. Ah well, so much for my ego!'

Maria couldn't help but laugh at his droll expression of mock sadness. 'Paolo Valier,' she said, as enlightenment dawned. 'I haven't seen you since that night. I believe you left Venice to live in Verona?' She did not miss the sad expression that crossed his face, quickly replaced with a neutral smile.

'That's true. Unfortunately, my father caught a fever while he was visiting the family estates in Verona and I had to go to look after the business.'

'How is he now,' enquired Maria.

'Sadly he died about five months ago and I've just returned to Venice to see my sister, who married the eldest son of Hector Quirini. My mother died some years ago and my sister is my only remaining close family.'

'I'm so sorry, Paolo,' said Maria. 'I've been very ill myself and have completely lost touch with events.'

They made polite conversation for a little while then Ricardo asked Maria if she had received his message.

'I did, father and if Paolo will excuse me saying so, I'd hoped it was Giam who was with you.'

'Giacomo, here in Venice?' said Paolo in amazement. 'I heard he was killed in a galley fight.'

Ricardo smiled. 'It's a long story, but yes, Giacomo is here in Venice at last and cleared of any wrongdoing.'

Paolo still looked puzzled. 'I've been out of touch with events here myself, since I remained in Verona to sort out the problems with the estates and business. I only returned to Venice two days ago.' He regarded Maria with a strange expression. 'I'm a bit confused about what happened. I heard you married Adrian Ragazoni and went with him to England as his wife, but he died there, I believe.'

Maria couldn't help the expression of pain that crossed her face as memories of Adrian's cruelty came flooding back. Even now, he had the power to hurt her from beyond the grave.

Realising the situation, Ricardo quickly changed the subject. 'Yes indeed, Giacomo has returned to Venice at the invitation of the Capituary. He is Glassmaker to the English Queen now.'

Maria brightened up at Giam's name. 'When will he be coming here, father?'

'There are a few bits of protocol to sort out, but there will be a meeting with the Capituary to sort out the problems in two days' time. Until then he must stay on board his ship.'

'It seems I have come at an inopportune time,' said Paolo, with a tinge of regret in his voice. 'When I met your father in the Palazzo Ducale, I inveigled him into allowing me to accompany him to see you. I'd hoped you might be persuaded to accompany me to the Casino tomorrow night. There is an excellent programme that evening.'

Maria hesitated. It was so long since she'd gone out, but Giam was here, even though he couldn't leave his ship. But then again, Paolo was rather handsome! What if Jacob really didn't want anything to do with her and the child?

Maria shook her head in dismay. She was behaving like a silly adolescent girl! This will not do she told herself. Turning to Paolo, she thanked him for the invitation, but said she must decline. 'I must be here in case Giam is able to visit,' she said, and her tone gave Paolo little hope that she would reconsider.

He bowed. 'It was rather presumptuous of me to come at such short notice,' he said sadly, 'but my sister thought it might be good for both of us to get out.'

So, he's been discussing me with his sister thought Maria, taking great satisfaction in the thought that she could still be attractive enough for an old suitor to be interested. She smiled prettily at Paolo and extended her hand. 'I'm sorry that I can't accept your invitation.' She paused for a moment to consider, then added, 'On this occasion.'

Ricardo gave her a sharp look, but said nothing.

Paolo seemed to take heart from her comment and bowed over her hand. 'I do hope that we might get together on another occasion. It would give me the greatest pleasure to renew our acquaintance again.' He turned and acknowledged Ricardo, thanking him for his forbearance and took his leave.

Maria braced herself for some comment from her father, but apart from a rather puzzled look, he said nothing further on the matter of Paolo, simply enquiring about his grandson.

Maria was grateful she did not have to explain. She was not at all sure why she'd said it herself. Linking arms with him, she took him up to see Rico and they spent a lovely half hour watching his antics. After he'd left, Maria sat in her room and thought about why she'd encouraged Paolo. It wasn't as though they had ever been lovers, or even close friends. He'd simply been one of a number of young men, including Adrian Ragazoni, vying for her attention and once she'd met Giam, she had eyes for him only.

However, the past five years had wrought a lot of change, not only in Maria, but in Giam as well. When she had first known him, he was different to all the other men she knew. He was kind, intelligent and had a strong sense of purpose. Not bad looking and a good lover too, she thought and flushed as she felt the warmth flooding into her groin: just thinking about making love to Giam filled her with desire.

Calming herself, she came to a decision. If Giam couldn't come to her, she would go to him. Excitedly, she called Anna and began to change into her latest day clothes. All thoughts of Paolo forgotten, she hurriedly dressed. She must look her best if she was going to see Giam.

When Anna arrived, Maria sent her to organise a gondola, requesting her to find Angelo Robusti if he was available. A short while later Angelo helped her into the gondola. She ducked down under the covered awning, sat down and drew the curtains closed.

'Where do you wish to go today, my lady?'

When Maria explained about Giam's ship, he became very animated. 'I know the very one, my lady, I passed it only this morning. It's at anchor about fifty metres from the main battery of the Armoury.' He steered out into the main canal and then chattered away about the ship. 'I saw the English flag, but I never thought that Master Bellini was on board. And you say it's his ship? He seems to have done very well, a ship like that must have cost at least a hundred thousand ducats.'

Maria let his chatter flow over her as she looked anxiously for her first glimpse of the ship. She might even see Giam on deck. It was not to be however and she had to be patient as they came alongside the ship. Angelo shouted up to the sailor on watch and he disappeared. There was a delay of some minutes and then a stunned Jacob came to the rail and looked down at the beautifully dressed woman looking up with an expression of supreme happiness as she saw his face.

The look of delight when Jacob saw her chased away most of Maria's doubts. The hug he gave her when they were in his cabin confirmed the feeling. She clung to him with fierce determination as if she was determined that he would never leave her. They kissed until Maria nearly swooned and she was forced to break away and sit down.

Jacob regarded her anxiously. 'Are you ill?' he said, his voice betraying his anxiety.

Maria's flashing smile and the shake of her head reassured him. She held out her hands and Jacob took them and sat beside her. 'It's just been too much,' said Maria weakly. 'I wanted to see you so much, but when we kissed, it was as if all of my strength went into the kiss and my legs turned too jelly.'

Jacob threw his head backed and laughed in relief. 'I know what you mean, mine felt rather shaky too. It was such a surprise to see you after so long. I'd been building up our first meeting in my mind. I haven't the words to describe the feeling as I looked down from the rail and saw your lovely face. When your legs went funny, I thought you might still be ill and coming here was too much for you.'

He kissed her again and Maria felt the heat rising in her body and she pushed herself against Jacob's hard body, gasping as he reacted strongly to her. Jacob pulled up her skirts and she opened her legs wide, pulling him down to her. Pulling her drawers to one side he entered her at once, thrusting forcibly, her body shaking as she matched his frantic rhythm. They reached a searing climax almost simultaneously and lay shuddering, clutched tightly together, until at last they lay quietly, bodies moulded together.

Jacob nuzzled her neck and then leaning on one elbow studied her carefully. 'You are still as beautiful as I remember you, but you're much slimmer. It must have been a terrible illness.'

Maria laughed. 'You should have seen me straight afterwards, I looked like a bag of bones. I had no appetite at all. Anna has been feeding me up since I could eat again.'

She snuggled close to him and regarded him with a loving expression. 'I've waited so long for this moment, Giam. I couldn't bear the thought of you being so near and yet not see you, even though it was only for a few days. I hope sneaking on board like this won't cause you any problems.'

Jacob shook his head. 'I can't see why it should, but I'm pleased that you took the initiative. I can't leave the ship until I hear from the Signory.'

'My father said as much,' said Maria, looking slightly puzzled, 'but I don't understand why you can't come ashore. After all, you have been cleared of any wrongdoing and you have returned as the Giunta instructed.'

'It's a little more complicated than that, Maria.' Jacob paused as he decided how much he could tell her. He decided it was better to tell her it all. 'Please understand that what I am about to tell you is very confidential. It is important for Venice and England that the true reason for my visit remains a secret. I am here not just to sort out my own problems, but as Special Envoy for Queen Elizabeth of England.'

Maria was only a little surprised, since she was aware of the high regard that Giam enjoyed from the Queen and Lord Burghley. She saw immediately that Giam's return was a perfect cover for the talks. It was unlikely that anyone would guess without receiving information.

Jacob went on to explain the full story behind his mission and his own personal ambitions for the talks about his status as a glassmaker in England.

'I want you of all people to understand my reasons and my hopes,' he said, looking earnestly into her eyes. 'In England, I have standing, respect and thanks to the Queen's generosity and the Crouched Friars Glass-works, I am becoming a rich man. Venice has treated me badly, thanks to the Ragazonis whose lies orchestrated it all, but I was sacrificed in the name of politics. I have thought long and hard about this and I believe my future probably lies in England. However, I could never commit myself to it without discussing it with you. Do you love me enough to leave Venice and make a new life with me in England?'

Chapter Twenty-Six
Venice, June, 1571

Before Maria could even begin to think about this stunning request, there was an urgent knocking on the door. It was Captain Roberts. Maria got to her feet immediately, hurriedly adjusting her clothing. Having straightened his own clothes, Jacob called for the Captain to enter.

'I'm sorry to interrupt, Jacob, but a representative of the Doge is asking to come on board. I've told him I will send down the bosun's chair as soon as I have informed you.'

Maria looked worried. 'It might be a good idea if I was not seen here,' she said. 'You know what they're like about protocol. People might jump to the wrong conclusion.' She blushed furiously when Jacob raised an eyebrow and gave her a look that spoke volumes.

'I don't see that it matters too much, but I suppose you are here without a chaperone.'

Captain Roberts interrupted. 'It might be better if Lady Maria was not seen. If she will come with me, the gondolier is still on the seaward side of the ship, and we can get her down to it before the other party comes aboard. Once they're in your cabin, we will signal the gondola to leave. That way, it is highly unlikely that anyone will see her.'

'Good thinking, Captain Roberts, but will you give us a moment.' When the captain had left, he took Maria in his arms and kissed her, and after a short pause she responded eagerly. Stepping back and holding her at arms length, he looked deep into her eyes. 'I know I have presented you with a difficult request. Please give it some careful thought and we will discuss it properly as soon as I am free from seeing the Doge and his Councillors.' He kissed her hand. 'Until then, my love, take care of yourself.' Opening the door, he watched as Captain Roberts led Maria to the ship's side and sitting in the bosun's chair she was lowered down to the waiting gondola. As soon as she was clear, the chair was swung round to the other side of the ship ready for the official party to come on board.

The following morning, promptly at ten o'clock, Jacob was shown into the sumptuous reception room in the Palazzo Ducale. He had arrived an hour earlier and had passed to the Doge the letters that the Queen had sent. As he looked around the assembled Councillors of the Signory, he was pleased to see at least one friendly face. He bowed in recognition of Ricardo Morisini and sat down in the indicated chair.

The Doge spoke briefly to the Advocate General who then stood up and addressed Jacob. 'Master Bellini, the Signory are pleased to welcome you back to Venice and to officially inform you that your status as a nobleman of Venice has been re-recorded in the Libro d'Oro. On behalf of the Signory, we ask you to accept our apology that the courts failed to prevent the terrible injustice that you suffered. It is of little consolation to you, but I can assure you that your case has brought about a significant change in the law that will prevent any individual from perverting the system as Ragazoni did in your case.'

He paused a moment to see how this was being received. When Jacob indicated his acceptance of the statement, he continued. 'We also wish to welcome you in your role as Special Envoy to Queen Elizabeth of England. We recognise the signal honour that the Queen has bestowed on Venice by appointing one of our noblemen as her spokesman and invite you to speak to the Signory.'

Jacob stood up and bowed. 'Serenissimo, I bring you greetings from her most august majesty Queen Elizabeth of England. She has asked me to tell you that she has always held the Venetian Republic in the highest regard both before and since she became Queen of England. She has supported your ambitions wherever possible and maintained a fierce stance against those in France and Spain who would seek to reduce the power of Venice in the Mediterranean.' He noted with satisfaction the many murmurs of approval from the Signory.

'Her majesty has set out her thoughts in the letters you have seen, but has instructed me to further tell you that she will continue on her chosen path, even if the Signory feel that the time is not yet ripe to send a full ambassador to England. She is fully aware that La Serenissima is treading a path between the twin ambitions of France and Spain that make it difficult to openly support England. However, there is one more point her majesty wanted you to know. England has a most efficient spy system and they have discovered information about the Holy League fleet you should know. You may already have discovered this yourself, but we will see. There have been talks between Spain and the Pope about the situation in the Eastern Mediterranean. Whilst Spain is eager to limit the expansion of the Ottoman Empire, even if the Holy League win a battle against the Ottoman fleet, they will not support Venice in regaining Cyprus.' All around the room the Councillors were looking surprised and shocked. It was obvious that the revelation on Spain's intentions were unknown to them.

Having made the points suggested by the Queen, Jacob sat down.

The Doge rose to his feet. 'Master Bellini, we find ourselves in some difficulty at the gracious support, information and promises from the Queen. As you say, we tread a difficult path. I want you to assure the Queen that we appreciate the support of England and will do our best to modify and stifle the worst intentions of our allies. As to their intentions towards us, we will have to wait and see. Nevertheless, with your warning in mind, we will make plans to take account of this possibility.'

He turned to his Councillors. 'I believe from our discussions we can agree on a favourable reply to her majesty, but regret for the moment, we cannot openly establish full ambassadorial relations with England. We will however send an envoy who, whilst not carrying the credentials of an ambassador, will nonetheless have full ambassadorial powers. Regrettably, those will not be public knowledge to preserve our position with France and Spain.'

He turned to Jacob again. 'Your own position puts us in some difficulty. It is very beneficial for Venice to have a nobleman who has the ear of the Queen of England, but our laws make it necessary to recall you to Venice and for you to cease glassmaking in London.'

Since Jacob was obviously anxious to take up this point, the Doge indicated he should speak and sat down.

Taking a short while to compose his thoughts, Jacob stood up.

'Serenissimo, I thank you for your kind words and I will certainly convey them to her majesty. As for myself, I believe that Venice is in a position to have the best of both worlds, with a little goodwill on her part.'

Looking around Jacob could see that the Councillors were certainly looking interested in this thought. 'There are aspects of my title of Glassmaker to Queen Elizabeth that may have escaped your attention. The title also includes Letters Patent from the Crown that convey on me the right to control the making and import of glass to England for twenty-one years.'

This announcement provoked a round of whispered comments between the Councillors, and the Attorney General leaned over and made a comment to the Doge.

When the hubbub had died down, Jacob continued. 'In addition to the legal rights that I enjoy, I am also the major shareholder in the Glass-Sellers Association as well as the Crouched Friars Glass-works. Since the Crouched Friars is the only glass-works in England producing drinking glasses of quality and the Glass-Sellers control the importation of all of the glass to England, I effectively control all of the glass trade in England.'

He paused again to allow this point to sink in. 'What I propose is this. Allow me to continue to make glass at the Crouched Friars and I will ensure that, as far as the market will bear it, the Glass-Sellers will increase trade with Venice year on year. I will also use my position of trust with the Queen of England and Lord Burghley to further the interests of Venice. As long as they do not jeopardise the interests of England.' With that, he sat down to another buzz of conversation.

The Doge spoke to the Advocate General and he asked Jacob to withdraw to the anteroom while the Signory considered his offer. Having volunteered to answer any questions they might have, Jacob was escorted into the other room.

Over the next half-hour, Ricardo was despatched to ask Jacob questions. Another Councillor accompanied him on each occasion. He still managed a wink at Jacob as he went back to give Jacob's replies.

Encouraged by this Jacob waited patiently. He was beginning to feel rather hungry by now having only had a light meal before he left the ship. Just as he was about to ask for some refreshments, he was summoned back into the reception room. Taking his seat again, Jacob waited as the Doge gave some instructions to one of the waiting servants who scurried off. The Doge, with a final word to the Advocate General, stood up and addressed Jacob. 'We have listened to your offer with interest and I am pleased to say that, subject to certain safeguards as to trade with England, the Signory is unanimous in accepting it. The Advocate General will issue a proclamation freeing you from the restraint of the glassmaking laws since, in view of your special position, you will be able to increase trade between Venice and England.'

Jacob was ecstatic, he had won, but the Doge was continuing, so he forced himself to listen carefully. 'This proclamation will not of course mention your Special Envoy status for obvious reasons. We are grateful that you have shown you retain strong ties with Venice, despite the grave injustice that you suffered. We are also mindful that it is well past noon and we invite you to celebrate this agreement with a small banquet that has been prepared.'

Once the meal was over, Ricardo came over to speak to him. 'I can see that you have learned a lot more than glassmaking skills since you have been in England. Your strategy was brilliant.'

Jacob smiled. 'I will pass on your praise to Lord Burghley, for in truth, the main thrust of the strategy was his. I only added a few touches from my knowledge of Venice.'

'I will bear that in mind,' said Ricardo, 'if I am ever in negotiations with Lord Burghley. He is without doubt a master of stratagem.'

'There is no doubt about that,' said Jacob. 'I have seen him operate at close quarters and he is brilliant. And devoted to the Queen even though she tries him sorely at times.'

Ricardo glanced across at the Doge. 'I suppose that is true of all heads of state, but a Queen, believing in the divine right to rule, has less restrictions than a Doge.'

Over the next hour Jacob was introduced to most of the Councillors and received many offers of contact for trade and many invitations. Before he left, the Attorney General also informed him that he had issued instructions to the port authority that his ship was to be allocated a berth at the main quayside for the rest of his stay and that the usual inspections must be waived by decree of the Doge. Jacob himself was free to come and go as he pleased, with his full rights as a noble restored.

The Attorney General then informed him that there was to be a State banquet in his honour in three days' time at the Palazzo Ducale. Doge Moncenigo had agreed with his councillors, that Jacob should be granted the accolade of Honorary Councillor, in recognition of his services to Venetian trade and would announce this at the banquet.

It was an honour that Jacob had not expected and asked the Attorney General to pass on his thanks. Shortly afterwards he made his way back to the ship. He was met on the quay by the bosun who informed him that the ship was now berthed some little way down the quayside. 'The port authorities are falling over themselves to be helpful,' the bosun said, unable to keep the surprise out of his voice. 'Apparently, they have strict instructions to give the highest priority to the replenishing of our supplies.'

Knowing how slow the port authorities could be at times, even Jacob was surprised at the speed with which matters had proceeded. Going on board, he asked Captain Roberts if he could spare him a little while from his duties. When the captain arrived, he explained that he had successfully concluded his negotiations with the Signory and was not only free to go as he pleased, but that they were making him an Honorary Councillor.

'You certainly were successful, Jacob. You must be very pleased.'

'I certainly am. I am free to return to England and to continue with the business.'

'That is good news. Are you planning to buy any glass while you're here?'

'I am indeed,' said Jacob. 'Will you make sure that the hold webbing is in place, ready to accept the special crates.'

'Certainly, but we may have to re trim the ship once I see how much glass there is.'

'Possibly quite a lot: I propose to purchase as much as I can from the glassmakers' stock. They will have little time to make any as I plan to set off for England in about ten days or so.'

'Will you be going ashore now?'

'I certainly intend to do so, but there is the small problem of where to stay. Lady Maria is using the house I had before, so it will probably be with my father on Murano.'

That is indeed how it turned out and later that afternoon Jacob was sitting with his father in the shady upper terrace overlooking the main canal. He was pleased to see that his father was looking well. Despite all the stress and worry of the past few years, he looked remarkably fit.

Eduardo listened with pride as Jacob explained all that had happened since the trial. When Jacob had finished his story, Eduardo was full of admiration for the way his son had handled all the trials and tribulations.

'I am so proud of you, Giam,' he said, his voice heavy with emotion. 'As a father, you worry that your children have not had time to learn how to cope with life by the time they leave you.' He sighed expressively. 'You were taken away from me by the machinations of a truly evil man: despite my best endeavours to prevent it. You have had to face death on more than one occasion and struggle to make your way, against all the odds, in an alien country. Despite all of this, you have not only survived, but also come through it all with good cheer, new friends and the high regard of people of influence in England and Venice.' He embraced Jacob and patted him enthusiastically on the back. 'You have fulfilled all and more that your mother would have expected of you. Not only that, but you have reflected the greatest credit on your glassmaking roots.'

Jacob returned the embrace and his voice shook with emotion when he spoke. 'Thank you, father. You have made me so happy that I have not thrown away the heritage of my mother.' He moved back a little. 'I think we'd better change the subject before I burst into tears. Tell me more about Maria and the baby. I'm anxious to see them both, but the details are rather sketchy.

'I told you that Pietro Ragazoni died shortly after the trial.'

Jacob nodded.

'Pietro also changed his will and left everything to his grandson. This means that until he is of age, Maria controls the whole of the Ragazoni estates. Ironic isn't it?'

Jacob had certainly not expected this development and listened with mounting worry as his father continued. This was going to affect his plans more than a little.

'Maria has been forced to take over the running of the Ragazoni estates,' continued Ricardo, stressing the forced. 'Fortunately, there are some good men handling the day-to-day affairs, but it has involved a lot of hard work. She told me she was looking at ways to sell some of the assets to make sure you received some benefit.'

'I'm glad you explained, father,' said Jacob, not at all sure he wanted anything from them. 'I must admit that I found it difficult to accept the news that Maria's baby was named for Ragazoni.'

Ricardo regarded him fondly. 'It was only to be expected in the circumstances. Forced to live in an alien country, unable to speak, or communicate with the people you love, it was inevitable that you would be concerned. Maria's illness complicated everything.'

Jacob was silent. He wished now that he had not told Maria of his plans to stay in England. It was going to make his next meeting with her very uncomfortable.

Chapter Twenty-Seven
Tower of London, April, 1571

Charles Baillie sat shivering, hunched against the wall of his dark cell. Not from the darkness: nor from the damp and cold that ate into his bones. It was the echoes from scream after scream reverberating down the corridor from the torture room that terrified him. His jailers had dragged him into the room only that morning and shown him the rack again. They told him they would be putting him on it later that day. It was to be the third time. Later that morning they'd taken his cell mate William Herle and promised Charles that he would soon be next.

Suddenly the screams stopped and Baillie gave a sigh of relief. A short while later, two gaolers appeared dragging a sobbing Herle between them, his feet dragging along the floor. Throwing him unceremoniously into the cell they looked at the cowering figure against the wall.

'It looks to me as though Master Herle is somewhat taller than he used to be,' said one to the other, with a nasty smirk.

'I do believe you're right,' said the other. 'They never believe me when I tell them to save themselves the trouble and speak now. They all tell you in the end.' He gave an evil grin. 'Shall we do the same for Master Baillie now?'

'Nah!' said the first man, 'it's thirsty work turning those wheels, especially with all those red-hot irons heating in the brazier. We'll go and have a bit of a rest and a cool drink before we start on him. We don't want Lord Burghley thinking we're giving him an easy time and he particularly wants him to talk today.'

When they'd left, Charles helped the groaning man to sit up against the wall. 'I'm sorry, Charles,' William said in distress, 'I tried not to tell them, but in the end I gave them what they wanted.' He sobbed and hung his head. 'I've told them all I know about the Earl of Northumberland. I didn't want to betray my cousin, Lady Northumberland, but this was the third time they've put me to the rack and I couldn't stand it any more,' he cried, curling up into a foetal ball.

Charles shivered. 'I'm sure I don't know how I'm going to keep quiet about the letters I brought into England. I've sent letters to the Bishop of Ross and to others, but I haven't any money left to bribe the servants again and they've done nothing to help me.'

'My cousin is just the same,' said Herle, unwinding a little and raising his head. 'All they want to do is save their own skins. This Bishop will be just the same. They love the rich life too much. You don't see any thin Bishops, now do you?' He sniffed expressively sitting up against the wall next to Baillie, wincing as he stretched his legs. 'You were foolish to send letters though. They'll know all about what's in them. Burghley, damn his eternal soul, will have read them already.'

'He won't be able to,' said Charles, his voice full of bravado. 'They're all in cipher and even that damned Phelippes won't be able to crack it.'

William sat with his head down, hands over his knees rocking back and forth until suddenly he sat up. 'What are we going to do, Charles,' he said brokenly. 'I don't want to die in this awful place.' He began sobbing quietly to himself.

Charles tried to comfort him and after a while William fell into a fitful sleep. Left to his thoughts, Charles contemplated his own future. He was dreading the thought of being tortured again. Question followed questions: they never stopped asking questions. And every time he refused to answer, another turn of the wheel, until he thought his arms would be torn from his body. He closed his eyes wearily. How did I ever get involved in this mess? It's not as though I'm part of a plot or something, I'm just a messenger.

Just then, there was the sound of keys jangling and heavy footsteps in the corridor. 'Blessed Virgin Mary protect me,' he whispered in terror as the door opened. But they hadn't come for him this time. Seizing William by the arms making him scream in pain they dragged him away without a word. The door slammed shut and Charles was left to his terrified thoughts again.

He would have been amazed if he had seen what happened after the trio had left the dungeons. Releasing William, the two gaolers helped him to his feet, grinned and then went off to their rest. William made his way up to Burghley's room where the Queen's Secretary was waiting.

'Will you take some wine, William? You must be dry after all your histrionics. He lifted a handsome wine flagon, made in the Murano fashion.

'Indeed I would, my lord. Spying is very thirsty work.'

Burghley watched as he took a long draught. 'And how is your friend Baillie today. I confess I grow impatient for some results.'

William shrugged. 'It is difficult to be sure, but I have the feeling he is ready to crack.' He regarded Burghley with an odd expression in his eyes, a mixture of sympathy, pride and grim amusement.

'I confess to feeling sorry for the fellow. He is only a messenger after all, but he told me about the letters he has sent to the Bishop of Ross and others asking their help to secure his relief. They are not all they seem. Apparently he has added a secret message using a cipher.' He saw the flicker of interest in Burghley's eyes and shook his head. 'Before you ask, I was unable to get the cipher from him, but now you know about it, I am sure you will be all the more determined to crack him.' His words were delivered in a slightly facetious tone, but he felt a pang of conscience that he was likely to cause Charles more pain with this disclosure.

Charles meanwhile was sleeping fitfully, tormented by dreams of torture and pain. So much so, that when they came for him late in the afternoon it was almost a relief: until they took him into the torture cell.

Without a word, they stretched him on the rack and tightened the wheels until all of the slack was gone. Charles knew very well that the next turn would hurt a lot. He turned his head to see what they were doing, but the were simply standing there waiting. What now he thought? What are they going to do to me this time?

After what seemed to be hours, but in reality was only about a half hour, the door opened. The jailers bowed respectfully as Lord Burghley with his man Phelippes came in. With a nod to the jailers, Burghley stood impassively looking down at him as they tightened and tightened the wheel and the terrible pain began. He screamed for them to stop and Burghley made a gesture to the gaolers. They slackened the wheels again and the pain subsided and became almost bearable.

Burghley looked at Charles with something akin to compassion in his eyes. 'I will spare you any more pain if you tell me about the letters you sent to the Bishop of Ross.' He indicated his companion. 'Phelippes tells me they were in cipher. I will stop the torture and give you twenty gold royals if you will explain the cipher to him.'

Charles began to cry and the iron resolve that had sustained him so far cracked into a thousand pieces. 'I will tell you what you want to know. Just don't torture me any more.'

By the fifteenth of the month, using the alphabet that Baillie had given them, Phelippes had translated all of the letters that Baillie had sent to the Bishop of Ross. Two things were obvious to Burghley: the Bishop of Ross was up to his eyes in a plot and there had been a number of letters brought over from France in the box of books intercepted at Dover.

Baillie's letters named Ridolfi, the Earl of Westmorland, the Countess of Northumberland, and several others. But what had happened to the packet of letters? The men, who had intercepted Baillie at Dover, were trustworthy and had simply delivered everything to Lord Cobham, Warden of the Cinque Ports. It was inconceivable that Baillie would lie in his letter to the Bishop of Ross, so Burghley was sure that the letters must have been amongst the packages. 'Perhaps Lord Cobham can shed some light on this matter? He delivered the books to me, but why would he remove the letters?' he thought.

When Lord Cobham arrived, he was shown into Burghley's study straight away. Burghley asked him to sit down without his usual friendly greeting and Cobham was uncomfortable and wary.

'I will not beat about the bush, my friend, I have loved you too well and too long for that,' said Burghley sadly. 'I know about the letters.' In the silence that followed this revelation, Burghley could see from Cobham's expression that he understood exactly what he meant. He looked him squarely in the eyes watching for his reaction, forcing himself to be civil.

'Did you remove them?'

Cobham's face fell and dull colour suffused his pallid cheeks. 'It was my brother,' he said reluctantly at last, 'and I regretted the decision as soon as he'd left with them.' Fidgeting with his belt buckle, Cobham continued, his voice full of shame, 'I should have realised, but it was too late. He was ever the renegade.'

He regarded Burghley sadly. 'It is no excuse, but he persuaded me that the letters put Norfolk and the Northern Earls at risk. I'm related by marriage, you know. He told me it was in the best interests of England that the letters did not become common knowledge.'

He shook his head sadly. 'Having thought about it after he'd gone, I realised that they may have been plotting against the Queen and I should have informed you straight away.' He held his hands forward, palms upwards and looked at Burghley helplessly. 'But he's my brother. I love him too well and I just couldn't bring myself to inform against him. I know I was wrong, and worse, I betrayed my friendship to you.' Regarding Burghley with tears in his eyes, he pleaded with him. 'Please tell me it is not too late to make amends.'

Burghley came round and put a reassuring arm on his shaking shoulders. 'Don't worry, my old friend. All will be well, if you tell me the whole story.'

Once the floodgates of confession had opened, Cobham held nothing back. He told Burghley everything he knew from start to finish. One thing Burghley found particularly interesting was the fact that the Bishop of Ross had been the recipient of the letters and had prepared forged letters in case Burghley found out about them.

Turning to his friend, his voice full of sadness, Burghley chided him. 'What you did was indefensible. Nevertheless, your brother put you in an impossible position. You have freely confessed your part in this wretched business and from what you have told me I believe it is likely that no harm has been done.'

Burghley tugged distractedly at his moustache. 'In fact, you have given me some leads that could help me to conclude this matter. You must remain in my house until it is ended. You may not bring your entourage and you will stay out of sight. Do you agree to these terms?'

Cobham did not hesitate. 'Yes I do.'

Burghley took him by the arm and they walked towards the

door. Now that the interrogation was over he was more relaxed and his eyes were gentle and kind. 'I have loved you well, my friend of many years, therefore I am sorry at your offence. I am sure from what you have told me, that the loss of the letters will not prove to be too much of an obstacle in my investigation.'

Cobham visibly relaxed for the first time since he had entered the room. 'Looking back, I can see that my actions were in grave error,' he said sadly. 'I can only apologise and hope that I have not lost your friendship as well as my honour.'

Burghley too was more relaxed now he knew the full story. Deliberately lightening his voice, he gave a warm smile. 'Have no fear on that score, my friend. I will not throw you to the wolves. Since you have agreed to my terms without any attempt to modify them, for friendship's sake, I will suppress your part in the loss of these letters.'

Chapter Twenty-Eight
Tower of London, May, 1571

Despite the excellence of the furniture and hangings in the room, the austerity of the stone walls and the arrow slits told a different story. This was a castle and not the stately house that would have been expected as the location of such splendid furnishings. The flickering candles on the desk sent their shadows dancing around the walls, but the sombrely dressed, grey-haired man sitting at the desk reading a letter was oblivious to them.

Putting the letter down, Burghley sighed deeply and picking up a quill, carefully sharpened the end with the quill knife from the box. Reading the last paragraph with brows furrowed in concentration, he composed his thoughts before finishing his report to the Queen. There was a Privy Council meeting the following morning and the Queen always had full details of any information that Burghley intended to impart. Not only that, but she expected to know what emphasis and import he intended to place on the facts.

He began to write. "Further examination of Baillie revealed that among the letters he had written were three special ones in cipher. The first to Ross, the others without address, but carrying Arabic numerals, the second to 40, the third to 30. Baillie at first denied any knowledge of their contents, but later admitted that 30 and 40 were two English noblemen, although he was unaware of their identities. The letters concerned a plot inviting the King of Spain, the Duke of Alva, and the Pope, "to cause war in this realm and to have a force of strangers enter into the realm".

"I have no doubt that your majesty and the Privy Council will wish to pursue the accuracy of this information. To my mind, Baillie has told us all he knows. Nor have I any doubt that the Bishop of Ross knows the truth of it and should be charged therewith and forced to disclose what he knows."

The decision of the Queen in consultation with the Privy Council was that four members of the Council should visit Ross immediately and charge him with knowledge of the Baillie letters. Accordingly, the following day, the Earl of Essex, Sir Ralph

Sadler, Sir Walter Mildmay and Burghley attended Ross in his London house.

They were informed that Ross had taken to his bed ill, but undaunted they proceeded to question him. After many vehement denials of most things plainly confessed by Baillie, when he realised that his letters to Baillie both at Marshalsea prison and the Tower were discovered, he confessed that Baillie brought letters from Ridolfi. Of the two letters, the one addressed to 30 referred to the Spanish Ambassador and one to 40 referred to the Queen of Scots.

Burghley was delighted that he now had a connection to the Queen of Scots. As he told Elizabeth the following day, 'I have no doubt that Mary Stuart is well aware of this developing situation. However, the Earl of Shrewsbury is guarding her closely and I am surprised that nothing of this letter has been discovered. Either she has a new means of smuggling letters, or she has not received it.'

Elizabeth shrugged. 'No matter, the truth of it will out soon enough. What of De Spes?'

'He too denies receiving any letter since Ridolfi left England. Neither Sir Walter nor Sir Thomas Smith could persuade him to say otherwise.' Burghley could see the Queen was getting impatient at the lack of progress. 'I believe we must put more pressure on the Bishop of Ross,' he said, 'but we will need to tread carefully or we will have the church up in arms.'

Elizabeth scoffed contemptuously. 'They will not dare to cross swords with me over Ross. Put some pressure on him, sick or not. I want the truth of this matter. I like not the reports coming from Walsingham in Paris. There have been some terrible speeches against me both there and out of Flanders.'

She gave Burghley one of her imperious glares. 'Ross will be very sick by the time I have done with him if he continues to defy me over the Scots Queen. Tell him so from me.' She gave a bleak smile. 'Better still, root him out of his comfortable house and send him to the Bishop of Ely's house in Holborn.'

A thought struck her and her mood turned to amusement.

'Make sure that Ely does not make him too comfortable. A little austerity may concentrate his memory. Especially if he's reminded that the Tower is even less welcoming.'

Burghley tried hard to suppress a smile. 'I'm sure you're right your majesty. It will be as you command.'

Later that day, after prolonged questioning and many denials, he admitted that the letters and alphabet of the cipher had not been sent to the Queen of Scots, but destroyed. Despite his protests and threats of church reprisals, Ross was hauled unceremoniously out of bed and transported to Holborn.

Over the next few weeks despite much frenzied debate in both Parliament and Council, no further progress was made in determining the identity of the two Lords mentioned only as thirty and forty in the Ridolfi letters. As time passed, Burghley became more frustrated.

Late in May, on an impulse, he decided to take the long way to his room in the Tower via Harte Street. As he passed the home of Jacob Bell, he regretted, not for the first time, that he was absent in Venice. I'm sure the Ring would have found something out, he mused, but I can't wait until he comes back.

Reaching the corner of Harte Street and Woodroffe Lane, he was about to turn towards the Tower, when a thought struck him. Without further ado, he hurried along to the Crouched Friars Glass-works.

Roberto ushered his unexpected visitor into the office and offered him some refreshment. Burghley refused the offered wine, but accepted a glass of fresh orange juice with gratitude. Sipping it slowly, he studied Roberto. That worthy returned his gaze without the slightest sign of embarrassment or apprehension and Burghley was impressed by his easy manner. It reminded him so much of Jacob Bell.

The similarity was not accidental. Roberto had modelled his behaviour and attitudes on his former Master and now friend and partner. Thanks to his own hard work and Jacob's patronage, he was now a successful and prosperous partner and happily married man. Noticing that Burghley had put down his glass Roberto enquired how he could be of service.

'I will come straight to the point, Master Rosso,' said Burghley. 'It occurred to me that to cover for his absence, Jacob Bell would probably have made arrangements for the Ring to continue about its business of supplying information.'

Roberto nodded. 'You are correct, my lord.' He volunteered no further information, but waited for Burghley to explain the purpose of his visit.

Burghley's lips twitched. Jacob had trained Roberto well. He must treat Roberto with the same respect he reserved for Jacob.

'In that case, I assume you may be aware of the matter that is taking up so much time in Parliament and the Council.'

'Oh, the two mysterious numbers in the Ridolfi letters.' Roberto's face maintained its composure. 'I'm sorry, my lord, but I'm afraid I've no news on that score. Do you want me to make it a priority?'

'Most certainly. My present sources have dried up and I fear that without some sort of breakthrough, it will founder without trace.'

Roberto's face became animated. 'I regret I'm unable to supply that, my lord, but the reports that Quiff is receiving leave us in no doubt that the Duke of Norfolk is plotting with the Queen of Scots. You could do worse than concentrate your efforts on the Duke.' He gave a grimace. 'Unfortunately, despite our best endeavours, we have been unable to prove it to our satisfaction, let alone yours.'

Burghley rubbed his fingers against his chin considering his next move. 'What if I apply some pressure on the Duke?' he said, gesturing with a pointed finger, emphasizing his point. 'It might precipitate him into actions that would give your people the chance to find the proof.'

'So long as we don't put them in jeopardy. I have strict instructions from Jacob to keep them safe.'

Burghley was not sympathetic. 'This is a matter of national importance. Her majesty could be at risk.'

Roberto shook his head and his reply was not at all diplomatic.

'You care only to protect the Queen and your own position. The Ring put their lives on the line. Oh yes, I know they get paid, but most of them do it because they might be able to make a difference, not for money.'

With a deep sigh Burghley looked Roberto squarely in the eyes.

'I'm sorry, Roberto, I have played the statesman's role too long and forget the part played by ordinary people.' He gave a rueful smile. 'Except that those I call ordinary often go to extraordinary lengths to help. Without them this England would not be what it is.' He nodded gravely. 'My apologies, lad. I will leave you to what you do best and await any news with as much patience as I can muster.'

Roberto returned the gesture and escorted him to the entrance.

'Rest assured that we will do our best to find out what we can. Until then, fare you well, my lord.'

When Burghley reached his room in the Tower he spent the next hour going through the reports coming in from all the capitals of Europe. Several of them were reporting conversations among exiled Catholics. There was a common theme that confirmed the existence of a plot. In each case, the Catholics were expecting to return to England in the near future and that theirs would be the main religion of England following an invasion by the Duke of Alva supported by the Pope.

He spent the next hour composing a note to the Queen advising her of the gist of this information. He begged her to reconsider her avowed intention to carry on with her Progress, visiting many of her nobles along with her court. As they vied with each other to favour the Queen with ever more lavish receptions and entertainment, the Queen was vulnerable to an assassination attempt: especially as she had no intention of restricting her riding and hunting. Burghley had little hope that the Queen would heed his words of caution. Nevertheless, he felt honour bound to try.

The following day, he was summoned to the Palace of Placentia at Greenwich. The Queen made it plain, that assassination threat or not, she had no intention of cancelling the Progress to become virtually a prisoner in London. 'Fie on you, Burghley,' she said, but there was no anger in her voice. 'I know you mean well, but I will not shy away from my duty like a coward.' She smiled mischievously. 'Besides, my nobles assure me that this year they will surpass themselves with their entertainment. They must not be allowed to spend their money in vain.' Her smile became radiant as she thought about the festivities to come. She loved all the pageant, presents and above all the music and dancing.

As was her wont, her mood changed abruptly and she was all business. Calling to a lady-in-waiting she instructed her to inform the Lords Leicester and Essex to attend her immediately. When they arrived her ladies-in-waiting were giggling and whispering like silly schoolgirls and the Queen became annoyed. Turning to her chambermaid Agnes Sutton she instructed her in unequivocal terms. 'Take the ladies-in-waiting into the far room and see that none of them comes unless I call. While they are waiting, I suggest you instruct them in the way to behave before their Queen and senior nobles of the realm.' Agnes bowed and shooed the ladies into the other room. They departed with deep curtsies and frightened looks, well aware of the lengths to which the Queen could go if she was really angry.

Once they had gone, the Queen gave a sigh of relief. 'Thank goodness for that. Now mayhap we can get down to a serious discussion. Have we made any progress on finding out the identity of the two Lords referred to in the Ridolfi letters?' she demanded. 'What say you Robin?'

Leicester, sensing her mood, dispensed with his usual flattery. 'I have no definite proof, but I suspect that one of them is Norfolk and the other, either the Queen of Scots, or De Spes.' He looked across at Burghley. 'Have you received any more information from your spies?'

Burghley stroked his beard absent-mindedly. 'I have received much information, but precious little fact, I'm afraid. I have squeezed Charles Baillie dry and the Bishop of Ross has provided more: with the exception of that which we desire, namely the identities of the two Lords.'

'Who would be your most likely suspect?' said Elizabeth. She was obviously becoming irritated by the lack of progress.

'There is a considerable amount of circumstantial evidence that Norfolk is still in communication with Mary Stuart.' He shook his head sadly. 'I had high hopes that his stay in the Tower would have taught him the error of his ways, but he and his family were ever overly ambitious.' He glanced at the Queen to see how she was reacting to this statement, but her face remained neutral. 'I have kept him under close watch and I have strong suspicions that he is one of the two Lords. I ...'

Essex, who had been listening to the discussion with mounting impatience, interrupted him. 'Enough of this dissembling,' he said in exasperation. 'We are all agreed that Norfolk is one of the Lords. Why do we not throw him in the Tower again, search his home and put him to the question?'

Elizabeth gave a short barking laugh and the pearls at her ears danced as she shook her head. 'You were ever impetuous, Essex,' she said scornfully. 'That which you propose is a certain way of antagonizing the maximum number of Catholic families and many waverers to boot. I have been patiently building up goodwill for too long to jeopardize it by throwing the premier Catholic Duke into the Tower without certain proof of his treason.'

Burghley nodded in approval. 'I agree, your majesty, but I think we are agreed that there are sufficient doubts about Norfolk to warrant careful monitoring of his comings and goings.'

When the others signified their agreement, Elizabeth stood up.

'I too will keep my eye on Norfolk. I intend to visit him during my progress this year and I will take the opportunity to ask some searching questions.' The others exchanged glances. They all knew what a formidable and inexorable opponent she could be.

Elizabeth meanwhile was in full flow. 'He will earn my intense displeasure if I discover he is plotting to marry my cousin, Mary Stuart, and will quickly find himself in the Tower once more. Should he be involved, he will find it will be very much more difficult to get out than last time,' she concluded ominously.

Chapter Twenty-Nine
Venice, July, 1571

Despite Jacob's impatience to see Maria and the baby since moving into his father's house, nearly two weeks passed before he was able to visit her. Maria lived in the house formerly owned by Jacob opposite the glass-works in Murano. From time to time, she spent a few days in Venice at Pietro Ragazoni's large house. She had moved to Venice the day that Jacob joined his father, in order to deal with problems at the Ragazoni estates.

Looking around the atrium, Jacob noted the ostentatious decorations and many examples of Ragazoni family armour and military paraphernalia on the walls, continuing up the wide curving staircase to the upper floors. He was getting rather restless when he heard footsteps on the stairs. Looking up eagerly, he was disappointed to see it was the Sigisbei.

'My lady sends her apologies and asks that you be patient for a little while longer. Meanwhile, she has asked me to make you comfortable in the salon upstairs.'

When he had left, Jacob strolled around and looked at the rich silk hangings and paintings. His eyes were drawn a painting of a student and his tutor, by Giorgione. The tutor was holding a scroll on which was inscribed in Latin, "Talent has no worth unless accomplishment follows". Jacob smiled. He always tried to live his life according to this sentiment.

Before he could look at the other paintings, the door to the study opened and Maria emerged talking to a well-dressed man. By his servile manner, and clothes, Jacob assumed he was the Fattori of the estate.

Bowing low, the Fattori addressed Maria. 'I will see your instructions are carried out to the letter, Lady Ragazoni. I will return in a few days time to discuss the disposition of the Verona properties as soon as I receive an answer to your questions.' He bowed himself out with only a brief bow in Jacob's direction.

As soon as he'd gone, Maria hurried over and taking Jacob's hands in hers, held him at arms' length and studied him. 'You are looking better than when I saw you on your ship, Giam. I assume you are more rested now that you have accomplished your mission. How does it feel to be a pillar of the establishment: a full member of the Council no less? It's a well deserved honour.'

Jacob had been studying Maria carefully as she spoke. The piled up hair encrusted with seed pearls set off the beautiful banded white and yellow dress, with its pointed bodice and fan-like lace collar. The large matching pearls in the choker at her neck confirmed her wealth and status. Despite the slight pallor in her cheeks, she looked every inch the wealthy matriarch.

With a start he realised she was looking expectantly at him. Before he could speak, there was a discreet cough and turning round, he saw the Sigisbei.

'What is it now, Sigisbei,' said Maria. She was becoming very exasperated. 'I can't get a moment to myself. I told you I didn't want to be disturbed again.'

'My apologies, Lady Ragazoni,' he said, 'but the galleass and trading cogs have returned with the silks from Bursa. The overseers are awaiting your instructions for the distribution of the cargo and Captain Carreras is downstairs asking for an urgent word with you.'

'Captain Carreras!' exclaimed Jacob. 'Is that Lunardo Carreras?'

Maria sighed expressively and turned to Jacob. 'It is indeed. An invasion of Cyprus has been going on since last year and the Turkish invaders captured Nicosia. Famagusta has been under siege, but is still holding out.'

She frowned and rubbed her neck nervously. 'This trading voyage has been a huge gamble. Although the silk merchants wanted to do business with Venice, the Ottoman galleys have been a constant threat and many cogs have been intercepted. My father and I made a deal with the silk merchants for a rendezvous and despatched three cogs. We hired a fighting galley and persuaded the Doge to let us have a galleass as escort: at huge expense of course. It's a great relief if they've returned safely. I'm sorry, Giam,' she said apologetically, 'I must have a word with Lunardo. It won't take long, I promise.' She glared at the Sigisbei. 'Then there will be no further interruptions, will there, Sigisbei!' she said emphatically.

With a faint smile, the Sigisbei bowed himself out. Jacob

stood up. 'Don't worry about it, Maria. It's obviously a very busy time for you. Anyway, it will be good to see Lunardo if you don't mind me staying?'

Maria smiled gratefully. 'Of course I don't mind. It will be good for you to see Lunardo again. He's very much one of the senior captains in the fleet now.'

When Lunardo saw Jacob, his face lit up with pleasure and after a quick bow to Maria he seized Jacob in a bear-like hug, pounding him on the back as Jacob returned the compliment.

'I knew you'd do well in London, you old fox,' he said, with a grin that threatened to split his face in half. 'I saw your ship at the dock as we came in. Where on earth did you get her? She's an absolute beauty.'

Maria gave a loud cough, as the questions seemed to be getting out of hand and releasing Jacob, Lunardo bowed to Maria and offered his apologies for ignoring her.

'It's no matter, Lunardo, but I would be grateful for your report. Did you make the rendezvous and collect the silk?'

'We did indeed, Lady Maria and I'm happy to say we have brought it all to Venice without losing a bale.'

Maria crossed herself. 'Thank heaven for that. You have done well, Lunardo.'

'We have indeed, but it could have been very different. As the cogs were loading up, four Ottoman galleys attacked us. Fortunately, the galleass was in a good position to shield the cogs and after the first two engaged us, our fire-power destroyed one and left the other badly crippled. Before the others could board our war galley, we were able to turn our attention to them. We inflicted a lot of casualties with our swivel guns and they turned tail and ran for it.'

Maria and Jacob were fascinated by this account and Maria told Lunardo that he'd earned a large bonus for seeing them home safely. She excused herself for a moment and went into the study.

Lunardo took the opportunity to have a word with Jacob about his ship. 'I assume from the name 'The Crystal' that she is your ship, Giam.' When Jacob confirmed this he looked at him shrewdly. 'An interesting design: quite well armed on the deck, with bow and stern chasers.'

When Jacob simply confirmed this, keeping his face as blank as possible, Lunardo grinned. 'So are you going to tell me how many guns there are on the lower deck?'

Trying to remain casual, Jacob replied. 'What guns, The Crystal is only an armed merchant ship.'

Lunardo laughed. 'You were never very good at bluffing games, Giam. We passed close to your seaward side and I was examining the ship through my spyglass, when I noticed the hinges on the lower ports. They could only be gun ports.' He shook his head in mock sorrow. 'Assuming I'm right, I hope we never have to meet in battle. I suspect you carry far too much fire power for my galleass and with that low profile, you'll be a lot more manoeuvrable, even in the light Mediterranean winds.'

Jacob held up his hands. 'I should have known I couldn't deceive you. Why don't you come on board this evening and I'll show you around? In the meanwhile, I would take it as a huge favour if you said nothing to the authorities, or anyone else for that matter.'

Before Lunardo could reply, Maria came hurrying in from the study. 'I'm sorry to be so long, but I couldn't find the warehouse schedule for the Morisini warehouse. It was mixed up with some other papers. Anyway here it is.'

After a quick glance, Lunardo nodded and then took a list out of his doublet. He handed it to Maria who looked at it in surprise. 'What's this, Lunardo? It appears to be a bill of lading for a large number of extra bales of silk and spices. These aren't part of the agreed schedule.'

'That's correct, Lady Maria. The Bursa merchants brought them as insurance, in case the war with the Ottoman forces drags on and they are not able to ship any more goods to Venice. Kasim Bey asked me to give you this message.

'My lady, our thanks to you and your father, for risking so much to do business with Bursa when we are officially at war. We appreciate your trust in us and we can do no less. The bill of lading is for an extra quantity of silk and spices. We humbly request that you sell it on our behalf and put the money safely in Venice. When the war is over, Allah willing, we will reclaim it.' Lunardo paused. 'Kasim Bey then asked me to give you this personal message. "My partners and I applaud your business acumen in persuading your father in this venture and look forward to a long and mutually beneficial relationship. I, Kasim Bey, believe that you have demonstrated that you are truly your father's daughter."'

The flush of pleasure on Maria's face on hearing this accolade, made Jacob realise that the task of persuading her to come to London would be more difficult than he'd first thought.

Having delivered his message, Lunardo took his leave of them, promising to visit Jacob's ship later that evening. As soon as he'd gone Maria led Jacob to the settle again. She looked at him demurely, then with a twinkle in her eye said, 'Aren't you going to kiss me then?'

Jacob needed no further encouragement and kissed her soundly. After a short while Maria broke away and stood up, holding Jacob's hand. She led him to a flight of stairs and they went up to the roof.

Maria indicated the structure at the far end. It was made of wood with slatted bamboo sides that could be rolled up in very hot weather. There was a very large bed with large piles of cushions made up in the Arab style. Leading him to it, she sank down on to the cushions, drawing him down to her.

Although Jacob was in a highly aroused state, he curbed himself, stroking her body, kissing her deeply and slowly removing her clothes. By the time they were both naked, Maria was equally aroused and wrapping her legs around his waist, she drew him in, her whole body throbbing with desire. Even now Jacob controlled his actions and slowly but surely raised the tempo. Maria moved her body in matching rhythm, until finally, she cried out and Jacob too reached the final ecstatic climax.

They lay together with bodies entwined: Jacob stroking the silky skin of her back and buttocks while Maria nuzzled his neck whispering endearments. It was a long time before either moved and then detaching herself a little Maria propped herself up on one elbow and gazed at him adoringly. 'I have waited so long for that moment, Giam.' She smiled. 'I know we made love on your ship, but that was lust, while this was real loving.' She stroked his face gently. 'You were so patient and willing to make me feel as you were feeling. It was a very special moment which I shall always treasure.'

She sat up and Jacob raised himself so they were side by side. Regarding him with a very serious expression, Maria looked deep into his eyes. 'I wanted us to have this time to ourselves, but I think it is time I introduced you to our son.' Seeing the flicker of doubt that was quickly suppressed, she took his hand in hers, pressing it to her breast. 'I know you must have some doubts after all this time, Giam. Especially over the Ragazoni name and now the estates.' She frowned. 'Had it not been necessary to return to Venice to clear you, I would happily have stayed in London at your side. Once I was here, events took over and before I knew it, not only was Rico named a Ragazoni, but he was heir to the whole Ragazoni estate.'

Jacob wisely decided it was pointless opening the old wounds by telling Maria of his thoughts for the long months before he could come to Venice. Indeed, the discussion with his father had cleared away a lot of his former doubts and their lovemaking had removed the remainder. Rising to his feet, he helped Maria up. 'I think it would be a good idea to put on some clothes before we go downstairs,' he said, with a happy smile.

Jacob was entranced with the boy. He was even more so when Rico boldly left the safety of Julia's skirts and tottered over to him as he crouched down on his haunches. With a triumphant smile he reached his goal and seized Jacob's hand in a firm grasp, looking up into his face as though he recognised his father instantly. By the time Jacob retuned to his ship to meet Lunardo, he was full of pride in Rico, more than ever in love with Maria, but despondent about his chances of persuading Maria to come to England.

Chapter Thirty
Venice, July, 1571

Lunardo was amazed when Jacob showed him around the lower gun deck. 'I knew you had guns, but never such guns as these. My galleass, is one of the most powerful in the fleet, but it would be no match for The Crystal. You'd blow me out of the water with one broadside.'

'Lucky we're on the same side then,' said Jacob, with a beaming smile. 'However, I meant what I said earlier. Please do not report this to the authorities. This design is not the finished product, but is a trial of what Admiral Hawkins hopes will be a blueprint for the future of the English Navy.'

'With a fleet of ships like these, England will have one of the strongest navies in the world. Even the Spanish will not be able to defeat them.'

'They might if they get wind of what the Admiral is planning. There are people in the judiciary who are very much in favour of Spain and they would pass on this information if it becomes common knowledge in Council circles.'

Lunardo nodded. 'You're right about that, Giam.'

They had made there way back to the main deck as they talked and Jacob took Lunardo into his cabin for a drink. Sitting in the stern window, sipping a glass of wine, Lunardo pointed to the shrouded shapes of the two stern chasers, which had been rolled away to their storage positions. 'Long guns I suppose,' he said enviously, 'and big ones at that.'

'Big enough to sink an Ottoman galley,' said Jacob, with satisfaction. 'They would get a rude welcome if they tried to come round our stern.' He looked at Lunardo who was looking very serious. 'I think you had better tell me what's the matter,' he said.

'I was just thinking that as you are a Doge's Councillor now, I can trust you with some news.'

Jacob's curiosity was aroused. 'What sort of news?'

'I have received orders to rendezvous with Don Juan of Austria with my galleass and the final contingent of war and lantern galleys in the vicinity of the Gulf of Lepanto.'

He explained that there was a huge fleet of Christian galleys assembling at Lepanto. There would be galleys from Venice, Spain, Genoa, Savoy, the Papal ships and the Knights of St. John of Malta. The intention was to bring the Ottoman fleet under Müezzinzade Ali Pasha to battle as soon as possible. Venice was providing more than half of the ships and men in the hope that they could defeat the so far invincible Ali Pasha and raise the siege of Cyprus.

'I wish this ship was going with us,' said Lunardo intensely. 'The galleasses will be a prime force with their fire-power, but we've so few. Even one ship like this would make a huge difference. Do you think you could?'

Jacob was silent for quite some time as he considered Lunardo's request. As a Doge's Councillor, he certainly had the right, but what about Maria and his mission for the Queen?

'You don't know what you ask, Lunardo,' he said at last. 'It's not that I don't care about Venice, but there are so many other considerations.'

He paced around the cabin thinking furiously. It was very tempting to find out what the ship could do, but his men had not signed up for such a venture and he was not sure he could order them to go. After all, it wasn't their fight!

Lunardo looked at Jacob's worried face. 'I'm sorry, Giam,' he said contritely. 'I was carried away by the power of your ship. This is not really your fight, despite your new status. Your crew is English and your Queen may not be pleased if you get involved.' He put an arm round his shoulder. 'Not to mention the fact that you've only just returned to Maria, after all of the traumas you've both been through. It was wrong of me. Please forget I asked. It was just in the heat of the moment and shouldn't be taken seriously.'

But of course, he did! Long after Lunardo had left, Jacob sat in his cabin wondering what he should do, weighing up the various options. He decided it would be a good idea to talk to his father first, so he set off for Murano. When he arrived, he was surprised to see Ricardo Morisini.

When he had sat down, his father was the first to speak. 'I hope you understand our reasons, but we have been discussing the situation between yourself and Maria.'

Jacob was not sure what to make of this, so he simply said, 'Perhaps you'd better enlighten me.'

Eduardo looked across at Ricardo, who nodded his approval, so Eduardo began. 'Ricardo came to see me because he was worried about Maria. Apparently, you have asked her to go to live in England with you, when you return. Is that true?'

Jacob simply confirmed this, but made no further comment, waiting to see their reaction. He did not have long to wait.

'You must realise what you are asking Maria to give up. She is now an extremely rich and powerful woman.' He looked at Jacob for some signs of a reaction, but Jacob remained silent, his face neutral.

'I can't understand your reasoning,' said the puzzled Eduardo. 'You have many advantages to re-establishing yourself here in Venice, now you are free of the sentence against you. Both Ricardo and I would be happy to return all of the property and businesses you signed over to us at the time. What more could you want?' He looked at Jacob expectantly.

Jacob turned to Ricardo. 'Have you anything to add?'

'I don't think so, Giacomo. Your father has summed up our discussion very well.'

Jacob nodded and regarded them very seriously. 'I know you have the best of intentions, but you are looking at this from only one side, yours and Maria's. I understand why this should be so, but I would like you to hear my side.' When they both indicated their willingness, he continued. 'When I arrived here in Venice, I had three things on my mind. To see Maria and the boy, to carry out my mission for Queen Elizabeth and to clear the way for me to carry on making glass in England. I wanted to resume the life I have built up there.'

He shook his head and pursed his lips. 'When Maria visited me on my ship, I had severe doubts that she still loved me. Those were blown away by her visit. I was so jubilant at this that I asked her to share my new life in England, with no thought for the consequences of that request.' When they did not interrupt, he went on. 'Since that day, a number of events have opened my eyes to the reality of what I asked. In many ways, it would have been better if I had never asked it of her. However, that is not possible. What I must do, is to talk it out with Maria as soon as we can get a chance to sit down undisturbed.'

Ricardo was the first to speak. 'My apologies, Giacomo, we should have had more faith in your judgement. I can see how this came about and it is understandable. The main point is what do you intend to do now. Are you still set on going back to England?'

Jacob nodded. 'I must, Ricardo. Not just for myself, but also for Venice. You were privy to the discussions, so you know I must report to the Queen in person. It would be too dangerous to commit the report to writing. If it fell into the wrong hands it would do untold harm to Venice's relations with the other Catholic countries.'

'How long can you stay?

'About a week, or maybe a little longer.'

In all honesty, Jacob had not really worked out how long he would stay. When he set off, there were so many imponderables that he had not even tried to make an estimate. In the event, things had progressed far quicker than he had ever thought possible. Certainly, he had to make the rounds of the Murano glass-works, but that would only take a day or two. He was only going to take glass from stock, so he should have it all stowed away by the end of a week. That was not the deciding factor however. It was Maria, his son and their long-term future he was worried about.

Eduardo, guessing from Jacob's hesitation what was bothering him spoke up. 'What about your son? It must be hard to discover him and then have to think about leaving him so far behind.'

'Only if Maria decides to stay here, although from what I've seen and from what you've told me, that seems more than likely,' said Jacob sadly.

'There's only one thing you can do, Giacomo,' said Ricardo gently. 'You must speak to Maria, you'll be able to in the morning. She asked me to apologise for all the problems and she has arranged to spend whatever time you can spare tomorrow.'

'Where will she be?' said Jacob eagerly. 'I'm happy to go anywhere to meet her.'

'She'll be back at the house behind the glass-works tonight, so any time tomorrow will be fine.'

Ricardo took his leave and after a short discussion with his father, Jacob went up to his room. Tomorrow was going to be a very important day and he wanted to be sure he was well rested. His future happiness was at stake and Maria and Rico were part of it.

Maria was up early that morning and by eight o'clock she was sitting on the balcony outside the garden room enjoying the morning sunshine. She smiled at Anna as she came fussing around. 'Don't worry Anna, I'm perfectly all right.'

'You've been so busy since Senator Pietro Ragazoni died,' said Anna, smoothing the wrap around her shoulders. 'You've hardly had a minute to yourself.'

'I know, Anna. I tried so hard to have some time with Giacomo, but every time we tried to talk, something else came up. He was very patient, but I'm sure he wasn't pleased.' She settled herself comfortably in the chair, as Anna adjusted the cushions. 'I'm just going to take it easy until Giacomo comes.'

'Is there anything else I can get you?'

'Just make sure that when Giacomo arrives, no one is admitted; unless there's a real emergency. I don't want to see anyone at all until we've had a chance to talk.'

'I'll just get the fresh orange juice that Master Giacomo likes and then I'll guard the door. Don't worry, Maria, not a soul will get past me!'

When Jacob arrived, he sat down and sipped the offered orange juice. They sat in silence for a short time, both feeling reluctant to be the first to broach the topic on both of their minds. At last, Maria sat up. 'I'm sorry we haven't had chance to talk properly.'

Jacob smiled. 'As I recall it, we were otherwise occupied and by the time it came to talk, there wasn't enough time.'

Maria laughed. 'I can truthfully say that it was a case of absence making the heart fonder. Unusually, the event was even better than the anticipation.' She blushed a little and gave him a loving smile. 'I've missed you so much, Giacomo, I just wanted to make up for lost time.'

Jacob nodded and then with a sigh he changed the subject. 'I spoke with our fathers last night and they were urging me to change my mind about returning to England.'

Maria kept her voice neutral with difficulty. 'And what did you tell them?'

Sitting up and leaning forward to look her straight in the eyes, Jacob took a deep breath. 'I said that although I have many things tugging at my heart to stay here, I do not have any choice, but to return to England.'

Maria's face fell as Jacob confirmed her fears. Before she could say anything, Jacob came over and kneeling beside her, took her hand in his. 'My darling Maria, I want you to know that it will be the most difficult thing I have ever done. To leave you and Rico will tear my heart in two. But I must! Not for me, but for Venice and the Queen who has trusted me with her commission. The reply from the Doge must be kept as secret as my mission. It can never be put on to paper in case it falls into the wrong hands.'

Maria leaned forward, placing her forehead against Jacob's. 'I understand, Giam, I really do. The Queen has shown her trust and regard and you cannot betray that. But what then, my love: what will you do then?'

Jacob sighed again and put his arm round her shoulder and Maria leaned her head on his shoulder. 'When you came to my ship I asked you to return to England with me.' He sighed expressively. 'Would that I had not! It was a purely selfish request and had I known your circumstances I would have hesitated to ask.'

Maria took his face in both hands and kissed him gently. 'I know what prompted you. It was a very emotional moment for us both. But we know there is a lot more than just ourselves to consider. We both have responsibilities that will not be easy to shed.'

'There is something else to do with my ship,' said Jacob. 'Only Lunardo knows about it, apart from my crew.'

Maria was intrigued. 'I know it is quite well armed, but what else is there to know?'

'It is not all it seems,' said Jacob. 'I know that the cannons on deck look quite formidable, but what you cannot see and Lunardo found out by accident, is that there is a second gun deck hidden behind concealed gun ports. Those guns make The Crystal the most powerful ship of its size afloat.'

'Why have you told me?' said Maria and Jacob could see that she was worried.

'Lunardo told me that he and a number of war galleys will be leaving for the Gulf of Lepanto to rendezvous with a Christian fleet of the Holy League. They intend to bring the Ottoman fleet to battle as soon as possible.'

'Won't that be very dangerous? The Ottoman fleet has never been beaten for a hundred years or more. The last time they fought, it was a very bloody encounter and neither side could claim victory. But what has it to do with you?' she said, looking at Jacob fearfully.

'Lunardo thinks my ship with its powerful guns could make all the difference to the battle. They expect the galleasses to be very effective, but there are only six. My ship is far more powerful than any galleass.'

Maria clung to him tearfully. 'I don't want you to go, Giam. I've only just found you again and I couldn't bear it if you were killed.'

Jacob comforted her, stroking her face and kissing her forehead. 'Don't worry, I'm not sure I would be allowed to go. The Queen will expect me to return to England as soon as my business with the Doge and Council are complete. Also no English ships are involved in the Holy League, since the Pope has excommunicated the Queen.'

Maria was puzzled. 'So why have you mentioned it,' she said.

'Because my ship could make a real difference to the outcome of the battle,' said Jacob. 'I still care about Venice even though I was badly used by the courts. The future of the Eastern Mediterranean and even the existence of Venice itself is at stake in this battle and the outcome could affect both you and my child.'

Maria clung tightly to him for a long time without saying anything. Jacob just held her close and waited for her to come to terms with what he'd told her.

Eventually she sat up and resting her hands on his shoulders regarded him seriously. 'It's taken me a long time to understand that some decisions have to be made that don't sit well with your own feelings. This is one such decision. You must do what you think is right.'

'I have a final meeting with the Doge in two days' time,' said Jacob carefully. 'I'll think about it and probably discuss it with the Doge. I also need to think about the reaction of the Queen if I get involved. Meanwhile, there's the all-important decision as to what we do next.' He hugged her and then with his arm round her asked the question. 'I want to be with you, but I must return to England. Can you give up all that you have here in Venice and come with me.'

Maria shook he head sadly. 'I don't see how I can. There are so many persons depending on me. I'm trying to make it easier, but it will take time to get the right people. Perhaps in a few months time…'

She broke off at Jacob's forlorn expression and hugged him, sobbing against his shoulder. 'I'm so sorry, Giam. I want to be with you, with all my heart, but my head tells me I can't. Not for a while, at least.'

Jacob kissed her tenderly, reassuring her it was all right and that he understood. Off course he understood! But his heart was aching at the thought of having to part with her again.

They made love that afternoon desperately clinging to each other afterwards, with the knowledge that this could be the last time for many weeks.

A few days later there was a very tearful parting as he said goodbye to Maria and Rico. His father and Ricardo Morisini were also there and after a final embrace, his father handed him a carefully folded flag. 'I had this made up for you. It's a Venetian flag incorporating the Bellini arms.' He looked puzzled when Jacob laughed. When Jacob explained about the flag from the Queen, he too laughed. 'You will have quite a selection to use. Fly them all at the same time and you'll confuse anyone.'

There was time for one last embrace for Maria and Rico and then Jacob went on board. As they pulled away from the quay and headed out into the main channel, he waved until they were out of sight.

Standing by the port rail as the skyline of Venice disappeared into the haze Jacob wondered when, if ever he would be able to return and be with Maria and his son.

Chapter Thirty-One
Adriatic Sea, 7th August, 1571

On the third day after they'd left Venice, Captain Roberts asked Jacob to come on to the quarterdeck. The ship had been running downwind for some time, but there had been quite a change in conditions. The wind was veering round and was no longer in their favour.

When Jacob joined him on deck, the captain had just finished his midday sighting. 'What progress are we making for Messina, Captain?' Jacob was resigned to heading directly home. They'd discussed the possible intervention in the Christian Alliance's battle with the Ottoman fleet before they left Venice. The captain said the crew wouldn't pose a problem, especially if they received a bonus, but his advice was to go back to England.

'A conflict like that,' he shook his head and grimaced, 'it could finish in disaster. We'd be up against large numbers of galleys in conditions that favour them.' He smiled when Jacob seemed about to interrupt. 'I know we have more than enough fire-power to defend ourselves, but a lucky shot could bring down a mast and leave us at their mercy.'

Nothing more was said and now they were close to the turning point for Messina. Captain Roberts was looking concerned. 'The way the wind has shifted round, we're going to have the devil of a job to reach Messina,' he said, indicating their position on the folded chart. 'It might be prudent to settle for the longer way round and head for Malta.' He pointed to the island on the chart, moving his finger to show the revised route. 'Even that will require much tacking to achieve.' He made another grimace. 'It seems the weather has other thoughts. It's conspiring to push us straight into the Gulf of Lepanto.'

This was startling news for Jacob. 'How far away from the Gulf are we?'

'Almost the same distance as from Messina, in fact, Lepanto is about 175 miles and Messina about 210 miles, but with the prevailing wind, we could sail direct to Lepanto. To reach Messina will take a lot of tacking, unless the wind veers round again. Mister Marchant, the sailing master, is very experienced in these parts. He thinks there'll be some rough weather sometime in the next twenty-four to thirty-six hours. I'm inclined to trust his judgement in these matters.'

The thought running through Jacob's head was that perhaps fate was conspiring to change his mind. He hesitated a moment longer. 'Just supposing I said to head for Lepanto,' he said, to the captain's surprise. 'Do you have the charts and experience to take us there safely?'

Captain Roberts was silent for a moment then with a searching look at Jacob, strode over to the wheel where the master was at the helm. 'Any problems from here to Lepanto, Mister Marchant?'

'Aye captain a few, but none that I don't know about. I've been up that way a time or two over the years.'

Jacob had followed the captain to the wheel and came to a decision. 'Lepanto it is then, captain. Would you have me talk to the men?'

The generous bonus and the chance to show what the ship could do was too good to miss and so it was that the following day, shortly after midday, close- hauled, they cautiously entered the Gulf of Patras.

The sounds of the battle could be seen and heard from several miles away. First, they saw red flashes piercing the dense clouds of smoke shrouding the scene, like lightning in low clouds. Then came the sound of a continuous cannonade, like one huge thunderstorm. Jacob was anxious to have a better idea of how the battle was proceeding and asked Captain Roberts for his suggestion.

'I think the best plan would be to edge forward until we can make out a few details and then use the crows nest,' he said, pointing to the lookout's vantage point atop the main mast. Seeing the look of horror, he gave Jacob an amused look. 'Don't worry, I'll be up there with you.'

'It's not the going up that worries me,' said Jacob, looking up apprehensively. 'It's the coming down.'

There was a snorting laugh from Marchant at the helm. 'It's safer than climbing a tree in this weather,' he said. 'You want to try it in a full gale and furl the sails at the same time.'

'Not me, master, I'll leave it to the real sailors.'

'Very wise, Jacob,' said Captain Roberts with a laugh, 'but it will give us a bird's-eye view. Now if you don't mind, I'd like to clear the ship for battle.'

The crew sprang into well-drilled action. The splinter and anti-boarding netting was soon in place and the gun crews had the guns primed and ready to run out on the lower deck. They were chocked forward and ready to fire on the main deck. At Jacob's suggestion, the upper deck guns were all loaded with chain. 'Bring down a galley's mast and the rowers are hampered and steerage way is lost,' he advised.

Captain Roberts had spoken with all of the gun crews. Long hours of practice had created a bond of comradeship between them. He spoke to each man by name, urging him to make every shot count. The upper deck guns were to fire high on the upward roll. On the lower deck, the thirty-two pound ship breakers were loaded with solid balls and would fire on the downward roll. The former to bring down spars and masts: the latter to strike the waterline and sink the low-lying galleys.

By now, the master had brought The Crystal to within a half-mile of the nearest ships. Stripping down to shirt and breeches, Jacob and the captain began their climb.

'A shilling the captain gets there first,' said the master.

'You're on,' said the mate. 'Master Bellini is very fit and agile.'

'Very true,' said the master, 'but he's a landlubber.'

Captain Roberts held out his hand and helped Jacob into the crow's nest. Down below, the master held out his hand for his shilling. Holding tightly to the hand rope, Jacob surveyed the scene laid out before him. Despite the clouds of smoke that obscured individual conflicts, he could clearly see the tactics and formations of the opposing commanders.

The Christian fleet was organised in four divisions. The north division, as close to Point Scropha as the rapidly shoaling waters would allow, had been forced to turn to meet the threat of an outflanking move by Ottoman galleys exploiting their shallower draft. They were now more than holding their own and seemed to be inflicting heavy damage on the Ottoman galleys.

The centre division was locked in a desperate confrontation

and from their vantage point they could see individual conflicts going on everywhere.

'Look at the south division, Jacob. They've been drawn out of position and a block of galleys is heading in to engage the centre from the side. It's a very dangerous development..'

'What's the reserve squadron doing. Do you think they've realised the danger?'

'They don't have our bird's-eye view and so far there's no sign they appreciate the danger the centre is in.'

The captain took out his compass and took some bearings then checked the wind. 'I think if we tack to the right of the reserve fleet and then go on to the opposite tack as we clear them, we should have time to cut between the centre and the Ottoman galleys. It will be a close run thing, but it's worth a try. We'll have to be careful though, or we'll lose the weather gauge. We lose our advantage if we're forced to tack or close haul.'

'I understand the risks, captain. Lets do it,' Jacob said.

Then remembering his father's words about the flags he called to the captain. 'And fly both the Venetian flag and my personal flag. The reserve fleet will either take us for a Venetian, or with the crusader cross, belonging to the Knights of Malta. The last thing we need is for them to fire on us.'

The captain had not waited to answer but was sliding down a rope to the deck, at risk of rope-burned fingers. By the time Jacob had made his more careful descent and joined him on the quarterdeck, the ship was bounding forward on its new course with both flags flying boldly in the freshening breeze.

They were not spotted until they were almost level with the reserve, since all eyes were on the battle watching for signals. Steering within hailing distance, Jacob called out in Spanish that the Ottoman galleys had broken through the Christian lines and they were going to the aid of the centre.

As they came about on to the new course, the captain cursed. Several Ottoman galleys at full dash speed had closed the gap and were already engaging the ships of the centre. As they watched, they saw the commander of the Maltese Capitana struck by several arrows from the highly effective composite bows of the Ottoman archers and fall to the deck. Desperate hand to hand conflict was going on everywhere and the sea was littered with wreckage and bodies.

As they drew level with the conflict, the deck guns laid down a withering fire. Joining in as they came in range, the swivel guns did their deadly work, sweeping the decks of the nearest galley clear of boarders. Its scuppers running red with rivulets of blood.

The port side guns fell silent as The Crystal drove on its course. Calling for the master to ease off a point, the captain ordered the starboard guns to be manned. As they swept towards the clutch of galleys surging to engage the Christian centre, Jacob spotted a great trireme flying a large green banner, decorated with the Moslem crescent and inscriptions in Arabic. As he pointed it out to the captain, one of the leading galleys in this group turned to intercept them with the obvious intention of ramming. As it came into range, its forward guns fired. Holes appeared in the fore and mainsails and there was a clatter as severed blocks ricocheted down into the splinter nets.

'Ease her half a point, master.'

'Half a point it is, sir.'

'And another if you please, master. Now hold her steady.'

'Stand to your guns. Patience now. His eye calculated the distance and just as Jacob began to worry as the next upward roll began, his raised sword slashed down.

'Fire!' roared the captain and there was a rippling broadside from the lower deck. When the smoke cleared, the galley no longer existed. All that was left to mark its passage was a swirling mass of debris and bodies aimlessly turning in a spreading red stain on the sea.

Jacob crossed himself in shock and turned to the captain. 'I can't believe what we just did to that galley. It was a slaughter.'

'That's what war is,' said Captain Roberts grimly. 'It's kill, or be killed. They would have shown us no mercy if they had succeeded in ramming us.' He pointed to the arrows sticking in the deck and the rail to his left. 'Those Ottoman archers are good. If they'd been a little closer, they'd have hit one of us for sure.'

They were bearing down on the flagship now and the other galleys were giving them a wide berth. 'Full broadside on my command,' roared the captain and all of the starboard guns were run out.

The whole reloading process had taken little more than a minute and a half, as the powder monkeys scampered madly, bringing a constant stream of cartridges. The sweating gun-crews stripped to the waist worked furiously to swab the guns down, load, ram, and then run out.

'We'll only get one chance at the flagship,' shouted the captain over the noise of the battle. 'We're running too fast and I can't risk clewing up and backing the foresail. If we lose way, the other galleys will be on us like flies. Our safety lies in speed.' He checked his compass.

'A point on, master.'

'A point on it is, sir.'

'Now,' said the captain, 'let's see what the flagship is made of. Those triremes carry some cannon forward and have a small broadside. I've heard that one or two have fifty pounders. We may take a hit or two as we pass.'

He studied her through his glass. 'What the devil is he up to!' The bows of the trireme were starting to swing away and their closing speed was decreasing.

'He's backing his port oars to swing her round, captain,' said Jacob in a flash of insight.

'Two points off, master.'

'Two points it is, sir.'

As they closed in again, the trireme's bow came swinging round on to his original course.

'By the saints, it was a ploy to make us narrow the gap so his guns will be more effective and his archers can give us a hard time. I should have realised he wouldn't risk exposing his stern.' He smiled grimly. 'He has guts, I'll give him that, but it'll do him no good.'

The flagship was about four hundred yards away and closing fast. They were going to be swapping broadsides at about three hundred yards. The roar of the battle seemed to fade as Jacob concentrated on the oncoming flagship. Suddenly there was a cry from one of the sharpshooters on the main top. 'Deck ahoy, lantern galley two points off the starboard bow.'

The captain gave a curse and swung his glass round. Sure enough, a lantern galley, a larger version of the standard war galley, had just appeared from behind the stern of the flagship. It was on an intercept course and moving fast.

'This is going to be close,' said the captain and strode over to the master. 'When we've fired our broadside at the flagship, I want you to lay off two points to port and then back again on to the original course as soon as she's settled on to the new course.'

'Ay, sir,' said Mister Marchant. 'Should just about give you time to reload and hammer the lantern galley.'

'Quite right, master, quite right: we'll make a commander of you yet.'

'I'll settle for an extra tot if it works.'

'Let's hope so, but it will be a damn close run thing.'

The captain went chuckling back to stand next to Jacob. 'You'd better be prepared for more arrows and possibly some grape. Lie flat behind the wheel if they get a shot in.' He moved forward a little shouting to the mate. 'Have the gun crews lie beside their guns until my signal.

The captain's attention was now on the lantern galley and the trireme. They were closing fast. He turned his glass on the lantern galley and saw the figures around the bow guns on the front platform above the gleaming beak of the ram. 'Lie flat,' he roared, throwing himself down. Jacob did the same, just as grape howled over the deck, a little too high, but tearing away the port jib and riddling the sails. The captain sprang to his feet, sword raised. Jacob on his feet at the same time, looked across at the lantern galley.

'Ready the broadside. Rapidly, each gun captain raised his fist in the air to signify his readiness, eyes peering aft for the signal. Wait for it...The sword slashed down…Fire.'

Just before the captain roared out his orders, the lantern galley turned to a parallel course and went up to full dash speed.

Jacob stood frozen as the broadside began its deadly ripple of noise. The first few shots of the cannonade hit the flagship and she staggered as her front platform was reduced to matchwood. Not a single other shot found its mark. Watching in fascinated dismay, he saw the lantern galley, now shielding the flagship, blown apart by the fury of the weight of shot at less than a two hundred yards.

Even as their ship disintegrated beneath them, the archers kept up their deadly shower of arrows, until they too were mangled along with the rest of the ship. Jacob felt a stunning blow in his side and looked in disbelief at the arrow, which had gone right through the overlapping plates of his brigandine. Fortunately, it was only a flesh wound, but the assistant helmsman was not so lucky, lying dead beside the wheel, pierced to the heart by another arrow.

'Man the port guns,' roared the captain and the guns were run out. Once more the sword slashed down and the port guns roared their lethal tune reducing yet another galley to bloody ruin.

Jacob, unable to tear his eyes from the remains of the lantern galley rapidly falling astern, watched as it quickly settled below the waves. He slumped down beside the wheel, still scanning the shattered debris, twisting and bobbing in the down pull, but there were no survivors.

Even the gun crews were silent now as they surveyed their handiwork, reloading in mechanical rhythm. The captain looked around for another target, but their precipitous charge down the wind had sent The Crystal running clear of the remaining Ottoman galleys and they sailed on in subdued silence.

Chapter Thirty-Two
Gulf of Patras, 7th August, 1571

The Crystal rocked gently in the swell as the crew went about the business of making good the small amount of damage they had suffered. Jacob, the arrow removed, his wound cleaned and bound, sat in his cabin talking to Captain Roberts. Shortly after the last engagement, they had turned into the wind to make their way back into the fight. Progress was slow as they were forced to tack repeatedly in this narrow part of the Gulf. As they continued their slow progress, the lookouts reported that the battle was over. They could see the remaining Ottoman galleys fleeing, with a number of fast galleys in pursuit.

Seeing a sheltered cove, the captain conferred with Jacob. Not wishing to have his ship subject to prying eyes, Jacob decided they should anchor and make repairs. The wind was freshening. Mister Marchant had predicted they were in for a bit of a blow!

'We'd better get them done now then, rather than have something carry away in the storm,' said the captain. Once the repairs were in hand, the captain joined Jacob in his cabin for a well-earned glass of wine.

'How long will the repairs take, captain? We must continue our journey to England as soon as possible.'

'A few hours at most. My main concern is to replace the damaged sails and yards. We have suffered a little damage to the main structure, but we can see to that on the journey.'

Jacob took a long drink. 'This is a new sort of warfare for me, captain. And I must admit it troubles me. I would have no qualms about killing an enemy in a sword fight, but what we did to the Ottoman galleys was absolute slaughter.'

Captain Roberts looked thoughtful. 'I know what you mean, but I have to look at it in terms of my responsibilities as captain. Had one or more of those galleys boarded us, it would have led to many, if not all of my men losing their lives. Because we have a powerful ship, we were able to destroy several of the enemy and tip the balance of the battle in our favour. That saved a lot of Christian lives.'

Jacob nodded sadly. 'I can see that argument, captain, but the sight of that lantern galley and its crew being blown apart will live with me for a long time.'

The captain raised his glass. 'They were very brave men. The captain of the lantern galley knew what he was in for when he put himself between his flagship and our broadside. He sacrificed his ship and men for his leader. I give you a toast to a very brave man. The captain of the lantern galley!'

Jacob stood up. 'To the captain of the lantern galley,' he said, echoing the toast and drained his glass.

They sat down in silence for a while and then there was a knock on the door. 'What is it now, Caton,' said the captain.

'Begging your pardon, captain,' he said, pressing his knuckle to his forehead, 'but the master requests you join him on deck. The lookouts have spotted a Venetian galleass heading this way.'

'Very well, Caton, tell the master I will join him directly.'

'Very good, sir,' said Caton and hurried off.

Jacob gave a huge grin when, using his spyglass, he was able to read the name of the galleass nosing its way into the bay. It was the Galliano, Lunardo's ship.

When Lunardo came on board, Jacob introduced him to Captain Roberts. 'Captain Roberts, may I introduce my oldest friend Captain Lunardo Carreras of the galleass Galliano.'

The two captains exchanged courtesies then they all sat together in Jacob's cabin. 'I see you took a little damage, Captain Roberts, but little enough compared to what you handed out from what I've been hearing. I must say though, you have created rather a mystery.'

'A mystery?' asked a surprised Jacob. 'What sort of a mystery?'

Lunardo laughed. 'Your identity, off course: the Spaniards in the reserve fleet have identified you as Venetian and several other galleys swear you belong to the Knights of St. John of Malta. There is only one thing they can agree on and that is that you have the most powerful ship afloat.' He was obviously amused at their expressions and sat back in his chair. 'However, that's about the only thing they agree on. You have been described variously as a man-of-war with two decks, a large cog with added guns and a converted galleon of three decks.'

There was a lot of laughter about this and Jacob poured

Lunardo a glass of wine. 'How did you know where we were?'

'I didn't for sure, but I guessed you wouldn't be keen on allowing the Spaniards a close look. This is the safest anchorage for miles around and hidden from prying eyes.' He sipped his wine slowly then addressed the captain. 'I see you have the lower gun deck snugly stowed beneath its ports. I'll be glad to report that you are just an armed merchantman belonging to Councillor Bellini, if that is your wish.'

When Jacob inclined his head in confirmation, Lunardo continued. 'You look as though you intend to stay here until the storm has passed. Do you mind if I keep you company? My galleass is none too good in shallow water and rough conditions. Besides, it will explain the delay. Perhaps we can help you with supplies, or men to help with your repairs.'

'You are most kind, Lunardo, but for the same reason of secrecy, it would not be a good idea to have your people on board. However, you and your officers are welcome to join us for a meal this evening. I venture to suggest we have a bit more room and I'm sure we can put on a decent meal for you all. What say you, Captain Roberts.'

By next morning the storm had blown itself out and shortly after the hands had broken fast, with the wind now in a more favourable direction, they set off in company with the Galliano.

The meal had been a pleasant affair, but Jacob was nursing a thick head after imbibing rather too much of the wine that Lunardo had insisted on bringing. Fortunately, the motion of the ship did not cause him any distress and the master had the ship under very restricted sail so that the Galliano could keep up.

The site of the battle was deserted of ships now, but the ferocity of the conflict was still evident in the huge amount of wreckage and bodies scattered over a wide area. Lunardo had told them that the provisional estimate was that the Ottoman fleet had lost about two hundred ships, of which over a hundred galleys were captured and in good enough condition to keep.

The loss of life was enormous, with Ottoman casualties estimated at over 20,000 dead and 3,000 captured. In addition, over 10,000 Christian prisoners had been released. Sadly, the Holy League had lost about 10,000 men, with twenty galleys destroyed and thirty damaged so seriously that they had to be scuttled.

Ali Pasha, the leader of the Ottoman fleet, had been killed and beheaded, when his flagship was stormed with enormous losses on both sides. For the Holy League, Pietro Gustiniani, Prior of the Order of St. John was severely wounded by five arrows, but had been found in his cabin alive. The captured Maltese flagship was recovered from the fleeing galleys of Uluj Pasha, commander of the Ottoman right wing. He was forced to cut the tow in order to escape.

His clever tactics and attack on the centre had so nearly turned the battle, but The Crystal's intervention and the arrival of the reserve fleet had forced him to flee.

Once they were clear of the Gulf of Lepanto, Lunardo hailed them. 'Thank you for your company, but we are holding you back. May you have fair winds for England, God keep you safe and my thanks for your help. Until we meet again, fare you well.'

Jacob stood and watched until the galleass had been left far behind, then set his thoughts on England. The homeward journey was largely uneventful except for an encounter with a Portuguese carrack off Lisbon in Portugal. The carrack in company with a cog of about twenty tons had the weather gauge and on sighting The Crystal, crowded on all sail. Despite the master's best efforts, they were unable to make any headway against the carrack, but they were able to intercept the slower cog. A shot across his bows soon had the desired effect and he heaved to. To their delight, the cog was carrying a cargo of silk and spices, destined to provide money for the Duke of Alva's occupying army. They had no compunction about seizing them as they would fetch a pretty price in Plymouth. There was also a box containing jewels. The box was fairly small, but there were some fine emeralds and rubies and a particularly fine matching black pearl necklace.

The captain of the cog was most indignant. He was also bitterly disappointed that having completed the arduous trip from Cathay to Portugal, he should have been captured so close to safety. After consulting with Captain Roberts, they decided to put a prize crew on board and set the cog crew ashore near Porto.

Jacob, as a small act of compensation, handed the captain a fine emerald and ruby. This cheered him up no end.

They received a very enthusiastic welcome from Admiral Hawkins when they tied up at the Hawkins family quay. Jacob immediately sent a message post-haste to London, to notify Lord Burghley of their safe return to England. Hawkins also wasted no time in making arrangements for the disposal of the cog and its cargo. Knowing that there were sure to be some awkward enquiries by officious persons, he sent a present of ten pounds to the Lord Admiral's officer at Plymouth and smoothed the way. The Hawkins family owed much of their wealth to the efficient disposal of plunder, with the least possible loss to officialdom. On Hawkins advice, the box of jewels was not declared.

The Crystal was also unloading part of its cargo of glass. Some of this was destined for local merchants and some for shipping on to France. Despite the battle they'd fought, there were less than five percent breakages, thanks to the special cargo nets and crates designed by Roberto.

Once everything had been settled, Hawkins invited Jacob and Captain Roberts to join him for a meal at his home. He was most anxious to hear how The Crystal had performed. When Jacob, with animated help from Captain Roberts and many searching questions from the admiral, described the action in the Gulf of Lepanto, he was elated. Signalling to the servants to recharge everyone's glasses, he got to his feet.

'Gentlemen, I invite you to stand for a toast.' When they had done so, he raised his glass.

'I give you the toast of The Crystal, the finest ship I ever built.'

'The Crystal,' they chorused and drained their glasses in one go.

The discussions went on for some time, with Hawkins and Captain Roberts getting into technical details of the ship's performance. Feeling the effects of the journey and the wine, Jacob made his excuse and went to his room. Hawkins had insisted that they stay as his guests.

The next morning Jacob was awakened by a servant to inform him that a letter had arrived from Lord Burghley and the messenger was waiting for a reply. Putting on the robe that had been provided, Jacob had a quick wash and took the letter. Scanning the opening courtesies, Burghley informed him that the Queen desired his presence at court at the earliest opportunity. He was therefore to come post-haste to London, rather than wait for the ship to be replenished.

When he informed Hawkins, he told him that he was leaving for London himself and invited Jacob to share his coach. This suited him well and after giving explicit instructions to Captain Roberts, he set off with Hawkins.

Despite the fact that the coach was of the latest design, it was still a bone-shaking journey. By the time they reached London next day, Jacob was exhausted, stiff and sore. On reaching Harte Street, he despatched a message to Burghley at Greenwich and took to his bed.

An excited Mistris Simpkin woke him next morning with the news that a message had arrived from the Queen. Guessing it was a summons to court, Jacob hurried to open it. Sure enough, he was to attend the Queen at Greenwich, immediately after she had attended morning service. Jacob had lost all sense of the days and was surprised it was a Sunday. Fortunately, he had bought a new set of clothes before leaving London so at least he would be suitably attired. All of his other clothes were in dire need of cleaning from the travelling he'd done.

When he was dressed, he went to the small box of jewellery taken from the Portuguese cog. He examined the beautiful diamond and sapphire ring he had picked out for Maria. It would make a lovely gift when they became betrothed. Taking out the wash-leather bag, he opened the top and examined the black pearl necklace. Fit for a Queen, Captain Roberts had described it and so it would be his present to the Queen.

Arriving at Greenwich, he was not shown into the presence chamber where those invited usually waited. Instead, he was directed to a small antechamber just off the Queen's private apartments. He waited patiently for almost an hour, and then the door opened and a lady-in-waiting appeared. With a deep curtsy, she told Jacob that the Queen was ready to receive him. Following her into the Queen's private reception room, he fell on to one knee and bowed his head.

'Get up at once, sit down over there and explain yourself,' said Elizabeth brusquely, indicating a chair set in front of her.

Jacob got up with alacrity and sat down wondering how he'd displeased her. 'I'm sorry, your majesty, I'm not sure what it is you want me to explain.'

The Queen looked even fiercer if that were possible. 'Master Bell, did I or did I not instruct you to return to England at the earliest possible moment once your business with the Doge was concluded? Well!'

'You did, your majesty, but…'

'But me no buts, Master Bell, you disobeyed me and sailed off to battle at Lepanto. I've heard about it from Admiral Hawkins.'

Jacob was lost for words and sat wondering how he was going to explain. He looked at the Queen appealingly, but it only seemed to make things worse.

'Don't look at me with that little boy caught scrumping apples look,' she said angrily, 'I...' She broke off, muttered something about him being too easy to tease and then started to laugh. 'Jacob Bell,' she said, shaking her head. 'I don't know whether to send you to the Tower or make you a peer. You're always going your own way and getting yourself into one scrape or another. You remind me of the young John Hawkins, he was just the same.'

She patted the settle next to her. 'Come, sit beside me, pour me some wine and tell me about the battle. I hear my good ship The Crystal was magnificent.'

For nearly an hour, Jacob explained everything about the battle, his dealings with the Doge and the honour he'd received. He gave her the personal message from the Doge and explained how he'd come to get involved with the Holy League fleet. He then told her about the brush with the carrack and cog off Lisbon and presented her with the black pearl necklace.

When the Queen took it out of the wash-leather pouch, she exclaimed in delight, 'This is wonderful, Jacob Bell, I have never seen its better. I will wear it with pleasure,, rest assured on that score. Thank you for such a lovely gift, I do so love it when men give me gifts.' Jacob, noting the acquisitive gleam in her eye, was sure that she did, and often.

Placing the pouch carefully on the nearby table the Queen

turned to him with a gentle smile. 'And what of Lady Maria Morisini? You have said nothing about her. I trust she is well?'

'She is, your majesty and she has a wonderful, sturdy son,' he said.

The Queen looked at him shrewdly. 'I detect a note of pride when you mention the boy. Do I take it that you are the father?'

The question caught him off guard with its directness. He was silent for a moment and then a smile spread across his face. 'Yes, your majesty, you most certainly can.'

The Queen smiled in delight. 'In that case, I will only say one more thing on the matter. Should you wish to be married in England, which would very much be my own wish, I will expect an invitation.'

She sat back and straightened her dress. 'Now, Jacob Bell, there are other matters to discuss.' She picked up a small hand bell from the table beside her and rang it vigorously. When a lady-in-waiting appeared the Queen instructed her to arrange another chair, and to inform Lord Burghley that his presence was required.

When Burghley arrived, Jacob had moved to the other chair and Burghley sat down beside him. He added his congratulations on a successful mission and the Queen asked him to bring Jacob up to date with the investigations into the affairs of Count Ridolfi.

'We are most grateful to you and that Ring of apprentices of yours, for bringing Charles Baillie to our attention,' said Burghley. 'Without your forewarning, he may well have slipped into the country undetected.'

'I take it he has yielded some useful information.'

Burghley then went on to explain the current state of affairs. 'Much tooing and froing has been happening throughout the time you were in Venice. From the letters we have courtesy of Baillie we know that there are two principals involved. Ridolfi seems to be the brains behind the plot and both the Bishop of Ross and De Spes, the Spanish Ambassador, are involved.' He gave a gesture of annoyance. 'We have wasted an inordinately long time trying to discover the identities of forty and thirty, but without the cipher, we are no nearer proving anything. I am inclined to believe that one of the people identified only by a number is Norfolk and the other is Mary Stuart herself.'

The Queen who had been listening patiently to this account took up the story. 'As you know, I usually go on Progress during the summer. Because of the terrible speeches against me reported out of Flanders, the Council moved that I should remain in London. I would not forebear my Progress, but I agreed to remain near London.

Accordingly, after St. Bartholomew's tide, on 24th August, I repaired to the Duke of Norfolk's house at Walden in Essex.' She took a sip of wine. 'The Duke was very voluble in his denials that he was involved with Count Ridolfi, or with Mary Stuart, despite the Bishop of Ross having named him.' She smiled bleakly. 'I lent him a favourable ear, but even though he swore that he had learned his lesson and forsaken the matter of the Queen of Scots, I thought he protested too much.' Again the bleak smile. 'I assured him that he was not suspected of being one of the ciphered persons forty or thirty, but I strongly suspect he may well be so.'

Burghley nodded in agreement. 'We have been friends for a long time, but the Howards were ever an ambitious family, even for the throne itself. Should it be proved he is guilty of treason, I will have no compunction in bringing him to trial, friend or no.'

'So there you have it, Jacob Bell,' said Elizabeth. 'Once more, we are requesting your help.'

Jacob stood up. 'Then I will be honoured to give it, your majesty,' he said with a bow. 'However, I hope to go back to Venice in about two months time, or sooner, if I can arrange matters here in London. In the meantime, I will seek out the answers to your questions.'

Chapter Thirty-Three
London, 21st September, 1571

Roberto was waiting at Harte Street when Jacob returned from Greenwich. He embraced Jacob enthusiastically and begged him to tell all about his travels, what had transpired in Venice and if his mother was well.

Jacob told him that his mother was well and very much the trusted confidante of Maria. He then suggested that the rest should wait until everyone was present. 'I can't bear the thought of having to tell the tale repeatedly to all manner of people. I suggest that tomorrow evening, we meet here for a meal, assuming Mistris Simpkin can arrange it at such short notice.'

Once they had decided who should attend, they had a word with Mistris Simpkin, who promised to put on a meal fit for the Queen. Jacob told Roberto he was going to spend the rest of the day sorting out his things and writing up some notes so he didn't forget anything important. 'When you get back to the glass-works, will you ask Quiff to call in at Harte Street before he goes to the Swan. I want the Ring to concentrate on the Duke of Norfolk. Lord Burghley thinks he may be the key, now that Ridolfi is out of the country.' When Roberto promised he would, Jacob said, 'Off you go then and give my best to your lovely wife Elizabeth. Tell her she was right about Maria and I look forward to seeing her tomorrow.' Roberto gave him a puzzled look.

'Don't worry about it,' said Jacob, with a smile. 'I'll see you, bright and early tomorrow morning at the Crouched Friars.'

When Quiff arrived, Jacob asked if they still had a member of the Ring in Norfolk's house at Walden.

'Certainly,' said Quiff, 'and since you said he might be important, I've recruited two more while you were away. There's now a footman, Henry Goodman and his wife, Margaret. She's an upstairs maid. There is also a groom, who's prepared to pass on information to Henry. The footman is very useful, because he often gets sent out with messages to deliver.'

'Very useful indeed, Quiff,' said Jacob. 'Has he turned up anything valuable yet?'

'Not so far, Master Jacob, but I've asked him to make sure he lets us know about any letters that go to the Bishop of Ross and the Spanish Ambassador.'

Jacob rubbed his chin thoughtfully. 'It might be a good idea to ask him to widen the search a bit. Can he be trusted?'

It was Quiff's turn to look thoughtful. 'Yes, Master Jacob, I believe he can. He didn't join us just for the money. He'd heard from the groom that we helped to foil the Maldini plot and he thinks the Queen has done a lot for the people. He knows we are doing it to protect her, so he wants to help. The Queen was kind to his wife when she was at Walden during her Progress, which has impressed him even more.' He thought a moment. 'The only problem is we will have to wait until he comes to London with a message.'

'That's fine, ask him to use his own judgement and let us know about anything he thinks is suspicious. Even if it proves to be nothing, that's better than missing something.'

Since Quiff was not due at the Swan for another half hour, Jacob asked him if anything had been heard of Jed Sutton. Quiff made a face. 'He's a bad lot, that one. To my knowledge, he's badly beaten several of the servants at the house. Not to mention giving the women servants a hard time.'

'What sort of hard time?'

Quiff shrugged. 'The usual, groping them, making them share his bed when he feels like it and hitting them if they don't.'

Jacob was appalled. 'Why do they stay, then?'

Quiff gave a sad smile. 'Because they have to, Master Jacob, they don't have any choice. Jobs are not easy to get and there are not so many employers like you,' he said with feeling. 'You really don't know what it's like to be an indentured servant. Your master controls your life and the law is on his side. You must take whatever he hands out, or you, or worse still, your loved ones, will starve,' he said bitterly.

Despite the false accusations, prison and the sentence to the galleys, Jacob had never experienced that sort of desperate existence. He'd been extremely lucky that his family and friends had rallied round to ensure that the worst aspects of his conviction had been removed from him. He tried to imagine how it must be to suffer degradation as a part of everyday life, because the alternative was death. He lived a rich man's life far removed from the life of a servant, so he could only guess. Recalling the first time he had seen Quiff he saw why he sounded so bitter. He too had suffered from a vicious master.

'I want you to keep me informed about Jed Sutton. The man is evil and I want to find a way to stop him.'

'I wish we could, Master Jacob. I'm sure he's done away with Jenkins the servant from the Ridolfi house. I've had the Ring ask everywhere and all we can find out is that Sutton is supposed to have dismissed Jenkins for stealing and that he'd left the house for good.'

'I suppose it might be true,' said Jacob doubtfully.

Quiff shook his head emphatically. 'It's too much of a coincidence. He was found stealing when all the other staff had been sent out of the house on various pretexts. Besides, we haven't been able to find him anywhere. He'd have been in touch if he had been dismissed.'

'Perhaps your right,' said Jacob, but proving it is going to be difficult. That chute in the cellar leads straight to the river and where the house is, the body would go far downriver, or even to the sea. If that was his fate, we are never likely to be able to prove it.'

Reluctantly, Quiff had to agree, but said he'd keep trying to find Jenkins. 'Perhaps you could ask Lord Burghley if a body has turned up downstream that answers to his description.'

'An excellent suggestion, Quiff, I'll see to it. In the meantime, the word for the Ring is the same, use extreme caution in dealing with these people. They are playing for high stakes and will try to bury their mistakes, literally.'

He would have been even more concerned had he been privy to the scene at the Ridolfi house later that afternoon. Jed Sutton had received a note by hand from Count Ridolfi. It wasn't signed, but only he knew about the door into the cellar. It was a way of entering and leaving the house without being seen. The note said to unlock the door at three o'clock.

Jed opened it for the count and looked worried. 'You were safe in France, father, what possessed you to come back now?'

'Because the Guise family have ordered me to arrange the transfer of a large sum of money from the Duke of Norfolk to Scotland, for the use of the Queen of Scots,' he said wearily. 'I can't trust the Bishop of Ross, or De Spes with it. Burghley has his spies everywhere and is watching them both. He's sure to be intercepting letters. The Bishop in particular is a weak-kneed coward. He'll tell everything sooner or later and I've been forced to risk being caught to come and make sure it gets done.'

'Do you want me to dispose of this Bishop?' said Jed fiercely. 'I'll make sure he doesn't betray you.'

'It would be too dangerous,' the Count warned. 'He's under constant guard and you couldn't get in without detection. Besides, I need you here.'

He started to change into the clothes that Jed had brought for him. It wouldn't do for the servants to see him dressed as a fisherman.

They went upstairs to the study. 'Once I've contacted the Duke of Norfolk to arrange about the money, I will arrange to slip away to France. It'll not be easy, as all the ports are being watched. The fisherman who brought me, landed me at a small fishing port, but even he had his boat inspected. I was dressed like a seaman, so the revenue man didn't suspect me. In any case he was looking for contraband. After that, the fisherman wouldn't risk coming back.'

They discussed how the matter might be handled for some time and then, while the count kept to his study, Jed sent all of the staff away for seven days. He made the excuse that he was closing the house up while his master was away. He paid them their dues at the Count's insistence to stop malcontent's causing trouble and speculation.

Once they had left, the two men decided on how the matter could be arranged. After much discussion, the Count wrote a letter in cipher to Norfolk and Jed set off to deliver it next day. Although they were not to know it, it was this decision that enabled Jacob to make good his promise to Quiff.

Not a man to be easily impressed, even Jed Sutton felt a little intimidated by the sheer scale of luxury and importance of

Norfolk House. He had been forced to pass through the hands of a series of servants, each one more senior, until at last he was granted admittance to the main house.

Jed gave the footman a letter addressed to the Dukes secretary, Higford, prepared by Count Ridolfi. The footman told him to wait while he contacted Master Higford, to find out if he was available. Shortly afterwards, Jed was shown into the secretary's small room, off the main reception room. 'I'm sorry Sutton, but your being here today is very inconvenient. His Lordship has only just finished being questioned by Sir Thomas Smith and Doctor Thomas Wilson. They came from the Queen's Council to ask about the letters in cipher, of which you are aware.'

He went to the window and looked out. 'They were still here when you arrived and it would have been most unfortunate for everyone if you'd been seen. It would have confirmed their suspicions of a link with Count Ridolfi.' Suddenly he turned round and sighed with relief. 'They're leaving now. Thank goodness the grooms had the good sense to put your horse in one of the stables.'

He indicated a chair and they both sat down. 'Now that they've left, what can we do for the Count?'

Jed handed over a sealed letter. 'As you will see from the seal, it is from Mary of Guise. My master has just returned from France where he has been a guest of the Guises.'

'Do you know what they want?'

'I believe they sent certain sums of money to you from France.' Higford nodded.

'They wish for six hundred pounds of it to be sent to Scotland, to the usual place in Edinburgh. Queen Mary is running low on funds and the money is needed to pay the mercenaries who will cross the border to join up with the Northern Earls when they move against London.'

'I will see his Lordship gets the letter immediately. I assume you will wait for a reply?' He rang the bell on his desk and a footman appeared. 'Arrange for some refreshments for Master Sutton, while he waits for the Duke.'

When the footman hurried off, Higford nodded to Jed. 'I will attend the Duke and inform him of the letter. He may want to speak to you, but otherwise, I will bring the reply.'

It was almost an hour before Higford returned carrying a letter. He passed it to Jed and sat down. 'The Duke asks that you forward this letter to your master. He assumes he is still in Paris?'

Jed was just about to say that the Count was in London, when caution held his tongue. Since the Duke was already being questioned, it might be as well to keep the counts whereabouts secret. He simply nodded and Higford stood up. 'I will send instructions and the money to Bannister, my lord's steward in Shrewsbury. He will arrange to send the money on to Edinburgh. It will be much safer than sending it directly from here.'

Jed nodded. He could see the sense in being cautious. He stood up and placing the letter in his doublet, said his farewell. On the way back, he took a circuitous route, just in case he was followed. Despite a very careful lookout, he could not discover anyone remotely interested in him.

After Jed Sutton had left, Higford rang the bell. 'Ah, Henry, the very man,' he said, when the footman entered. 'I assume that Thomas Browne, the carrier, will be well on his way to London by now.'

'Yes, Master Higford, he left almost an hour ago.'

Higford made a gesture of annoyance. 'I thought as much. It's typical: when you want someone in one place, they're in another,' he said testily, sorting through the papers on his desk. 'Ah, here it is,' he said holding up a piece of paper. He peered short-sightedly at the address. 'Porter's Key, off Thames Street,' he read, 'do you know of it, Henry.'

'I believe so, Master Higford, it'd be down near the Tower. Between there and London Bridge.'

'Excellent,' said Higford. 'I will want you to go to the warehouse as quickly as you can with some saddlebags and letters. They are to be sent to Shrewsbury for delivery to Bannister, the steward. The carrier's cart only goes slowly, so you should catch up with him. If not, go to the warehouse.' He began to bustle around. 'I want you to get ready for the journey and take a couple of the grooms with you. Make sure you have decent horses and they'd better be armed, since there'll be fifty pounds of silver coins in the bags.'

As they rode along the track towards London, Henry Goodman was thinking furiously. When he'd hefted the saddlebags, he realised at once that there was far more than fifty pounds of silver coins in them. There were several heavily sealed letters too. Usually, it was Higford that sent instructions, but these bore his Lordship's seal. There was also the matter of Jed Sutton: he'd recognised him immediately from Quiff's description. It was too much of a coincidence that shortly after his visit, a hurried delivery of money and letters was being sent to the steward at Shrewsbury.

Before he could decide, one of the grooms came up alongside. 'We been talking, Henry,' he said indicating the other groom. 'Neither of us 'as been to London afore. Will us 'ave time to see some bear-baiting at Southwark. We 'eard all about it from one of the Queen's grooms when 'er came on 'er visit.'

'I don't see why not,' said Henry. He'd realised at once that this gave him the opportunity to pass on a message to Quiff. He'd have to use the emergency drop at The Swan, but it wasn't far from the Tower. With a bit of luck, Quiff would get the message and come to the warehouse while he was there.

Once he had worked it out, he replied. 'The warehouse is only just the other side of London Bridge and I'm not likely to be robbed in full view of everyone. You two can go off to the bear pit while I sort out with the carrier. I'll meet you outside, when I'm done.' He looked sternly at the groom. 'Mind you,' he cautioned, 'not a word about this to Higford, or we'll all be looking for jobs.'

The landlord's message found Quiff at the Crouched Friars. When he read the message, he rushed excitedly to the house on Harte Street to find Jacob. 'Master Jacob,' he cried breathlessly. 'I've received this message from Henry Goodman. He's at a carrier's warehouse at Porter's Key, just below London Bridge.'

Jacob read the note in rising excitement: this could be the breakthrough they'd been seeking. When he reached the warehouse, Henry was talking to Thomas Browne the carrier, who was hefting the saddlebags. 'I see what you mean, boyo,' he said in his lilting Welsh accent. 'And who might you be?' he said, putting the saddlebags down and looking suspiciously at Jacob and Quiff.

As soon as Jacob explained and said he wanted Thomas to bring the saddlebags to Lord Burghley, his manner changed. 'I was just thinking it might be a good thing to alert his Lordship. His men have asked me to keep my eyes peeled for anything suspicious. They pay well too.'

Henry Goodman was sent on his way to meet up with the grooms, richer by five gold royals. Jacob set off in company with Thomas Browne to see Burghley.

Fortunately, Lord Burghley was in London and Jacob soon tracked him down. The saddlebags yielded six hundred pounds in gold and three letters. These were given to Phelippes who was present with Burghley. Thomas Browne was well rewarded and went on his way rejoicing, while Jacob and Burghley waited impatiently for Phelippes report.

It turned out that one of the letters was in plain English, with just mundane instructions for Bannister. The others though were in cipher. Phelippes was sure that they were in the same cipher as the letters obtained from Baillie.

Burghley became very excited. 'By my faith! I do believe we have them.' He rang his hand bell vigorously and when a servant appeared instructed him to send for Colonel Young immediately. When the Colonel arrived, he nodded friendlily to Jacob and when Burghley had given his instructions, set of at once to take Higford into custody, preferably without Norfolk's knowledge.

Chapter Thirty-Four
The Tower, 30th September, 1571

The arrest of Higford set in motion a chain of events that quickly led to settling many of the vexed questions held over from the discovery of the Baillie letters. Jacob was summoned to see Burghley at the Tower on the 30th September to be brought up to date.

Higford had confessed to Burghley that the Duke of Norfolk had sent the money to Bannister. Following further examination Higford deciphered the letters as best he could and confessed that the cipher would be found at Howard House, 'under a mat, hard by the window's side where the map of England doth hang'.

Sir Henry Neville was sent to take charge of Norfolk and confine him to Howard House. A search for the cipher proved fruitless, although a further letter in cipher was found. It appeared that the Duke had been forewarned, possibly by the arrest of Higford, and had 'gotten away with it', as Neville reported.

'Where is he now?' asked Jacob.

'I have him safe here in the Tower,' said Burghley smugly. 'He will be left to stew for a few days, while he thinks over what I said to him.'

'What was that, my lord?'

'I told him that although he was my friend of many years, having supported me in my disputes with Leicester's faction, I would not hesitate to send him to the rack if so ordered by the Queen.'

'Is that likely,' said Jacob in surprise. 'He is the premier Earl.'

Burghley smiled bleakly. 'You have not had the doubtful privilege of seeing the Queen in a foul mood. When she learned that Norfolk was plotting at the time she visited him on Progress, she was in a fine fury.' He regarded Jacob with a kind expression. 'You have only seen the good side of her majesty and on my oath that can be very good. I hope for your sake you never see the reverse of the coin.'

He leaned back in his chair. 'Now we must get to the reason I asked you to come. Once more you have aided me with vital information. Under normal circumstances you would have received a more tangible sign of our gratitude. Unfortunately, to show you are in the Queen's favour now would put you at risk for what I have in mind.'

The hairs on Jacob's neck began to bristle. A sure sign that he was receiving strong warning signals. He looked warily at Burghley. 'I have a feeling I'm not going to like this,' he said, but there was no humour in his eyes.

'I won't insult you by saying it won't be dangerous.' Burghley leaned his elbows on his desk and locking his fingers, he rested his chin on them. He then rested his cheek against his hands looking down at the desk deep in thought.

At last, he sat up and leaned back again. 'First I must give you some background, so you may fully understand the situation in Europe. Walsingham's spies have reported that Count Ridolfi has disappeared from Paris. He has received an unconfirmed sighting of the Count near Calais. Despite intensive surveillance in England, no trace of the Count has been found at any of the ports. This does not mean he is still in France. I suspect he may have slipped in to England in disguise, at one of the smaller ports.'

'Surely he must know that would be dangerous.' Jacob was surprised Ridolfi would even contemplate returning. 'He must have been told that both Ross and Norfolk have been questioned. Why would he risk his life?'

'It would have to be something important,' agreed Burghley, 'but Higford has confessed that Sutton brought instructions from the Guises about the money. Where would that have come from except the Count?'

Jacob had no answer and Burghley sighed. 'It fits in well with the word that Hawkins sent a few days ago.'

'Has Fitzwilliam returned?' asked Jacob excitedly.

'Indeed he has and all of the prisoners that have survived starvation, disease and the rack have been liberated. They have each been given five Spanish gold crowns and passage on a merchant ship to England.'

Jacob was overwhelmed by this news. 'God is great in his mercy,' he said solemnly. 'I was not sure when we started this enterprise we would ever see this day. And what of Hawkins?'

Burghley laughed. 'I swear that man would fall in a midden and come up smelling of roses. He has a full pardon for his indiscretions in the Indies, a patent of nobility whereby he becomes a hidalgo of Spain and a promise of money for his ships.'

He picked up a letter from his desk. Indicating a passage, he passed it to Jacob to read, "they have granted me very great titles and honours from the King of Spain, from which God deliver me!"

When they had stopped laughing, Jacob asked what else was in the letter, which Burghley had reclaimed. 'I now know the whole of Ridolfi's plan,' he said in a very self-satisfied voice. 'Hawkins was to desert his post in the Channel the moment the rising took place in England. The Queen of Scots was to be liberated and married to Norfolk.'

He gave a very bleak smile. 'What was to be Queen Elizabeth's fate is not stated, but it doesn't take much intelligence to guess. The Duke of Alva would launch his army against the South Coast, while the Duke of Medina Celi approached with the Spanish fleet from Spain. Hawkins was to receive 45,000 ducats, about £11,000, to maintain twelve ships and sixteen hundred men for two months and he would join with Alva and Medina in subduing England.'

Once he had savoured the news, it occurred to Jacob that Burghley had something dangerous in mind for him. 'And what do you want of me, my lord? Isn't this enough?'

Burghley was once more the efficient statesman. 'Not by a long chalk, Master Bell.' He regarded Jacob as though deciding something. 'I know you are not one for prating, but this is very close to home. I have personal reasons for either making sure Ridolfi is dead, or out of the country. You may well guess why?' He looked at Jacob expectantly.

Jacob nodded. 'Both Walsingham and yourself were using Ridolfi as an advisor; on finance of course. It would not sit well if he were brought to trial and gave all of the names of other prominent people he'd fooled as well.'

Burghley nodded. 'Better dead, or long gone and that is where you come in. I want you to find out if the Count is in England

and either get him out of England, or kill him, if you must.'

Jacob shook his head emphatically. 'Kill him I will not, not unless he tries to kill me. I am no assassin.'

'Nor would I have you be, Jacob Bell. I know you to be an honourable and God-fearing man.' He rubbed his forehead. 'I only meant that you might place yourself in a position where this Jed Sutton, or the Count became suspicious.' The smile became mischievous this time.

'Should you be successful in arranging the Count's departure from these shores, it will do no harm at all to your standing with the Spanish.'

Jacob had to smile. 'I can see that the Spanish are not the only ones John Hawkins has been plotting with.'

'He did mention something along those lines,' said Burghley, trying to keep a straight face.

They discussed how this might be achieved for a little while and then Jacob said he would talk to Quiff to see what the Ring could discover. They could plan nothing until they knew for sure that the count was in England.

Before he left, Jacob had one final question to put to Burghley. 'Have you enough proof to charge the main principals in this plot?'

Burghley shook his head. 'Not yet, but I do not think it will be long. I am sure we'll discover the key to the cipher of the Baillie letters shortly and once we have that, it will just be a matter of convincing the culprits to confirm the details. We have the right of it I'm sure and soon we'll know it all.'

Chapter Thirty-Five
Murano, 4th October, 1571

Maria awoke feeling tired and rather queasy. She sat up in bed and thought about the events of the past few weeks. For too long the Ragazoni estate had dominated her waking life, but for once she had no appointments. Maria had been working to arrange matters so that it was not necessary, as at present, to consult her on every decision. She was determined that the estate would no longer dominate her life. After all, she had a young son to consider.

August had been a most difficult month. Events in the Eastern Mediterranean had dominated the moods of the city. On the seventeenth, news reached Venice of the fall of Famagusta, the main town of Cyprus. There were eight thousand Venetian soldiers defending the port and they were besieged by thirty thousand Ottoman troops.

All of the islands in the Republic were represented there and the despair was universal. Churches were running out of candles as families prayed for the survival of their loved ones. Little news was available due to the blockade by the Ottoman fleet. Indeed it was weeks after the fall of Famagusta before a ship managed to squeeze through and bring the news home to Venice.

The following morning at six o'clock, a number of people saw a galley approaching with the Ottoman colours trailing behind it in the water. It had made the trip from Lepanto in ten days, when eighteen was the accepted norm.

As the word spread rapidly through the city, large crowds began to gather at the Piazzetto San Marco. As the galley approached the quay outside the Palazzo Ducale a salute was fired by the forward guns and loud cries of, 'Vittoria! Vittoria!' could be heard.

At once the crowd began to roar Liberta! Liberta! now they realised that the Ottoman fleet had been defeated. The city became gripped in collective euphoria, surpassing the levels of despair from the day before. Some of the crowd rushed to the Piombi to release the prisoners, but only those confined for debt were allowed to go. Shops all over the city were closed as the celebrations continued with notices everywhere announcing "per la morte de' Turchi".

All around the city the delight was so effervescent, that strangers were embracing in the streets everywhere. For the next four days, throughout the Republic religious processions paraded the street playing music and chanting hymns. At night there were illuminations, masquerades and other rejoicing. The Fondaco de' Tedeschi was so splendidly decorated and lighted that it resembled an enchanted palace.

The celebrations became a little more restrained as news of the losses started to filter through. For Maria this was a particularly difficult time. What if Giam had changed his mind and gone to the battle after all? Fortunately the arrival of Lunardo Carreras ended her worry, but not at first. Lunardo, in answer to her worried query, admitted that Giam had been wounded. He soon reassured her that the injury was only a flesh wound and healing well when he last saw Giam.

Maria's first reaction had been one of anger. How could he put her through this? He'd said he would go straight back to England. Then when she thought she might have lost him, the realisation hit her hard. No matter what, she loved him.

Just then, Anna came in with some fruit and Maria tried to eat. Anna fussed around saying how tired she looked and she should rest. Shortly after eating the fruit, Maria was sick. Although she took Anna's advice and rested, she felt listless, tired and queasy for the rest of the day.

The situation did not improve and by the fourth day, Maria agreed that Doctor Nguyên should be called. Having questioned both Maria and Anna as to the onset of the illness, he proceeded to examine Maria. It was very thorough and when he'd finished, he said he would make up a potion for her. He returned with a small phial and asked her to drain it, which she did. She was then asked to lie down on her back, legs together and hands down by her side. 'Relax, my dear,' said the doctor. 'You must relax.'

Maria closed her eyes and shortly her breathing became deeper and she began to feel as though she was floating. In a detached way, she saw the doctor holding a jade pendulum over her abdomen. He was making a deep humming noise and appeared to be in a trance. At first the pendulum was still, but after a little while it began to move, haphazardly at first and then after a while, it settled into a steady clockwise circle.

When Maria woke up, she felt very relaxed. The doctor was sitting in a chair close by, with his eyes closed. When she sat up, he opened his eyes and smiled. 'Ah, Lady Maria, you are awake at last.'

'How long have I been sleeping,' said Maria with a yawn.

'About two hours, you were sound asleep, so I made up a tonic for you and some ginseng tea.'

'Have you found out what is wrong with me. I hope the measles haven't returned?'

Doctor Nguyên smiled gently. 'Certainly not, you're not ill at all.'

'But the sickness and the feeling of tiredness all the time, have I been working too hard?'

'That may have a bearing on your tiredness,' said the doctor thoughtfully, 'but it's more likely to be the fact you're with child.'

Maria was stunned. 'With child!' she exclaimed in astonishment. 'Are you sure?'

'Your breasts are slightly swollen and a little sore and the skin around the nipples is a lot darker than I remember. Together with the nausea and the extra passing of fluids they are all common signs of an early pregnancy. Quite early I believe, but in all probability your flux will cease next time it is due. Besides, my pendulum confirms you are having a girl child.'

This was too much for Maria to take in and she sank back on the pillows shaking her head in disbelief. She closed her eyes thinking it might be a dream, but it wasn't.

Doctor Nguyên was adamant that she was to have a daughter. 'My pendulum is always correct. Occasionally when another problem obscures the flow of higher energy from the qi, the results are not conclusive. In your case, I am certain.'

After he'd left, Maria thought back to the previous month. So much had happened, Famagusta, the battle at Lepanto, when she'd missed her flux, she'd forgotten all about it. After all, she'd missed it before without being with child!'

It was not long before Anna came in to congratulate Maria. The doctor had told her on the way out. 'Do you want me to send word to your father, in Verona?' The Senator had been away for a week now, but was expected back the following day.

'That won't be necessary. He is sure to come and see me the minute he gets back. If for nothing else than to tell me how the negotiations went with the local silk merchants.'

They were planning to offload part of their combined silk business. With the Ottoman forces in control of the Eastern Mediterranean, the merchants at Bursa would be forced to ship overland. These extra costs, plus the trade being taken by the Portuguese and English with ships capable of withstanding the sea route round Africa, made trade more difficult, risky and much less profitable.

When her father received the news, he was overjoyed. However, this was tempered by the thought that Maria was unmarried. Not that it was much of a problem if a wedding could be arranged soon. After all, the baby wouldn't be born until June if the doctor's predictions were correct.

'We must contact Eduardo and start making arrangements,' he said gleefully.

Maria would have nothing of it. 'Tell Eduardo the news of the baby by all means, but I will not countenance making any sort of arrangements until Giam has been told. He may have decided he doesn't want to marry me.'

When her father had left, she sat on the balcony outside the garden room. Rico was happily playing in the garden with Julia in close attendance. She smiled as he took a tumble and got up and carried on without crying. A sturdy lad and brave too: he looked more like Giam every day. It was good he would have a sister and perhaps another brother, who knows, she thought with a blush. She wanted to have a large family.

Thinking back to her father's visit, he'd made a very good deal with the Verona merchants and this was only the start. Maria was determined to reduce the size of the estates to more manageable proportions. Besides, having her wealth in money, not property and goods made it easier for her to be with Giam wherever that might be. With the acceptance of her condition had come the realisation that it changed everything. More than ever she must be with Giam, whatever the cost.

Chapter Thirty-Six
London, 10th October, 1571

Quiff burst into the sitting room at Harte Street, startling Jacob and Roberto. He was breathless from running all the way from the Swan.

'He's here! He's here!' he shouted excitedly.

'Who are you talking about, Quiff and where is he?' said Jacob calmly. 'Just sit down, catch your breath and tell me slowly.'

Quiff sat down for a short while then explained. 'It's Count Ridolfi, he's here in London.'

'Are you sure, Quiff?'

'I'm certain. One of our liverymen works in a very exclusive tailor's shop frequented by some of the most influential men in London, including Count Ridolfi. Earlier today, Master Sutton goes in and asks for the a new doublet, Venetian breeches and matching hose that the Count ordered a few weeks ago, to be delivered to the house this afternoon.'

'Perhaps this Sutton fellow intends to wear them himself,' said Roberto.

'Not a chance,' said Quiff with a scoff. 'They're totally the wrong size, because I asked the same question of the liveryman.'

'So how can you be sure it's the Count?'

'Because I've seen him myself,' said Quiff triumphantly. 'When I heard about this at midday, I went along to the Count's house at the time the clothes were due to be delivered. I kept a careful watch and when Sutton met the liveryman at the door, I saw the Count peering out through the curtains in the room overlooking the front.' He jumped up excitedly. 'It has to be him. Sutton has sent the servants away and there's only supposed to be him in the house. Anyway,' he said defiantly, 'I'm sure I recognised him from the description you gave me. Trust me on that, Master Jacob.'

'Very well, Quiff, we'll proceed on the assumption the count is there. Well done, Quiff, an excellent piece of sleuthing. We'll discuss it after the meal. I don't want Mistris Simpkin chasing me because the meal is cold.'

After they'd finished, they discussed various ways of dealing with the situation. Knowing how dangerous Jed Sutton could be, Jacob was not prepared to put any of the apprentices at risk. It was getting late and they'd still not decided, so Jacob called a halt. 'I think it would be better if we sleep on it,' he said with a yawn. 'I'm rather tired, so I'll bid you good night.'

The following morning, Jacob decided to call a small conference on the situation. He sent Quiff off to the Crouched Friars to ask Will to cope without Roberto and himself and sent a message to Colonel Young. Jacob also sent a message to Captain Roberts, who had brought The Crystal up to Somers Key, just below London Bridge. It wasn't the best of districts, being near the Petty, a notorious haunt of thieves, but it was very convenient for both the Glass-Sellers and the Crouched Friars.

The warehouse on the Key was very well guarded and the crew of The Crystal helped to keep it secure. Word soon got around among the thieves to leave it well alone, unless you liked living dangerously!

As requested, they all met for the midday meal. Colonel Young was much taken with Mistris Simpkin's pasties. 'Much better food than we get in the mess,' he said, helping himself to another one. Jacob promised to get Mistris Simpkin to make some for him.

While he had been waiting for them to arrive, Jacob had formulated a plan. 'We have identified that Count Ridolfi is hiding in his own house,' he explained. 'Now that it's certain he is the leading figure in the plot against the Queen, it was expected he would stay in France. It must have been very important for him to come back. He entered the country without detection and we know he sent a letter to Norfolk instructing him to send money to Scotland.'

He paused to see if there were any questions and continued when there were none. 'For reasons of state, which I am not able to disclose, Lord Burghley wants him out of England and has commissioned me to arrange it.' He turned to Captain Roberts. 'Can The Crystal put to sea on the next tide?'

'I don't see why not if it's to be a short trip. We'd have to leave without a cargo, but we have enough supplies on board. We've only just finished unloading the glass from Murano.' He looked questioningly at Jacob. 'Where would we be heading?'

'I want to put the Count ashore at Calais. The plan is to bring him to the warehouse dressed as a seaman and then have him come aboard carrying something in case of prying eyes. When we get to Calais we will escort him safely to his house and come back to London.'

'In that case, I'd best put a little sweetener the way of the local customs officer,' said Captain Roberts with a wink. 'We don't want any of his minions snooping around.'

'What do you want me to do?' said Colonel Young.

'Is that sergeant who was shot by Ragazoni, when we arrested Maldini, still with you?'

'He most certainly is. What did you have in mind?'

'From what you told me that day, your sergeant is more at home in the city than tramping about in the woods.'

The colonel laughed. 'Well there aren't many twigs to step on in the city and he knows his way around. I'd go so far as to say he's my best man at following someone. Did you have something like that in mind?

Jacob nodded and went on to explain. The colonel and a body of his men were to be well hidden near to the Count's house. Jacob would go to the house and once he was inside, he wanted the colonel to march up to the house with a good show and announce they'd come to arrest Sutton and the Count. The sergeant and a few of his best men were to be on watch at the rear of the house. They were to keep out of sight and only get involved if Jacob was in trouble.

'I'm sure that there is a door from the cellar to the back alley,' Jacob explained. 'With the colonel at the front door, they will use the other exit. The sergeant and his men are to follow and watch my back in case of treachery, but keep out of sight. I hope they'll not be needed.' In reality, he was not sure, but it was best to be careful.

Roberto was all for coming, but Jacob told him that for the plan to work, he must go alone. 'The idea is to convince him I am just one step in front of the men coming to arrest him,' he looked at the colonel. 'With you hammering on the door and me telling Ridolfi that Burghley is after him, I hope to keep him off balance.

The trick will be to ensure he doesn't have too much time to think. Just give me a few minutes inside and then march up to the door.'

Jacob could see that Roberto was not happy. After further words with him, he agreed he could join the sergeant. 'Good enough,' said Roberto, 'I'll bring my crossbow. It might come in useful.'

'Don't forget the knives as well,' said Jacob, 'it will be a big comfort to know you're close by.'

High tide was at four that afternoon so speed was of the essence. With everyone in position, Jacob, wearing the repaired brigandine, marched up to the imposing front door of the Ridolfi house carrying a small wrapped parcel. A very wary Jed Sutton opened the door to him. He regarded him in a very unfriendly manner. 'What do you want,' he said in a very aggressive tone.

Jacob looked at him disdainfully. 'Is this the way you normally greet visitors to your master? I will inform him of your rudeness.'

Jed gave a snorting laugh of disdain. 'You'll have to go to France, he's not here,' he said, starting to close the door.

Putting his foot in the door, Jacob looked him squarely in the eye. 'I know he's here and so does Lord Burghley. I only learned a short while ago from Admiral Hawkins that they have found the missing cipher to the Baillie letters. The Count's part in organising the plot has been discovered and the Duke of Norfolk has been arrested and is in the Tower. Hawkins was told that Burghley was despatching a troop of men under a colonel to arrest both of you.'

'What sort of child do you take me for,' blustered Jed. 'I told you the Count's not here and if you don't leave, I'll make you.'

'It's no wonder the best chance to put Queen Mary on the throne has been wasted because of idiots like you,' he said loudly, pretending to be angry. 'This is your last chance to save the Count. Now, take me to him at once. There's not a moment to lose if we are to prevent him from being arrested.'

Before Jed could reply, the Count, stepped out of the shadows to Jacob's right. He held a pistol loosely in his right hand. It was not pointing at Jacob, but held by his side.

Jacob bowed. 'My apologies for forcing my way in, count, but we have little time if we are to avoid your arrest.' He indicated Jed. 'Let your man keep watch. From what Hawkins told me, the troops could be here any minute.'

The Count considered for a moment and motioned Jed to the window overlooking the door. 'Now Master Bell, you say the plot is discovered. Why should I believe you?

Jacob put on a worried look. 'We haven't time for this. The troops could be here any moment and then I will be arrested as well.'

The Count shrugged. 'It's a chance we will have to take.' He raised the pistol a little. 'Explain!'

Jacob repeated the story and then added, 'Why would I come to you warn you like this if I was a spy. What do I have to gain? I promised Queen Mary at Chatsworth I would try to help her and all I get is threats.' He looked the Count squarely in the eyes and told him the truth. 'The only reason I am here, is to help you to escape to France. My ship The Crystal is just by London Bridge. I have brought some seaman's clothes so you can get on board without detection. The captain has his orders and will sail as soon as you are on board. Please do as I ask and quickly. I am no threat to you, I simply want to see you safely out of the country.'

The Count could see that Jacob was telling the truth and lowered the pistol. 'Give me the parcel and I will change at once.' Jacob gave him the parcel and went to the window. 'Any sign of the troops?'

'Nothing,' said Jed and put his mouth near Jacob's ear. 'I don't trust you Bell,' he whispered threateningly. You're up to something and even if my…the Count,' he corrected himself, 'believes you, I don't.'

He looked out of the window again and stiffened as a troop of soldiers headed by a colonel, marched out of the street opposite and headed towards the house. Quickly shooting the bolts closed, he shouted to the Count. 'The troops are coming. We must leave by the cellar door.'

By now, Colonel Young and his men were making a fine noise at the front door. The colonel was shouting, 'Open in the name of the Queen,' and the troops were battering at the door. While they were busy at the front of the house, the three of them slipped out through the cellar door and headed for the river. They were seen by the waiting sergeant and shadowed all the way to the warehouse.

Twenty minutes later Jacob stood on the quarterdeck and watched as The Crystal slipped quietly away down river. The Count was safely stowed in Jacob's cabin. Jed Sutton after a hurried conversation with the Count had remained behind. Unfortunately, as he learned from Roberto, who joined him on board just before they sailed, Jed had somehow managed to escape in the maze of alleyways behind Somers Key.

Chapter Thirty-Seven
France, 11th October, 1571

Walsingham flew into a rage when he read Burghley's message for a second time. What had possessed Burghley to let Ridolfi leave the country? He was ever the appeaser. His policies were based on not upsetting Spain and France. Once I am in his position, he thought, things will be different. Nothing and no one must be allowed to threaten the Queen's reign. There was only one way to deal with threats to the Queen, remove them permanently, and be done with it.

He looked at the clock and after consulting the tide tables for Calais and London, decided what he must do. Ringing the hand bell vigorously, he waited impatiently until his secretary entered and then gave him a stream of instructions. Sitting back in his chair, he shook his head sadly. Burghley had made a bad mistake and now it was up to him to rectify it. Count Ridolfi must die.

The journey to Calais was uneventful. The Count promised to make sure that Hawkins and Jacob received due credit from the Guises and the Spanish King, for his escape. Jacob again reiterated his desire to help the Queen of Scots and Ridolfi expressed his gratitude. He apologised for Jed's behaviour and in a burst of confidence, told him the story of their relationship.

Jacob then went to have a word with Roberto. He did not want the Count to see him, as that might be important at some time in the future. Having made this clear, they discussed the future. Roberto was delighted when Jacob told him of his plan to return to Venice to persuade Maria to join him in London. 'As soon as we return to England, I will instruct Captain Roberts to prepare The Crystal for the trip to Venice. Would you like to come with me?'

Roberto took his time answering. 'It depends on what Elizabeth has to say. I'd love her to come with me. I've told her so much about Venice, she's dying to see it.'

'I'm sure she is. It's what to do with the children I suppose.'

Roberto nodded. 'They grow up so fast. It would be dangerous to take them, but if we left them behind, it would be at least five months.'

They agreed to talk further after Roberto had spoken to Elizabeth. They were interrupted by the lookouts call that land had been sited. As they went on deck Jacob remarked that since they were in France it was a pity they would not have time to go to visit Walsingham in Paris. 'The last time I saw him, he told me what a beautiful city it is and if I came there he would show me around.'

As soon as they were tied up, Jacob told the captain to be ready to leave when he returned and set off in the gig with the Count and a couple of sailors. Reaching the quay, Jacob left one of the sailors to guard the gig and the other accompanied him to escort the Count to his home.

When they reached the door, the Count held out his hand. 'I am in your debt, Master Bell and I will not forget it.'

Jacob took his hand, but before he could reply, a number of men burst out of the shadows and attacked them. Pushing the Count towards the door a servant had just opened, Jacob drew his sword. Turning to confront the attackers, he was hit on the head by a cudgel. As he staggered, two more assailants armed with cudgels battered him to the ground. The last thing Jacob saw as he sank to the ground under a flurry of blows was the Count darting into the doorway and a servant pointing a pistol at the men.

The Count had frozen for a moment as the men attacked them, but Jacob's push and intervention gave him enough time to dart into the house. The servant holding a pistol fired and the attacker running towards the door with raised cudgel was hit and fell clutching his shoulder. By now, the Count had freed his own pistols and fired at the men attacking Jacob. One of the men was hit in the leg and lurched away. As suddenly as they began, the attackers fled, taking their wounded companions with them.

Warily the Count and the other servant went to Jacob's assistance. He was lying still and his face was a bloody mess. To the Count's relief however, he could feel a pulse. The servant was examining the sailor who had accompanied them. He looked at the Count and shook his head.

'Master Bell is still alive,' the Count told the servant. 'Help me to get him into the house and then tell the coachman to get the carriage ready as soon as possible.' They carried Jacob into the living room and laid him carefully on the settle. A quick examination revealed no other injuries except the vicious beating he had endured. His breathing was shallow, but steady and of course, he was unconscious.

The servant returned at that moment with a bowl of water and some clean cloth. Carefully cleaning around Jacob's badly swollen left eye, he cleaned the cut above it and another on top of his head and bandaged it. Smelling salts produced no reaction from Jacob and the Count realised he might be unconscious for some time.

Getting to his feet, he retrieved his travel bag and removing some money, gave it to the servant. 'Close up the house for now and if anyone enquires, I have gone to Paris on business, you know nothing about Master Bell, or about anything else.' He straightened up and instructed the other servant who had just returned to help him put Jacob into the coach when it arrived.

'What about the sailor who was killed?' The servant looked at him questioningly.

'We don't have time to explain what happened. Get rid of the body. I fear that there will be another attempt on my life and we must leave for Paris and the safety of the Guises' château in the Marias. No one will touch us there.'

When Jacob and the sailor didn't return as promised in an hour, Roberto and Captain Roberts became anxious. 'I'm worried,' said Roberto. 'It shouldn't have taken as long as this.'

'I agree,' said the captain. 'From what the Count said, it was only about twenty minutes walk each way.' He looked at Roberto's strained face. 'We'll give him ten more minutes and then start a search.'

Fortunately, Roberto had overheard the directions to get to the Count's home so with a strong, armed party Roberto led the way. The Count's house was in darkness, the servant who eventually answered the door said the Count had left for Paris and he assumed the men who had escorted him had returned to their ship. Despite further questioning, the man could not, or would not give them any more information.

Captain Roberts ordered the men to spread out and search all the alleys on the way back to the harbour. A short distance from the Count's house they discovered the body of the sailor. With rising apprehension, they carried out an extensive search for Jacob, but no trace of him could be found. When all of the sailors had reported to the ship, Roberto and Captain Roberts discussed their next move. It was agreed to keep the authorities out of it. Remembering his conversation with Jacob about Walsingham, Roberto suggested he should go to Paris and enlist his help. Captain Roberts would go back to London and report to Burghley. 'Between them, surely they will be able to find the Count and discover what has happened to Jacob.'

Captain Roberts agreed suggesting that Roberto should take a good supply of money in case he needed to bribe officials, or hire men. The following morning he waved goodbye as Roberto took the mail coach to Paris and when it was out of sight, he strode purposefully towards the harbour.

Chapter Thirty-Eight
Paris, France, 12th October, 1571

When Walsingham heard the news of the failed attempt on Count Ridolfi he was not amused. He brushed aside the agent's excuses about Ridolfi's men saving him. 'The fact you have killed two of his men, or so you claim, is neither here, nor there. It was a mistake to use local ruffians, they're incapable of thinking for themselves. They should have gone straight for the Count and bypassed his men.'

When the man had left, Walsingham turned to his secretary. 'I want you to put the word round all of my agents. I want Count Ridolfi found.' He thought for a moment. 'Make sure the men we have close to the Guises know first. I suspect the Count may run to them for a safe hiding place if he thinks I'm behind the attack.' He waved the secretary away, saying he didn't want to be disturbed and considered his next move. He did not intend to tell Burghley about the debacle, if there were an enquiry, he would say his agents had investigated and thought it was the work of some local footpads. However, it was unlikely that Burghley would hear of it, or query it.

For the next two hours, he sifted through the many reports from his agents, making copious notes, ready for his next report to Burghley. His network of spies was very extensive and even included a man high up in court circles in the Spanish court. He was annoyed when there was a knock on the door. 'What do you want, I thought I said not to disturb me'

The secretary looked contrite. 'My apologies Ambassador, but you have a visitor with some disturbing news. Since it is about Count Ridolfi, I thought you would want to see him.'

'Very well,' said Walsingham, 'you'd better show them in. Does our visitor have a name?'

'I'm sorry, Ambassador, I should have said. It's a Master Roberto Rosso and the matter concerns the Queen's Glassmaker, Jacob Bell.'

Walsingham was astonished. 'Young Roberto Rosso, Bell's business partner, what in heaven's name is he doing in Paris? Show him in at once please.'

When Walsingham heard the story of the missing Jacob and the dead seaman, he realised at once what must have happened. Those idiots! Not only didn't they kill Ridolfi, it looks as though they may have killed one of his most useful agents. Despite this devastating news, not by a flicker did he disclose that he knew anything of the matter. Instead, he rang the bell for his secretary and reassured Roberto he would investigate the Count's whereabouts immediately.

'I can only assume that Jacob has gone somewhere with the Count,' said Walsingham, giving Roberto a kindly smile. 'Perhaps an opportunity arose to find out more on the people involved in the plot.' Not that he believed anything of the sort. The men from Calais thought they had killed two men. From that it would appear that Jacob was probably badly hurt and the Count had taken Jacob with him. Had he been dead, it was certain his body would have been left with the seaman.

'What about the dead seaman?' asked Roberto.

'Perhaps Jacob sent him back with a message and he was set on by footpads. There have been a number of reports about a gang operating in Calais.'

Roberto began to look less worried. 'Perhaps you're right. Do you think you can locate the Count to find out?'

Walsingham turned to the secretary who had been waiting patiently. 'Ask all of my agents to discover the whereabouts of Count Ridolfi as a matter of the utmost priority. They should also look out for Master Jacob Bell, who might be injured.'

He told Roberto who was looking alarmed that he should not worry, but it was a small possibility that he might have been hurt as well. 'The Guise château in the Marias might be a good starting point. Check if any doctors have been there in the last day and a half.'

The secretary departed and Roberto looked around in a rather lost sort of way. 'I don't suppose you've thought about where to stay? You are very welcome to stay here. That way you will be able to hear any news as soon as I get it.'

When a servant had taken Roberto to his room, Walsingham sat back and assessed the situation. He could expect a missive from Burghley not later than the following day. It would be disastrous if his part in this affair came out. The possible loss of Jacob Bell was also a disaster. Not only was he a very valuable agent, he was a favourite of the Queen. Should the worst happen and Jacob Bell was dead, all hell would break loose when she found out.

The priest looked down at the young man lying still and pale in the enormous four-poster bed. His badly swollen face was mottled with purple, yellow and blue bruises and bandages almost covered the top of his head. The beautiful, white damask sheets only enhanced the effects. He looked at the pretty nun standing quietly at the side of the bed. 'Will it be long before Monsieur le Comte arrives?'

'I cannot say, father, I was just told to ask you to wait until the Count arrived before beginning the last rites.'

He indicated the patient. 'How long has he been like this?'

'Three days now, he's been unconscious ever since he was attacked in Calais. I doubt the coach ride helped.'

The priest shuddered and crossed himself. 'He has taken a terrible beating. It is a wonder he is still alive.'

The nun nodded. 'I told the Count as much this morning. He told me that he owes his life to the young man and he will do everything in his power to see he recovers.'

'What has the doctor said about his chances?'

'Only that if he doesn't come out of this coma soon, he will waste away and die. Even if he does, the doctor thinks he may be paralysed. There is no reflex action in his legs.' She wiped his face carefully and put another damp cloth over his forehead. 'I have managed to moisten his lips with a little water, but he cannot swallow. Unless he does he will just get weaker. I think the Count is worried that he might die, that is why he sent for you.'

A few minutes later the Count arrived accompanied by Mary of Guise. Acknowledging the priest's respectful bow, he asked him to carry on and give Jacob the last rites.

Like rising to the surface of a deep pool, the man became aware of his surroundings. Through pain-filled slits of eyes, he could determine shapes, but had no sense of where, or who he was. There was sound. A deep, man's voice: words without meaning. He tried to understand, but he was too tired. He slept.

Time passed and he opened his eyes again. Only flickers of light shone in the room. Candles he thought triumphantly, that's what they are, candles. It was a huge effort to think and exhausted, but pleased with his small triumph, he slept again.

More time passed. Someone was saying a prayer in Latin: a woman's voice. Cautiously he opened his eyes and discovered that he no longer saw through slits. The woman gave a gasp. 'Praise be to God,' she said, making the sign of the cross, 'His mercy is great.' She wet a cloth in the bowl by the bed and gently moistened his lips.

The man was grateful and tried to speak, but only managed a croak. The woman smiled and it lighted up her lovely face. She spoke, but he didn't understand. The severe black and white clothes with the high starched white collar were familiar. A nun, he thought, perhaps I'm in a convent. He closed his eyes again and when he opened them again, the nun was supporting his head and holding something to his mouth. Warm liquid trickled into his mouth: it was delicious. He managed to swallow a little and the nun gave a delighted smile and held the spoon to his mouth again. He swallowed it a little more easily this time and the nun looked pleased. The man tried hard to please her, but after a few more spoonfuls, he drifted wearily into sleep.

The next time he awoke, he felt a little better. His head still ached, but was quite bearable. He tried to sit up, but he couldn't move. The door opened and the nun came in. 'You're awake,' she said in Italian and hurried to prop up his head with pillows.

'What is this place?' He could tell from the ornate bed, luxurious sheets and the wall hangings, that this was no convent.

'You are in the Château de Lorraine in the Marias district of Paris, Monsieur Bell.'

The man was quiet for several minutes as he digested this information. Monsieur Bell she had called him, but it didn't seem right. She must know him to say his name, but somehow it wasn't right. He tried to think why it was wrong, but nothing came. He thought about the other information, but that made no sense either. Try as he might he could not recall a château in Paris.

'How long have I been here and what happened to me?' It was obvious he'd been injured, but he had no memory of how.

'You were attacked by some ruffians and badly beaten. Count Ridolfi was very grateful to you for saving his life and brought you to Paris six days ago so you could get the best treatment here at the home of the Guise family.'

The man closed his eyes again. Names! All these names and not one familiar, he gave a deep sigh and opened his eyes.

'Do not worry, Monsieur Bell,' said the nun, regarding him kindly. 'Your head has been injured and it could take a little while for you to remember things.' She picked up the bowl from the bedside table and took the spoon. 'Don't fret about it for now. You must eat some of this delicious broth and build up your strength.'

Chapter Thirty-Nine
Paris, France, 20th October, 1571

Roberto had just come back from yet another fruitless search of the Paris streets when the secretary informed him there was news of Jacob. A short while later he sat in Walsingham's study as he explained. 'My agents have discovered that Jacob is alive, but injured. Count Ridolfi and the Guise family are caring for him at the Château de Lorraine and it would appear he is recovering from a serious injury.' Roberto was obviously full of questions, but Walsingham held up his hand to stop him. 'How he came to be injured I am not able to say.' Not even by a flicker did his face betray this was not true. He had become adept at lying in his many battles with traitors and politicians. The line between these two was often blurred, as he was fond of quoting.

Since Roberto was upset, he explained further. 'My agents have discovered that Ridolfi left Calais almost as soon as he arrived home. He went straight to the Château de Lorraine taking with him a badly injured man. A nun and the doctor of the Duke of Guise have been attending him. Five days ago he was still unconscious and was given the last rites.' When Roberto looked alarmed, he hurried to explain that since then the man had recovered somewhat and was taking food.

'Are we sure it's Master Jacob?' asked Roberto.

'From the information I have, I believe it is. I am confident enough to advise Lord Burghley that I have found him.' He anticipated Roberto's next question. 'Please be patient for a little while longer. I hope to have confirmation of the man's identity later today. Then we shall see what we can do to assist in his recovery and get him back to England.'

It was all the man could do to stop himself from crying out in pain as the two burly footmen lifted him into the chair beside the bed. The doctor had told him that morning that the blow he had received on his spine was the cause of the paralysis in his legs. 'I believe the paralysis will be only temporary and will ease when the swelling subsides.'

It had been another blow. Firstly, he couldn't remember who

he was and now he was paralysed from the waist down. It was all very well for the doctor to say he thought he would recover, but what if he didn't! He was also suffering from hallucinations.

The nun had given him some watered down wine to drink with his last meal. She said it would make a change. It certainly had. As soon as he handled the glass, he had this nightmarish vision of hell. The glass started to change shape as though it was liquid. He was trying to stop it running off the end of a rod-like thing while putting it into a red-hot opening from which intense heat was blasting out.

As quickly as it had come, the image faded and he was holding a glass in his shaking hands with wine spilling everywhere. The nun told him not to worry, but he didn't tell her about the nightmare. The same thing had happened a few hours later when the doctor was examining him. Suddenly it was a woman leaning over him and telling him to wake up. It felt as though his mind was on fire. The more he tried to explain what he was seeing, the more it hurt. Suddenly the image was gone and the doctor was there once more. He didn't seem to notice anything was wrong, but simply told him he wanted him to try to sit up for a while.

He sat in the chair for about an hour and despite many attempts, he could find no trace of feeling in his legs, even when the doctor stuck pins in. The doctor then had a word with him about his loss of memory. 'It is entirely possible you will get fragments of memory triggered off by things that remind you. It's usually the strong memories that come first. Have you had anything like that?'

He told the doctor about the two nightmares as he called them. He was assured that this could be his memory returning and he should view it as a good sign and try to make sense of the scene. The doctor called a halt for now and the man was grateful to lie down again. Just before he fell asleep, he wondered if he would ever know who he was.

The following morning after a good sleep, he woke up with his head feeling clear for the first time. The nun told him that after he'd broken fast, Count Ridolfi was coming to see him. 'He has some important matters to discuss with you and the Duke of Guise is coming with him. We'd better make a little effort with your appearance, Jacob Bell, you have quite a straggly beard now.'

The man looked at her with a strange puzzled look. She had called him Jacob Bell again, but that wasn't right. The name Giam came into his mind, but Giam Bell didn't seem right either. It was very perplexing. Both names seemed slightly familiar, but neither was quite right. The nun came back with some scissors, a comb and a brush and began to trim his beard.

When the visitors arrived, the man was sitting up in the chair by the bed with his beard freshly trimmed and his hair carefully combed into a queue. Ridolfi was delighted. 'Good day to you, Jacob Bell, it is good to see you looking better. Allow me to present the Henri de Lorraine, Third Duke of Guise.'

The man inclined his head in a small bow. 'Forgive me for not rising, my lord: I seem to be having a little problem with my legs.' He gave a bright smile, but it was a little forced. Suddenly, an expression of intense surprise crossed his face, followed by a deeply, indrawn breath. He closed his eyes for a moment as if in pain and then let out the breath he'd been holding.

He opened his eyes again and his face was wreathed in smiles. 'And a very good day to you too, Count Ridolfi and yes I am Master Glassmaker Jacob Bell of the Crouched Friars Glass-works!'

The Count was elated and the Duke clapped his hands in delight. 'Capital, capital, you have regained your memory. When did this happen?'

'This very moment,' said Jacob excitedly. 'When the Count called me Jacob Bell, everything suddenly fell into place.' He was silent for a short while as he concentrated on what had happened to him. Try as he might, the last thing he could remember was leaving the ship to escort the Count to his home.

'I've been having flashes of memory a bit like nightmares, but nothing seemed to make sense,' explained Jacob. 'Until now, that is. I can remember everything clearly up to the time we left The Crystal at Calais. After that, everything is a blank.'

When the Count learned this, he recounted all the events that had happened up to the present, praising Jacob for saving his life. The Duke was also very generous in his praise and Jacob felt like a fraud. It would be instinct that had made him push Ridolfi to the door and turn to face his attackers, not any strong desire to save Ridolfi's life. Not wishing to discuss this further, he changed the subject and asked Ridolfi what it was he had come to discuss.

'I confess that it is a matter of some embarrassment to me, that despite my debt to you, I have not informed anyone of your presence here in Paris.'

This created quite a quandary for Jacob. He'd assumed that Ridolfi would have sent a message to the ship by the sailor. When Ridolfi told him the assailants had killed the sailor and that he had fled to Paris taking Jacob with him, he became angry. 'Surely you could have instructed your servant to give the search party a message,' he said. 'They were sure to come and look for me.'

'I'm sorry, Jacob Bell, but I am not a fighter. I am just a banker.' Cheeks flushed with embarrassment, the Count admitted that he had panicked. 'I should have sent a message to your ship, but I did not. When we got to Paris, you were likely to die. The Duke suggested I waited to see how you fared before we took a decision.'

The Duke of Guise held both hands palm up in a gesture of contrition. 'I regret my part in this after your efforts to save the Count cost you so much. We did not inform the Ambassador in Paris of your whereabouts, since I have no love for Walsingham.' He gave a rueful smile. 'In any case, I respect his talents and it would greatly surprise me if he doesn't know already. That man has spies everywhere.' He gave a very typical shrug. 'However, more than ever now that you have recovered your memory, we wish to rectify the matter. Your partner at the Crouched Friars, a Monsieur Rosso, has come to Paris to look for you. He has been asking questions about you everywhere. We suggest, with your approval, that we send a message for him to come here to see you as soon as possible.'

That Roberto was here in Paris was not much of a surprise for Jacob. His friend was very smart and tenacious. He had no doubt remembered that Walsingham was English Ambassador and come to alert him of Jacob's disappearance. He readily agreed to them sending the message with all speed and shortly afterwards they left to arrange it.

Long before the messenger had left, they were forestalled by the arrival of Roberto at the gates of the château. Alerted by Walsingham that Jacob was at the château in Marias, Roberto had set off at once. At first, there was a language problem since Roberto's French was very poor and so was the servant's English. A second servant was called who spoke some English and denied that either the Count or Jacob were at the château. When Roberto persisted, the servant made him wait in the entrance salon and went off into another room.

Roberto looked around the ornate atrium with its ostentatious decorations. On the far side was a flight of stairs, which curved gracefully upwards, while in serried ranks along the walls, were portrait after portrait of elaborately dressed noblemen and women, presumably members of the Guise family.

Roberto wandered across to look at them and had just finished studying the first, when a discreet cough came from behind. The servant begged his pardon for the delay and misunderstanding and conducted him up the stairs to the bedroom where Jacob was waiting.

When Roberto saw Jacob for the first time, he was appalled at how thin and frail he looked. The short beard and moustache were strange, but he was easily recognisable: his face seemed paler by contrast, except for the multi-coloured bruises on the left side of his face.

Jacob apologised for not getting up as Roberto hovered uncertainly in front of his chair. He held his arms wide and Roberto embraced him.

'That wasn't so bad, Roberto,' said Jacob. 'I may be injured, but I won't break.' When he explained about his legs and his memory loss, Roberto was appalled.

'At least I've got my memory back,' said Jacob with a querulous smile. 'Well, most of it at least, except the bit from the ship at Calais to here.'

They talked for some time and Jacob made it clear that despite the problem with his legs, he wished to return to London as soon as possible. The nun, keeping a watchful eye on Jacob saw he was getting very tired and asked Roberto to let him rest. Roberto promised to come back the following day and Jacob rested, elated, but apprehensive about the future.

Chapter Forty
Murano and France, 21st October, 1571

Ricardo regarded his daughter with pride and not a little surprise. During the last few years, she'd contended with more than some people had in a full lifetime. Whereas many would have wilted under the pressure, Maria seemed to go from strength to strength. They had just completed a meeting with a group of merchants from Verona to dispose of a substantial part of their joint assets in the silk trade.

Maria had shown a grasp of the business that equalled his own: no mean feat considering he had many more years of experience. Luckily, they had a more detailed grasp of the effect that the loss of Cyprus would have on the trade with Bursa. The merchants there had sent a substantial amount of stock to Venice via the Morisini ships, to be held on their account. They had been fortunate to get it out during the confusion following the Battle of Lepanto. Despite the defeat of the Ottoman fleet, they were still able to enforce a blockade of the Eastern Mediterranean that was unlikely to be broken. Already there were rumours of forests being denuded for wood to replace the galleys lost at Lepanto.

During the negotiations, Maria had disposed of a substantial part of the Ragazoni business and estates in Verona. She played on the fact that as a woman and a pregnant one as well, she could not cope with running them. Nevertheless, if they thought they would acquire them for very little, they were swiftly disabused. The eventual price agreed was well into the top echelon of the forecasts that Ricardo had made.

He smiled indulgently at his daughter taking her ease in the cool of the shaded part of the central courtyard. Maria herself was feeling very well at the moment. Her morning sickness had gone and she looked a picture of health.

'What have you decided about Giacomo and the wedding. With the money you acquired today, you are a very rich woman indeed. Never mind the residues of the Ragazoni business and property in Venice. There will be suitors queuing at your door from all over the Republic.' The latter remark was delivered with a sparkle in his eye and a sly smile.

Maria gave an amused chuckle. 'If Giam doesn't hurry back, I'll have to start looking at these other options.' She gave her father an oblique look. 'As to the Ragazoni property, I have already disposed of more than half.' She smiled at her father's look of surprise.

'You have been busy, Maria,' said Ricardo, looking at her shrewdly. 'This seems to be part of some plan. Are you going to enlighten me?'

Maria became serious and going over to her father sat down beside him and linked arms, leaning her head against his shoulder. 'I know you want me to marry Giacomo and settle down here in Venice. In many ways, I wish that was possible, but there are things you should know.' She squeezed his arm and gave him a loving look. 'I have been most fortunate to have a father like you. You have ensured I was well educated; allowed me far more freedom than any other daughter I know and always showed your love and support when I needed it.' She hesitated, because she knew that what she was about to say would cause him pain.

Ricardo made it easy for her. 'After a statement like that, there has to be a "but".' His eyes showed his sadness, but he gave her a smile. 'You want to go to England to be with Giacomo. That's why you have been disposing of many of the Ragazoni assets.'

'You read me like a book, father. But I want you to know that it's a decision that took a lot of making. The final clinching factor was the new baby.' She put her hands on her stomach that so far was showing no signs of a bump. 'Giam has made it plain he wants to stay in England. I think that although he still has affection for the Republic, the Old Families hurt him too much by their total dismissal of his birthright. From what he told me, England is a place where a man can carve out his own destiny. He has found acceptance, wealth and favour from the English court because of the deeds he has performed on their behalf. I could not ask him to turn his back on that, nor could I deprive him of his two children.'

Ricardo sat up and turning to her embraced her tightly. When he released her he simply asked when she would be leaving. Maria kissed him on the cheek. 'Thank you for your understanding, father. I hope to leave in not later than two months time. I must arrive in London well before the baby is born in April.'

In Paris, Walsingham was delighted at the news that Jacob was recovering, but was troubled by the report of his paralysis. He told Roberto that he would do everything in his power to smooth the task of getting him home.

When Roberto returned to the château, his reception was entirely different. The servants were very respectful and he was shown into a room where the Count was sitting. 'Monsieur Rosso, come in, sit down. I was hoping to have a word with you. Jacob Bell has told me of his plan to leave for London as soon as possible. The doctor has advised that should he attempt such a plan without building up his strength, the journey would have a very deleterious effect on his health. Not only that, but the jolting of a coach may cause permanent damage to his back and make the paralysis permanent.'

'Does that mean that the doctor believes he can recover,' he asked eagerly.

'Most certainly,' said the count, 'but only if he is prepared to work hard.' He leaned forward and spoke confidentially. 'The nun who has nursed similar cases is concerned by his refusal to discuss the future treatment of his condition. It is almost as though he has accepted that this will be permanent and therefore there is nothing to discuss.'

'That doesn't sound like the Jacob I know,' said Roberto in a puzzled voice. 'Even when things look desperate, he always remains positive.'

He regarded the Count warily, being very aware that one word out of place could jeopardize Jacob's position. After all, despite the Count's obvious concern for Jacob, it was built on sand. Jacob was not an ally, but a spy working for Lord Burghley. Should that be discovered, Jacob's survival was likely to be very short.

'The doctor tells me he has come across this before,' the Count went on, oblivious to Roberto's wariness, mistaking it for concern. 'Particularly in the case of men who lead an active life: it seems they become depressed at the thought of not being able to have an active life again and give up.'

'I will not allow that to happen to Jacob,' said Roberto fiercely.

'Leave it to me, Count and thank you for telling me.'

'Not at all, Monsieur Rosso, I am in Jacob Bell's debt and I will do my best to repay it. Which leads me to the other matter I wanted to discuss. When I was at court in England towards the end of Henry Tudor's reign, he became very overweight and couldn't ride. A chair with carrying poles was made for him. It took four chairmen to carry him, but it occurs that while Jacob Bell is incapacitated, a similar contraption might be useful. What do you think?'

Roberto gave a smile. 'I doubt Master Jacob would need more than two chairmen, but it seems an excellent idea. He could get about in reasonable comfort in London. I have seen one or two such chairs with influential merchants in them.'

'Excellent,' said the Count, 'because I have already taken the liberty of purchasing one from a leading coach maker in Paris. It will be ready in about a week. That also happens to be the length of time the doctor recommends that Jacob Bell should rest and build up his strength with some good nourishing food.'

Two weeks later, Jacob was back in Harte Street and Elizabeth Rosso and John Jacob had moved in too. They had a further addition to the household in Jack and Bob Petts, Jacob's chairmen. Jack was of medium height, barrel-chested and immensely strong. His brother Bob, had the same fair hair and ruddy complexion, but was slightly taller and thinner. Brought up on a farm near Tottenham, they were used to manual labour and had been recommended by the husband of Rebecca, Elizabeth's sister. They found lodgings nearby and were always the last to leave and the first to arrive.

Jacob was finding it difficult to be positive about his paralysis. Despite the assurance of the French doctor that he would slowly recover, he suffered from severe mood swings. Had it not been for Elizabeth Rosso, who simply refused to allow him to feel sorry for himself, he would have become totally apathetic.

On hearing of Jacob's situation from Burghley, Queen Elizabeth immediately dispatched the Royal Physician, Doctor Bayly, to attend him. When he had examined him thoroughly and talked to him at length, he pronounced that Jacob was suffering from the melancholy and prescribed a regular concoction containing St. John's Wort.

His examination of Jacob's injuries confirmed the view of the French doctor that it was simply a matter of time for the paralysis to ease. He confided to Roberto that he was less sure that Jacob would recover the full use of his legs.

In the meantime, he told Elizabeth Rosso that Jacob must exercise regularly to prevent the muscles from wasting and he must be encouraged to work hard at trying to walk.

The part that Elizabeth liked the most was "he must exercise the muscles regularly, or he runs the risk of losing them".

Jacob became heartily sick of Elizabeth quoting "use them, or lose them" to him when she was trying to cajole him into trying to walk. Despite all of the advice, Jacob simply didn't believe he was going to walk again. He'd no feelings at all below the waist and as the days passed he began to feel he should accept his situation and adjust his life accordingly. What future did he have with Maria? He was no longer the man she loved.

Chapter Forty-One
Venice and London, 1st December, 1571

Looking back towards the deep-water quay, Maria stood by the rail of her flagship galleass and looked at the familiar sights of the city of her birth. Apart from short trips to Verona, she had never left it for long. Now she was committed to leaving Venice, possibly never to return.

She turned and embraced her father. Holding him tight, the tears coursed down her face. 'It is so hard to leave you, father,' she sniffled. 'I owe you so much.'

Ricardo too was having difficulty in holding back the tears. He held her at arm's length and in a voice choking with emotion, told her what she needed to know. 'Maria, my dear child, you owe me nothing. You have repaid my love over and over again.' He wiped her tears with his kerchief and she gave a tremulous smile. 'You will find that one of the most difficult things a parent can do is to know when to let your child go.' He indicated his grandson standing a short distance away with Anna's protective arm around him. 'You will feel the same when it is time to let Rico go.' He caught Maria's instinctive gesture of feeling her abdomen and smiled. 'Yes, and your daughter-to-be too.' He smiled. 'Daughters are the worst of course,' he said and was rewarded with a smile. He took her hand and led her across to Rico. Bending down, he regarded him seriously. 'I will miss you young man,' he said ruffling his hair.' Turning to Anna, he told her to take good care of Maria and Rico and then with a final embrace with Maria and a gesture of farewell, he climbed down into the waiting gondola.

When he had disappeared from sight, Maria made her way to the stern deck to have words with the captain. As Maria climbed the steps to the upper deck, Captain Carreras offered a helping hand. Lunardo was resplendent in his new uniform of Commodore of the combined Morisini-Ragazoni fleet. Maria had paid a high price to purchase both the Galliano and to release Lunardo from his contract with the Arsenale.

When they were at the discussion stage, two months earlier, Maria had outlined her plans for the future to Lunardo and invited him to join her. The fleet now consisted of two great galleys and three large cogs, which had been partially rebuilt to lower the centre of gravity and improve their armaments. Lunardo had based the design on certain aspects of The Crystal.

Because of the incursions of the Ottoman ships, the Galley to Flanders summer fleet had ceased two years ago. Maria believed after her discussions with Lunardo, that a well-armed fleet such as she now possessed, would be a match for any Ottoman galleys, pirate, or fleet: especially since the main Ottoman fleet had been decimated at the battle of Lepanto.

Maria was convinced that the Portuguese and English ships, better suited to open waters outside the Mediterranean, would continue to erode Venice's trade with the Far East, particularly now the route from the Eastern Mediterranean was blocked by the occupation of Cyprus.

However, Europe remained a good market for Murano glass, silk and spices. Giam controlled the trade of glass in England, so sales would increase. Accordingly, Maria had used the Ragazoni money to buy out a couple of the major glass-works. The three cogs carried a good cargo of glass from her glass-works and spices and silk garnered from the supplies held for the Bursa merchants.

'Has Doctor Nguyên and his wife settled into their cabin satisfactorily, Lunardo?'

Ricardo had insisted on paying the doctor to accompany Maria, to ensure that the baby was protected. He was to return with the Galliano. Maria had remonstrated with Ricardo when she learned he was paying the good doctor 25,000 ducats, but when he said it was a price well worth paying for peace of mind, she was secretly very relieved.

'He has, Lady Maria and he told me he was looking forward to visiting London, of which he has heard many tales.' The sailing master interrupted them and informed Lunardo that all of the ships were ready to sail on his orders. Lunardo looked quizzically at Maria and when she nodded, gave the order to weigh anchor and send the signal to the other ships to follow.

Totally unaware of Maria's plans, Jacob was being carried to his chair in the living room at Harte Street by Jack Petts. He swung Jacob into his chair with effortless ease, while Elizabeth Rosso fussed around fluffing up cushions to make sure Jacob's back was supported.

'Stop fussing, woman,' said Jacob testily, 'I'm quite capable of sitting in a chair without your help.'

Elizabeth scoffed. 'It's high time you walked here for yourself then, instead of having this big lump carry you about,' she said, indicating the grinning Jack Petts. Roberto who had watched the scene in high amusement, laughed as Elizabeth pretended to storm off in high dudgeon, barely pausing as she gave him a kiss and a wink. The indignant scowl when Roberto slapped her playfully on the bottom turned into a beaming smile and a chuckle as she left the room.

The reason the house was in upheaval was the imminent visit of Lord Burghley to discuss the latest developments in the Ridolfi plot. When he arrived, with Colonel Young, he made no reference to Jacob's situation at all, but got straight down to business.

Burghley said he was delighted that the Count had been whisked out of the country, but was less than pleased with the disappearance of Jed Sutton. He had immediately issued instructions that Sutton was to be arrested and arranged for a description of him to be sent to all of his agents and the Watch.

On Jacob's advice, the colonel's men had made a thorough search of the basement area, but apart from some recently burned papers in the fire grate, the only other thing they'd found was a copper ring with a bell and number engraved on it, which was found in the corner of the cellar, close to the wall chute.

When Jacob heard about the ring, he became agitated. 'Do you have the ring with you?'

'As a matter of fact I do,' said the colonel, holding it out for Jacob's inspection.

Jacob recognised the ring at once, as did Roberto when Jacob passed it to him.. It was the one given to Jenkins, the missing servant. There seemed no doubt now that Quiff was right, Jenkins was dead.

When Jacob enquired if there was any news of a body being

found downstream of the Ridolfi's house, Burghley shook his head sadly. 'I'm afraid not, but I will arrange for the river authorities to organise a search of the riverbanks right down to the estuary.'

He commiserated with Jacob on the probable loss of one of the Ring members and promised he would arrange for the Jenkins family to receive a pension from the Crown.

It was also agreed that from now on, Burghley would have little direct contact with Jacob. 'It's possible that Sutton may try to follow you, or have you followed. I am anxious to ensure that he is captured, since I have recently learned that his mother Agnes Sutton is a chambermaid in the Queen's service. It is entirely possible that she has been passing information to her son and hence to Ridolfi.'

'What have you done about her?' asked Jacob. 'Are you going to question her about her son?'

'Not at present,' said Burghley. 'I prefer to have her watched to see if she will lead us to him.' He gave a slight smile. 'I've made sure she is not in a position to divulge any serious information, although it's impossible to stop the gossiping of the ladies-in-waiting, so she might hear something.'

Jacob said that the Ring would keep looking for Sutton, but a messenger interrupted them at that point and when Burghley read the message, he couldn't contain his delight.

'At last!' he burst out delightedly. 'Higford has disclosed where the cipher was hidden and they found it where he said, under the tiles at Howard House. Phelippes has used it to decipher the letter we found at the house earlier.'

'That's excellent news, my lord,' said Jacob, 'but does it get us any further in sorting out the plot?'

'Indeed it does. The letter was from Mary Stuart to the Bishop of Ross written in February. In it, she expressed the opinion that Count Ridolfi would be the best man to send to Spain, but that she left the decision to the Duke of Norfolk.'

Jacob was sad, because it definitely linked Mary Stuart and Norfolk with Ridolfi's plans and purposes. He had been sorry for Mary, having fallen a little under her charm. Not the first to do so, but with far less disastrous consequences than many who had.

'What now, my lord?' he asked, knowing that this letter would probably seal the fate of Norfolk at least.

Shaking his head sadly Burghley thought for a moment before replying. 'Norfolk has been my friend of many years, but I am afraid that after this disclosure, I see a very bleak future for him.'

Shortly afterwards the meeting ended and the ever-willing Jack Petts carried Jacob, who was in considerable pain now, up to his bed. Lying back against the mound of pillows, Jacob contemplated his own prospects. With no sign yet of any improvement in his legs, his own outlook looked equally as bleak.

Chapter Forty-Two
London, December, 1571 - February, 1572

Jacob, having carried out his commission successfully, despite the cost to himself, now concentrated the efforts of the Ring on finding Jed Sutton. Unfortunately, despite their best efforts, no trace of him could be found.

With the help of Colonel Young, Jacob engaged two former comrades of his to act as guards at Harte Street. Not a soul could get in without being checked in by them. At night, they took it in turns to keep watch and everyone slept sounder for their presence.

Towards the end of the December, he learned that Francis Drake had arrived back in England. Hawkins visited Jacob to find out how he was getting on and to pass on some interesting information. He informed Jacob that he had received news that Drake's expedition had done well by seizing various Spanish cargoes and ships.

'Where is he now,' enquired Jacob. He had not thought of Drake at all for months and now there was the exciting prospect that they might make a lot of money.

'Lying outside Plymouth, awaiting a reply from the Queen confirming her acceptance of his prizes as legitimate privateering,' said Hawkins. 'Not that it's likely she'll turn down the chance to make a substantial return on her money,' he said, with a knowing smile.

They did not have long to wait for news. It came in the form of a letter from Drake that informed him that if he presented the enclosed receipt to the London Goldsmiths, he would receive his share of the expedition profit. The letter was signed 'your humble servant and grateful friend Francis Drake'.

When Jacob looked at the enclosed receipt, he couldn't believe his eyes. His share amounted to two thousand, two hundred and fifty pounds. John Isham would receive a similar sum and Roberto, a half share. Their gamble in backing Drake had been most successful. As Elizabeth said when she heard the news, 'If that doesn't cheer you up then nothing will!' The medicine was also helping and he began to try a little more with his exercises.

Christmas had come and gone and even Jacob had roused out of his depression a little at the antics of young John Jacob. The house had been full of people with the Isham family in full attendance. Even Rebecca and her husband had come, proudly showing off their new baby.

Things settled down into a steady routine afterwards, with the Petts brothers taking Jacob wherever his fancy took him and Elizabeth cajoling him to try to walk. Indeed there were a few signs of progress, but the painful swelling at the base of his spine still made sitting difficult and painful.

Early in January, Jacob received a report from Quiff. It was not from one of their usual sources, but from the landlord of the Swan. He told Quiff that the previous evening some men had been drinking and in his hearing had made a virulent verbal attack on Lord Burghley and one of the two younger men was making threats against Lord Burghley.

The landlord had recognised the older man. His name was William Herle and he was a regular in the Swan. The landlord was sure that Herle was an informer. He was known as such by a number of the less salubrious customers, who were very wary when he was around.

The name was also familiar to Jacob. He remembered Burghley telling him that Herle had been put in the same cell as Baillie to gain his confidence. Lord Burghley didn't like the man, but he was useful, so long as you realised he would sell his own mother if the price were right.

Jacob was not sure what Herle was up to, but he was sure that Burghley needed to be told. If this were one of his own plots, no harm would be done: if it wasn't, then Burghley needed to be warned.

When Roberto took the message, Burghley said he was not involved in anything that Herle was doing. 'Thank Jacob Bell for the warning please, Roberto. I will have words with Master Herle and see what he's up to.'

When Roberto told him how Lord Burghley had said it, Jacob had the feeling that it might be a slightly uncomfortable meeting for Master Herle!

And so it turned out. Jacob learned from Burghley that Herle said he had befriended the two men, to find out what they were doing. Berney and Mather were being very vocal in their condemnation of Burghley and his arrest of the Duke of Norfolk. Mather was boasting about his friendship and regular conferences with Guerau de Spes, the Spanish Ambassador.

Herle was instructed to further ingratiate himself with Mather and Berney and to keep Burghley informed of any developments. Herle later sent a letter to Burghley that resulted in the two men being arrested and sent to the Tower. During questioning, it emerged that Mather was the active spirit. He admitted that De Spes suggested the idea of assassinating Burghley and that his steward, Borghese, had actively promoted it.

Burghley slipped in to see Jacob a few days later.

'Following the disclosures of Mather, De Spes was called before the Queen's Council,' Burghley explained. 'He accused me of being the orchestrator of all the problems between his king and the Queen's majesty.'

'I cannot believe he had the gall to suggest such a thing,' said Jacob in astonishment. 'He's been an active party to most of the plotting that's been going on.'

Burghley nodded. 'Indeed, that is so and the Council left him in no doubt that was the opinion of them all. Lord Sussex confirmed everything to De Spes in his fluent Italian.' Burghley looked amused throughout his account of the De Spes arraignment. 'The upshot is that De Spes continued to abuse me and has been dismissed from these shores and is now under house arrest.'

'And what is it you wish of me, my lord?' Jacob was curious to know what Burghley had in mind. He was extremely surprised by the answer.

'De Spes is under house arrest and is waiting for a ship to transport him to Calais. Admiral Hawkins has been deputed to escort him once the Twelve days are over. Apparently, the former ambassador still has a good opinion of Hawkins.'

Jacob laughed. 'Hawkins could sell glass to Murano.'

Burghley joined in the laughter. 'That's very true. Meantime, the Queen wishes to commission The Crystal to take De Spes to Calais. I'm sure you will find the terms of the commission to be very favourable. We may not be able to acknowledge you in public, but at least we can show our approval in other ways.'

'What if De Spes finds out about the other gun deck? He'll report back to Spain.'

'I'm sure Hawkins will manage to keep him locked in his cabin,' said Burghley, obviously enjoying the thought of De Spes's discomfort. 'He'll be told it's a condition of his release. In any case, the word will get out soon, since Hawkins and his father-in-law, Benjamin Gonson the Navy Treasurer, are already converting ships to a similar design. With many more ships in service, it will be impossible to keep it a total secret.'

Having received Jacob's agreement to the commission, he brought up the matter of Jed Sutton. 'I thought you ought to know, a man answering his description was seen getting off the Dover packet at Calais by one of Walsingham's men.'

Jacob thanked him. 'If only it's true,' he said with feeling, 'I'll breathe a little easier if it is!

Hopefully, Sutton would be informed by Count Ridolfi of Jacob's part in saving his life and it would take the edge off his suspicions.

Jacob was given no time to dwell on the news, because Elizabeth came to cajole him into his walking exercises. She instructed Jack Petts to pick him up and bring him down to the small walled courtyard at the rear of the house. When Jacob had been put into a chair placed for him, he looked in surprise at the contraption that Bob Petts had just finished.

It had two frames about three feet apart, with a rounded bar at the top of each at waist height. The contraption was about twelve feet long and Jacob wondered what it was for. He didn't have to wait long. Jack picked him up, carried him to the near end of the poles and lowered his feet to the floor, holding him securely by the waist. Instinctively, Jacob seized the poles in each hand for security and Elizabeth clapped her hands in delight.

'Well done, Jacob, you have the idea already. Now try to use your legs to walk.'

Chapter Forty-Three
London, January/February, 1572

January was very cold and although the snow had not been very deep, there had been a series of very severe frosts that had frozen the Thames over so that people could walk from one bank to the other: even a wedding was held on the ice.

Fortunately, the house at Harte Street was always warm. The large cooking fire at the rear of the lobby and the fires in each room were kept well supplied with wood from the glass-works store.

Relaxing after the evening meal Jacob, was sitting in his favourite chair in front of the roaring fire. Replete with food and wine, he was drowsily going over the information he'd received that day from Lord Burghley concerning the trial of Norfolk a few days earlier, on the sixteenth.

"With the weight of evidence we provided," Burghley wrote, "the verdict was a forgone conclusion. So much so, that the Duke did not seek to bring witnesses to rebut it, despite being given the opportunity. He was found guilty and condemned to a traitor's death, but I feel the Queen will be loathe to sign the Royal Warrant so the verdict can be carried out.

The Queen's majesty has always been a merciful lady, to her own detriment. She hesitates, because she believes she is more beloved of the people for being merciful: even to the extent of doing herself harm."

Despite the certain guilt of Norfolk Jacob agreed with Burghley that Norfolk was a reluctant traitor. While he stood ready to profit by treason, he was never an active agent in Ridolfi's plans and purposes. As Norfolk pointed out at the trial, he never took any steps to organise his very considerable following in support of domestic rebellion.

There was a huge surprise at the end of the letter when Burghley told him that the Queen had granted Norfolk's request that his two children should be fostered by Burghley. In his postscript Burghley wrote, "For love of a friend I have agreed to this request, where for his treason I was obliged to condemn him for love of my Queen and country, which was the stronger."

Jacob was lost in admiration for the compassion, strength and loyalty of Lord Burghley, who could no more have concealed his friend's treason than he could turn away his poor orphans. He was becoming a huge influence on Jacob's life and he counted it a privilege that Burghley trusted him with his confidence.

Over the next few weeks Burghley's predictions of the Queen's vacillation became evident. It was true she issued warrants to carry out the execution of Norfolk, but hastily recalled them before sentence could be carried out.

Towards the end of February, the weather took a turn for the better and there were a few days of unseasonable warm sunshine. Elizabeth Rosso of course insisted he should continue his work with the bars. The depression that had so hampered him at first was much better, thanks to the potions of St. Johns Wort, but his legs were still a matter for concern. He was now able to move his feet to give a semblance of walking, but without the bars could not even get around using sticks.

Even Doctor Bayly was less optimistic. When Jacob insisted he be honest in his diagnosis, he was forced to admit for the first time that a full recovery might not be possible. He had examined the lump on Jacob's lower spine that was still refusing to go down, even after blood-letting with leeches. Jacob hated the creatures and was not at all sure of the benefits of using them. In fact, after the last session, he told the doctor he would not countenance further use of them.

The day following the consultation, he was sitting in the chair by the fire drinking a pewter mug of ale when Roberto came in. There was a strange expression on his face. He announced that some visitors had arrived and asked if he should show them in.

Puzzled by Roberto's manner Jacob asked him to do so and enquired who they were. Roberto shot out of the room without an answer and shortly after, Jacob heard excited voices on the stairs. He turned to put the mug on the table by his side and when he straightened up, he had the surprise of his life. Just inside the room stood a beaming Maria with her arm around the shoulders of her son.

Jacob's jaw dropped and he struggled to speak except for a strangled, 'Maria?'

'Is that the best greeting you can manage after we've come so far to see you?' she scolded, but there was laughter and joy in her voice. 'Go and say hello to your father, Rico.'

The boy hesitated a moment, but after a little push towards Jacob and a reassuring nod, he shot across the room into Jacob's open arms. Jacob swept him up into an embrace that threatened to crush the life out of him, but Rico didn't complain, throwing his arms round his neck.

'Let me have a good look at you,' he said, holding the boy a little way from him and balancing him on his knees. 'My, you've grown so much since I saw you last.'

Rico regarded him quizzically and ran his fingers over Jacob's beard. 'I didn't recognise you at first, father. You are very pale and the hair makes you look different. Have you been ill? It's horrid when you are ill. I remember when my mother and I were so ill it took many weeks to recover.'

Maria interrupted what threatened to be a long explanation. She lifted him up and sent him to Anna who had just come into the room. She curtsied to Jacob and the boy took her hand trustingly. 'Come along, Master Rico, Mistris Simpkin the housekeeper has promised to find some cakes with you. We'll leave your mother to talk to Master Jacob while we go and help her to look.'

And talk they did, far into the night, but not before they had embraced and kissed each other with love and affection. 'I never thought I would see this day,' said Jacob, with wonder in his voice. He indicated his legs. 'These damnation legs made me feel that we could never have a life together.'

Maria looked at him in surprise. 'How could you think I would spurn you because of your legs. And yes, Elizabeth has told me the full situation. She sat back on her heels and drew attention to her swollen stomach and Jacob's eyes were wide with wonder again. 'Besides, I did not wish my daughter to have the bad start that Rico had.'

'Daughter!' mouthed Jacob. 'A daughter? How can you possibly know.'

'Because the good Doctor Nguyên insists it is a daughter and that his method is never wrong.'

Moving towards him again Maria took his hand and placed it on her abdomen. After a short while, Jacob felt a strong kick from the baby and drew his hand back in surprise. Quickly replacing it, he waited for the next kick, which produced an ecstatic reaction from him.

Maria pretended to grumble. 'It's all very well for you to be pleased. I'm the one your daughter kicks every few minutes. She's going to be a very active young lady, mark my words.'

Jacob pulled her close again. 'It's so good to see you. I thought this day would never come. What about the estates and businesses, who's looking after them?'

With a contented sigh, Maria leaned her head on his shoulder. 'It's a long story, but really all you need to know at the moment is that I decided that I was not prepared to have my daughter grow up without her father. Rico has already had a bad start and I didn't want to repeat that mistake. So really the estates, or what's left of them, are only of secondary importance.'

She gave him a long lingering kiss and then stood up. 'My father insisted that Doctor Nguyên came with me on the journey. He brought his wife and Anna and Rico too. I'm not sure where we are going to put everyone here at Harte Street.'

'That's shouldn't be too difficult to solve,' said Jacob, after a moment's thought. 'John Isham is back in Northampton, but his large town house is available. I'm sure Elizabeth will be able to arrange for the doctor and his wife to stay there. Roberto and Elizabeth can go with them, as can Quiff. That will leave room for you, Rico and Anna here at Harte Street.'

A couple of days later after breakfast, Jacob and Maria sat in the living room talking. Maria had told Jacob about the changes she had made in Venice and Jacob was very impressed. 'It looks as though you have inherited your father's head for business,' he said proudly, 'but it must have been a wrench to leave him.'

Maria admitted as much then changed the subject. 'I have a confession to make,' she said. 'I've arranged for Doctor Nguyên to come and have a look at you this morning.' She put a finger over his lips as he was about to say something. 'I know I should have asked, but I wasn't prepared to have you find some excuse for not doing it.' She understood how depressed Jacob had been and Elizabeth had told her that Jacob had told her he could not be with Maria as half a man.

'He is a wonderful doctor and I will only believe that your condition is permanent if he says there is nothing he can do. I haven't come all this way to be rejected because you've given up.'

Jacob felt ashamed. He loved her more than life itself, so he agreed at once. Jack Petts carried him up to bed and Maria helped him to undress. The doctor examined his tongue first and then proceeded to check his pulse and examine his chest and legs very carefully.

Next, with the help of Jack, he was turned over. Using his fingers, the doctor pressed them hard into points near the base of Jacob's spine. Studying the lump at the base of the spine more carefully, he pressed against two more points on either side of the spine.

He peered intently at the lump again, let out a short 'haa' sound and then with his finger pressed hard into the point on Jacob's left side, stuck a needle into the top of his thigh. Jacob yelped in surprise as he felt the sharp prick of the needle. Normally there was nothing. The doctor then stuck the needle into his calf and then his foot. Jacob felt nothing. Releasing the pressure on the point the doctor made to move away, but stuck a needle in the same area as before. This time, there was no reaction from Jacob at all and the doctor nodded in satisfaction. Indicating he had finished his examination, he sat down patiently while Jack helped Jacob to dress. When he was finished, Jack left Maria and the doctor to speak with Jacob.

'What have you discovered, doctor?' asked Maria anxiously. 'Do you think the paralysis is permanent?'

Jacob looked at the doctor apprehensively as he took his time in answering, not daring to hope he might be able to do something.

Seeing his agitation, Doctor Nguyên smiled kindly at Jacob. 'Calm please, Master Bellini, not believe your condition permanent.'

'I did feel a pin prick in my left thigh just now,' said Jacob eagerly. 'It's the first time I've felt anything since the attack. Can you explain what happened.'

The doctor nodded. 'Will try to put in terms you understand. Chinese traditional medicine believes qi, your life energy source, flows through meridians of body together with the blood. Qi has two parts, yin and yang. Must be in balance as they flow through the meridians.' He touched a point on Jacob's back. 'This meridian point, near edge of lump caused by severe blow, hold key.' He touched four points on Jacob's back and legs. 'Believe these points are cold and preventing balanced flow of qi.' He pressed the point on the left side of the lump. 'Pressure on that point, gave feeling in leg. Think pressure on four meridian points same side, reduce or cure paralysis.'

Jacob sank back against the cushions with a sigh of relief. 'I was hoping you could do something. Will it take long?'

'Please to understand, this not simple technique,' said the doctor carefully. 'Need study notes. Think moxibustion give best result.' He held up his hand, palm outwards and shook his head. 'No questions, please, tomorrow I explain. Must study to make right way: wrong way could make worse. You get plenty sleep tonight. Need rest for tomorrow.'

Chapter Forty-Four
London, February/March, 1572

Doctor Nguyên sat opposite Jacob and regarded him with a very serious expression. 'You ask me explain how I treat you. Last night I study notes, very long time. Must tell you there is a risk to what I do.'

'I understand, doctor,' said Jacob, 'but there has been no change for weeks now. Without some way to make a change, I fear it will get no better than it is now.' He gave a strained smile. 'Besides, what you did yesterday gave some feeling in my thigh that was not there before.'

'This is true,' nodded the doctor. 'But please to understand, results may not be for always. Must try once and see what happens. Most usual to take at least five treatments for full effect.'

'You mentioned moxi- something last night.'

'Ah yes, moxibustion. This is what I plan to use.' Opening his bamboo medicine chest, he took out some sticks and handed one to Jacob. They had quite a pungent smell.

'What are they, some sort of herb?'

'Indeed, in Chinese we say Aiye, in the West, name is Mugwort.' He indicated the sticks. 'These are called moxa and can be burned and held near the meridian point to heat it.'

Accepting the stick back, he placed it with the others in his medicine chest and took out some very thin needles. 'I will use acupuncture needles with moxa wrapped around the end. The needles are inserted through the skin into the meridian point and twisted carefully. Moxa then lighted and heats needles. Heat goes into meridian point, drives out cold.'

He smiled when Jacob looked a little dubious about the idea. 'Do not worry, Master Bellini, all will be well. Heat will stimulate the meridian line through the damaged and stagnant area of your back and legs allowing qi to flow freely. It will also help flow of blood.'

After the first treatment, as Jacob lay relaxing in his room, the strong pungent smell of the moxa still lingered. He was disappointed that there had been little improvement, but the doctor had warned him that at least five applications would be needed. He concentrated on doing what the doctor had ordered and that was to lie down and relax all of the muscles in his legs and back.

After about an hour, the doctor returned and said he would now massage Jacob's back and legs. Having applied some sweet scented oils, he began. The massage lasted for about half an hour and then the doctor told him to lie still. He went to sleep almost immediately and did not wake up until next morning.

When it was time for his next treatment, Doctor Nguyên examined him thoroughly. He checked his tongue, his pulse, in six places, and examined his lower back and legs for changes in colour and warmth.

When asked how he felt, Jacob said that he'd had the best night's sleep for weeks. 'I feel very relaxed, but my legs feel no better.'

'Do not attempt to walk until treatment is finished,' said the doctor earnestly. 'Most important for best chance for qi to flow freely.'

By the sixth day, Jacob was in a ferment of impatience. When the doctor had carried out his usual examination, Jacob could contain himself no longer. 'Well! What do you think, will I walk again?'

The doctor made no answer, but walked to the foot of the bed and crouched down by Jacob's feet. Out of sight of Jacob, he produced a feather and brushed it lightly over the soles of his feet. Jacob experienced a strong tickling sensation and without realising what he had done, jerked his foot away. 'What on earth are… Ohhh…' The sound was full of surprise and relief as the realisation sank in that he'd moved his leg.

Raising himself up on his elbows, he peered at the grinning face that had bobbed up from the bottom of the bed. 'You tickled my feet and I felt it,' Jacob said and burst into a fit of laughter. Throwing his arms wide and throwing back his head, he shouted at the top of his voice. 'I have feeling in my leg isn't it wonderful.'

The doctor gave an enigmatic smile and stuck a needle in his calf muscle. 'Oww!' yelled Jacob, 'that really hurt.'

But his indignation lasted only a few seconds and then he

roared with laughter. Even the normally inscrutable Doctor Nguyên was smiling as the whole household rushed up to see what was happening. It was absolute pandemonium for some considerable time.

When things had quietened down, the doctor told Jacob to take things slowly. 'Must build up muscles again, Master Bellini. Although you try use them before treatment, they in poor condition. Walking frame outside, good idea of Mistress Elizabeth, suggest you use, but carefully, please. Too much, no good.'

That night Maria came to Jacob's bed for the first time since she had arrived. 'I know we can't make love yet, but I've missed cuddling up to you. That's all I need for now.' Jacob held her close and they fell asleep in each other's arms.

It was early when Jacob woke and he opened his eyes to see Maria leaning on her arm studying him.

'Good morning, darling, you've slept well.'

'Yes I have and I want to ask you something.'

'Of course,' she said, kissed him and then sat up, hugging the bedclothes round her shoulders. 'What do you want to know?'

'Well,' Jacob said hesitantly, 'I know this may not be the most romantic time, but will you marry me, Maria. I love you to distraction.'

'Silly boy,' said Maria hugging him. 'You don't think I would have two children by you and come all this way to be with you, if I didn't want to marry you. There is a condition though.'

'Condition? What's that?'

'That we don't get married until you can walk down the aisle with me after the ceremony. I'm not having Jack Petts carrying you to and from the altar.'

Chapter Forty-Five
London, March, 1572

Maria sat huddled in front of the fire, wondering if her decision to come to London was a wise one. Although it was almost midday, the candles were lit because of the dark, snow-laden clouds casting their gloom over the city. It was such a cold place.

At first, the snow that came in late February had been a novelty. She made snowmen with Rico in the rear courtyard and threw snowballs until they were thoroughly cold and wet. It had been great fun at first. As more snow fell however, the winds of early March piled it up into ever deeper drifts and Maria longed for the sunshine and warmth of Venice.

She sipped the mulled wine that Mistris Simpkin had made for her and read the note from the Queen again. In it, her majesty had invited her to come to Whitehall for a private audience that afternoon and she had spent the last two hours trying to decide what dress to wear.

The door opened and Jacob came in walking with the aid of two sticks. Maria beamed at him as he came across and sat down in the chair opposite. 'Your walking is coming on by leaps and bounds, my love. You'll soon be able to walk me down the aisle.' She gave him a loving look. 'We'll have to make the situation plain to everyone and set a date.'

'It's funny you should say that,' Jacob said, with a happy smile. 'I've just heard about your invitation to Whitehall and it seems like a good time to let her majesty know of our intentions. I've been informed that it would be a good idea to consult her, rather than just announce it. I don't need her approval as I'm not related, but as her Glassmaker it would, I am told, be the courteous thing to do.' He gave a cheeky smile. 'Unless you've changed your mind that is?'

Maria gave him an enigmatic smile in return, went across and knelt down between his legs. Wrapping her arms round his neck, she gave him a kiss that sent his senses reeling. When at last it ended, she sat back on her heels and regarded him quizzically. 'What does that tell you?' she said innocently and laughed uproariously as Jacob rolled his eyes and pretended to faint.

She slapped him playfully. 'Be serious, of course I haven't changed my mind.'

'In that case,' Jacob said, taking something out of his doublet, 'you'd better have this.' He took her right hand and slid a ring on to her third finger.

Maria looked at it in delight. The centre stone was a large oval cabochon diamond, with a flat surface on the top, which increased the brilliance: set around it in a band were fine-looking sapphires.

'It's so beautiful,' she said, holding it up so it reflected the candlelight. 'I absolutely adore it.'

They kissed again and it was some time before Maria disentangled herself. She regarded him lovingly. 'You have done so well in the past week.' She gasped as she felt his manhood pushing against her. Giving him a sultry look, she pushed herself against him. 'Your legs are not the only thing that's recovering,' she said bawdily and threw her arms round him again. Unfortunately, at that moment, there was a knock on the door and Maria hastily returned to her chair trying to straighten her clothes.

Roberto entered with a message and gave a knowing glance at their dishevelled clothes. 'Sorry to interrupt,' he said, with a cheery grin, 'but Elizabeth has just come over with a message from her father. He has taken the liberty of enquiring if you can use the Mercer's Hall for your wedding celebration and the answer is yes. It's available any day after the nineteenth of March.'

Noticing the ring on Maria's right hand, which she had been holding in a manner sure to attract his attention, he came over to look at it and offered his congratulations. 'I thought my father-in-law was a bit precipitous booking the Mercer's Hall,' he said, 'but it seems he has it about right.'

They thanked Roberto and asked him not to spread the word outside until they had told the Queen. 'We will tell the family and household, but others will only be told after Maria has seen the Queen this afternoon.'

When Maria was shown into the Privy Chamber at Whitehall it was a surprise. Maria was aware that the Queen regarded her kindly, but to be admitted to her private apartments was a great honour. When Maria swept into a deep curtsy, the Queen came over and taking her hand told her to rise and join her on the settle. Waving her hand in dismissal to the maids of honour, they curtsied and left them alone. Another surprise.

Taking her hand in hers, the Queen looked her over. 'I am pleased to see you have fully recovered from the ordeal you suffered when last you were in my company.' She smiled. 'In fact you look an absolute picture of health. When is the baby due?'

'Early May, your majesty.'

'And what of the father? Is it that handsome devil of a glassmaker of mine, by any chance?'

Maria gave an embarrassed smile. 'It is, your majesty and we would like your permission to be married.'

'Would you indeed,' said the Queen, but Maria could see she was pleased. 'Hm-m-m, and about time too. I suppose it had better be soon then, in view of the new baby. And I will expect to be invited. Has he given you a ring yet?'

Maria had not been wearing the ring, but had it on a chain round her neck. Taking it off, she showed it to the Queen.

'Put it on then,' she said in mock disapproval, 'a ring as pretty as that should be in plain view. What about the nuptials, Maria, have they been discussed? Oh, and when we are alone like this, you must call me Elizabeth. But only when we're alone mind you,' she cautioned.

'Of course, your…er, Elizabeth.'

The Queen smiled. 'There you are, Maria, that wasn't so bad.'

They talked for almost an hour and Maria told her all the events since she went back to Venice. The Queen told Maria all about English marriage contracts and explained some of the wedding day customs. 'You must come and join me again, Maria, when the weather improves. It is refreshing to talk to a woman of your education and breeding. English women are seldom as well educated. Unless they are being groomed to be Queen, or marrying royalty,' she said, with a twinkle in her eyes. 'Besides, they are all looking for my favour, but few have helped to save my life from the plots around me.'

She led Maria to the window. 'I have a beautiful garden, which I love to stroll in particularly in the spring and late autumn. Oh and by the way. You tell Jacob Bell from me that if he doesn't treat you well, I'll send him to the Tower.'

They laughed and on that note, said their farewells with Elizabeth embracing her warmly. Promising to consult with the Queen on the date of the wedding, Maria set off happily to tell Jacob all about the meeting.

The next three weeks went by in a blur as the wedding preparations took over every facet of their life. Jacob was working especially hard on his walking. He was determined that he would not only walk Maria down the aisle, but he would do it without the aid of sticks. He was also determined to buy a new house for Maria and himself. The house at Harte Street, whilst convenient, was much too small for his new family. He finally settled on a newly built stone house in Mark Lane, near the far end of Harte Street. It had been built for the Earl of Shrewsbury, but because of his duties as gaoler for Mary Stuart, he had decided to sell it.

He told nothing to Maria about the house. It was to be a wedding day surprise. The date had been set for Tuesday the 21st of March, that being the only day before Easter that the Queen could attend. This also presented a large problem, since where the Queen went, many from the court would go too. Jacob was determined that his glass-blowers must be present at church and at the celebration. At least, the Queen was going to arrive when they had reached St. Olaves, so as long as his men where early, they would be able to get in to the church and places had been allocated to them at the Mercer's Hall.

When Jacob spoke to the rector, Rad Bentley, he was horrified when he learned that the Queen was attending the service. 'This is one of the smallest churches in the city,' he said, rolling his eyes heavenwards, 'it will only hold about two hundred people and there are about two thousand at court.' He blanched at the thought. 'We will also have to provide a throne for the Queen. The cost will be terrible.'

'Don't worry about that, rector,' said Jacob. 'I will cover all the costs and make a healthy donation to the church. And as for numbers, I don't suppose many courtiers will attend.' Privately he was worried that he was mistaken. Where the Queen went, many followed.

The rector cheered up immediately. 'It will be an honour to have your wedding here.'

Jacob looked around as the rector told him the church dated from 1450 and was dedicated to King Olaf II of Norway. It was a square church in stone with a simple oak roof with bosses. The rector was right though; it was going to be impossible if many from the court attended. Having arranged for the banns to be called on the next three Sundays, Jacob returned to Harte Street. Only to find that Maria and Elizabeth had taken over the living room with bolts of silk everywhere, brought from the cargo now in the warehouse at Somers Key.

'What on earth is going on,' queried Jacob, standing in the doorway.

Maria surfaced from underneath a mound of silk, followed by a tousled Elizabeth. 'Go away, Giam,' she said impatiently. 'Can't you see we're busy?'

Jacob gave a sigh and did as he was told. He might have known that choosing the fabric for the dress would take a long time. As the days passed, he realised he'd radically underestimated how long it would take. He'd settled on his own clothes more than a week earlier, having grown very fond of the raven's-wing colour that Walsingham had recommended. Nobleman and rich merchants in Venice often wore black, although trimmings of ermine, or leopard, were common for best clothes and heavy gold chains called catenina d'Oro were often worn.

In his capacity as Glassmaker to the Queen, he was entitled to wear a chain of office and one of the luxuries that the money from Francis Drake had furnished was an ornate chain of office incorporating his coat of arms. The cloaks habitually worn by nobleman in London were designed to go over one shoulder. The fur-trimmed Venetian equivalent was more like an academic gown, almost reaching the floor. Jacob's was in a matching colour to his doublet and hose and the cloak was lined in a lighter version of the colour, matching the fabric showing through the slashed sleeves of his doublet.

Despite a considerable amount of pressing from the Reverend Bentley, he had still not settled the thorny matter of his name and the one that Maria would adopt. There was also the same problem with Rico's name. Normally in Venice, Maria would have used Morisini-Bellini as her surname after marriage and she still preferred to call him Giam. In London and at court, he was known as Jacob Bell. Of course, the Queen, Burghley and Walsingham were all aware of his true name.

Strange to tell, although Jacob tended to think of that as his name in London, in Venice, he reverted easily to Giacomo Bellini as though he'd never changed it. In the end, they decided to use the English name in England and Maria would be Lady Maria Bell. In Venice, Maria would drop the Ragazoni and became Lady Maria Morisini-Bellini.

Finally, all the arrangements were in place and the wedding took place at St. Olaves church with the procession starting from the house in Harte Street. For Maria, getting dressed was not a simple process and had taken the best part of an hour. Her hair had been parted at the middle and hung well down her back in cascading waves. By the time she had put on her stockings, pearl earrings, shoes, chemise undergarment, a petticoat for extra warmth, and willow-stiffened farthingale, she was already feeling harassed. Next came the corset stiffened with wood to flatten all lumps and bumps. Maria did not usually wear one, but both Elizabeth Rosso and her sister Rebecca, her bridesmaids, had insisted. This was followed by the bumroll worn on the hips to give extra flare to the skirt.

Rebecca held up the heavily bejewelled parlet that was worn over the top of the bodice. 'It's absolutely stunning,' she breathed in admiration. 'I've never seen golden diamonds before.'

'I'm told they are quite rare,' said Maria, who absolutely adored them. Once the parlet was in place, Maria heaved a sigh of relief. They only had the heavily brocaded silk kirtle, the main underskirt and the gown to put on. The kirtle was in gold and cream with sewn- in sleeves, slashed to reveal a light cream lining. The silk gown, with its plunging neckline, was in a wonderful warm orange shade, split at the front to reveal the kirtle. The two women busied around putting on Maria's crescent-shaped cap in matching silk brocade adorned with flowers and matching small flowers.

Maria had insisted that both of her bridesmaids should have silk dresses that complemented hers and they both carried tussie-mussies, small bunches of sweet-smelling herbs with flowers added.

Rebecca handed Maria her large flower-ball over a pomander filled with fragrant marjoram, sage, thyme and rosemary, which she held demurely in front of her. Stepping back, both girls looked at the radiant bride and breathed deep sighs. Almost in unison, they told Maria how beautiful she looked then led her off down the stairs to the waiting guests.

Chapter Forty-Six
Harte Street, London, March/May, 1572

It had rained hard during the night, but a watery sun was peeping through the leaden skies as they left for the church. Maria was led to the church between two sweet twin boys with bride laces and rosemary tied about their silken sleeves. The boys were the sons of Peter Tyzack. There was a glass bride cup with twin handles, specially made for Jacob in the Crouched Friars by Roberto, with the Bellini arms engraved in diamond point on one side and the Morisini arms on the other. It contained a large branch of rosemary and was hung about with silken ribands of all colours.

Musicians came next, then a group of maidens, some bearing great bride-cakes, others garlands of wheat finely gilded, and thus they passed into the church. Jacob, resplendent in his ermine-trimmed gown came next, followed close behind by Roberto and the other men. The streets were lined with hundreds of people who cheered the couple as they processed past, regaling them with many ribald comments and advice.

At the church door, Maria joined Jacob who gave her a loving look and a squeeze. The Reverend Bentley joined them and together they waited for the Queen to arrive with her entourage. Suddenly, there was a huge burst of cheering at the far end of Harte Street and they braced themselves for the Queen's arrival.

The Queen in her beautifully gilded coach arrived shortly afterwards to loud cries of 'God bless the Queen. Long live good Queen Bess.'

A dazzling entourage followed her from the court and Jacob was astonished to recognise Lord Burghley, Leicester, Essex, Sir Christopher Hatton, Admiral John Hawkins and other familiar faces. Fortunately, the entourage was more prominent for its quality rather than quantity, but even so, it was going to be a tight squeeze.

The Queen approached, looking stunning in her favourite black and white, with a huge fanned ruff. The Queen's dress was absolutely dripping with seed pearls and other jewels and the parlet contained some of the largest jewels Maria had ever seen. She had been warned not to outdo the Queen even if it was her wedding, but there was little chance of that.

The waiting party gave her their obeisance and Queen bade them rise, complimenting Maria on her dress and then preceded by the rector and the two churchwardens in their formal dress, holding their staffs of office proudly aloft, they escorted the Queen to her throne beside the altar. Jacob took Maria's hand and then the bridesmaids escorted them into the church followed by the courtiers.

The service was a formal affair and events passed in a blur, until at last, they were all seated in the magnificent room of the Mercer's Hall, with the Queen holding centre stage. The wedding feast was sumptuous. Since his arrival in England, Jacob had continually marvelled at the quantity of meat eaten at one meal. The former Spanish Ambassador had reported to his master that the English consume more at one meal than would a Spaniard in a whole week. Jacob could readily understand his report.

The Mercers had enormous pride in being first in precedence of the Livery Companies and thus no expense was spared at their feasts. On this occasion, the presence of the Queen ensured that they had outdone themselves with the meal. There were bucks, swans and peacocks, all presented on elaborate dishes with their feathers used for decoration. After two courses, Jacob was already full and when the table was cleared of the meat, he was astonished at the plethora of fancy jellies made into exotic shapes of flowers and birds, march panes and pies of all sorts, fruits, cheeses and sweetmeats. All of this was washed down with ale, or wine, all in vast quantity and excellent quality.

Throughout the meal, the musicians provided delightful music and when the food had been cleared away, it was announced that Leicester's men, the Queen's favourite acting company, would perform a play especially written for the feast. The Queen was delighted and applauded the troupe enthusiastically as Leicester made an elaborate bow to the Queen and announced them. She favoured him with a flashing smile and with a gracious incline of her head. 'You will love this Maria,' the Queen whispered, leaning over close to Maria's ear. 'They are very good indeed. Look out for James Burbage the lead actor. I believe he is the finest in the world.'

When the play had finished, the musicians struck up a loud chord, then it was announced that the first dance would be in honour of the newly-weds and that Jacob and Maria together with the Queen and the Earl of Leicester would lead off. Fortunately, both Maria and Jacob had spent many long hours under the strict eye of their tutors, mastering the most popular dances of the times, so it was not an ordeal. Indeed, they were so engrossed in each other, that they barely noticed anyone else.

Eventually, in the early hours, they were escorted to the waiting coach with the musicians playing loudly and much merriment. When the happy couple sank back into the seats with a sigh of relief, they kissed and held each other tight. It was only when they heard the coachman giving a discreet cough that they realised the coach had stopped. Jacob handed her down from the coach and Maria was astonished to see they were not at Harte Street, but in the extended entrance to a large house.

'Where are we Giam?' she asked in surprise.

Jacob pointed to the servants lined up outside the door, including those from Harte Street, with a beaming Mistris Simpkin at the front. She gave a deep curtsy and bade them welcome to their new home. Maria's eyes were wide in astonishment as Jacob, who had worked hard for this moment, swept her off her feet and carried her over the threshold to the applause of the servants.

For the happy couple, the weeks flew by and it was a very happy time as the pregnancy proceeded normally under the watchful eye of Doctor Nguyên. Maria went into labour early in the morning of the sixth of May. Much to the surprise of Elizabeth and Rebecca, Maria had insisted that Doctor Nguyên must be in charge of the birth, although she agreed to have their well-recommended midwife in attendance.

Unknown to the midwife, who would not have approved, the doctor had given Maria an infusion containing a pain-dulling opiate. Whilst he was aware that current religious dogma insisted that women should bear the pain of childbirth to atone for the sins of Eve, he thought it was barbaric. He was wise enough however, not to express the opinion aloud.

Being a second child, the birth proceeded normally and shortly after midday Jacob became the proud father of a baby girl. When he was shown in to the bedroom, having been forced to pace the corridors outside, with and equally anxious Roberto, his first enquiry was for Maria.

'Is she well, doctor?'

The smiling doctor indicated the bed where a radiant, but tired Maria was proudly holding her new daughter. Jacob looked at Maria adoringly and then with great care, pushed back the shawl from his daughter's face and drew in a deep breath.

'She is absolutely perfect,' he said, gently caressing the baby's sweet face with a forefinger, 'and she is going to be as beautiful as her mother.' He caressed Maria's face and she nestled it against his hand. 'I love you very much,' he murmured and bending down, kissed her gently.

Just then, Anna arrived with young Rico who was anxious to see his new sister. Jacob picked him up and held him close to his sister and Rico gave her a loving kiss.

Roberto and Elizabeth came in with John Jacob and it became quite a joyous, but noisy occasion, until the doctor called a halt. 'Everyone must leave now, please. Mother and daughter in need of rest, come back tomorrow.'

Epilogue

Events in France following the massacre of the Calvinist Huguenots on St. Bartholomew's day had an enormous effect on the people of England. The political consequences were huge. The Catholic world, including the Pope applauded the massacre, whilst the Protestants condemned it. Reaction in London was almost universal as survivors of the slaughter told their stories of the horrible atrocities in Paris and elsewhere. The evil deeds struck the English people with horror. Clergy from their pulpits cried out for bloody revenge and the populace demanded the French Ambassador should be driven out and all peace treaties with France be torn to bits. Trust in France, previously high, became eroded to the point where most people would have agreed with Walsingham's comment to the Privy Council, "Considering how things stand, I think it less peril to live with them as enemies than as friends."

On 2nd June 1572, Thomas Howard, 4th Duke of Norfolk was executed at the Tower of London, for his part in the Ridolfi Plot. Jacob felt that he was to some extent a scapegoat for Ridolfi.

Conversely, the past year had been kind to Jacob and Maria. Their children were thriving and life was extremely pleasant. Much as he loved his son Rico, Jacob was totally besotted with his daughter, Eleanor. Sitting with Maria on the settle in the drawing room of the house at Mark Street, Jacob gave a heartfelt sigh.

'This last year has been perfect,' he said, leaning over to kiss her cheek. 'I can't believe it is more than a year since Eleanor was born.'

'Neither can I,' said Maria, with a warm smile. 'I missed the sunshine when I first arrived, but England in the spring is very special.'

Jacob gave her a loving look. 'To me, anywhere would be extraordinary with you present, but I do agree. The blossoms have been splendid this year.'

Maria stood up and leaning down, kissed his forehead. 'I promised Anna I would have a word about Rico's clothes. They are in need of replacing. He's such an energetic child. He tore his doublet on a tree branch yesterday and it's beyond repair.'

'Just get him some new ones, darling. It's not as though we can't afford it.'

Maria nodded and with a wave departed. When she had left, Jacob took out the note he'd received from Lord Burghley. It was very cryptic and asked him to be at the end of Mark Street that evening after dusk and to get in the coach that would stop for him. He was not to tell a soul about the letter, or the meeting.

Making the excuse he was going out for a breath of fresh air and refusing company, he made his way to the meeting place. He had hardly time to draw breath before a coach stopped by him and the familiar voice of Lord Burghley bade him get in quickly. He climbed into the coach with its drawn curtains and it set off immediately.

When he turned to sit beside Burghley, he was surprised to see Walsingham on the seat opposite. After the cordial greetings were over, Burghley asked Walsingham to outline the need for the secret meeting. Having given a brief résumé of the political scene, Walsingham explained their fears raised by the rise of the Guisan faction after St. Bartholomew's day.

'We believe that very soon there will be another attempt to put Mary Stuart on the throne. Certain steps have been taken to mitigate attempts at stirring up the English and Scottish Catholics, but there are consistent rumours from the Louvre that something is being planned.

'Can't your spies keep an eye on things in France?' asked Jacob.

'Unfortunately, my intelligence has dried up in recent weeks. A number of my spies have disappeared, or met with untimely ends, many of them seeming to be accidents, or illness.' He sighed expressively. 'It is too much of a coincidence. I believe the Guises are deliberately targeting my spies to ensure their plotting goes undetected.'

Burghley added his voice to this. 'We are sure that a number of leading Catholic sympathisers have been contacted and that something is afoot. We badly need some intelligence so we can counteract any move they make.'

'I suppose you wish me to use the Ring to find out what's going on.'

Walsingham nodded. 'More than that though, we badly need

someone on the inside of the plot, someone they trust.'

The realisation of where this was leading struck Jacob with the force of a physical blow. 'Oh no,' he gasped, 'you can't ask me to get involved with the Guises again. I was lucky that my injuries convinced them I was an ally.' He shook his head. 'I will not put my family in jeopardy. There would be reprisals if they find out.'

Walsingham produced a letter from his doublet and handed it to Jacob. 'I think you should read this. A courier was intercepted at Dover and a letter to the Bishop of Ross was found. The original is now on its way to him, this is a fair copy, after the cipher had been broken.'

The early part of the letter mentioned that a considerable sum of money had been deposited with the usual banker in Edinburgh for the use of Mary Stuart. The middle paragraph leaped out of the page. It commended Jacob Bell, the Queen's Glassmaker, to the Bishop as a true believer and friend of the Guisan cause and one to be recruited as an active member of the group attempting to release Mary Stuart from her captivity and put her on the throne of England.

Jacob handed the letter back to Walsingham in silence and sat considering what he must do. Eventually, Burghley ordered the coach should return him to Mark Street.

'You have set me a puzzle I do not know how to solve,' said Jacob with a sigh. 'I cannot give you the answer you desire, without a concession on your part.'

'What do you require, Jacob Bell?'

'I must have your permission to explain about this plot to my wife and the dangers it might bring to her and the children. I am mindful of Jed Sutton's threats and I cannot keep this from her, nor can I agree to it until I know her response.'

'This is no more than I expected, my Lord,' Walsingham said to Burghley. 'All our efforts have failed to apprehend Jed Sutton who has no love for Jacob Bell. We must bite the bullet, agree to his request and hope that in the meantime the situation does not deteriorate.'

There was no more to be said. As the coach returned to Harte Street, Jacob knew that no matter how Maria responded, his idyllic life would never be the same again.

Historical Notes.

The Ridolfi Plot-1571.

In 1571 a plot was discovered involving, Felipe II of Spain, Pope Pious V, the Duke of Norfolk, Mary Queen of Scots and her advisor, Leslie, Bishop of Ross. The conspirators were led by Roberto Ridolfi, a Florentine banker based in London since the reign of Queen Mary Tudor. As an international banker, he was able to travel between Brussels, Rome and Madrid without attracting too much suspicion. Ridolfi had been questioned by Walsingham after the Northern Uprising two years before, but Ridolfi managed to convince him, he was simply a banker. Indeed his services were used in that capacity by many establishment figures, including both Walsingham and Cecil.

Ridolfi had discussed his plans with the Duke of Alba in the Netherlands and travelled to Rome and Madrid to raise support for an invasion of eastern England. There was to be an uprising of Catholics, followed by the marriage of Thomas Howard, 4th Duke of Norfolk to Mary, Queen of Scots. Ridolfi called for Spain to intervene with troops to support the marriage and put Mary on the throne.

The Spanish were at first doubtful as to the value of the plan. King Felipe disliked the idea of assassinating Queen Elizabeth - a stable England was needed as a counterweight to France. There was also no guarantee that the English population or its nobility were as Catholic in sentiment as the success of the plot demanded.

With the full knowledge of Cecil, Admiral John Hawkins, pretended to be part of the Ridolfi plot to betray Queen Elizabeth. He offered his services to the Spanish, in order to obtain the release of prisoners that he'd been forced to leave behind on one of his voyages. He also hoped to discover plans for the proposed Spanish invasion of England that Cecil suspected was being prepared.

When relations between England and Spain worsened, due to the activities of English privateers. The detention in England of Spanish ships carrying large sums of money destined for their armies in the Netherlands was the final straw. Encouraged by petitions from English Catholics for deliverance, the plot went ahead.

When Charles Baillie, a Scot favourable to Mary's party, was arrested at Dover, incriminating letters from Ridolfi to Bishop Leslie were seized. Baillie revealed the existence of the plot under torture. Leslie, was interrogated and under the threat of torture, laid all the blame on Mary and Norfolk.

Mary admitted giving Ridolfi a financial commission but strongly denied any other part in the scheme. Elizabeth was reluctant to authorise the execution of a fellow queen, but Mary was kept under ever-tighter surveillance.

Norfolk was arrested, tried for high treason, found guilty and executed on Tower Hill on 2nd June, 1572. Ridolfi was abroad when the plot was uncovered and escaped this fate.

Although unsuccessful, the plot concentrated the minds of the English government on assassination attempts on Elizabeth, and, more importantly, exacerbated the Puritan demand that Mary be executed in order to safeguard the English church and state.

Hawkins for his help in foiling the plot, was rewarded, and became Member of Parliament for Plymouth. He was later appointed Treasurer and controller of the Royal Navy (1573-1589). His brilliant redesigning of the fleet laying the foundations for the long prominence of the Royal Navy.

Although pilloried by twenty-first Century values for his part in the slave trade, by the values of his own time, he was a hero. He was held in enormous esteem by Queen Elizabeth and the common people, to them, he epitomised the courage and resourcefulness that made England great.

The Battle Of Lepanto

In 1571, the Christian powers in the Mediterranean assembled a large fleet to confront the growing menace of the Ottoman Empire. Assembling at Messina, Sicily in July and August, the Christian force was led by Don John of Austria and contained vessels from Venice, Spain, the Papal States, Genoa, Savoy, and Malta. Sailing under the banner of the Holy League, Don John's fleet consisted of 206 galleys and 6 galleasses (very large galleys with mounted artillery). Rowing east, they encountered the Ottoman fleet of Ali Pasha off Greece in the Gulf of Patras.

Commanding 230 galleys and 56 galliots (small galleys), Ali Pasha had departed his base at Lepanto and was moving west to intercept the Holy League's fleet. As the fleets sighted each other, they formed for battle. For the Holy League, Don John, aboard the galley Real, divided his force into four divisions, with the Venetians under Agostino Barbarigo on the left, himself in the centre, the Genoese under Giovanni Andrea Doria on the right, and a reserve led by Álvaro de Bazán in the rear. In addition, he pushed galleasses out in front of his left and centre divisions where they could bombard the Ottoman fleet.

Flying his flag from Sultana, Ali Pasha led the Ottoman centre, with Chulouk Bey on the right and Uluj Ali on the left. As the battle opened, the Holy League's galleasses sank two galleys and disrupted the Ottoman formations with their fire. As the fleets neared, Doria saw that Uluj Ali's line extended beyond his own. Shifting south to avoid being flanked, Doria opened a gap between his division and Don John's. Seeing the hole, **(See Author's note) Uluj Ali turned north and attacked into the gap. Doria responded to this and soon his ships were duelling with Uluj Ali's.

To the north, Chulouk Bey succeeded in turning the Holy League's left flank, but determined resistance from the

Venetians, and the timely arrival of a galleass, beat off the attack. Shortly after the battle began, the two flagships found each other and a desperate struggle began between the Real and the Sultana.

Locked together, Spanish troops were twice repulsed when they tried to board the Ottoman galley and reinforcements from other vessels were needed to turn the tide. On the third attempt, with aid from Álvaro de Bazaar's galley, Don John's men were able to take the Sultana killing Ali Pasha in the process.

Against the wishes of Don John, Ali Pasha was beheaded and his head displayed on a pike. The sight of their commander's head had a severe impact on Ottoman morale and they began withdrawing around four in the afternoon. Uluj Ali, who had success against Doria and captured the Maltese flagship Capitana, retreated with sixteen galleys and twenty-four galliots.

Aftermath & Impact.

At the Battle of Lepanto, the Holy League lost 50 galleys and suffered approximately 13,000 casualties. This was offset by the freeing of a similar number of Christian slaves from the Ottoman ships. In addition to the death of Ali Pasha, the Ottomans lost 25,000 killed and wounded and an additional 3,500 captured. Their fleet lost 210 ships, of which 130 were captured by the Holy League. Coming at what was seen as a crisis point for Christianity, the victory at Lepanto stemmed Ottoman expansion in the Mediterranean and prevented their influence from spreading west.

**Author's note.

It is this hole that The Crystal exploits in my fictional account of the Battle of Lepanto.

Peter Cooke, Yorkshire, July, 2008